The Great Heinlein Mystery

Science Fiction, Innovation and Naval Technology

Edward M. Wysocki, Jr.

Copyright © 2012 Edward M. Wysocki, Jr.

All rights reserved.

ISBN: 1477410201
ISBN-13: 978-1477410202

To the memory of my parents

CONTENTS

1	How Did the Mystery Begin?	1
2	The Early Quotes	9
3	The Virtues Quote	19
4	Analysis of Quotes	38
5	Technology and the Navy	45
6	The Class of 1929	64
7	Naval Science Fiction	87
8	Science Fiction and Inventions	108
9	Prediction and Inspiration	126
10	Naval Innovation	146
11	Analysis of Stories	160
12	Interesting, But Not the Answer	181
13	Device Analysis	191
14	What is the Answer?	215
	Appendix 1 – Graduates of the Class of 1929	233
	Appendix 2 – Electromechanical Computing	240
	Notes	250
	Bibliography	264
	Acknowledgements	276
	Index	278

LIST OF TABLES

1	Stories by Robert Heinlein	12
2	Naval Electronics	59
3	Naval Postgraduate Education	84

LIST OF FIGURES

1	Manuscript Page from Virtues Essay	35
2	Naval Academy Class Sizes	67
3	Naval Science Fiction	92
4	Land Battleship	103
5	Block Diagram of Battle Tracker	224
6	Mark 2 (Baby Ford) Rangekeeper	247

1

HOW DID THE MYSTERY BEGIN?

In this book, we will consider what I have always called ***The Great Heinlein Mystery***. The Mystery concerns the claim by the late science fiction author Robert Anson Heinlein (1907-1988) that one of his early published stories contained a fictional electronics device that inspired one of his Naval Academy classmates to develop a real naval system used during World War 2. Unfortunately, Mr. Heinlein left no record that I have been able to locate which identified the story, the classmate, the fictional device, or the naval system. Once I became aware of this puzzle and decided to solve it, I have investigated many diverse topics in my attempt to arrive at a solution. Some of the topics visited in the chapters which follow are Heinlein's early writings, his Naval Academy classmates, naval technology in the period between the World Wars, and the process of invention. In these chapters I will present various facts that I have uncovered in the course of my research which may not have a direct bearing on the solution, but I hope will be of interest to fans of Robert Heinlein and science fiction in general.

How did this quest to identify Heinlein's Mystery Device come about? I begin with a recounting of the events connected with this project. The purpose is to show how certain facts became available and directed the course of research. With the background out of the way, I then proceed to cover each of the topics in more detail. The one point I would like to make is that this was never a full-time effort. My degrees are in the field of Electrical Engineering, not literature or history, and I was employed for my entire working career in the defense industry, not in academia. I was dealing with this task as a spare-time personal effort. One might consider it a hobby, although at times I have felt that it should be characterized as an obsession.

It all started at the 1983 WorldCon, ConStellation in Baltimore, Maryland - the city in which I was born and where I lived the first 45 years of my life. At the Con, I was wandering through the dealer's room, and a book happened to catch my eye. Nothing special there, books are always catching my eye. In this particular case, it was *Heinlein in Dimension* by Alexei Panshin, published by Advent. The interest in Heinlein is easy to explain. The first work of science fiction that I can definitely remember reading was Heinlein's *Space Cadet*, when I was nine years old. There may have been other earlier works, but any memory of them is long gone, probably with good reason. Although I have read many works by other science fiction authors over the years, my favorite has been and remains Heinlein. It did not take me more than a few seconds to decide to purchase the book.

After I had finished reading *Heinlein in Dimension*, I noticed there were other interesting books available from the same publisher. I placed my order for *In Search Of Wonder* by Damon Knight, *A Requiem for Astounding* by Alva Rogers, *Of Worlds Beyond,* edited by Lloyd Eshbach, and the book which turned out to be the initial trigger to this research, *The Science Fiction Novel: Imagination and Social Criticism*. My only reason for purchasing the last two books was, of course, that the listing indicated that they contained essays by Heinlein.

Heinlein's essay in *The Science Fiction Novel* is titled "Science Fiction: Its Nature, Faults and Virtues." (From this point, I will refer to it as the Virtues essay.) As I read this essay, I encountered the mention of the fictional electronic device and the naval system that Heinlein claimed was inspired by it. At the time I probably thought that the fact that Heinlein had not identified the device was interesting, but did not pursue the matter further during the years that remained of Heinlein's life.

I have often asked myself that had I written to him and asked the identity of the device, would he have told me? Probably not. He considered it to be a military secret. I never had a chance to ask him in person. The closest that I ever came to meeting Robert Heinlein was being in the audience when he delivered the Forrestal Lecture at the Naval Academy in 1973. I was seated at the end of a row and was no more than 15 feet from him as he was escorted out at the end of the talk.

I was affected by Robert Heinlein's death in 1988 in much the same way as many other readers. Although we had never met the man in person, we all felt that we knew him well through his works and mourned him as we would any friend.

If I gave any thought to the device at the time, it was probably that any chance of discovering the identity of the device was now gone. No effort was devoted to the problem for the next two years. Then *Grumbles from the Grave*, hereafter referred to simply as *Grumbles*, was published. This was in the spring of 1990.

For those of you not familiar with *Grumbles*, it is a collection of excerpts from letters both to and from Robert Heinlein, edited by Virginia (Ginny) Heinlein. The very first letter quoted is the one which accompanied his submission of his short story "Life-Line" to *Astounding Science-Fiction* in April 1939. The letters cover both his writing career and various details of his personal life. Throughout the first two chapters of *Grumbles,* the letters are exclusively to and from John W. Campbell, Jr., the editor of *Astounding*. During the first chapter and the beginning of the second, the topics are exactly what you would expect between a writer and the editor of the magazine in which most of his works were being published - suggestions of story ideas, rates of payment, and reasons why certain stories were rejected, interspersed with the occasional threats of Robert Heinlein to retire from writing.

Then we reach the letter dated December 9, 1941. This is two days after the Japanese attack on Pearl Harbor. By the time he wrote this letter, Robert Heinlein had already made an attempt to get back into the Navy. He later said he was rejected for medical reasons; the most critical of these being that he had been given a medical discharge from the Navy seven years before for having contracted tuberculosis. The primary subject of this and the letters that followed for the next few months was, as might be expected, the war. More specifically, he discussed the Navy and how it was or was not responding after the attack. Most were Heinlein's attempt to address statements in Campbell's letters which he felt represented misinformation and perhaps ignorance on Campbell's part regarding naval matters. In the course of these discussions, Heinlein referred to the naval device taken from one of his stories. At this point, I recalled the earlier mention in the Virtues essay. In spite of now having multiple references to the fictional device, I again took no action.

We move forward another two years, a delay you will see was very critical in my efforts to identify the device. In early 1992, I purchased a copy of *Requiem: New Collected Works by Robert A. Heinlein and Tributes to the Grand Master*, edited by Dr. Yoji Kondo. This consisted of many of Heinlein's works which had never been reprinted, accompanied by the texts of many speeches and articles paying tribute to the Grand Master. The appearance of the book again stimulated my interest in identifying the device, although it did not make reference to it in any way. Later that spring was the death of Isaac Asimov. I told myself that I had better try to find out the answer while there were still some people around whom I could ask.

My first step was to contact Dr. Kondo and explain the objective of my search. He listened to my question and said that he did not know the answer, but that he would pass on the question to Virginia Heinlein. He promised to call me back within the week. I told myself that I would have the answer and that would be the end of it.

When he called me back later that week, he told me that Virginia Heinlein had said that she did not know the answer either. She said that the person who would have known was Robert Heinlein's Naval Academy classmate, Admiral (actually Rear Admiral) Caleb Barrett Laning. She added that it might have had something to do with Laning's work with the Combat Information Center. Unfortunately, Laning had passed away the year before. This is the critical delay to which I referred earlier. If I had contacted Laning in 1990, I might have been able to get the answer from him. Laning was mentioned briefly in *Heinlein in Dimension*. Panshin identified him as a friend of Heinlein at Annapolis, the source of part of the pen-name "Caleb Saunders," the person to whom *Beyond This Horizon* was dedicated, and the co-author of the 1947 *Collier's* article "Flight Into The Future." Until *Requiem* appeared and I passed my question along to Ginny, I had no knowledge of the importance of Laning to my quest.

From this point the research concentrated on Caleb Laning, then on the surviving members of Heinlein's Naval Academy class, and finally on the stories.

I obtained from the Naval Academy Alumni Association a copy of Rear Admiral Laning's obituary which had appeared in *Shipmate*, the Alumni Association magazine. This did verify that Caleb Laning had been a member of the Class of 1929, the same as Robert Heinlein. It also stated that "Early in the war he received the Legion of Merit for the development of the Combat Information Center principle in all Navy Combat ships."

Those members of Laning's family whom I was able to contact at times throughout my search - both of his daughters, a grandson and a cousin - have been unable to supply me with any information relevant to my search. My next step was to obtain a copy of Laning's naval biography from the Naval Historical Center. While it gave no direct answer to my question, it did provide certain information which will be discussed in subsequent chapters.

I contacted the Alumni Association again and requested a list of the names and addresses of the surviving members of the Class of 1929. There were approximately 60 names on the list. It was surprising that 25 percent of the graduating class was still alive over 60 years after graduation. I sent a letter to everyone on the list and received about 30 responses. The details of these responses are presented in the chapter on the Class of 1929. Although the focus of the research into the classmates was Caleb Laning, based on Ginny Heinlein's comments, it was recognized that she could have been in error. Consequently, an effort was made to obtain the naval biographies of as many of the classmates as possible from the Naval Historical Center.

With a bit of assistance from Yoji Kondo, I sent letters to L. Sprague de Camp and J. Hartley Bowen. Although de Camp was also well known as a science-fiction author, the main point of interest to me was that he had worked at the Naval Aircraft Factory in Philadelphia during the war, as had Heinlein and Isaac Asimov, and where Mr. Bowen had been a supervisor. It was thought that since they had been in contact with Heinlein in the years immediately after the device had come into existence, they might have heard of it from him. But, as was becoming the case no matter which path I pursued, no useful information was obtained.

The next step was to look at the stories. The date of the earliest letter in *Grumbles* which referred to the device allowed me to place an upper limit on the last story to be examined. This limit was obviously December 1941. In my research I had become aware that at least one of the stories which had been reprinted after the war contained various details that could not have existed in the pre-war version. This made it obvious that I would have to acquire the original published version of each and every story within the time range. At that time I already possessed a collection of *Astounding*s and *Analog*s covering many years, but not quite as far back as would be required. For a number of years I was locating and acquiring those magazines in which the stories had originally appeared. For those of you that have never attempted to buy specific issues of science fiction pulp magazines published more than 50 years previous, there are not that many sources. Also be prepared to pay a *bit* more than the original 25 cent cover price.

Based on the information from stories in the few issues I then possessed, the quotes from the Virtues essay and *Grumbles*, and what I had been able to learn about Laning and from the classmates, I decided to present my question to a science fiction audience. I wrote a short article "The Great Heinlein Mystery" that briefly described my research and asked if anyone knew the answer. I submitted it to *Analog*, but it was rejected. I felt that the only other logical audience was the alumni of the Naval Academy. So I revised the article slightly and submitted it to *Shipmate*. In a phone conversation with the editor, I was told that the *Shipmate* does not usually publish an article by someone who is not an Academy alumnus. There was then a long pause - at least it seemed like a long pause at the time - and he said, "But in this case, we will make an exception, as it concerned such a famous Academy alumnus." The article appeared in the January-February 1995 issue of *Shipmate*. Although I received a number of responses, no one was able to provide me with any useful information. In other words, everything was proceeding according to an established pattern.

I was still interested in presenting my question to a science fiction audience. Although I had been unable to get an article published in *Analog*, I was successful in getting a short letter published in the November 1996 issue. The letter briefly described my search and asked if anyone had any details. I emphasized that I was only interested in definite information, not guesses. It happened that my issue was late arriving in the mail, so I began receiving responses before I knew that my letter had appeared in print. I received a grand total of four responses. Unfortunately, the four responses that I did receive were either guesses or the recollection of reading of the device in an article by Heinlein that never appeared at the time or in the magazine suggested.

I became aware of the existence of *The Heinlein Journal* shortly after the first issue had appeared in 1997. It provided me with a whole new venue. The *Journal* is edited and published by Bill Patterson, the author of the Heinlein biography which has recently appeared. I was able to learn various facts about Heinlein from the *Journal* which probably would not have appeared elsewhere. I was able to pose my mystery question to the readers of the *Journal*, who did not know the answer. Over the years, as my research would lead me to interesting facts about Heinlein and his works, I would occasionally write a short note or an article and submit it to the *Journal*. The topics have included The Naval Aircraft Factory where Heinlein worked during World War 2, the article "Flight to the Future" which he co-authored with Cal Laning and the appearance of pieces of naval technology in his stories.

It was recognized that Laning's service record might contain some useful information. The story of the effort to obtain that service record will be presented in Chapter 6.

Although we had communicated by phone and e-mail, I was very fortunate to have had the chance to finally meet Ginny Heinlein in person once before her death in January 2003. My visit in November 2001 was an enjoyable one - I can still recall standing in her living room and looking at the row of Mr. Heinlein's Hugo awards upon the mantelpiece. As pleasant and memorable the day was, my conversations with Ginny did not yield any information useful in my search.

A very productive trip was taken in October 2003 to examine the Heinlein Archives in the McHenry Library at the University of California Santa Cruz. I had the assistance of Bill Patterson, who was then working at the McHenry Library's Special Collections. His position was funded by the Heinlein Prize Trust to integrate new material into the Archives. I was able to examine the manuscripts of several of the stories of interest. I was also able to obtain a copy of the script for the talk at the University of Chicago upon which the Virtues essay was based and a copy of the final markup of the essay. Finally, I was able to examine, in the few days available to me, the Heinlein-Campbell correspondence file from which the letter excerpts published in *Grumbles* had been obtained.

It should be noted that the files which had required my trip to UCSC to examine are now available online from the Heinlein Archives (http://www.heinleinarchives.net/). One can search for the file or files one desires, and with the payment of what I consider very reasonable fees, may then download PDFs containing the scanned material. This has permitted me to examine again and again those files which I had only a few days to examine in Santa Cruz. I have also downloaded and examined many additional Archives files as well. I consider the availability of these files from the Archives to have been one of the greatest aids to my research.

By this time I had been able to obtain copies of all of the magazines in which the stories had been published. Just reading the stories did not result in the answer jumping out at me. That would have been far too easy. It was necessary to go through all of the stories and pick every mention of technology for later evaluation. This process and its results will be covered in Chapter 11.

A good part of my research concerned naval history and both electronics technology in general and naval technology in particular. I have been interested in naval and military history since my high school days. I was fortunate that the branch of the public library in Baltimore closest to my home had the entire 15 volume set of Samuel Eliot Morison's *History of the United States Naval Operations in World War II.* I had always been interested in the history of science and technology. So trying to solve the Mystery just combined these two other existing interests with science fiction.

As I had stated earlier, my degrees are in Electrical Engineering. My interest in matters electrical and electronic was no doubt stimulated by the environment in which I grew up. My father had taken the National Radio Institute course for Radio and Television Repair. Part of our basement was filled with his old course books, various boxes of electrical parts, and items of test equipment. But neither that early exposure to electronics nor my subsequent education had provided me with much knowledge of electronic technology of either the inter-war period or World War 2. Like many people, I knew that radar had been used during the war, and that was about the extent of my knowledge. It became necessary to find articles and books that described the technology of the time and when the various portions of it were developed. It was also possible to find various naval technical manuals from the period to get a better feel for the technology. Another useful source of the history of technology was the *N.Y. Times* online archives, which permits you to purchase PDFs of the old articles which you desire. These were most useful in determining what technologies or devices portrayed in Heinlein's stories were already in existence.

There was also a trip to the National Archives in Washington, D.C. to examine the log of the U.S.S. *Philadelphia*. This was the ship on which Cal Laning served during the period of interest.

Another important source of information was Special Collections and Archives Department of the Nimitz Library at the Naval Academy. This enabled me to find information on the classmates that was not available by other means, and learn about naval education at both the undergraduate and postgraduate level, as it existed during the interwar years. With regard to Naval Academy information, perhaps the most useful document that I was able to acquire was an edition of the *Register of Alumni*.

Another source of information which became available relatively late in the research was Heinlein's *For Us, The Living* (*FUTL*). The manuscript of this unpublished work had been thought lost. It predates all of his early published works of science fiction. Various ideas and concepts which appear in his published works can be traced back to *FUTL*, as is seen in different parts of the analysis.

If I had been an academic in an area where I would have been able to devote many more hours each week to the research, with the assistance of graduate student "peons," I can only speculate how much sooner this might have been completed. If I had known that this process was going to take so long, would I have undertaken the search?

Performing such research on my own would have been impossible without the Internet and email. Although occasional use was made of the telephone and, on even rarer occasions the U.S. Postal Service, the primary means of contact and information exchange has been email. Old books and navy manuals were located and purchased online. Sometimes very useful things were discovered and a whole new line of inquiry initiated just by something popping up in a browser search for a name or some other piece of information. But as anyone who has done any kind of serious research using the Internet can tell you, a great deal of care must be exercised with regard to what you find online. I have tended to use the Internet to point me to a person or some book or published article rather than to directly employ any of the information found online.

The next chapter will consider the information extracted from letters in the Heinlein Archives.

2

THE EARLY QUOTES

The various quotes that define The Great Heinlein Mystery are considered in their original order of occurrence, rather than the order in which I had discovered them. This means that the discussion of the Virtues essay and its key quote occurs in the next chapter. Although all of the quotes to be covered in this chapter are ultimately from the Heinlein-Campbell correspondence files in the Heinlein Archives, those which also appear in *Grumbles* will be identified as such in the Notes.

As noted in Chapter 1, the first reference by Robert Heinlein to the attack on Pearl Harbor occurs in the letter to Campbell dated December 9, 1941. This letter is primarily concerned with Heinlein's attempts to return to naval service in spite of his bad eyesight and having been discharged from the Navy for having had tuberculosis, and also presents his personal feelings about the war.

We do not encounter anything relevant to the mystery until a letter to Campbell dated December 21, 1941. The first portion of the letter that is quoted in *Grumbles* is concerned with comments made by Campbell and his father regarding the war and the Navy in a long rambling letter dated December 17. Heinlein admits that some of the supposed faults identified in the letter are real, but that others are based on insufficient knowledge on the part of both Campbell Sr. and Campbell Jr. One implication by Campbell Sr. is that junior officers are not allowed to criticize or disagree with the status quo. Heinlein admits that some faults are due to the nature of the organization and goes on to say:

> The navy is an involved profession; it takes twenty-five years or so to make an admiral --- and older men are not quite as mentally flexible as younger men. I see no easy way to avoid that. Is your

father as receptive to new ideas as you are? Will he step down and let you tell him how to run AT&T? Is there any way of avoiding the dilemma? Nevertheless the brasshats are not quite as opposed to new ideas as the news commentators would have us think. The present method of anti-aircraft fire was invented by an ensign. Admiral King encouraged a warrant officer and myself to try to invent a new type of bomb (Note: We weren't successful). You may remember that one of my story gags was picked up by a junior officer and made standard practice in the fleet before the next issue hit the stands.

Heinlein makes reference to Campbell's father in connection with AT&T. As Campbell's father will be mentioned again shortly in another quote, it is worth investigating the exact nature of that connection. John W. Campbell, Sr. was employed by AT&T. He started in 1906 with what became New Jersey Bell Telephone, in Plant Engineering. After ten years, he transferred to AT&T. In 1939, he became Outside Plant Engineer in the Operation and Engineering Department. He was the co-author of a 1943 article on the subject of "War Emergency Stocks in the Bell System." His biographical data obtained from AT&T indicates that the company later loaned him to the Office of the Military Government in Germany, at the request of the Army. Was Heinlein engaging in a bit of exaggeration here, or was he misled by Campbell regarding the actual position of his father within the corporate structure?

We must consider the last sentence of the above quote, in which Heinlein refers to the "story gag." The biggest problem presented by this sentence is the implied time frame. Heinlein is making the claim that his story idea was spotted by the junior officer, recognized very quickly as something potentially useful to the Navy, then presented to his superior officers, and finally "made standard practice in the fleet" all within a one month time span. As long as this particular quote has been known, it has seemed extremely unlikely that such a process could occur as quickly as stated by Heinlein.

We could assume that Heinlein is simply engaging in a bit of exaggeration here regarding the time span. Another possible explanation is that Heinlein's story idea was interpreted in terms of a change to an already existing device or process. This could make the very rapid employment of the new idea a bit more plausible. But is a month a reasonable time frame even with such an assumption?

The accuracy of the information conveyed in this quote will no doubt be a subject for further debate. But there is one important feature of the letter in which it appears - its date. This allowed an absolute upper limit to be placed on the stories which had to be analyzed. All of Heinlein's works which originally appeared in print up to December 1941 are listed in Table 1. The version of each story with which most are us are familiar from later hardback or paperback collections may have been modified from the originally published versions. As stated in Chapter 1, it was necessary to obtain the magazines containing those originals. This was eventually possible for every story, with the exception of "Heil" (also known as "Successful Operation") which appeared in the fanzine *Futuria Fantasia*. As only a single version of this story is known to exist and it has been reprinted, it was possible to examine it and verify that it has no details even remotely connected to naval technology.

The next quote is from a letter from Campbell to Heinlein dated December 29, 1941. The letter starts out on the subject of photography, touches on a number of topics including L. Sprague de Camp and Willy Ley, and then finally returns to a discussion of the Navy and the war in a manner similar to the letter of the 17th. Then appears this quote, short and to the point:

> And --- you did <u>not</u> tell me about a story gag being taken over into fleet practice. Give!

There is not much to say about this quote as it stands. Its importance will become clearer as we consider later quotes. There are then three short letters in the correspondence file, two from Campbell and one from Heinlein, but none contain anything relevant to the mystery. The next quote to be considered is from a letter from Heinlein to Campbell, dated January 4, 1942. From the tone of the letter Heinlein is again finding faults with many of Campbell's opinions or statements about the Navy stated in his letter of December 29, as shown in the paragraphs reproduced in *Grumbles*. He accuses Campbell of being "brilliantly stupid" in such matters, cautions him about making statements which might be construed as destroying the morale of a member of the armed forces, and then attempts to educate him about naval topics. A discussion of the need for military secrecy leads up to the statement that:

> Lots of civilians are necessarily entrusted with certain naval secrets. I've sailed with many a G.E., Westinghouse, and AT&T engineer. The gadget of mine that was taken over by the fleet was developed by one of your father's engineers. I doubt if he personally had any occasion to know about it, but don't ask him about it and don't try to conjecture what it might be. Don't mention it to any one, lest they do a little guessing. By mentioning the <u>class</u>

Title	Magazine	Date	
Life-Line	Astounding Science-Fiction	August 1939	
Misfit	Astounding Science-Fiction	November 1939	
Requiem	Astounding Science-Fiction	January 1940	
If This Goes On—	Astounding Science-Fiction	February, March 1940	
Let There Be Light	Super Science Stories	May 1940	L
The Roads Must Roll	Astounding Science-Fiction	June 1940	
Coventry	Astounding Science-Fiction	July 1940	
Heil	Futuria Fantasia	Summer 1940	L
Blowups Happen	Astounding Science-Fiction	September 1940	
The Devil Makes the Law	Unknown	September 1940	
Sixth Column	Astounding Science-Fiction	January – March 1941	A
—And He Built a Crooked House—	Astounding Science-Fiction	February 1941	
Logic of Empire	Astounding Science-Fiction	March 1941	
Beyond Doubt	Astonishing Stories	April 1941	LW
They	Unknown	April 1941	
Universe	Astounding Science-Fiction	May 1941	
Solution Unsatisfactory	Astounding Science-Fiction	May 1941	A
Methuselah's Children	Astounding Science-Fiction	July – September 1941	
—We Also Walk Dogs	Astounding Science-Fiction	July 1941	A
Elsewhere	Astounding Science-Fiction	September 1941	C
By His Bootstraps	Astounding Science-Fiction	October 1941	A
Common Sense	Astounding Science-Fiction	October 1941	
Lost Legion	Super Science Stories	November 1941	L

of engineer that developed it I have shown greater confidence in you than I have in any other civilian. Let it stand that it is a proper military secret and that we hope that we are the only navy using it.

It should be noted that here we have the first specific mention of the "gadget," as opposed to the earlier mention of a vague something that was made "standard practice." That both quotes refer to the same object is indicated by each having been used by the fleet. It was once suggested to me that the above quote and the one from December 21 were referring to different objects, to which my reply was "Thank you very much. You now have me looking for *two* mystery devices."

Heinlein then states to Campbell that the gadget was developed by one of "your father's engineers." This could be interpreted to mean that although the gadget may have been quickly adopted by the Navy as a result of the actions of the naval officer mentioned in the first quote, it was also the subject of further development efforts. I would say that the reference to development work contradicts the earlier statement regarding the speed with which the device was actually put into use within the fleet.

We have an implied connection with AT&T. But with what segment of AT&T? In light of Heinlein's earlier remark about Campbell's father running AT&T, how do we interpret the comment regarding the engineers? Are we to assume the engineers were immediately junior to him, or was Heinlein assuming that Campbell's father was at a much higher level in the organization? The second alternative seems the most likely, that the senior Campbell does not have any knowledge of the work. If the men on the gadget project had been working directly for him, he would have had specific knowledge of their assignments. This makes it very difficult to say at what segment of AT&T the work had been performed. The rest of the sentence indicates that Campbell himself has no direct knowledge of the device, as he is requested by Heinlein "not to conjecture what it might be."

Before proceeding, we must ask if the fact that AT&T was involved in the development work provides us with any means of identifying the gadget. First let us consider the structure of the pre-breakup Bell System. AT&T was the central organization of the Bell System. Associated with AT&T were a number of subsidiary telephone companies throughout the United States. The manufacturing and supply segment of the Bell System

Table 1. Stories by Robert Heinlein from his first story in August, 1939 until the end of 1941. They appeared as by Robert Heinlein except as indicated by the letter in the rightmost column, where A = Anson MacDonald, C = Caleb Saunders, L = Lyle Monroe and LW = Lyle Monroe with Elma Wentz.

was the Western Electric Company. Finally there was the Bell Telephone Laboratories, founded in 1925. Campbell's father, being concerned with the day-to-day operations of the phone system was properly identified as working for AT&T, as opposed to the research or manufacturing segments. I would suggest, however, that we should be considering the Bell System as a whole in this search.

The wartime work can be divided between research and development of military devices and systems at Bell Laboratories and the manufacturing of these devices and systems at Western Electric. The basic study of the wartime efforts of the Bell System is *A History of Engineering and Science in the Bell System: National Service in War and Peace (1925 - 1975)*. This work divides these efforts into the areas of Radar, Electronic Computers for Fire Control, Acoustics, and Communications. Many individual devices are directly mentioned or implied in each of these areas. A study of many post-war issues of *Bell Telephone Magazine* containing articles on wartime development efforts failed to provide any useful information. An inquiry to the AT&T Archives in 2005 resulted in the reply that very little information existed in the Archives on military projects of the war years. The response also identified the study mentioned above as the best source available for such information. In general, research on the Bell System does not appear to directly identify the device solely on the basis of it being developed by that corporation.

Heinlein's use of the word "class" to refer to the engineer involved in the development has always been confusing to me. (The word "class" is underlined in the original letter.) He says "By mentioning the class of engineer," but to what mention is he referring? Does he mean the engineers employed by the companies listed in the second sentence of the quote, or does he mean the engineer working on the project for some segment of AT&T? Should we assume that he simply means an electrical or electronics engineer, or does the connection with AT&T suggest a further specialization?

There is nothing in the letter containing the above quote that addresses Campbell's objection that Heinlein never told him about the story gag. This is covered by an excerpt from another letter of the same date, January 4. What distinguishes it from most other letters in the correspondence file is that it was written by Heinlein's wife at the time, Leslyn:

> Your very request for further information about Bob's fictional gadget which is now in use in the fleet, ... I recall that Bob did mention the matter to you in your living room in New Jersey (the old place), and that you asked then what the gadget was, or what

story it was from, or something, and Bob told you then that it would be a confidential matter.

This is a very important statement, as it supplied me with information that was missing during the early phases of my research based only on what appeared in *Grumbles*. It indicates that the device was mentioned to Campbell when Robert and Leslyn were physically present in his residence. It also indicates that while Heinlein had originally related the existence of the naval system, he did not provide Campbell with any of the details which would enable him to identify it. This is consistent with Heinlein's January 4 letter in which he cautions Campbell not to conjecture about the gadget.

So the next question is when did Robert and Leslyn visited Campbell? We must jump backwards in the correspondence file to the point where the trip shows up as a gap. The last letter before the gap is dated May 4, 1940 and informs Campbell that:

We are leaving for the east in fortyeight hours. . . . We are coming to the east coast within ten days and expect to find some small summer resort and lie around in the sun for a month before doing much sightseeing.

The next letter which appears in the file is dated July 14, 1940 and is from Chicago. Heinlein was there to attend the Democratic National Convention, which ran from July 15 to July 18. But while in Chicago, he and Leslyn also attended a General Semantics seminar which started on July 8.

The Heinleins arrived in New York on May 18. They stayed in New York for almost a month, until June 13. During their time in New York, the Heinleins were staying at an apartment maintained by three ex-Navy men identified as classmates of Heinlein. One of these is identified as John Arwine, who is discussed in the chapter on the classmates. There does not appear to be any way of identifying the other classmates. Robert and Leslyn then went to New Jersey, spending approximately two weeks at a nudist resort. They departed for Chicago on June 28.

With the Campbells living in New Jersey, it is likely that the Heinleins could have visited them at some point during the entire time in the New York/New Jersey area. All that is really important is that the time in the Campbells' living room when the gadget was mentioned could have been no later than June 28.

This is a key point in the search for the device. Any story which appeared in print after the end of June 1940 cannot have contained the description of the gadget. This allowed me to eliminate "Blowups Happen" and all stories which appeared after it. Unfortunately, this information only became available after I had acquired copies of the magazines, and examined all of the stories listed in Table 1.

One question that remained was, should "Coventry" be retained or eliminated from the list of stories to be considered? To answer this, it was necessary to determine when the July 1940 issue of *Astounding* became available to readers. If we look at a modern issue of *Analog*, we discover, for example, that the May 2007 issue went on sale on March 5, 2007. If we were to apply the same publication schedule to the issue of *Astounding*, it would indicate that the July 1940 issue would have been available in early May. But is this a valid assumption?

Useful information concerning the publication dates of *Astounding* is contained in the first volume of Isaac Asimov's autobiography, *In Memory Yet Green*. He has a series of statements for the period from mid-1938 to mid-1939 concerning publication dates or the date on which the issue actually reached the stores. First consider Asimov saying that:

> On Monday, July 18, 1938, I traveled to Campbell's office . . . . gave me a copy of the August issue of *Astounding* . . . . three days before I would have had it on the newsstand.

Note that July 21, 1938 was the day before the fourth Friday of the month. Then we move to 1939, where he says that:

> On the way out on that June 21 visit . . . . I passed a pile of July 1939 *Astounding*s. It was due to reach the store the next day. . . .

Again the date in question, June 22, 1939 is the day before the fourth Friday. As we move forward another year, we can look at the Contents page of the June 1940 issue of *Astounding*. There is a square in the lower corner which contains the phrase "ON SALE FOURTH FRIDAY EACH MONTH." This holds true for the July and August 1940 issues. It is only when we get to the September 1940 issue that the box contains the more specific information that the October 1940 issue will be on sale September 20. This meant a change in the sale date, since the 20th was the third Friday of the month.

Even with minor shifts in delivery dates, we would have been misled by applying the modern publication schedule. The July 1940 issue of *Astounding* would have not been available until the fourth Friday in June, which was the 28th. This was the day the Heinleins departed New Jersey on their way to Chicago. Therefore the fictional "gadget" could not have appeared in "Coventry." The last possible story that must be considered is "The Roads Must Roll." Even then the naval officer would have had less than 5 weeks (May 24 to June 28) to obtain a copy of *Astounding,* spot the Mystery Device, develop the idea for use as a naval system and relay news to Heinlein in sufficient time for him to inform Campbell of its existence. Although the June 1940 issue is the last one considered, it is almost certain that we are talking about an even earlier issue.

With the dates established, we may now return to the original series of quotes. How did Campbell react to Leslyn's reminder? On January 8, he says:

> Re the request for information on the gadget taken over from your story: I'd forgotten your mentioning it when you were here. When you mentioned it to me in your recent letter, in an off-hand, of-course-you-remember way --- is it remarkable I reacted by saying that I didn't remember and what was it?

We must wonder if Campbell really remembered being told about the device eighteen months before, or was he just saying that he did.

Let us pause and consider the pieces of information that have been presented so far. First, we have Heinlein informing Campbell of the device in one of his stories being used by the Navy. This event occurred in mid-1940. Then, at the end of 1941, we have Heinlein mentioning the naval system in a letter and also referring to development work. We do not have any details concerning the development. It is not unreasonable to assume that this work occurred over the intervening months. But that brings up the question as to how Heinlein was kept informed of these details. One might assume that same naval officer who had told Heinlein about the use of the device was also connected with the development work and was able to keep Heinlein current on its status. It is interesting to note that in his January 4 letter, Heinlein referred to the matter as a military secret. Does this mean that the naval officer was violating security by informing Heinlein of its existence and ongoing work, even though the system was based on one of Heinlein's stories?

I have been able to locate only one additional letter that makes direct reference to the gadget. This one occurs on January 17, 1942. Heinlein is telling John Campbell and his wife Doña about the possibility of obtaining a position with the Navy. He speaks of being contacted by a naval officer. It was first a matter of speculation that the officer was his old friend Buddy Scoles. During the examination of another Archives file, a letter dated January 14, 1942 was located. This letter was from Scoles and was concerned with the high-altitude work for which facilities were nearing completion at the Naval Aircraft Factory. His thought was that useful technical ideas regarding high-altitude survival and pressure suits could be obtained from the writers and readers of science fiction magazines. Scoles even suggested that Heinlein could write an article to point out the need for such ideas. It was in the closing paragraph of the letter that Scoles made the suggestion that Heinlein come to work at the Factory.

Although such a full-length article was never written, a brief description of the problem written by Campbell did appear in *Astounding* in late 1942, and apparently some readers responded. An additional benefit of Scoles' suggestion was that the authors L. Sprague de Camp and Isaac Asimov did come to work at the Factory. After the war, de Camp performed work related to the design of high-altitude pressure suits.

Heinlein felt that he was limited in what he could say, but did let the Campbells know:

> This much I can say (still strictly for you and Doña only): I was thought of for the job because of the stories of mine you have published. It is not a writing job but I was picked because I am both a naval officer and a science-fiction writer. The officer who contacted me reads ASTOUNDING. (This has no connection with the gadget picked up from one of my stories. The officer who contacted me does not know of that incident.)

Since Heinlein mentions *Astounding* and then refers to his stories and the gadget, can we assume that story appeared in that magazine? This would permit us to eliminate "Let There Be Light" as it appeared in *Super Science Stories*. Or is such an assumption attempting to extract too much from the final quote?

Now let us look at the Virtues essay and the quote that it contains.

3

THE VIRTUES QUOTE

This chapter begins by presenting the quote which is the remaining source of information from Heinlein used to identify the mystery device. The background of the essay is considered and an analysis of the essay places the quote in the proper context. The quote is dissected to derive as much useful information concerning the device.

The key quote, as it appears in the essay "Science Fiction: Its Nature, Faults and Virtues", is as follows:

> I had a completely imaginary electronics device in a story published in 1939. A classmate of mine, then directing such research, took it to his civilian chief engineer and asked if it could possibly be done. The researcher replied, "Mmm . . . no, I don't think so—uh, wait a minute . . . well, yes, maybe. We'll try."
>
> The bread-boarded first model was being tried out aboard ship before the next installment of my story hit the newsstands. The final development of this gadget was in use all during World War II. I wasn't predicting anything and had no reason to think that it would work; I was just dreaming up a gadget to fill a need in a story, sticking as close to fact and possibility as I could.

The first question to be answered is why Heinlein created the essay in which this particular quoted appeared.

In 1957, there were a series of lectures by four science fiction authors at the University of Chicago. These were arranged by Mark Reinsberg who had long been involved in science fiction fan activities - fandom. He had attended the first World Science Fiction Convention in New York in 1939 and was instrumental in getting the second Worldcon, as they came to be called, for Chicago in 1940. Ginny Heinlein stated that she and Robert knew Mark and his wife Diane in the late 1940s when they were both attending Colorado College. According to Robert Heinlein, the lectures were arranged by Mark Reinsberg in conjunction with the University of Chicago Science Fiction Club.

If not for the efforts of Earl Kemp, these lectures might have been lost to history. Kemp was instrumental in having the lectures converted into essays and then published. In 1955, Earl Kemp and other members of the University of Chicago Science Fiction Club started Advent Publishers, which concentrated its efforts in the area of science fiction criticism. It was Kemp who came up with the idea for the collection of essays after he had heard about the lectures. He was acquainted with all of the writers, although in arranging for the publication of the essay Heinlein had insisted that Kemp work through his agent Lurton Blassingame. It was Kemp who arranged for Basil Davenport to write the introduction and who then assembled the material for publication. The collection of four essays and Davenport's introduction appeared in 1959 with the title *The Science Fiction Novel: Imagination and Social Criticism*.

In all four cases, the published essay is labeled as being "Based on a lecture by . . . ." With the exception of Robert Heinlein, however, the extent to which each essay differs from the delivered lecture is not known.

The first lecture was delivered on Friday, January 11 by C.M. Kornbluth (1923-1958). Many of Cyril Kornbluth's early works were written in collaboration and he made use of many pseudonyms. In the years following World War 2, he began writing science fiction under his own name. One of his better known short stories is "The Little Black Bag" which concerns a collection of futuristic medical devices that is sent back in time. The novel for which he is probably best known is *Space Merchants* (originally *Gravy Planet*), in collaboration with Frederik Pohl. The dedication in my copy of the collection of essays reads "In Memoriam C. M. Kornbluth."

Kornbluth's essay is "The Failure of the Science Fiction Novel as Social Criticism." On the basis of the title, we do not have to speculate as to his view of the topic. The essay begins by presenting some works of literature that have succeeded as social criticism: *Don Quixote*, *Uncle Tom's Cabin*, *The Jungle*, *The Good Soldier Schweik*, and *Babbitt*. Kornbluth then goes on to state that no work of science fiction has had the impact on society as the works that he has listed. The essay then discusses *Gulliver's Travels* and *1984*. He moves on to works that would be considered science fiction, starting with the Skylark series of E.E. "Doc"

Smith and Wilson Tucker's *The Long Loud Silence*, and disposes of the works of Olaf Stapledon at the rate of one sentence per book.

Kornbluth concluded that the science fiction novel does contain elements of social criticism, but that the nature and structure of the work makes it difficult to relate to individual and society.

The next lecture delivered was by Heinlein. For the moment we move on to the third lecture, which was delivered by Alfred Bester on February 22.

The first published science fiction work by Alfred Bester (1913-1987) was "The Broken Axiom" which appeared in *Thrilling Wonder Stories* in 1939. A number of stories were published until 1942, when Bester made the transition into the field of comic books. This was followed by work in radio and then finally in television. The works for which he is probably the best known are those that were created in the period following his return to science fiction in 1950 - *The Demolished Man* and *The Stars My Destination*. Following these works, in the late 1950s, Bester became a feature writer for *Holiday* magazine, and its senior literary editor for the remainder of the life of the publication.

Bester's essay "Science Fiction and the Renaissance Man," marginally the shortest work in the collection, is somewhat autobiographical in nature. The first section relates in greater detail the points of Bester's life mentioned in the preceding paragraph. Recollections of writing for Horace Gold and John W. Campbell, Jr. provide most of the science fiction content of this section. Bester continues with some interesting anecdotes and funny stories, but only at the very end of his work does he draw a picture of science fiction which even touches upon the topic of social criticism.

The final lecture was delivered on March 8 by Robert Bloch (1917-1994). The name might not be familiar as a science fiction writer, as his work in the field was relatively small. He is best known for his work *Psycho*, which served as the basis for the 1960 Hitchcock film. Much of Bloch's total output was in the areas of fantasy and horror.

Bloch's essay "Imagination and Modern Social Criticism" begins in a lighthearted manner by referring to those people who in the past have dared to criticize the status quo - people such as Harriet Beecher Stowe, Mark Twain, Ring Lardner and Will Rogers. He discusses a few more recent social critics and then arrives at the field of science fiction.

Bloch's approach to the problem is a bit more systematic, as he takes a collection of 50 science fiction works, selected at random, and divides them into 3 categories - Man against Nature, Man against Himself, and Man against Man. The final grouping, which contains 35 of the 50 works, is stated as providing an opportunity for social criticism. Bloch then lists a number of possible futures for our society that are presented by science fiction authors. Throughout his essay, he discusses individual works of science fiction, devoting the most space to Heinlein's *Beyond This Horizon*. Bloch concludes that science fiction has not been a failure in its function of social criticism. Basil Davenport, in summing up the conclusions of each of the essayists, appears to have missed that statement in Bloch's work.

Now that I have disposed of the other essays within the collection, we come to the subject of this chapter. The lecture on which Heinlein's essay is based was delivered on February 8, 1957. Heinlein's essay is the largest in the collection and appears first. The essay will be divided into 9 sections for the purpose of analysis.

1. Attempts to define science fiction. Heinlein begins by trying to decide what is meant by the term "science fiction." When you say that such a task is difficult, most people are likely to respond that they know what is meant by the term. The trick then becomes finding two people who will agree in their definitions. The alternative term for which Heinlein states a preference is "speculative fiction," but he goes on to say that he will use the two terms interchangeably throughout the essay.

Heinlein first provides definitions by others in the field - Damon Knight, August Derleth, Theodore Sturgeon and Reginald Bretnor. The definitions provided by the first three were criticized as being too broad or too restrictive. The one provided by Bretnor was considered the best and what is presented here is Heinlein's paraphrase of that definition:

> science fiction being that sort in which the author shows awareness of the nature and importance of the human activity known as the scientific method, shows equal awareness of the great body of human knowledge already collected through that activity, and takes into account in his stories the effects and possible future effects on human beings of scientific method and scientific fact.

After stating his preference for Bretnor's definition due to the amount of freedom it allows the author, Heinlein approaches the problem from a different direction. He begins with the broadest possible definition of fiction - "story telling about imaginary things and people." Fiction is then divided into two categories - what is considered as "imaginary-but-not-possible" is called "fantasy fiction" and what is considered "imaginary-but possible" is called "realistic fiction." Stories are then presented which fall into the first category, and the statement is made that all other fiction by default falls into the second category. Heinlein admits to problems with this approach noting that one must include time travel, faster-than-light travel and possibly even reincarnation and ghosts into the second category to admit certain stories, even though such concepts might not be considered "possible" by many people.

Realistic fiction is then divided into three into three groups: Historical Fiction, Contemporary-Scene fiction, and Realistic Future-Scene Fiction. Heinlein states that the final group contains nothing that is not science fiction, and contains 90% of all science fiction in print. The remaining 10% occurs, of course, in the other two groups. We may assume that the final group is what comes to the minds of most people when you say science fiction.

The discussion of science fiction then returns to his favorite alternative term "speculative fiction." Heinlein considers that our lives are always in the future, as the future is all that it is ever possible to change. This means that a form of literature which concerns itself with speculation is superior to any other type.

2. Science Fiction as Prophecy. The section of the essay begins with a question about the nature of speculation as discussed in the first section:

Are the speculations of science fiction prophecy? No.
On the other hand, science fiction is often prophetic.

We must first consider the meaning of the words "prophecy" or "prophetic." The most basic definition of prophecy is "A declaration of something to come; prediction." But for many people, prophecy has additional meanings. During the course of my research, I used the word in referring to the predictions of science fiction writers. The reaction that I received from one person led me to believe that this person feared that I was bringing in all sorts of mystical or spiritual or extra-sensory implications. I had to point out that I was using the term employed by Heinlein and others.

The main point is that a prophecy in the religious sense is considered to be a pronouncement as to what *will* occur. This is a different matter than a prediction which presents what *might* occur. We may then translate Heinlein's statements as saying that science fiction does not state what will occur, but has been reasonably successful in its predictions of what might occur.

And to what may we attribute this success? If you predict a great number of things, some small quantity will have the chance of occurring. In most situations, we tend to focus on the few successful predictions and tend to ignore the much greater number of failures. But successful predictions come, as Heinlein states, from those who are aware of the current states and trends in science and technology and are making a logical extrapolation. Heinlein uses the rest of this section to discuss the predictions in two of his works, "Waldo" and "Solution Unsatisfactory."

"Solution Unsatisfactory" is discussed first. For those unfamiliar with the story, it concerns the development of atomic weapons and the post-war implications for world peace and survival resulting from the nature of the weapons. Not bad for a story that appeared in 1941, before the entry of the United States into World War 2, and before the Manhattan Project. I will defer a discussion of this particular story until a later chapter.

Part of the story "Waldo" involves the use of remote control manipulators by a person with limited muscle power. The devices developed and employed in the Manhattan Project for the remote manipulation of highly radioactive materials are said to have been given the name "waldoes" by engineers and scientists who were readers of *Astounding Science-Fiction*.

Heinlein claims that his manipulators were inspired by a 1918 article in *Popular Mechanics* magazine. The subject of the article was a gentleman afflicted with myasthenia gravis, a disease of profound muscular weakness. This person developed mechanical arrangements to get the maximum use of what small amount of muscular strength that he did possess. All that Heinlein claimed to have done was to convert this mechanical system into a remotely controlled electromechanical one.

There does appear to be one problem with Heinlein's statements. I made an attempt to locate this article by scanning microfilm containing back issues of *Popular Mechanics* from that year. I found no such article. I then expanded my search to cover 1917 and 1919, also with no success. There are several possible explanations. I was scanning a lot of material and it is possible that I missed it, particularly if the article was smaller than I thought. Such efforts tend to make one appreciate search engines. The most plausible explanation, I would suggest, is that Heinlein was mistaken in recalling either the publication or the date. Consider that if he read the article as claimed in 1918, he would have been 10 or 11 years old. When he was planning for the Chicago lecture, he would have been 49 years old. How many of you can say that you could accurately remember details of such an article 38 or 39 years after the fact? I would also suggest that the article may have been in a different publication or may have appeared at later date, perhaps during the 1920s. If anyone out there wishes to spend hours scrolling thru reels of microfilm to locate the article, I wish them luck. Let me know if you find anything.

The final technical detail in this section concerns a brief mention of another supposed prophecy. Heinlein states that:

For example, in one story I described a rather remarkable oleo-gear arrangement for handling exceedingly heavy loads. I was not cheating, the device would work; it had been patented about 1900 and has been in industrial use ever since. But it is a gadget not well known to the public and it happened to fit into a story I was writing.

These devices were "waterburies" which are mentioned in "If This Goes On—" and described in my Note "Naval Technology in Heinlein's Stories" that appeared in *The Heinlein Journal* (Issue No. 14, January 2004). Briefly, they are a means of converting rotary motion into hydraulic pressure and then converting back to rotary motion at some other location. In Heinlein's story, they are used to drive the freighter on which the protagonist John Lyle obtains a lift, as well as the military craft appearing elsewhere in the story.

3. Interaction of Science Fiction and Science. We now come to the most important section of the essay - the one which contains the device quote. Heinlein begins by stating that science and science fiction do interact. He lists a number of authors of the time with some form of technical or scientific background, such as Isaac Asimov, L. Sprague de Camp, and George O. Smith.

Heinlein claims that "science fiction not infrequently guides the direction of science." This statement is followed by the reference to the mystery device which was quoted at the beginning of this chapter.

Later in this section, Heinlein presents another case to demonstrate the connection between science fiction and science. This connection involved the development of high-altitude pressure suits (space suits) at the Naval Aircraft Factory during the war. As opposed to the paragraphs concerning the mystery device, the paragraph concerning the space suits presented detailed information. The original plan in presenting this section was to contrast the amount of information provided in the two cases. When research was done in the area of the pressure suits, however, the claims of Heinlein began to look a bit questionable. Heinlein begins by stating that he was in charge of a laboratory concerned with the development of a high-altitude pressure suit. Heinlein claims to have worked on the problem and:

> then was relieved by L. Sprague de Camp, who is an aeronautical and mechanical engineer as well as a writer; he carried on with this research all through the war, testing and developing many spacesuits.

The difficulty appears when one reads de Camp's autobiography, *Time and Chance*. After the war, an article appeared in *The Philadelphia Record* which inaccurately represented the work done by Heinlein, de Camp and Isaac Asimov at the Naval Aircraft Factory. One of the erroneous claims made in the article was that the three worked together to develop a "pressurized space suit." De Camp claimed that the nearest that any of them got to a suit during the war was when one developed by a contractor was brought in for a test in the altitude chamber.

De Camp does explain a few pages later that he did work after the war while still in the Reserves in developing constant-volume joints. This type of joint prevents the pressurization of the suit from forcing the person into a spread-eagle configuration or from having to expend considerable effort when bending any of its joints. Heinlein does not refer to this particular development in the essay, but does mention "de Camp joints" in his juvenile novel *Rocket Ship Galileo*. So there appears to be a definite science fiction connection in this particular case, although not precisely the way that Heinlein presents it.

4. Peenemunde quote and its dissection. This section forms the logical bridge between the discussion of the connection between science and science fiction and the following discussion of the literary criticism applied to science fiction. When science fiction is mentioned, the type of story that most people will visualize concerns space travel. Heinlein points out that many people involved in the development of rocketry have at some time written fiction on the subject. He then produces a quote from *The Saturday Review* that he considers typical of the criticism applied to science fiction:

> Even before the German inventors created the first navigable rocket at Peenemünde the writers of this somewhat crude form of entertainment had developed the rocket ships which cruised to the moon and the solar planets and then burst into outermost space and explored the galaxies of the Milky Way. Driven by atomic power these apparently mad devices were as well known to the devotees of science fiction as the liners that cross our oceans. Nevertheless, it (space travel) remained unadulterated fantasy until scientists contemplated the experiments with rockets that have proceeded since the last war.

He takes the next three pages of the essay to tear the above quote into very small pieces. I will not repeat any of his dissection here, and suggest that the reader see how many misstatements and absurdities can be found.

5. Literary merit and standards. Should science fiction be judged by standards that differ from those applied to other fields of fiction?

Heinlein states that it should not. He makes an analogy between a person writing a historical novel and a person writing a science fiction novel. One would not sit down to write a novel concerning, as Heinlein suggests, 16th century England without having thoroughly researched the subject. A science fiction author must similarly research the technical topics which form the basis for his speculations.

Heinlein closes this section by suggesting that science fiction be judged only by those critics who are properly educated, unlike the author of the quote presented in the previous section.

6. Difficulty in writing science fiction. Having stated that science fiction should be judged according to same standards as other fiction, Heinlein states that science fiction does not in general measure up to those standards.

His primary reason for making that statement is his claim that speculative fiction is the most difficult to write. A science fiction author may be describing an alien race with particular customs or a radically different future form of human society or a new means of traveling through space. The author must, above all, make the reader believe in what he has created. He must do this without the ability to use the conventional assumptions that writers of historical fiction or westerns or detective stories may invoke with a few simple sentences. Each of these types of stories makes use of a common background shared by the writer and his audience. The science fiction author, unless he sets his story in the past or the present, has no such common background. He must create the unique framework required by his story and communicate it the reader without bringing the action in the story to a screeching halt.

7. Quality of the field. The argument for the general poor quality of the field continues with the statement that there is very little science fiction of any sort.

As Heinlein's reasons are presented, please remember that his comments are of the state of the field over fifty years ago. His claim is that the writers of speculative fiction are outnumbered by those writing historical fiction and contemporary-scene fiction. This is probably still true, though not to the extent that Heinlein claims. A good test would be to walk through the sections of a large bookstore and total up the number of authors in the various categories.

For the mid to late 1950's, Heinlein claims to know either personally or though his work, every writer of speculative fiction, of which only a small percentage are able to make a living by it. With such a small number of writers, Heinlein claims that demand exceeds supply. As a consequence, many works are published that would otherwise be rejected.

Although it is claimed by Heinlein that there is not a large quantity of good speculative fiction, his is willing to admit that there are some works which come up to the standards. The short list includes works by Asimov, Kornbluth, Clement, Stapledon, de Camp and Clarke.

Heinlein concludes this section by mentioning the only history of science fiction that existed at the time, J. O. Bailey's *Pilgrims Through Space and Time*.

8. Virtues of science fiction compared with other literature. Having made a number of judgments in preceding sections concerning science fiction, Heinlein then poses the following question:

> Of what use is science fiction? I have already said that it is not prophecy, that most of it is not very good from a literary standpoint . . . . and now let me add that much of it is not even very entertaining in my opinion. Good heavens! Does it have any virtue?

His answer is the assertion that speculative fiction is the mainstream of fiction as opposed the historical or contemporary scene novel. In doing so, he places science fiction at a higher level than the historical novel or contemporary-scene novel. Dismissal of the historical novel, excepting the merits of any particular work, is based on the reason that it looks backward. Not a very pleasing approach to someone used to looking to the future.

Heinlein's feelings with regard to contemporary-scene fiction are stronger. He begins by claiming that such fiction is not capable of dealing with the rate of change in the society of his time. Can we assume that he would make similar pronouncements regarding the literature of our time? The characterization of most serious literature of this type as "sick" is applied to the realist school of writers such as Henry Miller and James Joyce. He states that much of what passes for literature should ". . . . not be printed, but told only privately—on a psychiatrist's couch."

Speculative fiction, Heinlein claims, is the only form of literature which truly prepares the reader for dealing with the future. By its speculations, it can do what "mainstream" literature cannot - present problems facing the human race, perhaps disguised as alien civilizations on distant worlds. If not capable of coming up with solutions to these problems himself, the science fiction author should enable people to consider such problems and arrive at their own solutions.

9. Future of science fiction. Heinlein concludes with his expectations. His first is that science fiction will improve in amount and quality. We can point to a large amount of science fiction being published. I do not propose to become involved in argument regarding the quality of the current crop of science fiction. Whether the intervening years have, as Heinlein expected, led to the decline of "neurotic and psychotic fiction" is another topic that I will also avoid.

The body of the essay is followed by a short section in which Heinlein lists people and works that have influenced his thoughts. I present only a partial list - Reginald Bretnor, Arthur C. Clarke, John W. Campbell, Jr., William A. P. White, L. Sprague de Camp and Isaac Asimov. Of these, Heinlein singles out Reginald Bretnor as having the greatest influence.

The list of names is followed by a short list of references (omitted from a republication of the essay in *Turning Points*, edited by Damon Knight). The two references from the list I feel are of particular interest are *Modern Science Fiction: Its Meaning and Its Future*, edited by Reginald Bretnor, and J. O. Bailey's *Pilgrims Through Space and Time*.

Modern Science Fiction, published in 1953, is a collection of essays by, among others, Reginald Bretnor, Arthur C. Clarke, John W. Campbell, Jr., Anthony Boucher (aka William A. P. White), L. Sprague de Camp and Isaac Asimov.

It is not difficult to see the influence of the essays in this collection upon the Virtues essay. Many of the authors (Fletcher Pratt, de Camp, Rosalie Moore, Asimov and Gerald Heard) attempted to define science fiction. Several (de Camp, Heard and Bretnor) made specific use of the word "prophecy." One essay, by Rosalie Moore, attempted to discuss science fiction and its relation to mainstream literature but succeeded in demonstrating her lack of knowledge and understanding of science fiction. A poet, her only stated connection with the field appears to have been her marriage to a science fiction author.

The Virtues essay refers, in its discussion of "Solution Unsatisfactory," to comments by Campbell that a number of the prophecies have come true. This discussion of these prophecies, although Campbell uses the word predictions, occurs in his essay "The Place of Science Fiction." The Peenemunde quote, which Heinlein thanked Bretnor for providing to him, also appears in his essay "The Future of Science Fiction," although Bretnor's comments regarding the content of the quote do not even approach Heinlein's efforts.

There is one section of the Virtues essay which has no direct counterpart among the essays of *Modern Science Fiction*. Although an essay might make reference to the technological content of science fiction or as Campbell does, discuss predictions, there is no mention anywhere of the close coupling between science fiction and science as presented in the section of the Virtues essay that contains the gadget quote and the space suit story.

For such a discussion we must turn to the other of Heinlein's references noted above, Bailey's *Pilgrims Through Space and Time*. This work is an extension of Bailey's Ph.D. dissertation at the University of North Carolina in the 1930s. The scope of the original work only extended to 1914. The extension of the work to cover the period into the 1940s, as claimed on the book jacket, was not very successful. Clifford Simak and Murray Leinster do appear with works from the early 1930s. But there is no mention of John W. Campbell, Jr., Isaac Asimov, L. Sprague de Camp, or even Robert Heinlein. One might suspect that Bailey did not consider any stories later than the 1930s despite the claim to the contrary. But a search of the index reveals at least one story from the 1940s, George O. Smith's "Identity" (1945).

What makes Bailey's work important, despite its faults, is his approach to the problem of defining science fiction. His central thesis is that "scientific fiction" is based upon invention or discovery. The analyses performed upon the many stories that he presents are always in terms of such imaginary inventions or discoveries. In one of the later chapters of the work, significantly titled "Inventions and Discoveries," Bailey states:

> Even though a direct influence of imaginary invention upon actual invention can hardly be demonstrated, the course of important inventions and discoveries in scientific fiction is worth record.

I consider this quote to be of great importance. My contention is that Heinlein included the gadget and space suit stories within the Virtues essay in an attempt to refute Bailey's statement. Although Bailey's statement was encountered late in the course of my research, I would say that attempting to find and present additional means of countering his statement is a fair description of the aim of that research.

Let us now return to the Virtues essay. Having attempted to extract as much useful information as possible from the published version of the essay, I began to wonder if the script which Heinlein used for his lecture might contain additional information that had been edited out in preparation for publication. Fortunately, during my visit to the Heinlein

Archives at the University of California Santa Cruz, the script was located. The box that was provided to me contained 3 folders as follows:

FOLDER 1.
- Sticky note on front of folder "M. Baughman has part of this."
- A typed copy of the script marked "Lecture as delivered orally" - unfortunately with a number of pages missing.
- A typed copy marked "Lecture as revised for publication."

FOLDER 2.
- A page defining the talk, which also existed in folder 1.
- An index card which listed the missing pages of the lecture script.

FOLDER 3.
- Another copy of the lecture script with the same pages missing as in Folder 1.

The contents of folder 2 indicated that I was not the first to notice the missing pages, and then there was the implication that possibly "M. Baughman" knew where they might be. With no other information available, I had resigned myself to never locating the missing pages of the script, one of which contained the greater part of the gadget quote. It was not until some time later that I noticed that every page that was missing from the lecture script had been re-used in constructing the version for publication. This conclusion was based on the particular manner in which the lecture script pages were numbered.

Recognition of the re-use gave me three types of pages to consider: (1) Lecture script pages not re-used in manuscript, (2) Lecture script page re-used in manuscript, and (3) Manuscript pages that were newly typed. In the first group all deletions, with one exception, or additions were made using the typewriter. The exception was a single faint handwritten insertion of text. The last group, while it does contain a few deletions and insertions made using the typewriter, also contains many handwritten editorial changes in a very dark ink. These handwritten changes also affect the group of re-used pages, so that it becomes possible to strip away the final set of changes and view the lecture script pages in their original form.

It may have occurred to most of you that if the technology of the 1950s had included word processors, none of this valuable evidence of manuscript changes would have existed for us to consider. What does that imply about future historians looking back at the literary evidence of our time?

The final version for publication consists of 40 double-spaced pages, of which 12 were pages re-used from the lecture script. It is therefore not practical to consider every possible change that occurred between the two versions. Some were to remove comments to the audience at the beginning of the talk, while many others were the changes in words or sentence structure that would be expected in revising a manuscript for publication. There are, however, a few cases in areas of the script of particular interest where there were deletions of text.

The first of these involves Heinlein's reference to the waterburies in the section on prophecy. As it appears in the lecture script, it is of the form:

> For example, in one story I described a certain rather remarkable and exotic variable oleo gear arrangement for handling exceedingly heavy loads. I was not cheating anyone for the device would work. It had been patented about 1900 and has been in industrial use ever since -- I was required to learn to sketch and describe it at the US Naval Academy back in the twenties. But it was a gadget not well known to the public and it happened to fit beautifully into a story I was writing.

This may be compared to the published version quote appearing in the discussion of the Virtues essay section on prophecy. The deletion of a word or two is not significant, nor is the change from "variable gear arrangement" to "oleo gear arrangement." But I do wonder why Heinlein deleted the reference to the naval application of the device. Was he concerned about revealing any specific naval information, however inconsequential it might be? Or was he just cutting out extraneous text?

Omitted from the paragraph on the space suits is the statement that Heinlein was relieved of the Altitude Chamber work by the flight surgeon because of his having had tuberculosis. The other significant omission from this paragraph was a group of sentences removed from the very end, possibly viewed as redundant in its reference to the original space suit descriptions of Edmund Hamilton in 1931, but interesting in its view of the process of invention:

> A space suit has to be worn by a man and has to provide him with an artificial environment -- is it surprising that an intelligent man could speculate correctly about its obvious necessities? Twenty-five years ago? 25 year ago all that was lacking was the need for the invention; the correct shape of the invention could already be formed in a man's mind.

Finally we come to the gadget quote. As previously stated, I had hoped that the script would reveal some information deleted or modified for the final version which could aid in solving the mystery. There were in fact a number of such changes to these two paragraphs. Instead of simply presenting these changes, however, I would like to put them in the context of a more detailed analysis of the quote. The gadget quote as it appeared in the lecture script is:

> I had a completely imaginary electronics device in a story published in 1939. A classmate of mine, then engaged in direction of such research, took it around to his civilian chief engineer and asked if it could possibly be done. The researcher replied, "Mmm . . no, I don't think so -- uh, wait a minute . . . Well, yes, maybe. We'll try."
>
> The bread-boarded first model was being tried out aboard ship before the next ■■■■ installment of my story hit the stands. The final development of it was in use all through World War II. I can't tell you what it was because it was then secret, it may still be secret, and as far as I know the public has not heard of it. But mind you, I wasn't predicting anything and had no reason to think that it would work; I was just dreaming up a gadget to fill a need in story, sticking as close to fact and possibility as I could.

(Note: The four squares represent a typeover correction that I will discuss shortly.)

In comparing this with the published version at the beginning of the chapter, let us first dispose of some minor editorial changes:

1. "then engaged in direction of such research" versus "then directing such research"

2. "took it around to" versus "took it to"

3. "stands" versus "newsstands"

4. Deletion of "But mind you"

I think that it can be agreed that none of the above changes could have the slightest effect upon the mystery.

Now look at the entire sentence that was deleted from the lecture script:

I can't tell you what it was because it was then secret, it may still be secret, and so far as I know the public has not heard of it.

This statement concerning the secrecy of the device is considered important in the identification of the device. It is also consistent with one of the footnotes to the essay as published in *Turning Points* (1977). In this footnote, Damon Knight states "I asked Heinlein what this gadget was; he replied that as far as he knows it is still classified."

Now we come to the typeover. To understand its significance, two parts of the quote must be examined. It is stated that the story containing the device was "published in 1939." Later, it is stated that the idea was being tested before the "next installment of my story" appeared. To anyone familiar with Heinlein's works, the combination of these two quotes presents us with a problem. The only stories published in 1939 were "Life-Line" (August) and "Misfit" (November). These were each short stories that appeared within a single issue. So how could he speak of the next "installment" of the story? The first Heinlein story that consisted of multiple installments was "If This Goes On—" in 1940 (February and March). If we accept "1939," we must reject "installment." Conversely, if we accept "installment," then "1939" becomes impossible.

A section of the reused lecture script page which contains part of the quote is shown in the upper part of Figure 1. Now take a close look at the typeover in the enlargement in the lower part of the figure. Is there any objection to my suggestion that the first letter typed over was an "i"? The next two letters are similar in appearance. The top and bottom of both letters appear slightly rounded – compare the base of each with the straight base of the first letter. I suggest that both the second and third letters are "s". The final typeover character is an equal sign - there are many other typeovers in the lecture script that end with an equal sign. As he was typing the lecture script, did Heinlein actually start to type "issue"? If that is the case, and Heinlein had continued with the same thought, the sentence would then have read "before the next issue hit the stands."

But what does this mean? With the earlier statement of "1939," the alternative form of the sentence would have pointed directly to his first two stories. By typing "installment," Heinlein created a situation where the quote made it impossible to select any story. But why even say "1939"? Why did he not simply say "In one of my early stories"? Was the use of both "1939" and "installment" meant to defeat anyone attempting to locate the device?

My approach from the very beginning has been to ignore both "1939" and "installment" and simply consider all of his stories starting with "Life-

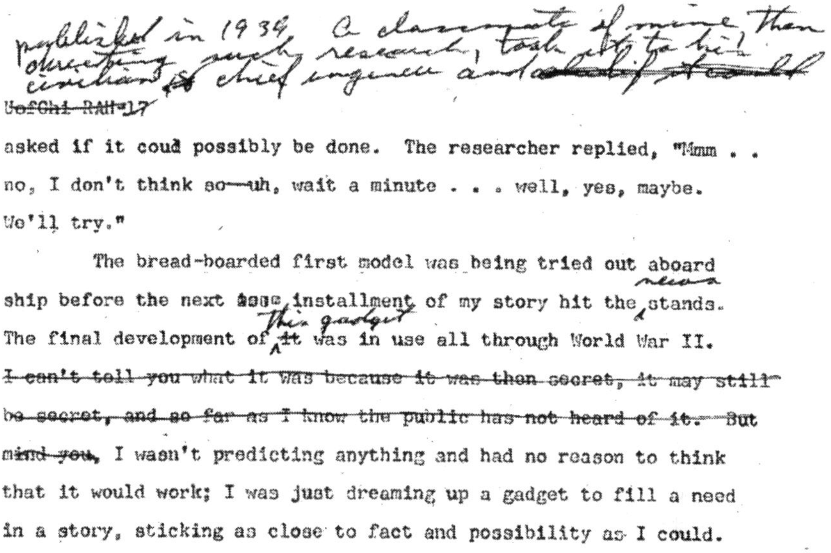

published in 1939, a classmate of mine then
our civilian ~~was~~ chief engineer and ~~asked if it could~~

asked if it could possibly be done. The researcher replied, "Mmm . .
no, I don't think so—uh, wait a minute . . . well, yes, maybe.
We'll try."

The bread-boarded first model was being tried out aboard
ship before the next ~~issue~~ *news* installment of my story hit the stands.
The final development of ~~it~~ *this gadget* was in use all through World War II.
~~I can't tell you what it was because it was then secret, it may still
be secret, and so far as I know the public has not heard of it. But
mind you,~~ I wasn't predicting anything and had no reason to think
that it would work; I was just dreaming up a gadget to fill a need
in a story, sticking as close to fact and possibility as I could.

Segment of Manuscript Page with Key Quote

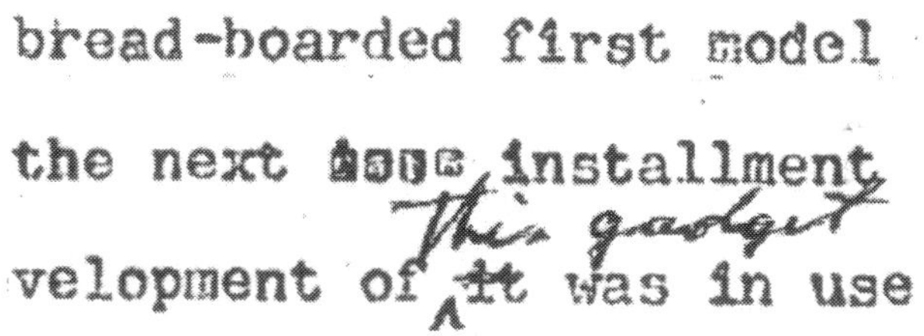

bread-boarded first model

the next ~~issue~~ installment

velopment of ~~it~~ *this gadget* was in use

Enlargement showing typeover

Figure 1. Manuscript Page from Virtues Essay (By permission of the Robert A. & Virginia Heinlein Prize Trust)

Line." In the absence of additional data, this meant considering all stories until December 1941. It is only with the evidence obtained from the letter quotes, as described in the previous chapter, that is was possible to limit the number of stories to be examined.

Now that the various changes have been presented, let us move on to the specific statements made within the quote:

1. The device is specifically identified as electronic in nature.

2. The person responsible is identified as a classmate of Heinlein. Obviously, he is referring to a Naval Academy classmate. He is also referring to a fellow member of the Class of 1929, rather than simply another Academy alumnus. To illustrate the distinction, in *Expanded Universe* Heinlein refers to Albert "Buddy" Scoles (Class of 1927) as "at the Academy with me, shipmates before then in USS UTAH," but never as a classmate. On the other hand, in a letter to Campbell dated January 5, 1942, Heinlein refers to a newspaper article featuring "my classmate and old friend, Bill Kabler," who was definitely a member of the Class of 1929.

3. The classmate was still in active service at the time, as the distinction is clearly made that his classmate's chief engineer was a civilian. The condition of active service is important as it is possible that a classmate could have resigned or have been retired, as Heinlein had been for medical reasons.

4. Only the bread-boarded version of the device was being tried out during the first month following the publication of the story containing the fictional device. This might be a convenient time to explain the term "bread-boarded." In this context, it refers to a version of a circuit hastily constructed to test the idea or serve as a proof of concept. The name comes from the breadboard used to construct it. Circuits using tubes or even transistors would have been constructed using sockets and connectors fastened to a wooden board with the dimensions possibly those of an actual cutting board for bread. The construction of such circuits would be done quickly and the overall appearance was usually sloppy. Integrated circuit breadboards take the form of plastic panels with rows of holes. Groups of holes are internally connected with conductive metal strips according to a known pattern. Circuits are assembled by simply plugging in wires, integrated circuit packages and the lead wires of discrete components. Breadboard circuits are

practical only when dealing with relatively low frequencies or operating speeds, where factors such as component placement and interconnection length are not critical.

5. There was subsequent development work before the device went into naval service.

6. On the basis of the sentence deleted from the script, the device was secret.

How much reliance may we put into the accuracy of any of these statements made by Heinlein in the gadget quote? A lack of accuracy in the Virtues essay has been demonstrated elsewhere in this chapter, both with regard to the date of the article that inspired "Waldo" and the details concerning space suit development at the Naval Aircraft Factory. The only way that it is possible to evaluate the statements is to compare each of them to corresponding material from the letters. This will be performed in the next chapter.

4

ANALYSIS OF QUOTES

One thing that is consistent between the two sets of quotes presented in the preceding chapters is the emphasis on secrecy. In the letter of December 29, Robert Heinlein told Campbell not to discuss the story device with his father or anyone else, lest they try to guess what it was. This concern over secrecy was emphasized in the letter from Leslyn Heinlein on January 4. She reminded Campbell that when the device was first mentioned in the spring of 1940, Robert refused to identify it because he said that the matter was confidential.

Then we come to the quote in the lecture script from 1957 (but not in the published essay) where Heinlein said "I can't tell you what it was because it was then secret, it may still be secret, and so far as I know the public has not heard of it." Finally we have Heinlein replying in 1977 to a question from Damon Knight about the identity of the system that as far has he knew the device was still classified.

This all adds up to a tremendous concern on Heinlein's part regarding people not being able to identify the naval system. ***If that is the case, then why did he mention the device at all in the Virtues lecture and essay????*** The naval system does provide an excellent example for Heinlein's discussion of the influence of science fiction upon science or, in this case, engineering. Prior to the delivery of the lecture and the publication of the essay, Heinlein had only discussed it with the Campbells. By mentioning it to a much larger audience and not identifying it, all he did was set out a challenge to people like me to try to identify it. I can only speculate that he removed the above quoted sentence from the published essay because he realized that it was acting as a big red arrow pointing to the naval system. Saying that the system is secret might discourage some people from trying to figure out what it was. Others might take it as even more of a challenge.

As previously noted, the Virtues essay was the first reference to the device that I encountered. It was much later that I became aware of the other quotes, first in *Grumbles* and then in the Archives. Therefore, the Virtues essay has always had a leading position in my mind among the entire collection of evidence. However, when I considered the question of why Heinlein presented the story of such a secret naval system, I have had to conclude that he had distorted the details contained in both the lecture and essay to make identification of it very difficult, if not impossible.

First, consider the sentence from the first paragraph of the Virtues quote: "A classmate of mine, then directing such research, took it to his civilian chief engineer and asked if it could possibly be done." In the quote taken from the letters, the person responsible for picking up on the idea was simply identified as a "junior officer." As noted in Chapter 2, this officer must have read *Astounding* (or possibly the issue of *Super Science Stories* that contained "Let There Be Light") and must have been able to contact Heinlein to let him know of the naval system derived from his story. This could have been possible for any number of naval officers, but it seems that we should be restricting ourselves to those officers who knew Heinlein personally, either Academy classmates or former shipmates. I am of the opinion that an Academy classmate is the type who would have known Heinlein better and would have been more likely to stay in touch. This would include, but would not be restricted to, his close friend Cal Laning.

So what may we conclude about the claim that the classmate was directing research and had a civilian chief engineer? As is shown in a subsequent chapter, this particular situation was not possible for Cal Laning. In addition, I do not think that any member of the class of 1929, with a rank of only Lieutenant in 1940, would have been in such a position. They might possibly have served on some type of research project, but not directed it.

A naval officer who would satisfy the conditions of doing research and having civilian engineers under him, ***without*** being a classmate, would be his friend and former shipmate Buddy Scoles. Starting in June 1939, he was Assistant Chief Engineer for Materials at the Naval Aircraft Factory in Philadelphia, with the rank of Lt. Commander and with civilian engineers working under him.

If we accept the reference to the direction of research as pointing to Scoles, are we then justified in disregarding the term "classmate" and saying that Scoles was the person involved? One thing in favor of Scoles is that his duty at the Naval Aircraft Factory covers the period of the publication of Heinlein's early stories.

I say *NO*, based on the evidence of Scoles letter to Heinlein on January 14, 1942. In the opening paragraph, Scoles says:

I have been a long time writing, I know, but I hope you won't get mad and throw this away without reading it. I have been reading all your stories and should have congratulated you on your success a long time ago. However, it is due to that success that you are even getting this letter, which indicates how bad I am at correspondence.

Unfortunately, Scoles says "a long time" and "a long time ago" without stating a specific interval of time. Since he is congratulating Heinlein on the success of his stories, may we conclude that he had not written since before the first of the stories appeared in print in the August 1939 issue of *Astounding*? This would make it impossible for Scoles to have been the person involved with the process in the spring of 1940 leading to a naval system. If he had been that person, how would Heinlein have known about this process without Scoles contacting him? This conclusion is reinforced by Heinlein's letter to John and Doña Campbell where he states that the naval officer who contacted him about the job did not know of the story gadget.

So we have another case of intentional misdirection. Just picture Heinlein in early 1957, working on the script for his lecture to be delivered at the University of Chicago. He wishes to mention the mystery device to provide an example of the influence of science fiction. To confuse anyone who might try to identify the device, he thinks back to his time at the Naval Aircraft Factory. He brings in this fictional director of research, based on his friend Buddy Scoles, and links him with the classmate that really did the job. He then has this person taking the idea to his civilian chief engineer. And what was Heinlein's job at the Naval Aircraft Factory? He was a civilian engineer under Scoles. I think that Heinlein is playing a game with us here.

Therefore, the conjunction of "classmate" and "directing such research" is as much of an effort to make the device unidentifiable as the pairing of "1939" and "next installment."

The supposed conversation with the engineer, which provides no information, also vanishes. All we are left with is a reference to an electronic device that appeared in a story in 1939. And that particular year is known to be questionable. As noted in Chapter 2, Heinlein does not identify the device as electronic in the letter quotes. His reference to the class of engineer involved in the development work following the mention of G. E., Westinghouse and AT&T engineers does allow us to conclude that the device was either electronic or electrical in nature.

The second paragraph begins by referring to the bread-boarded model being tried out aboard ship before the next installment of the story appeared. If we interpret the problem term "installment" as simply specifying a one-month interval with no connection to actual story segments, I see no problem with a bread-board of some new device being thrown together and tested in a month. This makes more sense than the statement in the letter that the idea was in use throughout the fleet in the same time interval. Any system proposed for either military or naval applications would not be placed in use as quickly as Heinlein claimed. It would have to undergo some form of development work to ensure that it was reliable, safe to operate, capable of providing the desired function and capable of operating in the projected environment.

If we then look at the remainder of second paragraph of the Virtues essay quote, which does not include the explicit statement of secrecy, we are left with two statements. In the first, Heinlein claims that "The final development of this gadget was in use all during World War II." This has the potential for being another piece of misdirection as well. Let us assume that a candidate naval system is identified. If it did not go into service until later in the war, strict adherence to Heinlein's statement could cause it to be rejected as the solution.

In the second statement, Heinlein says, "I wasn't predicting anything and had no reason to think that it would work; I was just dreaming up a gadget to fill a need in a story, sticking as close to fact and possibility as I could." Does this sentence mean that the device that he described bears a close resemblance to the final naval system? I would consider it very unlikely that the naval system corresponded closely to what was described in the story. The story device could still have served as the direct inspiration for a naval system that differed in some details of operation. Even if this difference existed, I would consider that the concluding sentence of the Virtues quote would remain valid. This should prevent us from too strict of an interpretation of the details of each story device as we attempt to match it with naval systems.

After the preceding discussion, exactly what remains? Very little:

- Classmate

- Electronic or Electrical

- One month Bread-board

- Naval system not required to exactly match story device

The above discussion regarding Buddy Scoles and the Naval Aircraft Factory shows that he could not have been the naval officer involved in basing a naval system on the story idea, starting in the spring of 1940. Nevertheless, there is an additional quote from a letter in the Archives that may indicate some later connection between Scoles and the system and might permit the system to be identified. It does not come from a letter written by Heinlein, Campbell or Scoles. It is from a friend of Heinlein, William Corson. (*I would like to thank Bill Patterson for pointing out this particular letter to me.*)

William Corson and his wife are the people to whom the novel *I Will Fear No Evil* was dedicated. William Corson was a friend of Heinlein in California before the war. He had one published science fiction story, "Klystron Fort," which appeared in *Astounding Science Fiction* in July 1941. Starting in 1942 Corson was also on the East Coast, either in Army training or stationed at different locations. He visited the Heinleins in Philadelphia whenever possible and there are many letters in the Archives from Corson to them. The handwritten letter from which the quote is taken was postmarked May 28, 1942, very shortly after Heinlein began working at the Naval Aircraft Factory. Please note that in the following quote, the emphasis of the word "gadget" is mine.

After a discussion of his adventures traveling back to Arlington, VA following his most recent visit to Philadelphia, Corson mentions Buddy Scoles and his wife and then launches into a technical discussion:

> Which reminds me. Robert, as a diffident suggestion from an unqualified guy: you remember Bud speaking of difficulty of getting a full record of accel. & decel. on a ship??? Seems like as if a lot of worries consequent on measuring from the deck could be circumvented by installing your **gadget** in the plane itself. Set up a measuring track at appropriate velocity, and graph off your curve from some kind of needle or words to that effect, and with your **gadget** undergoing the actual stresses you're trying to measure, you should be able to get quite a good reading. If you want immediate dope on take-off, pilot just looks at the **gadget** and phones it down. Shouldn't be too cumbersome. Any good at all? I suppose the scheme was considered & discarded for some flaw not apparent to me. Two methods of approach suggest themselves. One is a weighted needle between springs of known tension, and the other is a disturbance of electrical nature, occasioned by displacement of core or coil, & able to be registered by electrical

means. Both complicated, particularly the latter, but not any worse than Bud's "light-beams", I betcha, if as bad. Mebbeso your needle could be charged and & register against some of that fine electrically-sensitive paper.

In this discussion, we have repeated mentions of "gadget" with Corson speaking to Heinlein about "your gadget" in two places. Is there any chance that this relates in some manner to the mystery device? Or are we talking about some other device that was developed at the Naval Aircraft Factory?

Consider a few facts regarding Heinlein's employment. Having failed in his attempts to get back into the Navy, Heinlein's fallback position was to accept a civil service position as an engineer at the NAF. This acceptance occurred on May 11, 1942, which was a Monday and can be taken as his first day of work. According to the material presented in Volume I of Patterson's biography of Heinlein, his initial duties were the recruiting of engineers for Scoles and performing some work in connection with high-altitude chamber.

I wish that it were possible to find out more about the technical problem being discussed and the "gadget" as mentioned by Corson. I have not been able to locate any letters at all from Heinlein to Corson. An examination of other letters from Corson which are in the Heinlein Archives reveals that none of them discuss the gadget nor give any more details of the problem to be solved. No other material has been located regarding this device. We therefore have no background to Corson's discussion and no follow-up to indicate if his ideas were employed or what results were obtained.

There is nothing to indicate when this meeting with Scoles took place, but the flow of the letter leads me to conclude that it occurred during Corson's most recent trip to Philadelphia. This was the weekend of May 23 and 24, at the end of Heinlein's second week as a NAF employee.

If Scoles was the Assistant Chief Engineer for Materials, why would he have been involved with something as described by Corson? According to the Scoles letter, the primary technical concern at the time was the high-altitude chamber. Of course, the Scoles letter was written in January and the Corson letter in May. So any number of new technical problems could have popped up in the intervening months. It is possible there was a concern about stresses on various airplane materials, which would depend on its acceleration and deceleration, as mentioned in the letter.

May we assume that at some point after Heinlein came to Philadelphia, Scoles became aware of the mystery device and saw its potential application to a problem of his? I can see him discussing it with Heinlein, but why bring Corson into the discussion? The fact is that Corson was a good friend, someone who Heinlein could trust and whose opinion he valued.

Something else to consider was Heinlein's lifelong refusal to discuss in any detail the work that he performed during his time at the NAF. Is this refusal connected with his concern about the secrecy of the mystery device?

Heinlein's earlier process of misdirection appears to work for him here. If we accept that Scoles could not have been involved with the initial work with the naval system in 1940, we would be inclined to discount any connection with the Naval Aircraft Factory, even at a later point in time. This would have been my conclusion, were it not for the existence of the Corson letter.

Am I stringing together too many unrelated items? Or hanging too much on the use of the word "gadget"? The problem is that we have the gadget described by Corson magically appearing, or so it seems, at the very time that Heinlein started working there. Prior to the start of his employment, all that Heinlein was doing for Scoles was lining up other people for work at the NAF, such as L. Sprague de Camp and Isaac Asimov. No engineering work. Regarding the gadget discussed in Corson's letter, there are three possibilities: (1) It was something that Scoles had already been working on unrelated to Heinlein's device, (2) It was something new that Scoles and Heinlein came up with in the two weeks that he had been working there, or (3) It has a connection to the mystery device. It is just not possible to make a definite decision here. On the other hand, there is nothing that precludes it from being connected in some way with the mystery device.

The analysis of the quotes has not permitted any definite statement to be made regarding the identity of the story device or naval system. The next chapter will consider the problems connected with identifying the naval system.

5

TECHNOLOGY AND THE NAVY

In the course of most discussions or presentations concerning The Great Heinlein Mystery, I have occasionally encountered someone who thought that they had a possible solution. This solution turned out to be incorrect either because the person had a faulty knowledge of Heinlein's works, or had a similar defect in his knowledge of the state of naval technology when Heinlein was writing his early stories, or both. For example, several responses proposed radar as the naval system. This ignores the fact that there is nothing in the early stories that could be interpreted as radar and the fact that radar existed in some form before any of Heinlein's stories were published.

The solution to the first deficiency is obvious - ***Read what Heinlein has written!!!*** This chapter will attempt to rectify the second deficiency by presenting a view of the state of naval electronics technology at the time when the Device appeared in the story.

Suppose we were to ask the average American what happened of importance in the years between 1919 and 1939. What types of answers are likely to be received? If this person has any knowledge of history at all or is old enough to have lived through a portion of the era, he or she might mention Prohibition and its eventual repeal, and possibly by connection The Roaring Twenties. In the economic area, the response might be the stock market crash in 1929 and the Depression. In the area of politics, the response could be the election of Franklin Delano Roosevelt as President. Another event mentioned could be Lindbergh's solo flight from New York to Paris in 1927. In the area of world events, the rise of Nazi Germany and the actions of the Japanese in China might be the answers given. And that would most likely be the end of that person's knowledge of the period.

In our world with its cell phones, high-definition television, personal computers, the Internet, world-wide telecommunications, supersonic aircraft, Mars Rovers, medical transplants, and other modern marvels of technology, it may be the opinion of many that our current age is the only one in which scientific and technological advances have taken place. That opinion is not true. The objects and processes that have appeared relatively recently, and which we now cannot conceive of ever having been without, are themselves the result of a long history of discovery and development. When we look back at the 1920s and 1930s, we see that these years were a period of great change, both in the sciences and daily technology. As this chapter is not meant to be a comprehensive history of the period, I will consider just three areas of change.

The first area is aviation. There were a number of efforts to fly across the Atlantic immediately after World War I. Most of these were in response to a £10,000 prize offered by the London *Daily Mail* to the "first person who crosses the Atlantic from any point in the United States, Canada, or Newfoundland to any point in Great Britain or Ireland in 72 continuous hours." Entirely separate from this prize competition was a flight by the U.S. Navy involving 3 flying boats: NC(Navy Curtiss)-1, NC-2 and NC-4. The plan was to proceed from New York to Newfoundland, then to the Azores, to Lisbon and finally to Plymouth, England. The planes began on May 8, 1919. The only one to complete all legs of the flight was NC-4, arriving on May 31 with a total amount of actual flying time of 26 hours.

Slightly over two weeks later, John Alcock and Arthur Brown flew nonstop from Newfoundland to Ireland, a distance of 1890 miles in slightly over 16 hours, thereby winning the *Daily Mail* prize. Another prize was then offered in 1919, this one for $25,000 for the first non-stop flight between New York and Paris. There were many attempts to win this prize, all unsuccessful and some fatal, until May 1927 when Charles Lindbergh flew the distance of 3610 miles in approximately 33 and a half hours. This is quite an improvement in the course of only eight years.

In the years between the wars the nature of aviation changed drastically. The evolution began with fabric-covered biplanes, open cockpits and engines that gave speeds only in the neighborhood of 100 miles per hour. By the end of the period, we are looking at all-metal construction, enclosed cockpits and engines that, coupled with aerodynamic designs, gave speeds in excess of 400 miles per hour. At this point, aviation had also proceeded to multi-engine bombers and to commercial airliners that would permit people to travel in some degree of safety and comfort.

The associated field of rocketry moved past the long existent field of solid fuel rockets with Goddard's first flight of a liquid fuel rocket in 1926. Although Goddard continued his experiments in the United States, the greatest advances in the area of rocketry were made in Germany. These advances were made by the members of the German Rocket Society, initially in their civilian organization and then when some of their number worked for the German Army. These experiments at Peenemünde led to development in 1942 of the A-4, better known as the V-2.

The second area to be considered will be that of physics. Discoveries and advances in this area had little direct impact upon the life of the average person.

Although Einstein had published the Theory of Relativity during the war, it was not until 1919 that the opportunity existed to verify one of its predictions. By photographing the stars near to the sun during an eclipse, it would be possible to determine an apparent shift in the position of the star due to the deflection of the light by the Sun's gravitational field. This experiment was conducted by English scientists during an eclipse on May 29, 1919. That the results confirmed Einstein's theory was important news. But it was noted at the time that although their nations had recently been at war, the confirmation of a theory by a scientist from Germany had been performed by a group of scientists from England.

Some theories and discoveries of the interwar years concerned the world of the very small. Many experimental results were understandable only if electromagnetic radiation was considered as being composed of particles, while other results fit only within the long accepted representation of an electromagnetic wave. One result explained in terms of particles was the Compton Effect, in which the wavelength of X-rays scattered from metal varied according to the angle of emergence. The obvious question was how radiation could be both a particle and a wave.

Efforts to resolve these problems led to the appearance in 1926 of matrix form of quantum mechanics developed by Werner Heisenberg and the equivalent wave mechanics developed by Erwin Schrödinger, with related developments by others such as Louis de Broglie, Paul A. M. Dirac and Pascual Jordan. Heisenberg then employed a purely mathematical approach to define the limits on what might be known. It was shown that it was not possible to, as claimed in classical physics, precisely define the position and velocity of a subatomic particle simultaneously. Any steps taken to refine the accuracy of the one measurement causes the measurement of the other to become more uncertain, giving rise to name "uncertainty principle." Neils Bohr took a wider approach to address to wave/particle problem described above. His result was the principle of complementarity, which states that the experiments which determine the behavior as a particle and a wave are both valid within the limits of the instruments used to obtain the results. The solution is to accept both representations as mutually exclusive representations which were complementary to each other. This approach to the problem also encompasses the uncertainty principle if we consider that position and velocity are complementary variables.

Many advances in nuclear physics can be tied to the early 1930s. To resolve problems connected with the structure of the atomic nucleus, Ernest Rutherford proposed the existence of a neutral atomic particle, the neutron. One set of experiments performed in England then confirmed its existence. At about the same time in the United States, Harold Urey succeeded in demonstrating the existence an isotope of hydrogen, which came to be called deuterium. Unlike the better known form of hydrogen, whose nucleus consists of only a proton, the nucleus of deuterium must contain two bodies, a proton and a neutron. The development of the cyclotron by Ernest Lawrence removed the limitations of using radioactive materials as sources of particles for experiments. Experiments on cosmic rays led to the discovery of the first known type of anti-matter, what was originally called the anti-electron and what we now call the positron.

In the related field of astronomy, several important discoveries were made. Within the bounds of the solar system, the planet Pluto was discovered in 1930. Most of you should be familiar with the recent debate among astronomers whether Pluto, in view of the newer determinations of its size, should still be classified as a planet. If we move past the bounds of the solar system, the most important discovery of the period would have to be Edwin Hubble's "law of the red shifts." Based on extensive investigation of distant nebulae, it was discovered that the further away such an object was, the faster it was traveling away from us. It was also at this time that our conception of the size of the Universe began to change.

The final area to be considered is the one most closely connected with the search for the mystery device - electronics. The very term "electronics" appeared in the interwar period. The term was introduced by *Electronics Magazine* in 1930, with the meaning of the application of the vacuum tube in working with weak signals, as opposed to working with the larger quantities employed in the distribution and use of electric power. Unlike physics, as previously noted, the advances in electronics during the interwar years had a considerable impact on the average American. This was due to the appearance of broadcast radio. Prior to World War I, the focus of commercial, military and amateur radio communications was the sending of a signal from point to point. Shortly after the wartime restrictions on radio had been removed, the first of the broadcast stations began to appear. Although amateur operators had been transmitting music, the real beginning of broadcast radio is considered to be the Pittsburgh station KDKA in 1920. It took a year and half from the start of the operation of this station to the beginning of the radio (or broadcast) boom.

Some figures illustrate this phenomenon. By mid-1922, there were already from 500,000 to 700,000 radio sets in the United States, with almost 600 radio stations. By the start of 1923, the number of radio sets had increased to somewhere between 1,500,000 to 2,000,000. When we get to the end of the interwar years (actually 1940), the number of stations was only a bit larger - around 750 - but the number of radio sets was now over 45,000,000. This growth may be reasonably compared to the growth experienced following the introduction of personal computers.

It will be useful to investigate the history of radio as it will also tell us much about the history of radio communications in the Navy. The story of radio begins with James Clerk Maxwell (1831-1879), a Scottish mathematician and physicist. His equations established a series of relationships between an electric field, a magnetic field and an electric current. The consequence of his equations was the existence of an electromagnetic wave that will propagate at the speed of light. This meant that light itself was an electromagnetic wave.

Maxwell died at the age of 48 without ever witnessing the generation of electromagnetic waves at frequencies that would later be used for radio communication. It was nine years after Maxwell's death when Heinrich Hertz (1857-1894) succeeding in generating such waves in his laboratory, covering frequencies from approximately 31 to 1250 MHz. The range of his transmissions was very limited, but can be considered the first true generation and reception of radio waves. Hertz did not pursue his experiments past the point of demonstrating that Maxwell was correct and did not see any practical consequences of his work.

Just as Maxwell did not live to see the vindication of his theoretical predictions, Hertz did not live to see that he was incorrect regarding the consequences of his work. One of the people who was interested in building upon the discoveries of Hertz was Guglielmo Marconi (1874-1937) who was the son of an Italian father and a Scotch-Irish mother (Anne Jameson - some of you might be familiar with Jameson's Irish Whiskey). Marconi began his experiments in 1894, the year of Hertz's death. Through a series of discoveries and inventions, he was able to extend the range of his transmissions. All of these transmissions involved the use of Morse Code, as voice transmissions were still a number of years away. By the start of 1896, Marconi was able to transmit 3 miles at his father's estate in Italy. There was no interest in his work in Italy, so he went to England. By 1901, he had succeeded in transmitting signals across the Atlantic, from Poldhu, Cornwall to St. Johns, Newfoundland.

At this point it is necessary to explain the techniques employed in the early days of radio. The systems of Marconi, which built upon the work of Hertz, used a spark gap. This involves the buildup of voltage until it discharges across a gap. The far side of the gap is connected to a resonant circuit and the transmitting antenna. The energy entering the circuit will cause the generation of high frequency oscillations. These oscillations will then cause the electromagnetic waves to be emitted from the antenna. The loss of energy through the radiation of the waves will cause the oscillations from a single discharge to die out very quickly. The "damped" oscillations give rise to a number of RF frequencies, and the major frequency transmitted was determined primarily by the size and configuration of the antenna. Until a way was discovered to accurately tune the signal to a particular frequency, this meant that similar transmitters operating in a given area would interfere with each other. The major advances connected with this type of transmitter were the development of a system for tuning and ways to improve the means of generating the spark.

It was recognized that transmission of a series of damped waves was not the best approach, so the search was on for ways of generating a continuous series of waves. One solution was the Poulsen arc transmitter. An invention of the 19th century had been the arc lamp, in which the light was generated by the electrical discharge between two electrodes. This is similar to the spark gap, but the discharge is continually maintained rather than intermittent. It was found that by inserting a resonant circuit in parallel with the electrodes, an alternating electric current would be generated that was superimposed on the DC voltage maintaining the arc. This was initially found to be limited to the generation of audible sound, since any attempts to increase the frequency resulted in a decrease of efficiency. It was Valdemar Poulsen (1869-1942) who discovered the means to improve the efficiency to the point where it was possibly to generate radio waves at a useful frequency. His approach involved the discharge through a chamber containing hydrogen gas and used a magnetic field to stabilize the arc.

Another solution to the generation of waves was the Alexanderson Alternator developed by Ernst Alexanderson (1878-1975). The alternator is related to electric power generators which operate at very low frequencies, usually either 50 Hz or 60 Hz. Alexanderson developed the means to generate an output at frequencies up to 100 kHz. This means of generation resulted in a continuous wave of high purity. One disadvantage of such an approach was that it required a large electromechanical device not suitable for many applications where there was limited space, such as on ships. The equipment also required a great deal of maintenance. As the frequency depended on the rotation rate of the alternator, there was a practical limit on the highest frequency that could be generated. This made such an approach unsuitable as attempts were made to operate at higher and higher frequencies.

The solution to the problem of the generation of continuous waves was the vacuum tube, which made radio and other electronic devices of the interwar years possible. The vacuum tube appeared in practically every type of electronic system. It is still manufactured and used today in certain applications. Its primary application in the home during the greater part of the 20th century was first in radio receivers, and later also in television receivers. It is likely that many young people have never seen a vacuum tube, or if they were shown one could even tell you what it was or what its purpose was.

The basis of the vacuum tube is the incandescent light bulb invented by Thomas Edison in 1879. As part of investigations into the blackening that formed on the interior of the bulb conducted a few years later, a type of light bulb was created in which a metal plate was placed inside the bulb, near to but not connected to the filament, and was brought out as a third connection. Measurements showed that an electric current was flowing from the filament to the plate. This gave no answer to the blackening problem, but Edison obtained a patent on it anyway on the chance it might have a later application, and moved on to other projects.

It was this phenomenon, called the "Edison effect" that formed the basis for the vacuum tube. In 1890, Professor John Ambrose Fleming, as an advisor to the Edison Electric Light Company, performed some experiments with the three terminal bulb. A battery was connected between the filament and the plate. When the negative terminal of this simple circuit was connected to the filament and the positive terminal to the plate, he found that a current flowed. If the battery was reversed, with the plate negative with respect to the filament, Fleming found that no current flowed. The reason for this operation is clear. The electrons that are emitted from the filament are attracted to the plate if it is positive and repelled if it is negative. Any device performing this function is called a rectifier, as it converts a current that flows in both directions into a current that flows in only direction (rectification). In most circuit representations, it is assumed that the filament (heater) is electrically and physically separated from the cathode which emits the electrons and which forms part of the electric circuit. Another name for the plate is the anode. A device with only two elements active in the operation of the circuit (neglecting the filament or heater) is called a diode.

The real breakthrough came with the insertion of a third element, the grid, into the tube between the cathode and the anode. The addition was performed by Dr. Lee De Forest in late 1906, and the patent was filed in early 1907. The tube now had three active elements and was therefore called a triode. With the anode (plate) sufficiently positive with respect to the cathode, we would expect the flow of electrons just as in the diode. The difference in operation occurs as we change the voltage on the grid with respect to that of the cathode. If the grid is made positive, it will allow more current to flow to the anode. Conversely, if the grid is made more negative it will begin to restrict the current flow. If made sufficiently negative, it will cut off the flow completely. This allowed the triode to function as an amplifier, using a small voltage variation in the input (grid) circuit, to cause a larger voltage variation in the output (anode) circuit. With this simple amplifier began the path that leads to all electronic devices today.

It has been stated in the literature that De Forest had little understanding of how his creation worked or exactly what it was capable of doing. It was only through the work of others such as Edwin Howard Armstrong that the true potential of the triode was realized. By feeding back a tiny portion of the input, it was possible to greatly increase the amplification obtainable from a single tube. When the amount of feedback was increased beyond a certain point, the circuit would begin to oscillate. The frequency of the oscillations would be determined by the design of the circuit external to the tube and by properties of external components such as inductors and capacitors. This means of generating continuous waves made possible the elimination of all of the cumbersome methods previously employed in radio transmitters.

The early triodes were delicate and unreliable devices. One problem that the early triodes had was an insufficient vacuum. It was even thought by De Forest, erroneously as it turns out, that gaseous ions were the key to amplification. When the triode had been brought to a consistent and practical state, however, it still had certain operational limitations. One new version of the vacuum tube was the tetrode, which was developed during World War I. As the name indicates, the tetrode has four active elements, the fourth being the screen grid placed between the original (or control) grid and the anode. The screen grid is held a constant positive potential. This helps to reduce any undesirable effect that the larger anode voltage has upon the electron stream passing through the tube. A further major change was the pentode, which was developed during the 1920s. The fifth element is the suppressor grid, located between the screen grid and the anode. The suppressor grid is held at the same voltage potential as the cathode. A problem of the tetrode at low anode voltages is the effect of electrons that are knocked from the anode by the impact of electrons in the main flow from the cathode. These "secondary" electrons may impact the screen grid, which has an undesirable effect upon the operation of the tube.

The suppressor grid keeps the secondary electrons from reaching the screen grid.

With all of these improvements to the operation of the vacuum tube, there were still certain problems that were impossible to eliminate. The first was the construction of the tube. The outer envelope of many tubes was usually made of glass as in a light bulb. Even if the outer covering could be made to resist breakage through the use of metal envelopes, there was still the possibility of damage to the internal elements by shock or vibration. (This did not prevent the development of special tubes during World War 2 for use in proximity fuzes, where the tube had to withstand the shock of being fired from a gun.) The second is the heat of operation. It is necessary to raise the cathode to a temperature sufficient for electron emission. Tubes get hot and therefore heat their surroundings. When you have a large enough number of tubes in operation, cooling is a very important consideration. The final problem was that although tubes were made smaller and smaller, details of internal construction place a lower limit on just how small a tube can be. Consider also that if you do succeed in creating very small tubes and use this advantage to fit more tubes into an available space, you have now increased your cooling problems by having the heat from more tubes to be removed.

In applications of tubes that processed continuously varying (analog) electrical signals, such as radio and television receivers, the number of tubes employed was usually small enough so that the space they occupied or the heat emitted was not a serious problem. But you could still place your hand on the outer case of a radio or TV that had been operating for a while and feel some of the heat being generated within. Now consider that vacuum tubes may also be operated as electronic switches. The very first forms of electronic digital computers, as opposed to earlier much slower systems using relays, employed vacuum tubes. In designing a system to perform digital calculations of usable complexity, it is necessary to employ a very large number of switching elements. This is where the basic nature of the vacuum tube, as described above, begins to cause problems.

It would be safe to assume that most users of today's cell phones, computers and other electronic devices have no idea of the principles upon which these devices and the components of which they are constructed operate. They only care that these devices are light, easy to transport and consume relatively small amounts of power. The path to our present day devices began with the inventions of the bipolar junction transistor (BJT), various forms of field effect transistor (FET), and most importantly, the integrated circuit (IC). Prior to these inventions in the area of solid state electronics, all that a designer or engineer had to work with was the vacuum tube.

Using only vacuum tubes, one would not even consider constructing systems to perform the same functions that we obtain today from solid state devices. The degree of miniaturization possible these days allows the manufacture of a cell phone which contains several million transistors or a Pentium IV processor in a desktop or laptop which contains 44 million transistors. Consider the problem of trying to construct a Pentium IV processor substituting a vacuum tube for every integrated circuit transistor. This would require room after room stuffed full of large equipment racks, which consume tremendous amounts of electric power and emit enormous amounts of heat. Hardly something that is portable. With such a large number of vacuum tubes being employed, given their reliability it is questionable whether anything useful could be accomplished before tubes started failing. Finally, even if something of this magnitude could be constructed, the physical separation would mean larger signal propagation times between components, limiting the operating speed.

The focus of radio transmission before World War I was in point-to-point communications. After the war, the commercial sector turned to broadcast. But of course navies around the world were still interested in point-to-point communications. A ship must be able to communicate with a shore station or with other ships. Similarly, an airplane must communicate with other planes, a ship or a shore station.

The first major advance in naval and military communications was the telegraph in the 19th century. As telegraph lines were extended, it became possible for governments to communicate rapidly with very distant forces. The first major instance of this involved the English and French governments and their forces in the Crimea in 1854. The telegraph was also extensively used in the U.S. Civil War. Later, during the Spanish-American War, Washington communicated with Commodore Dewey by means of the transatlantic cable and then a series of other telegraph lines laid from Europe through to Hong Kong.

The story of radio in the United States Navy is the story of the growth of radio in general. The initial interest was in the work of Marconi. When the Navy performed a survey starting in 1901 to determine the best equipment for its needs, however, it was also possible to consider a number of European firms such as Slaby-Arco, Ducretet, Rochefort and Braun-Siemens. As there was some concern about being dependent upon Europeans suppliers, the survey also considered a British firm and two American manufacturers, the National Electric Signaling Company and DeForest's Wireless Telegraph Company. Although original purchases were made from Slaby-Arco, the equipment so acquired was gradually replaced or modified to work with newer American equipment.

The Navy followed the same progression from spark to arc to alternator to vacuum tube equipment that occurred in the commercial sector. Alternators were restricted to use in shore installations because of their size. As early as 1917, the Navy had acquired over 1000 CW 936 radiotelephone transceivers from Western Electric. These vacuum tube sets operated over a frequency range of 500 to 1500 kHz. Spark gap equipment remained in use until the early 1920s, when the use of such equipment was banned. So as we consider the types of electronic equipment in use during the interwar years, we will be looking at only vacuum tube systems.

It is worth mentioning the effect that the interest of the Navy in vacuum tubes had upon tube quality and price. In 1910, a naval reorganization had moved control of the acquisition of naval radio from the Bureau of Equipment to the Bureau of Steam Engineering. This might appear to have been a strange place to place control of radio equipment. But the decision was actually quite logical, as the Bureau was responsible for all shipboard equipment, electrical as well as steam. One problem with early vacuum tube equipment was that the tubes themselves were expensive and short-lived. Before World War I, the Bureau prepared a requisition for tubes with a long operating life and a lower price than those currently available. The conditions of the requisition were a life of 5000 hours and a cost of ten dollars each. Western Electric then proposed instead that the operating life be reduced to 2000 hours. If that was done, they would be able to provide tubes at a cost of only $4.50 each. The terms of the requisition were modified and the contract was awarded to Western Electric. One important effect was that less expensive tubes could then also become available to the public and for the manufacturers of radios and other electronic equipment.

Earlier it was stated that the growth in the number of radios with the start of commercial broadcasting could be compared to the growth in the number of personal computers. There are additional factors to consider in such a comparison. Early radio transmissions operated at very low frequencies. This meant long wavelengths, so the corresponding antenna structures were large and it required a considerable amount of power to transmit a signal. One might call it industrial-strength radio. Even though radio was a broadcast system, with radio waves going in every direction, the objective was to get a message from point A to point B, such as in a telegraph system. And the main users of radio were communication companies and the military. Then it was employed during World War I. All along amateur operators had existed, but they represented an extremely small number. One of the factors that made the broadcast boom possible was the lower priced more reliable vacuum tube mentioned above. Now consider that the first computers - that we can really call computers - were employed during World War 2. These were massive machines. So were the ones that were employed by industry following the war. (Slight difference here: radio was business, then war; computer was war, then business.) But even before the first personal computers that anyone could use came out, we had people trying to building their own computers, the equivalent of radio amateurs. The key to personal computing was the integrated circuit. It took the space program to bring down the price of integrated circuits in the 1960s. This led to the microprocessor and then to the personal computer.

In 1915, there were concerns about the United States being able to cope with the newer technologies and their effects upon naval warfare. An effort by Josephus Daniels, the Secretary of the Navy led to the creation of the Naval Consulting Board. This Board was chaired by Thomas Alva Edison and consisted of 24 inventors, engineers and industrialists including Elmer Sperry of Sperry Gyroscope, Leo Baekeland (the inventor of Bakelite plastic), and Willis Whitney (the director of the General Electric Research Laboratory). One result of the Board's activities was the recommendation of the foundation of a new laboratory for the Navy. Originally referred to as the Naval Experimental and Research Laboratory, the name was later changed to the Naval Research Laboratory (NRL). Money for the construction was appropriated during the war, but due to delays, the Laboratory was not commissioned until July 1923.

Existing radio facilities within the Bureau of Engineering (changed from the Bureau of Steam Engineering in 1920) were moved to NRL. These included the Naval Aircraft Radio Laboratory and the Naval Radio Telegraphics Laboratory. Also moved to NRL was the Sound Research Section. The Radio and Sound Divisions thus formed at NRL were later supplemented with other divisions or groups working in areas such as ballistics, optics and metallurgy. The important factor with regard to radio is that NRL became the organization with the responsibility for improving and advancing the radio capabilities of the Navy.

With regard to radio communications, the efforts included investigations into the propagation of radio waves under a variety of conditions as well as the design, construction and test of a wide range of radio transmitters and receivers. The design objectives were high power for shore based systems, sensitivity of receivers, and stability and reliability for all types of equipment. In looking at the years of development work, there is a clear progression to operation at higher and higher frequencies. The following discussion is not meant to be a comprehensive review of all naval radio systems up to the beginning of World War 2. Its purpose is to illustrate the evolution by considering the gradual increase in the operating frequencies of the various systems.

The very early spark gap sets operated in the Low Frequency (LF) range (30 kHz to 300 kHz) or the Medium Frequency (MF) range (300 kHz to 3 MHz). Shore stations operated as low at 111 kHz, while ships operated at 500 kHz. The previously mentioned vacuum tube CW936 transceiver also operated entirely within the MF band.

The Navy had originally wished to employ the frequencies from 600 to 1250 kHz for short range communication. But in the early 1920s, the problem was with the newly established broadcast radio stations operating within the same frequency band. The eventual solution was to force the Navy to give up this frequency band. The frequency band remains in use for AM broadcasting, with its range now extended slightly to cover 520 kHz to 1710 kHz.

With each step in the move to higher and higher frequencies, it became necessary to gain experience in how the equipment should be constructed and operated. The next range of frequencies that were employed are designated the High Frequency band, extending from 3 to 30 MHz. In 1924, a number of transmitters were developed that operated on the boundary between the MF and HF bands. Experimental models operating in the range from 2000 to 3000 kHz (2 to 3 MHz) at a power of 100 watts were tested aboard battleships. The success of these tests led to the acquisition of over 100 sets that were then placed in use on battleships, cruisers and destroyers.

Another portion of the work performed by NRL was with respect to the use of quartz crystals in oscillator circuits. The frequency of the oscillation is determined by the physical characteristics of the crystal and is more stable than those circuits in which the frequency is determined solely on the basis of capacitances and inductances. Crystal-controlled oscillators found use in shore stations as well as shipboard systems. Starting in 1926, the Model XA crystal-controlled transmitters were installed on a number of ships. These transmitters were capable of 500 watts output and operated over three High Frequency Bands: 4000 kHz, 8000 kHz and 12,000 kHz.

Most of the preceding discussion has concerned transmitters, but it should be obvious that development work in that area must be paralleled by similar work in the area of receivers. Receivers were developed for aircraft applications as well as for ship and shore installations. In the case of aircraft, designers had to cope with the additional problem of interference caused by the plane's ignition system. For regular shipboard use, the first High Frequency receiver was the Model RG, tunable over the range from 1000 kHz to 20,000 kHz (1 to 20 MHz). The Model RG remained in service for a number of years, and was followed by models with improved performance in many areas. These included the Model RAB in 1935, and the smaller and lighter models such as the Models RAL, RAO, RBB, RBC and RBS.

Although the various HF systems were successful, there was interest in moving to even higher frequencies. The primary factor influencing the work in the Very High Frequency (VHF) range (30 to 300 MHz) was the desire to develop systems that could be operated over a short range without the possibility of enemy interception. Tests in the lower end of the VHF range indicated potential propagation problems caused by sunspots. It was also found that operation as high as 40 MHz could occasionally result in transcontinental reception. All of the results indicated that a useful short range system would have to be operated at frequencies above 60 MHz. The first VHF communication system was developed for the Navy by NRL in 1929. This consisted of the XP series of transmitters and the XV and XJ series of receivers. Based on the knowledge obtained from the construction and use of these models, NRL was able in 1938 to introduce the Model TBS, which consisted of both a transmitter (40 watts) and receiver operating over the range of 60 to 80 MHz. This system was used for intership communication throughout World War 2, being known by the operators from its model designation as "Talk Between Ships".

Experiments were performed at even higher frequencies in the years leading up to the war, although operational systems at these frequencies did not come into use until much later. Systems capable of operating in the Ultra High Frequency (UHF) range (300 MHz to 3000 MHz) were being developed as early as 1936. Tests of a communication system operating at 500 MHz were performed on the destroyer U.S.S. *Leary* in 1937. Other system operating at 500 MHz were used in operational tests in the Fleet in 1938. Work was also done in frequencies above the UHF band. One system operating at 3000 MHz was also tested upon the *Leary* in 1937, using 40-inch diameter parabolic antennas. Although these various demonstrations were successful, there was more interest in this frequency range for radar, and work in the area of communications at these frequencies occurred after the war. The largest difficulty with such work, either for radio communication or radar, was in developing tubes or other devices capable of generating sufficient power at these higher frequencies.

The discussion so far has focused entirely upon radio communications. This was, of course, not the only way in which electronics was employed by the Navy in the interwar years. Table 2 shows the various categories which could conceivably be related to the mystery device. This table was based on three sources: the topics presented in a 1950 article "Electronics - Your Future" that detailed many of the wartime electronic advances in the Navy, the chapter headings of Gebhard's *Evolution of Naval Radio-Electronics and Contributions of the Naval Research Laboratory* and the chapter headings of *Shipboard Electronic Equipment (NAVPERS 10794-B)*. All of the categories, with the exception of radio communications which has already been covered, will be briefly discussed. If any category appears to be relevant to the search for the device, it will be considered in greater detail in a later chapter.

Communications
   1. Radio
   2. Infrared
   3. Remote Control

Navigation
   4. Radio Direction Finder
   5. Radio Navigation

Weapon Systems
   6. Radar
   7. IFF
   8. Sonar

Communications Security and Countermeasures

Table 2. Naval Electronics

Infrared. The discussion of systems of this type will be deferred until the analysis of story devices in Chapter 13.

Remote Control. There was considerable naval interest in radio remote control for a number of applications. The first was the attempt to determine if a naval torpedo could be controlled by radio. Experiments were conducted in the interwar years, although the results were not applied to any torpedo used before or during the war. The second area of interest was in the remote control of target ships, to provide a more realistic mobile target for planes and long range gunnery than the stationary German battleship *Ostfriesland* sunk by General Billy Mitchell in 1921. The ships employed as targets were the battleships U.S.S. *Iowa* (1921-1923) and U.S.S. *Utah* (1932-1933) and the destroyer U.S.S. *Stoddert* (1925-1928). The last application of remote control was for aircraft. The potential uses for a remote controlled aircraft were either as a type of radio guided missile, or as a target drone for use in the training of anti-aircraft gunners. No systems were developed for assault purposes in the interwar period, but considerable use was made of gunnery drones. The systems originally developed in the early 1920s for the control of aircraft were tested on a small three wheel cart at NRL called the "Electric Dog."

Radio Direction Finder. The principle of direction finding is the use of radio receiver with an antenna having a directional reception pattern whose orientation may be changed to determine the bearing of a radio transmitter. The principle is that described by Robert Heinlein in the episode from his early navy career that accompanied the short story "Searchlight" in *Expanded Universe*. Naval experiments in direction finding occurred as early as 1906. Starting in the last year of World War I and continuing until 1923, the Navy established a series of direction finding stations along the Atlantic, Gulf and Pacific coasts. These stations were used to provide position information to ships, with three station working together to obtain the ship's position on the basis of the intersection of their individual bearings. Shipboard systems were also developed, primarily for the purpose of purpose of aiding in directing naval gunfire. The primary difficulty connected with shipboard systems was the reflection of signals from the metal structure of the ship, which introduced an error into the bearing. Aircraft direction finders were used to provide navigation for planes searching for submarines in World War I. It was the use of such an airborne system that permitted the NC-4 flying boat to remain on course during the leg of its trans-Atlantic journey from the Azores to Portugal in 1919. Improved versions of the aircraft systems were developed by NRL during the interwar year and remained in use throughout the war.

Radio Navigation. The use of radio in navigation was not limited to the Radio Direction Finder just discussed. As is described in the analysis of story devices in Chapter 13, systems were developed in the interwar years to assist aircraft in landing at airports under conditions of poor visibility. Also described in Chapter 13 is the system used to guide planes back to their carrier. One important development by the Navy was an altimeter which determined the actual height of the aircraft above the surface, using the reflection of radio pulses. Another development worth mentioning was the use of pulses received from a number of shore transmitting stations. By means of equipment which permitted the small time difference between such pulses to be determined, the ship or plane could determine its position. This system was given the name LORAN (from Long Rage Navigation).

Radar. The full story of the development of radar, even naval radar, is far too extensive to present here. For anyone with an interest in the details, one of the better books on the subject is *A Radar History of World War II* by

Louis Brown. This book covers the development of radar in the United States by both the Army and the Navy, as well as systems developed by all of the major combatants in World War 2. Given our interest in the United States Navy, it is sufficient to consider the first radars that were tested in the Fleet.

Work on the development of systems for the detection of ships and planes by the reflection of radio waves occurred throughout the 1930s. At the end of 1938, two radars were installed on battleships for evaluation during Fleet exercises scheduled to occur in early 1939. The XAF radar, operating at 200 MHz and installed on the U.S.S. *New York*, had been designed and constructed by NRL. The CXZ radar, operating at 400 MHz and installed upon the U.S.S. *Texas*, had been designed and built by RCA. The XAF was the more successful of the two during the exercises, observing both ships and planes, and was even able to track shells fired from the large naval guns and their splashes. There were even reports of radar echoes from large birds. The problems with the CXZ were attributed to the speed with which it had been designed and constructed. The Navy was sufficiently impressed with the XAF to immediately order twenty copies made. These copies, designated Model CXAM, had been installed on a number battleships, aircraft carriers and cruisers by the time that the United States entered the war.

The above discussed systems were search radars used for determining the location of ships and planes. Radars were also developed for the purpose of the fire control, that is, the direction of naval gunfire. The first of these systems, developed by Western Electric, was installed on the cruiser U.S.S. *Wichita* in July 1941. The system operated a frequency of 700 MHz.

If you mention radar, the image that will occur to most people on the basis of what they have seen in movies of airport control towers or shipboard control rooms is the circular screen with the trace sweeping around every few seconds. But this was not the type of display that was used in the early radars. These systems employed the Type A or A-scope display where the information was presented as a single trace running horizontally across the screen. The left end represented the location of the radar and any return signal was shown as a line or hump rising above the horizontal line, with its distance across the screen corresponding to the actual distance of the target. The type of display with which we are all familiar today, in which the center of the screen represents the location of the radar and returns are indicated as bright blips as the trace sweeps around, is known as the Plan-Position Indicator (PPI). This was developed at NRL in 1939 and 1940 and given a shipboard demonstration in 1941.

There was independent development of the Plan-Position Indicator display by the British.

IFF. In warfare, a key requirement is the rapid and correct identification of ships, aircraft, vehicles and personnel, both to provide the appropriate response to enemy forces and for the avoidance of "friendly fire" incidents. The term IFF, which stand for Identification Friend or Foe, was coined by the British and so concisely describes the purpose of such a system that no alternative term has ever been in use. The original system developed by NRL in 1937 was based on the use of coded transmissions from an aircraft.

The introduction of radar led to the approach (developed independently by the U.S. and Britain) of using the radar beam to trigger a response that would be observable upon the radar screen. The first such systems were passive, simply reflecting back a portion of the original signal. A clearer indication was provided by an active system in which the radar beam triggered the generation of a stronger return signal from a vacuum tube oscillator circuit. One problem with this early version was that the trigger circuitry had to be adapted to the frequency used by a particular radar system. This difficulty was circumvented in the next version by the use of separate challenge and return frequencies that were independent of the radar frequencies, allowing such a system to be used with any type of radar. Subsequent developments in IFF systems were the result of collaboration between the U.S. and Britain.

Sonar. The discussion of this particular system is deferred until the analysis of story devices in Chapter 13.

Communications Security and Countermeasures. The discussion of these types of systems is deferred until the analysis of story devices in Chapter 13.

It is hoped that the preceding material has provided some useful information on radio communications to those unfamiliar with both the technology and its history. The intent was to give a feel for the level of technology that existed when Heinlein wrote his early stories. The quantity of material should also indicate that, even if we were to restrict ourselves to developments made only by the Naval Research Laboratory, the number of electronic systems that were designed and constructed makes the attempt to identify a specific electronic device far from a trivial matter. The problem is further complicated by the fact there were also many electronic devices developed for the Navy by firms such General Electric, Westinghouse, Western Electric and RCA.

The next chapter considers another possible approach to identifying the device - identifying the classmate responsible for developing the corresponding naval system.

.

6

THE CLASS OF 1929

Is there any way to identify the naval officer who converted Heinlein's story idea into a real naval system? In Chapter 2, the first quote presented contained a reference to a "junior officer" who Heinlein claimed was responsible for taking the story idea and converting it to naval practice. If that was the only information available to me, I would have had to consider the several thousand junior officers (i.e. Ensign, Lieutenant Junior Grade or Lieutenant) serving in the Navy in 1939 or 1940. Fortunately the quote from the Virtues essay refers to a "classmate" of Heinlein, allowing me to reduce the number considerably. This chapter considers the ways in which we might identify the responsible classmate, but also presents a number of interesting details about Heinlein's fellow members of the Naval Academy Class of 1929.

Let us begin by looking at the size of the class. The value given in many works about Heinlein is 243 graduates. This value occurs in works by H. Bruce Franklin, Leon Stover, Jim Gifford and Bill Patterson. I admit that even I used the value of 243 in my original 1995 *Shipmate* article "The Great Heinlein Mystery." But if we look at the essay "The Happy Days Ahead" in *Expanded Universe*, Heinlein himself gives a value of 240. This value is confirmed in my copy of the *Register of Alumni* (1992 Edition), which lists 240 graduates and 130 non-graduates. So where did the value of 243 come from? The earliest of the works mentioned above is Franklin's *Robert A. Heinlein: America as Science Fiction*, which was published in 1980. Franklin stated that his sources included the yearbook for the Academy, which is called the *Lucky Bag*. This led me to conclude that his research was the source of the higher value. But in the "Class News" section in the October 1973 issue of *Shipmate*, there was a long discussion for the Class of 1929 regarding the precise number of graduates and the discrepancy between the *Register* value (240) and number of biographies in the *Lucky Bag*. The number of biographies stated in this discussion was 244, not the value of 243 given by Franklin. It was suggested in the discussion that one cause was the fact that the *Lucky Bag* had been printed before the final determination of graduates had been made. I can only assume that the value determined and presented by Franklin was repeated by everyone else. The value of 240 stated by the *Register* and by Heinlein should be accepted as the correct value. The list of graduates of the Class of 1929, obtained from the *Register* and presented in Appendix 1, contains 240 names.

As all of the classmates are properly identified in Appendix 1 by their rank at the time of death or retirement as given in the *Register of Alumni*, I hope that no one will mind if from this point on I refer to them in most cases simply by name.

It was stated above that the class also included 130 non-graduates. The situation with regard to the non-graduates was best explained by Heinlein himself in "The Happy Days Ahead":

> 240 of my class graduated; 130 fell by the wayside. *One* of that 130 resigned voluntarily; all the others resigned involuntarily, most of them plebe year for failure in academics (usually mathematics), the others were requested to resign over the next three years for academic, physical, or other reasons. A few resigned graduation day through having failed the final physical examination for commissioning. Three more served about one year in the Fleet, then resigned — but these three volunteered after the attack on Pearl Harbor. 28 of the 129 who left the service involuntarily managed to get back on active duty in World War Two.

The situation with regard to the identification of classmates gets a bit more complicated. When I visited Virginia Heinlein I asked her about classmates that Robert had stayed in touch with over the years. I was trying to determine if there were any classmates to consider other than Caleb Laning, who had been the one she had suggested at the beginning of my search. One name that she mentioned was John Arwine. At first this appeared to me to be a mistake on her part, as the *Register of Alumni* listed him as Class of 1930, not 1929. But his obituary in the February 1966 *Shipmate* listed him as a member of the Class of 1929. The explanation was provided by the Special Collections and Archives Department of the Nimitz Library. Arwine did enter the Academy in June 1925 as a member of the Class of 1929. He was turned back to the Class of 1930 on account of illness in May of his plebe year, and subsequently resigned in January

1927. In spite of this situation, it was as a classmate that Heinlein first knew Arwine, and it is how he continued to think of him.

For the purpose of determining the classmate responsible for the naval system, I made the decision to consider those 240 who were specifically listed as graduates. Since Heinlein had referred to him as a "junior officer," we must conclude that this person was on active duty at the time. Although, in the quote above, Heinlein states that some number of the 130 listed as non-graduates returned to the service after Pearl Harbor, they were not serving at the time when the device was proposed and developed. By the content of the quotes in the first chapter, this activity occurred before Pearl Harbor. In restricting my search to the 240 graduates, I might be excluding someone such as Arwine who began as a member of the Class of 1929, but actually graduated as a member of another class. My thought was that it would be very difficult to determine if such a person even existed, and would interfere with the efforts focused on the actual classmates who graduated in 1929.

Another interesting thing about the Class of 1929 was its small size. The chart shown in Figure 2 presents the number of graduates and non-graduates for every Academy class from 1920 through 1939. The Classes of 1928 and 1929 had the lowest number of graduates of any classes during this interwar period. The Class of 1928 even styled itself as "The Biggest Little Class" as it had 173 graduates. But why was there such a drop in class size and then a recovery?

The personnel situation facing the Navy in the 1920s was very complicated. The first problem was demobilization - reducing the large wartime navy back to a peacetime level. Then there was the Washington Naval Treaty of 1922, which affected the number and type of ships that would comprise the navy and of course the number of officers and men that would be required to man those ships. Although the Act of 1916 that had created the plans for the wartime navy authorized 160,000 enlisted personnel for the peacetime forces, the actual numbers were much lower. Instead of the 90,000 enlisted and 4,160 officers that were requested in 1922, only 86,000 enlisted and 4,500 officers were actually authorized by Congress.

By 1924, the situation was such that the Navy had problems supplying officers for the ships in commission. The one good sign appeared to be the size of the total enrollment at the Academy, which in the fall of 1923 was 2,498. The fourth class (plebes) was very large, starting with 885 members. These plebes would eventually complete their first class year as the Class of 1927 with 579 graduates. This would help the personnel situation.

Figure 2. Naval Academy Class Sizes

The Great Heinlein Mystery

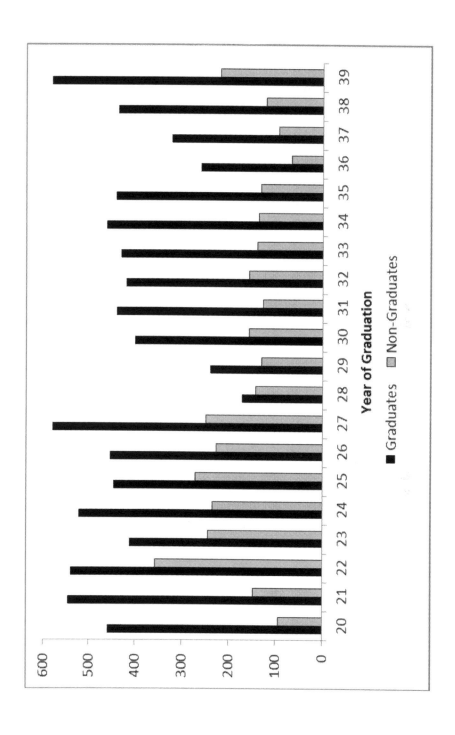

But then in stepped Congress again, this time with the naval appropriations law of 1924-25. A restriction was placed on the number of midshipmen allowed to each Senator, Representative and Delegate. It is very important to note that this was not the number allowed to be appointed in one year, but the total number allowed at one time at the Academy for that member of Congress. The maximum value was five, but could be limited to a smaller number by the appropriations. For 1924, the appropriation limit was set at three. With very large numbers already in the first, second, and third classes in the fall of 1924, this meant that only a very small plebe class was possible, which would graduate as the Class of 1928. The situation eased in the fall of 1925. Although the congressional restriction continued, the small third class that had originally entered in 1924 meant a smaller total for the three upper classes. It was therefore possible to have a slightly larger plebe class in 1925 which would then graduate as the Class of 1929.

With the smaller Classes of 1928 and 1929 graduating, it would be impossible for the Academy to supply the number of new officers each year to maintain the required total. The recommendation was made by the Chief of the Bureau of Navigation (personnel) that the limitation on the number of midshipman allowed for each member of Congress be removed, which would then permit the class sizes to grow to a level to meet the needs of the service. There were changes in the appropriation, but even in 1938 the value permitted by the yearly appropriation was only four.

Before attempting to search for the classmate responsible for the naval system, I wish to present pieces of information about the members of the class. Let us first consider their names. When I began looking at the class list from the *Register*, I noticed a few names that corresponded to characters in Heinlein's works. That began a careful rescanning of the list and checking of names in all of his works. The result was a Note published in *The Heinlein Journal,* a similar short article in *Shipmate,* followed by some additional *Journal* Notes with a few more names. Rather than repeat the entire list from the Notes and article here, I will just point out a few of what I feel are some of the more interesting names. The reader is then invited to look through Appendix 1 to see how many Heinlein characters can be found. I had only found a few character names among the non-graduates, so the Appendix contains the greater number to be located.

In most cases, it is only the surname of a classmate that matches with a Heinlein character. As I stated in the *Journal* Note, my listings omitted the more common surnames that matched, such as Burke, Davis, Ford, Johnson, Jones, McCoy, Smith, Walker, Wheeler, and Wilson. I had also commented "Whoever heard of science fiction characters named Smith and Jones?" There are two cases involving common surnames that I included only because the full name matched. The first such classmate was Samuel Anderson, who matches with Sam Anderson in *Starman Jones*. The other was Lowell Stone - the proper name of Buster, the youngest member of the Stone family in *The Rolling Stones*, was Lowell.

The classmate whose name appeared in the largest number of Heinlein's works, again excluding very common surnames, was Joseph Berzowski. He is listed among the graduates in the *Register* as Joseph Berzowski Berkley, which he used as his service name. It is interesting that in spite of the multiple uses of his name, none of them involved an active character. The earliest appearance was in the long lost and recently published *For Us, The Living*. The character Perry is discussing the history of the future age in which he finds himself with Master Cathcart and is told of the committee that drafted the new United States Constitution. The members of this committee were "Cyrus Fielding, Rosa Weinstein, John Delano Roosevelt, Ludvig Dixon, Joseph Berzowski and Colin MacDonald." It is the only case where Berzowski's first name was used by Heinlein. The second appearance was in *The Puppet Masters*, where one member of a tank crew killed in combat against the aliens is listed as "Powerman 2/C Florence Berzowski." The final appearance was in conversation in *The Door Into Summer* in which Daniel Boone Davis is reacting to the name "D. B. Davis" on a patent for a drafting system that he claims that he could not possibly have invented. His co-worker and drinking buddy advises him to find out the full name of the inventor and is commenting on first names, saying "But don't trip a breaker if it is 'Daniel,' because the middle name might be 'Berzowski' with a social-security number different from yours."

The character Delos D. Harriman appears in both "Requiem" and "The Man Who Sold the Moon." It was stated by Dr. Leon Stover that the surname was taken from the late nineteenth and early twentieth century financier and railroad owner Edward Henry Harriman. There were actually two classmates who could have provided the character's proper name: Reynold Delos Hogle and Delos Edwin Wait. It must be said that Delos is not exactly a common name. I have never been able to discover a reason why two men in such a small group, born early in the twentieth century (1906 and 1905 respectively), should share the name Delos. What was so special at that point in time about the name Delos?

There is yet another connection of the classmates with science fiction. I commented above that I had noticed that various classmates' names matched those of characters. The very first name that caught my eye was Dodson, used by Heinlein for cadet Matt Dodson in *Space Cadet*. The full name of Heinlein's classmate was Edwin Neil Dodson. At some later point in time, I was reading the on-line autobiography written by the physicist and science fiction author Dr. Robert Forward shortly before his death. In giving the details of his family, he mentions his father-in-law's name—Edwin Neil Dodson. I could have stated that they were most likely the same person, but with the assistance of David Hartwell who contacted the Forward family with my question, I was able to verify it.

Heinlein was not the only author in the Class of 1929. Kemp Tolley was the author of several books based on various stages of his naval career: *Yangtze Patrol: The US Navy in China*, *Cruise of the Lanikai: Incitement to War*, and *Caviar and Commissars: The Experiences of a US Naval Officer in Stalin's Russia*.

In Kemp Tolley's books, he has occasional mentions of other classmates who were encountered in the course of his travels and duty assignments. This points to yet another way in which member of the class of 1929 may be encountered. During the general course of my research I have been able to discover a number of historical works or biographies that contain references to members of the Class of 1929. These works, including those of Kemp Tolley, are presented with the names of the classmates appearing within, as follows:

Bluejacket Admiral: The Naval Career of Chick Hayward by John Hayward and C.W. Borklund.

    Flatley   Parish

Carrier Admiral by Admiral J. J. "Jocko" Clark with Clark G. Reynolds

    Flatley   Roy Johnson

Cruise of the Lanikai by Kemp Tolley

    Berkley   Bermingham
    Britt   Galbraith
    Jordan   Adolph Miller
    Roth

Commissars and Caviars by Kemp Tolley

    D'Avi   Frankel

Hellions of the Deep: The Development of American Torpedoes in World War II by Robert Gannon

Kirk   Triebel

Reaper Leader: The Life of Jimmy Flatley by Steve Ewing

Collett   Flatley
Hall

Silent Victory by Clay Blair

Benson   Davidson
Hardin   Carl Johnson
Kennedy   Kirk
Richard Lake   McGregor
John Moore   Rooney
Sharp   Stephan
Stone   Stovall
Triebel   Wales
Weiss

Thach Weave: The Life of Jimmie Thach by Steve Ewing

Benson   Flatley

The First Team: Pacific Naval Air Combat from Pearl Harbor to Midway by John B. Lundstrom

Fenton   Flatley
Raby

The First Team and the Guadalcanal Campaign: Naval Fighter Combat from August to November 1942 by John B. Lundstrom

Collett   Flatley
Paul Foley   Simpler

Wings for the Navy: A History of the Naval Aircraft Factory, 1917 - 1956 by William F. Trimble

Beardsley   Heinlein

In addition to the above, if you wish to look through the entire 15 volumes of Samuel Eliot Morison's *History of United States Naval Operations in World War II*, you are bound to encounter more mentions of members of the class of 1929. I do know that Morison's work contains mentions of at least Bermingham, Frankel, Laning and Ricketts, but I have not taken the time to locate any others.

There is one more way in which one might encounter names from the class of 1929. There have been five ships, none of which exists any longer, that were named after members of the Class of 1929. I feel that it is worth describing the circumstances under which each ship came to be named after a member of the class.

U.S.S. *Claude V. Ricketts* (DDG-5) was originally commissioned in May 1962 as U.S.S. *Biddle* (DD-955), a guided missile destroyer. It was renamed on July 28, 1964, to honor ADM Claude V. Ricketts who had died on July 6 of that year while serving as Vice Chief of Naval Operations. The U.S.S. *Claude V. Ricketts* was decommissioned in October 1989. Also named in honor of Admiral Ricketts is Ricketts Hall at the Naval Academy. If you were to go the Armel-Leftwich Visitor Center at the Naval Academy and arrange to take the walking tour, Ricketts Hall will be one of the first buildings pointed out to you when you start your tour. Ricketts Hall is part of the collection of building connected with athletics and contains the football locker room, physical training facility, weight room and offices for the Naval Academy Athletic Association.

U.S.S. *Collett* (DD-730) was a Sumner-class destroyer commissioned in May 1944. It was named in honor of LCDR John Austin Collett who was killed in action on October 26, 1942 during the Battle of the Santa Cruz Islands. At that time, he was serving as commanding officer of Torpedo Squadron 10 on the U.S.S. *Enterprise* (CV-6). The U.S.S. *Collett* was decommissioned in December 1970.

U.S.S. *John M. Bermingham* (DE-530) was an Evarts-class destroyer escort commissioned in April 1944. It was named after LCDR John Michael Bermingham. He had assumed command of the destroyer U.S.S. *Peary* (DD-226) after the commanding officer was wounded. Under his command, the *Peary* successfully made it from the Philippines to Australia. The *Peary* was bombed and sunk during a Japanese air attack at Darwin on February 19, 1942. In addition to LCDR Bermingham, approximately 80 of his crew were also lost. LCDR Bermingham was posthumously awarded the Navy Cross. The U.S.S. *John M. Bermingham* was decommissioned in October 1945.

U.S.S. *Pennewill* (DE-175) was a Cannon-class destroyer escort commissioned in September 1943. It was named after LCDR William Ellison Pennewill. While serving a commander of Escort Scouting Squadron Twelve at Kodiak, Alaska, he was killed in an airplane crash on June 23, 1942. He was posthumously awarded the Distinguished Flying Cross. On August 1, 1944, the U.S.S. *Pennewill* was decommissioned and leased to Brazil.

U.S.S. *Van Voorhis* (DE-1028) was a Courtney-class destroyer escort commissioned in April 1957. It was named after LCDR Bruce Avery Van Voorhis. While service as commanding officer of VB (Bombing Squadron) 102, he was killed during an attack on Greenwich Island during the Battle of the Solomon Islands on July 6, 1943. LCDR Van Voorhis was posthumously awarded the Medal of Honor. The U.S.S. *Van Voorhis* was decommissioned in July 1972.

Based on the information collected on the members of the Class of 1929 during the course of my researches, I could very easily continue to write about their wartime exploits, the levels that some eventually reached in their naval careers, and even pose unanswered questions about a few. To do so, however, would keep us from identifying the classmate responsible for taking the device as the basis for a naval system.

In the course of reviewing any information that could be obtained concerning any of the classmates, it would have been unlikely for me to have encountered a document that directly stated any connection with the device. To be able to evaluate whatever information was obtained with regard to each classmate, it was necessary to become familiar with the details of naval education of Heinlein's time as well as the career path and duties of a naval officer.

At the time when Heinlein was a midshipman, the basic curriculum included courses in the Department of Electrical Engineering. In spite of the name of the department, its courses for the first two years were more in the nature of the basic sciences, including chemistry and physics. Lectures included the applications of chemistry and physics in the navy. It was only in the third year that the course work began to include electrical concepts and electrical machinery, beginning the year with direct current and concluding with alternating current. When the midshipman reached his fourth year, the course topics began to include the principles and applications of the vacuum tube, which was identified in the previous chapter as the basis of all electronic devices of that era. The time in the electrical engineering course concerned with radio considered the basics of transmitters and receivers. The impression is that most midshipmen would have obtained some degree of familiarity with electronic devices but no great depth of understanding or capability in the field.

At this point, I present the typical course of a junior officer's naval career. It is not meant to be an exact description of every officer's path. It is very easy to present variations from the norm. After graduation and commissioning, an ensign would begin his first sea duty. During the first two years, the ensign would typically serve in turn in the various shipboard departments, such as gunnery, communications and engineering. Consider Heinlein's story of his early naval career as stated in *Expanded Universe* which involved the attempts to locate the plane piloted by his friend Buddy Scoles. Heinlein stated that he was assigned as radio compass officer. Since we know that by the end of his short naval career Heinlein was a gunnery officer, the question might be asked what he was doing in a position involving communications. As this episode occurred in 1931, we may conclude that Heinlein would still have been in his period of rotation among the ship's departments.

At the end of the two years, the young officer, still an ensign, might begin to specialize. He could request either submarine or aviation duty, or specialize, as Heinlein did, in a field such as gunnery. During these years, he would have been gaining much practical experience working with men and with the tools and equipment associated with his area of specialization. When he had reached seven years after graduation, the young officer, by now a lieutenant junior grade, could be selected for postgraduate education. This would have occurred in 1936 for Heinlein's classmates.

We know from the Virtues essay and letter quotes that the device was electronic. It is my contention that it is not likely that the classmate was able to recognize the potential of the story device and then be involved in the development of at least the bread-board version of the actual system without the benefit of any additional training or education in electronics past that what he would have received as a midshipman. He would have received such training or education either as a benefit of information acquired during duty assignments or through specialized technical education following graduation from the Academy.

The type of duty assignment that a classmate had during the time of the story's appearance is also of importance. If we could find a statement that a particular classmate was directly involved in electronic research or development work, it would be a strong indication that he was the one connected with the device. It is also reasonable to assume that an officer whose duty assignment involved electronics in any way would have the advantage of easier access to the materials and equipment required to construct and test the bread-boarded implementation.

Another factor to evaluate is contact with Heinlein. This may seem obvious, but let us consider the situation if the only existing reference to the device was the Virtues essay, written over 15 years after the fact. If such were the case, Heinlein could have acquired the knowledge of the naval system based on the story device from the classmate at any time in the intervening years. But we have the letter quotes from late 1941 and early 1942. If we believe the statements that the information of the existence of the naval system, but not the details, had been conveyed to Campbell at some point in the May - June 1940 time frame, then the information transfer between the classmate and Heinlein would have occurred before or during that time frame. It is also important to consider how Heinlein was kept informed on the subsequent development work for the system.

So, to repeat, the three major factors to be evaluated with respect to any candidate are:

1. Training and/or education in electronics in excess of that received as a midshipman.

2. Duty assignments that would have permitted experimentation with the naval system in the late 1939 to late 1941 time frame.

3. Contact with Heinlein in the mid-1939 to late 1941 time frame.

With these factors in mind, let us proceed to the information obtained concerning the classmates. The initial attempt was made to obtain information from the classmates themselves. As related in Chapter 1, I had explained the purpose of my search to Alumni Services in the summer of 1992 and was provided a list of those members of the class still living. The letter sent to each explained the objective of my search, and included the December 21, 1941 quote, the key sentence from the January 4, 1942 quote and the Virtues quote. I also mentioned that Ginny Heinlein had said that the classmate might have been Cal Laning, and then asked four questions:

1. Do you have any idea as to the identity of the system derived from the gadget or the classmate who could have developed it?

2. Do you know which members of the Class of 1929 were involved with any sort of research or development work in the 1939-1941 timeframe?

3. Is there any particular classmate who might know the answer?

4. Is there someone outside the Class of 1929, perhaps a historian, who might know the answer?

I received responses to approximately half of my enquiries. The majority of the responses can be summed up as "Sorry, I can't help you." and were received because I had provided a stamped and addressed return envelope with each letter sent. Some of the responses were written by a wife or daughter to the effect that the classmate had suffered a stroke or was afflicted with Alzheimer's or some other memory impairment. A few of the letters related the wartime experiences of the respondent, which were very interesting but did nothing to answer the questions. Some said that they had not had any contact with Heinlein since graduation.

There were only six who provided responses that at least attempted to answer some of the questions:

Ballinger: "I, too 'heard' of such a device. However, I think it was through the now deceased Caleb Laning."

Berkley: "Laning had some knowledge - never sharing with me."

John Davison: "Cal Laning would probably have known of the gadget you seek. We miss him!"

Ferrier: "If Robert Heinlein developed the gadget while he was assigned to the U.S. Navy (Naval?) Experiment station in Annapolis, which was across the Severn River from the Naval Academy, I don't think it was electronic" Aside from the fact that Heinlein has obviously been confused with some other classmate who had such an assignment, this response resulted from a misunderstanding of my question as it is concerned something that Heinlein was supposed to have done while on active duty.

Johansen: "Ginny Heinlein was right when she said that Cal Laning would have known, probably better than anyone else, what the gadget was that Bob referred to. Cal was a very close friend of Bob's, I was a very close friend of Cal's and I knew he was involved in electronic research in the Navy at one time. It is quite possible that he was the classmate Bob referred to who developed the gadget."

Ramsbotham: The response in this case was by phone, the only conversation with any member of the class. Ramsbotham tried to be helpful, but like Ferrier was interpreting my question as regarding something that Heinlein had supposedly done while he was still on active duty. In addition, he suggested the development of a torpedo targeting system developed while Heinlein was in submarines - but we all know that Heinlein never served in submarines.

The responses of Ferrier and Ramsbotham indicated that problems exist when asking for accurate long-term memories from gentlemen who were then in their mid-eighties. This might make the other four responses somewhat suspect. I had specifically mentioned the targeting of Laning by Ginny Heinlein. How much of an influence did that have on their responses? If I had not mentioned Laning, would Ballinger, Berkley, Davison or Johansen have responded as they did?

The next type of information obtained was the Naval Biography of several of the classmates. Such biographies are available only for those who have obtained flag rank (rear admiral or higher). The naval bio appears to be composed on the basis of information provided by the officer on a standard form. In some cases all that was provided to me was the form itself, or a portion of it. The biography gives minimal personal details, summarizing the period from birth through graduation from the Academy in the first paragraph. After noting the date of commissioning as Ensign, it continues with the details the officer's naval career, giving the name of ships or the location of shore duty assignments. Promotions may not be precisely noted, but changes of duty are noted, such as "on this date he was assigned as the Electrical Officer on board the U.S.S. . . . ." Postgraduate education is usually mentioned. Any combat awards are mentioned and the circumstances which led to that award are given, possibly quoting a portion of the text of the citation.

Two circumstances made it possible to obtain naval biographies for approximately one third of the graduates. The first was the small size of the class. The second was the existence for some period of time of a provision in the law known as "tombstone promotion." This Act of Congress allowed an officer who had received one or more awards for valor to retire at the next highest rank. For example, a Captain who retired in this manner could put "RADM (Ret.)" on his business cards, and of course that rank would also appear on his tombstone, hence the name. Until 1949, this meant receiving the higher retirement pay as well. For the remaining 10 years until the law was abolished in 1959, retirees received the higher retirement rank but not the higher retirement pay. Many naval biographies received show a file started when the officer was a Captain, but included the copy of a file card with supplementary entries including one that gave the retirement date and with a notation such as "Retired (Advanced to RAdm on the basis of combat awards.)"

Obtaining more information required the use of the Nimitz Library at the Naval Academy. The Special Collections and Archives Department maintains a collection of back issues of *Shipmate*. The "Class News" sections of many issues were examined to see if they contained anything useful. It was also possible to examine the Alumni Association file for any of the deceased members of the class. These files usually contained a form filled out by the classmate giving some personal information and the details of his naval career. Many of these forms gave very limited data, but at least provided something for those for whom naval biographies were not available.

At this point, someone is bound to ask why the service records of many of the classmates were not examined. One must submit a request for service records to the Military Records Center in St. Louis. If one is not the next-of-kin of the person for whom you are requesting information, one must have the written permission of the next-of-kin. As Caleb Laning had always been the "prime suspect" on the basis of Ginny Heinlein's statement **and** he was the only classmate for whom I had been in contact with family members, I have made the effort to obtain only Laning's record. And thereby hangs a tale.

In the summer of 2002, I submitted my request for Cal Laning's service record accompanied by a written permission from Judith, one of his daughters. I knew his social security number, but she was unable to provide me with his service number. After my request had been submitted I would make occasional telephone queries every month or so and each time was told that it was being worked, but no results ever appeared. When I called in January of 2003, I was given the same response, but it was suggested that I should submit another query. I did not see what good that would do, but I submitted it anyway. There were still no results for the next 5 months.

During a June 2003 call to check status, I was specifically asked for Laning's service number for the first time. When I said that I did not have it, I was told that the lack of the service number was the reason I was getting no action. I was able to obtain the service number and was then told that I would shortly receive my results. The months went by. In September 2003, I found that an email status request system had been started. It began to appear that my periodic status requests were triggering a standard response. When I got to December 2003, a period of 17 months gone and still no result, I decided that something new was required. It took a very long, highly detailed email to the Office of the Inspector General of the National Archives and Records Administration to finally get some action. ***17 MONTHS!!!***

After that painful and time-consuming experience, I was never inclined to try to obtain the service record for any other classmate. I was lucky enough to have been in contact with members of Laning's family. But as I stated in Chapter 1, none were able to provide me with any information connected with the device. For other classmates, there would be the problem of locating next-of-kin to request permission. If any of my readers wish to pursue this particular line of investigation for any of the other classmates, please let me know what you find out.

The following segment, which is taken from Laning's naval biography, may be considered typical of the other naval biographies that I was able to obtain:

> Following graduation from the Naval Academy in 1929, he joined the USS *Oklahoma* to serve until November 1932, interspersed with instruction, January - May 1931, in fire control (specialized in Antiaircraft Directors) at the Ford Instrument Company, Long Island, New York. Completing submarine training at the Submarine Base, New London, Connecticut, he reported in June 1933 on board the USS *S-13* and in September 1935 transferred to the USS *R-2*.
>
> He attended a course in general line at the Postgraduate School, Annapolis, Maryland, from June 1936 until May 1938, after which he had duty as Radio Officer on the staff of Commander Cruiser Division Eight, USS *Philadelphia*, flagship. In that capacity, he took part in some of the earliest micro-wave radio experiments in the Fleet. In September 1940 he was assigned to the USS *Sicard* as Executive Officer, and received a commendatory letter for his contributions toward the *Sicard*'s winning the Battle Efficiency Pennant in gunnery, engineering and mine laying in 1940. In June 1941 he joined the USS *Conyngham* to serve as Executive Officer and Navigator until October 1942.

If we consider Laning's time in submarines as indicated in the naval biography, we find in his Fitness Report (a part of his service record) for the period May 19, 1934 to September 30, 1934 the statement:

> This officer was commended by the Chief of the Bureau of

Ordnance and Gunnery for his zeal in designing a torpedo director for use in submarines.

This particular item is worth mentioning only because it appears to match with Ramsbotham's mistaken recollections concerning Heinlein. He was apparently thinking of Laning.

Four points should be noted from the large paragraph in the quote from the biography:

1. Postgraduate education

2. Duty as Radio Officer

3. Microwave radio experiments

4. Subsequent duties on *Sicard* and *Conyngham*.

Skipping over the first point for the moment, let us take the remaining three in turn. The period of his duty as Radio Officer ran from June 1938 until September 1940. This is from well before the appearance of Heinlein's first published story "Life-Line" until several months after the publication of "The Roads Must Roll" which was the last story that it was determined we must consider. It also brackets the time of the Heinlein's trip to the east coast when the information about the existence of the naval system was first conveyed to Campbell.

As noted earlier in this chapter, a duty assignment concerned with electronics would make that particular classmate a more likely candidate. The reference to micro-wave radio experiments should not be seen as correlating with any details presented in the Virtues essay or the letter quotes. In later chapters it is seen that there is no match with any material extracted from the stories. It does appear to match up, however, with the reference in Chapter 5 to experiments in communications at 500 MHz that were conducted in the Fleet in 1938.

Nothing is mentioned in Laning's naval biography or his service record that would permit us to attempt a match with some fictional device. But consider that while the naval biography specifically mentions his being involved in "microwave radio" experiments, this is not mentioned in his service record. I see this as leaving open the possibility that tests of the naval system based on the story idea could also have been conducted during his duty as Radio Officer, with no mention occurring in his service record.

The duty assignments after September 1940 do raise the question regarding the classmate's knowledge of the subsequent development work upon the device. How would Laning have obtained knowledge of such work being performed at some laboratory or by a manufacturer from his duty station on a destroyer? Of course, the information related to Heinlein could have been on development work of which Laning was aware only up to the end of his duty assignment as Radio Officer.

Now we return to the first important point mentioned in Laning's naval bio - his postgraduate education. The system for providing additional education to naval officers following their graduation from the Naval Academy has a history with many twists and turns. We consider the situation as it existed in the 1930s when the Postgraduate School was still located in Annapolis.

The postgraduate instruction received during the 1930s was based on a possible combination of the General Line course and some type of technical specialization. I used the term possible as some officers would take only courses in the General Line Curriculum where, according to the 1938-1939 catalog:

> The objective of this curriculum is to prepare line officers to perform efficiently the duties of a head of department of any type ship or those of a commanding officer of any small craft.

In the 1931-1932 year, the first year of postgraduate instruction consisted of the General Line Course. Those who completed this year of instruction and who were considered to be qualified were chosen for a second year of study in a particular technical area. This system continued for several years until it was modified in 1938. Under the new system, only those following just the General Line curricula course for a year would still receive the full course of study in that area. Those enrolled for work in a particular technical specialization would, during their first year, take a combination of general line and technical courses. Because of the mixture of courses, they would not receive the full range of instruction in General Line topics. They would continue with their technical courses during their second year. Note that the description of the curricula that follows is taken from the catalog for the 1938-1939 year. This represents the newer course structure. The members of the Class of 1929 would have begun their instruction in 1936 under the old system. Unfortunately, it was not possible to locate a catalog for the old system. It is assumed that although the distribution of courses among the first and second years would be different - only General Line courses the first year under the old system - the intent and overall content of the technical curricula to be discussed would not have changed appreciably from 1936 to 1938.

The only two curricula with which we shall be concerned are Radio Engineering and Communications. How did they differ? Again quoting from the 1938-1939 catalog:

The objective for the Radio Engineering curriculum is to prepare the Radio Engineering group of student officers

(a) To become competent supervisors over the operation, maintenance, test and inspection of all types of apparatus utilized by the radio and sound activities of the Naval Communication Service

(b) To become competent supervisors over work relative to the specification, design and research problems of Naval Radio and Sound Engineering

The objective of this [Communications] curriculum is to prepare officers

(a) To perform the various administrative activities of the Naval Communication Service

(b) To become competent supervisors over the service, operation and maintenance of all types of apparatus utilized by the Naval Communication Service

(c) To become competent tactical officers

While both refer to the operation and maintenance of the equipment, the important distinction is that the Radio Engineering officer would also be concerned with specification, design and research, where the Communications officer would be concerned with administration. It is considered possible that officers passing through either of these curricula would then have gained sufficient technical knowledge to bring Heinlein's story idea into realization.

Although both types of officers would have had classes in Physics, Electricity, Radio Engineering, Sound and Communications, there was minimal overlap in the exact courses taken. There were some interesting differences in the catalog. A first year Radio Engineering course was taken by each type of student. The Radio Engineering curriculum version of the course involved practical work, whereas the Communications version was lecture only. Radio Engineering curriculum courses would go into greater technical details covering topics such as network theorems, long line properties and filters that were not covered in the Communications curriculum courses. Another difference is that the Communications curricula did not include any Mathematics courses, but Radio Engineering did. Courses in both curricula did cover vacuum tubes and both included practical work with all types of navy issue equipment.

Both Radio Engineering and Communications had four additional weeks at the end of the first year at the Navy Department in Washington, D.C. for the purpose of practical instruction. They also both had four weeks at the end of the second year at the Submarine Base in New London for practical instruction in Sound and Sound Apparatus. There was one other important difference. At the completion of the second year, students in Radio Engineering could be selected for a third year of study at either Harvard or the University of California, most likely resulting in a Master's degree. Such an option was not possible for those in Communications. Of all of the possible technical curricula, the only two that did not have the option of graduate study at some university were Naval Engineering and Communications.

If we go back and look at the Class of 1929, who besides Laning had postgraduate education in these areas? To understand the difficulty in obtaining this information, note that the quote from Laning's naval bio indicates only that he did the course of instruction in General Line. The time indicated at the Postgraduate School, June 1936 until May 1938, makes that statement questionable, as it has been stated that General Line involved only one year of instruction. The indication of Communications rather than General Line does appear in his service record.

Although it appears that the Communications curriculum did not provide quite the technical depth of the Radio Engineering curriculum, I do not feel that this justifies eliminating from consideration those classmates whose study was in Communications. Laning, for example, ended the war in Washington as the head of the Radar and CIC Section in the Office of the Director of Electronics. It is clearly a question of what the officer was able to do with the education that he received.

It was possible to discover a total of 13 officers from the class of 1929 who had postgraduate instruction in either Communications or Radio Engineering. These are all shown in Table 3. Aside from the Naval Bio and service record employed in Laning's case, the sources of information were the contents of the Alumni Association files at the Nimitz Library, a number identifying any special qualifications appearing in the officer's entry in the *Register of Alumni*, and the content of any letter received in the

Name	Naval Bio / Service Record	Alumni File / Other	1992 Register of Alumni	1992 Letter
Berkley			927 – Radio Engineering	Yes (4)
Carmichael	Applied Communications			No
Dye		Navy PG School, Communications, 1936-1937	926 – Communications	No
Dyer		Postgraduate studies in Aviation Communications, 1936-1939 (Columbia University Oral History Research Office)	927 – Radio Engineering	No
Ferrier			926 – Communications	Yes
Folger		Naval PG School (2)	926 – Communications	No
Hutchins		PG School – Communications (2)	926 – Communications	No
Johansen	Communication Engineering		926 – Communications	Yes
Laning	General Line / Communications (1)		926 – Communications	No
Mains		PG School 2 years – Radio Engineering, 2 years EE at Berkeley (2)	927 – Radio Engineering	No
McCoy		PG School – Applied Communications (2)		No
Nelson, Paul		PG School, Major PG26 (2)	926 – Communications	No
Wait	PG School (3)	PG USNA & U of CA U of Cal Berkeley, MS (EE, Radio) (2)	927 – Radio Engineering	Yes

initial survey. (In the case of Dyer, the information came from an Internet search.)

None of the sources is ideal. There are naval biographies only for 4 of the officers listed in the table, and the one for Wait is extremely spotty in details. The strongest indicator is the qualifications number from the *Register of Alumni*. But notice that no number was listed for Carmichael even though it is clearly stated in his naval bio that he had the postgraduate course in Communications.

What may we conclude from Table 3? The most important thing to note is that I had received letters from Berkley, Ferrier, Johansen and Wait that indicated that they had no knowledge of the device. If we are to believe their statements, then we may remove them from the list. This leaves us with seven in Communications (Carmichael, Dye, Folger, Hutchins, Laning, McCoy and Nelson) and two in Radio Engineering (Dyer and Mains).

Among those remaining, the one for which a naval bio exists is Carmichael. His duty assignment following postgraduate was very similar to Laning where:

> From May, 1938, until December 1940, he was radio officer consecutively on the staffs of Commander, Training Detachment, United States Fleet; Commander, Atlantic Squadron, United States Fleet; and Commander Patrol Force, United States Fleet.

In the absence of additional information, I would consider Carmichael another potential candidate.

To summarize, it has not been possible to determine on the basis of available information which of Heinlein's classmates was the one connected with the mystery device. If my reasoning with regard to postgraduate education is accepted, the logical course at this point would be to attempt to locate any of the next-of-kin of the eight classmates resulting from the analysis of Table 3 (excluding, of course, Laning) and then attempt to obtain their service records in the hope that they will contain the necessary information that will permit the mystery to be solved.

Table 3. Naval Postgraduate Education
(1) Naval Bio states "course in General Line." Portions of Service Record indicate "Communications" and Applied Communications."
(2) Dates not given in Alumni Association Files.
(3) Gives span as May 1936 to May 1939.
(4) Makes reference in letter "In 1938 I was finishing 2nd yr off [sic] graduate school .... Berkeley U."

It is hoped that the appearance of this work might make it possible to locate the next-of-kin.

Any subsequent analysis remains based on the assumption that Caleb Laning was the classmate connected with the development of the naval system inspired by the mystery device.

The next chapter considers the type of science fiction story in which the mystery device might appear.

7

NAVAL SCIENCE FICTION

In attempting to identify a device in a science fiction story with a real world implementation that would have been of use to the United States Navy, it is useful to consider the type of story in which the device had appeared. While it is possible that the device could have appeared in any type of story, it seems more probable that it appeared in a story with some naval features.

If you were to ask someone not very familiar with science fiction what comes to their mind when they hear the terms "science fiction" and "fleet," the responses that you are most likely to receive are either *Star Trek* or *Star Wars*. Both of these contained a collection of spacecraft with some implied correspondence to the composition of the various naval fleets since the latter years of the 19th century. To someone more familiar with science fiction, a larger number of additional responses should be obtained. These responses could include the titanic space battles in the works of E.E. "Doc" Smith or John W. Campbell, Jr., the Miles Vorkosigan stories of Lois McMaster Bujold, the Honor Harrington stories of David Weber, and short stories such as Arthur C. Clarke's "Superiority." The preceding list is meant to show that the concept of a space navy is very well established in science fiction, and represents a small percentage of such stories in existence.

The largest ships in space navies are, by analogy with their waterborne ancestors, usually called battleships, dreadnoughts or even super-dreadnoughts. Then with the reduction in size and firepower, we would pass through various types of cruisers, eventually arriving at the destroyers. One advantage with creating space naval science fiction is that the capabilities and weapons of your types of spacecraft may be defined by the need to establish the constraints of your story. It is simply a matter of how much you wish to play with established physical principles or possibly invent new ones of your own. You could have very short range weapons with capabilities reminiscent of sailing ships firing solid shot cannon balls at near point blank range. At the other extreme, you could have the futuristic equivalent of a 20th century battleship hurling armor piercing shells more than twenty miles at targets barely visible on the horizon. Your weapons might be missile or torpedoes equipped with all sorts of specialized warheads, or you might rely on energy weapons projected from your ships. (In the *Star Trek* context, think "photon torpedoes" and "phasers.") When developing the weapons, the author must consider ways of resisting their effects, usually with "shields" or "force fields." If both sides possess weapons that may be easily countered, we have battles that are draws. If one side possesses weapons that are impossible to counter, we have battles which end quickly with few or no survivors on one side. Most authors tend to avoid such situations. One exception is *Off Armageddon Reef* (and its sequels) by David Weber which deals with the attempt to preserve humanity in the face of an enemy whose space fleets and weapons cannot be defeated.

In space navy stories, one must consider the problems of communication and the means of detecting the enemy. Unless your forces possess a faster-than-light communication system, even interplanetary distances present a situation equivalent to that prior to the introduction of radio into naval communications at the beginning of the 20th century, as described in Chapter 5. Spacecraft will be able to see or otherwise sense the presence of others unless the existence of some sort of invisibility shield or cloak is allowed. The most obvious example of this is the "Balance of Terror" episode of the original *Star Trek* series. The story featured an encounter with a cloaked Romulan ship which was attempting to return to Romulan space and was being pursued by the *Enterprise* intent on its destruction. This episode has been compared to the World War 2 destroyer versus submarine cat-and-mouse game in the film "The Enemy Below."

Returning to the opening observation of the chapter, it is suggested that not only would the mystery device appear in a story with certain naval features, but most likely in a story with a correspondence to conventional naval warfare rather than the space versions just discussed. This presented an interesting question - how much conventional naval science fiction actually exists? The purpose of this chapter will be first to explore naval science fiction in general and then to consider how the Navy appears in the works of Robert Heinlein.

To begin, let us consider two works which present slightly different types of naval fiction. The first is a novel published in 1925 that predicted a naval war between the United States and Japan. This is Hector Bywater's *The Great Pacific War: A History of the American Japanese Campaign of 1931 - 1933*. Bywater was a naval correspondent for a British newspaper and may be considered to have been very knowledgeable of the existing fleets of his time and capable of making logical predictions of ships that might have been added to the American and Japanese fleets by the time his fictional war was to have occurred.

Contrary to the statement on the cover of my copy of *The Great Pacific War*, the book did not predict the attack on Pearl Harbor. It did predict the conquest of the Philippines and Guam by Japan, and their eventual recovery by the United States. Although the novel does occasionally involve the use of aircraft carriers, the decisive battles are all actions primarily involving battleships and cruisers. This is consistent with the assumption of many naval officers at the time that the next war would involve large fleet actions similar to the Battle of Jutland. The names Bywater uses for some of the older capital ships on both sides are familiar as they were in existence when he wrote the novel and still existed by the time of World War 2. It is only when he comes to newer ships such as a few of the aircraft carriers and cruisers that names are encountered that seem strange to one familiar with naval history. The only detail of naval warfare suggested by Bywater that departs from what we would consider conventional warfare was the use of gas in both naval battles and attacks on islands. As gas was used in land warfare in World War 1, this cannot be considered a prediction of some new weapon. The basic premise of the novel was that Japan started the war based on the assumption that an external threat would help to stabilize the political situation at home. Very little of the work deals with the situation in the United States except to show its military responses. With no science fiction content, this book should be called future naval fiction.

The second work is the short story "Politics" by Murray Leinster (the pen name of Will F. Jenkins) which originally appeared in the June 1932 issue of *Amazing Stories*. The title of the story refers to the political situation in the United States which Jenkins contrived to be of an extremely pacifist nature. When the story begins, a large portion of the U.S. fleet had just been destroyed by an un-named Pacific enemy. You may fill in the name of the enemy if you wish. Preparations are being made for a final battle involving the remainder of the U.S. Fleet, while back in Washington the politicians are considering accepting the enemy's terms for peace. One important component of the surviving fleet is the fictional battleship U.S.S. *Minnesota*, which missed the earlier battle because of an engineering problem. The *Minnesota* had just been equipped with automatic infrared range finders.

The American ships go out for the final battle, which occurs close to the west coast of the United States. This enabled the Fleet to be aided by land-based Army planes. Without going into details, it is sufficient to state that the U.S. Fleet succeeds in destroying the enemy fleet, primarily due to the enhanced targeting capabilities of the *Minnesota*. Clearly the best point of the story occurs when the politicians have finally decided to accept the peace terms and issued a resolution which directed the President to order the Commander of the U.S. Fleet to surrender his ships to the Commander of the enemy fleet. Upon the receipt of that order, the U.S. Commander had the extreme pleasure of replying:

To the President of the United States:

There is no longer an enemy battle fleet off our coasts. We have destroyed it.

The key technical feature of the story was the automatic infrared range finders. The range finders, consisting of parallel telescopes, scan the horizon many times a second. Based on the differences of the times at which the image is detected in each of two telescopes, the distance to the target is automatically determined and fed to the fire control equipment. The speculative technical element is based on Jenkins making the detectors in the range finder sensitive to infrared light. This makes it possible for Jenkins to have the *Minnesota* accurately locate the enemy ships by spotting it through two smoke screens, one laid by each fleet. Although infrared is slightly better at penetrating smoke than visible light, it is technically correct to state that the battle could not occur in the manner that was postulated by Jenkins. If one were to say "fire control radar" instead of "infrared range finders," then one would have a technically feasible story in which a ship could accurately project its gunfire in spite of limits on visible target spotting. Feasible or not, I would claim that the inclusion of the fictional infrared range finders is sufficient to make this story naval science fiction.

Future war fiction is a sub-genre that that has been explored, most specifically by I. F. Clarke. Even though Clarke's papers have been published in *Science Fiction Studies*, it is necessary to ask how many of the stories that he has identified may be legitimately called science fiction. If we return to the problem of defining science fiction as discussed in Chapter 3, we could make use of Heinlein's preferred term and call these stories "speculative fiction." But consider a story predicting a future war, either simply set 1 or 5 or 10 years in the future or (as in the case of *The Battle of Dorking*) told from a standpoint 50 years in the future as the memories of someone who fought in the battle. Assume that this story does not contain any technology in excess of what existed at the time that the story was written. Just as with Bywaters's work described above, such a story should not be considered science fiction.

I have presented the works by Bywater and Jenkins in an attempt to distinguish between what I consider naval science fiction and what I do not. As I attempted to come up with a good succinct definition for "naval science fiction" I began to encounter problems. Somewhat like the problem of trying to define science fiction as discussed in Chapter 3. I could try to get away with saying something like "a science fiction story with naval features." A few of you might even accept that definition. But that raises the question as to what aspect of a particular work made it science fiction and what features related it to the Navy. A short list of science fiction stories, movies and even television series was compiled to illustrate what it means when I use the term "naval science fiction."

Having compiled such a list, an attempt was made to organize them in such a way as to make their similarities and differences clear. The best way found was to make use of a Venn diagram as shown in Figure 3.

The two large ellipses represent types of naval science fiction that will be described below. The region outside of both ellipses represents conventional naval fiction, with no recognizable science fiction features. One work that inhabits this outer region is Bywater's tale of the war between Japan and the United States. Other such works might be found among the future war fiction described by I. F. Clarke.

First consider the left ellipse, ignoring the area of overlap with the right ellipse. This area contains works that place conventional navy ships, equipment and personnel within a story that most would consider for other reasons to be science fiction. One of the best examples of this type of naval science fiction is the 1980 film *Final Countdown*. For those of you who are not familiar with the work, it involves the transposition of the modern aircraft carrier U.S.S. *Nimitz* to the time immediately before the attack upon Pearl Harbor. An attempt is made to warn Pearl Harbor of the impending attack, which fails since they have truthfully identified themselves as the *Nimitz* and are told that aircraft carriers are not named after serving Admirals. The ship eventually returns to their present, leaving behind a member of the crew in company with a woman rescued during their time in the past. This couple re-appears at the very end of the movie, having lived during the intervening years, thereby closing the time loop.

The mechanism by which the *Nimitz* travels through time is never explained. It simply occurs. One could argue that the failure to present some form of scientific or even pseudo-scientific explanation makes it possible to consider this story a fantasy rather than science fiction. In

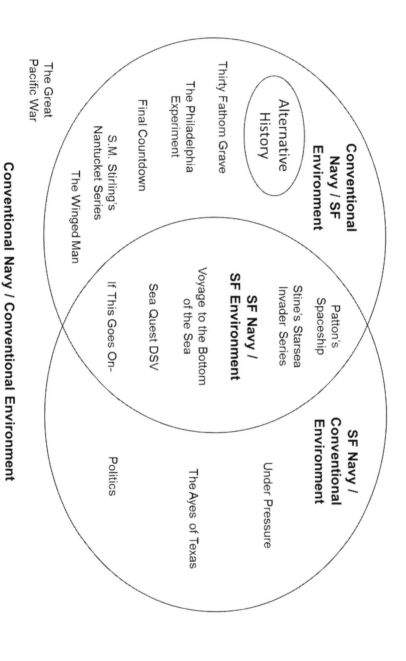

classifying this story as one form of naval science fiction, I consider it important that every purely naval feature of the story could just as easily have been applied to a plot involving contemporary warfare with the Soviet Union or Red China.

The Philadelphia Experiment is a 1984 film based on an incident that allegedly took place at the Philadelphia Navy Yard during World War 2. The destroyer U.S.S. *Eldridge* (DE 173) was supposedly used in an experiment to make the ship invisible to radar. During this experiment the ship was said to have vanished, or even to have been teleported to another location. All sorts of gruesome things are supposed to have happened to the crew. Judging from what may be found on the Internet, there are some people that believe it actually occurred and who are trying to explain how it happened. In any case, we may definitely consider the film to be science fiction. As we have a naval craft involved with science fiction concepts such as invisibility and teleportation, just as we were presented with time travel in *Final Countdown*, I would say that this film belongs in this first category.

A slightly older work is the *Twilight Zone* episode "The Thirty Fathom Grave" which appeared in 1963. The story concerns a Chief Petty Officer Bell played by Mike Kellin (perhaps chosen for the part due to his having also played a Chief in the 1960 film *The Wackiest Ship in the Army*). Bell was the sole survivor from a submarine sunk during the war in the same area where the destroyer on which he serves is now sailing. Bell has long been suffering from guilt at being the only survivor. As the site of the submarine is approached a sound is heard which is identified as someone pounding a hammer within the submarine. Chief Bell's torment worsens, and he kills himself by jumping overboard, finally joining his shipmates. This episode could probably more accurately be called fantasy, as were many *Twilight Zone* episodes, but again the purely naval features of the story are untouched.

The earliest work that I have been able to identify that places conventional navy in a science fiction environment is "The Winged Man" by E. Mayne Hull (the first wife of A. E. van Vogt). The story, which appeared in *Astounding* in May and June 1944, concerned a submarine that was transposed a million years into the future. This transposition was accomplished by one of the two forms into which the human race has evolved in the far future - the winged men of the title and submarine men. The submarine was chosen as a weapon by the winged men for combat on a future Earth which is totally covered by water.

A set of novels that may also be placed in this category belong to S. M.

Figure 3. Naval Science Fiction

Stirling's Nantucket series (*Island in the Sea of Time*, *Against the Tide of Years*, and *On the Oceans of Eternity*). By some never explained process, a circular area containing the island of Nantucket and all of its 20th century inhabitants is transposed back to 1250 B.C. Also transposed are nearby ships, including the U. S. Coast Guard ship *Eagle* and its crew. Although such modern technology as was transposed does work in the past, it was advantageous that the *Eagle* is a square rigged sailing ship used for training purposes. A group of Nantucket islanders and some members of the Coast Guard crew flee the island and attempt to set up their own empire in the Mediterranean and Middle East, and also to provide technological assistance to others who would threaten the existence of the Republic of Nantucket. A sufficient number of naval actions occur within the pages of the novels to permit them to be called naval science fiction. The naval technology employed can be classified, at least in the case of the *Eagle*, as conventional 19th and 20th century. Other ships are either constructed along the same lines or represent more ancient designs with some influence of the Nantucket island technology.

Completely contained within this region of the diagram are stories of alternative history. This is a well-known subset of science fiction, although it is possible to encounter alternative histories that are not presented as science fiction. The author of an alternative history picks a decisive point in history and changes some factor. He or she then develops the story on the basis of assumptions as to what would have then happened differently from the result we know. Some of the obvious changes are a battle being won instead of lost (or vice versa) or the fact that an important person died instead of living (or vice versa), although more subtle changes have been applied. Many works of this type have been written, from short stories to series of novels. Have any of you with an interest in naval history wondered during an idle moment what would have happened at Midway if there had been no codebreaking to warn of the coming Japanese attack, or if Task Force 34 had been in place at San Bernardino Strait during the Battle of Leyte Gulf? The list of such "what if" scenarios is endless.

One collection of alternative history short stories, *Alternate Generals*, contains four with a naval theme. "Vive L'Amiral" by John Mina assumes that Horatio Nelson becomes convinced that he cannot advance within the British Navy and instead fights for the French. The result is a victory for the French at Trafalgar, but Nelson meets the same personal end. In a similar vein, "The Captain from Kirkbean" by David Weber has John Paul Jones fighting for the British during the American Revolution. He still replies "I have not yet begun to fight," but does so in reply to a question from an officer of the French Fleet aiding the Americans. "Tradition" by

Elizabeth Moon considers a different outcome to the pursuit of the *Goeben* in the Mediterranean at the very beginning of World War 1.

The fourth story, "Billy Mitchell's Overt Act" by William Sanders, is the one which raises some interesting questions. The basic assumption is that General Mitchell remained in the Army following his court martial and was stationed in Hawaii at the time of the impending Japanese attack in December, 1941. Instead of the U.S. Pacific Fleet being caught totally by surprise, the story assumes that the Japanese Fleet was detected prior to the attack and bombed by Mitchell's forces. Mitchell dies by diving his crippled bomber into the aircraft carrier *Kaga*. The U.S. does go to war to war with Japan, with General Mitchell as its first hero. But without the definite event of a successful surprise attack on the U.S. Pacific Fleet, the American people are not united in the conflict. Considerable opposition develops, and the war is not ended in a decisive manner. The resulting political situation keeps the U.S. from responding to Communist domination of the Pacific nations in the post-war years. Absurd? Perhaps. Given the isolationist feeling in the United States prior to the war, can anyone confidently say what would have happened if there had been no Pearl Harbor as we knew it?

In a similar vein is Harry Turtledove's *Days of Infamy*, in which the Japanese attack on Pearl Harbor occurs as it did in our history, but is followed up by subsequent attacks, invasion and occupation of the Hawaiian Islands.

Now let us move to the right hand ellipse, again ignoring the area of intersection. These stories present a conventional story structure in which the ship, equipment or weapons have been enhanced or modified to operate in some manner in advance of existing naval capabilities. One story which fits into this category is Jenkins' "Politics."

Another story which may be placed in this category is Frank Herbert's "Under Pressure," which originally appeared in *Astounding* in late 1955 and early 1956. It was later republished as *Dragon in the Sea* and again as *21st Century Sub*. The story is concerned with the voyage of an atomic submarine, the *Fenian Ram*, which is involved in an effort to steal from oil deposits belonging to Eastern Hemisphere nations. The purloined oil is placed in a large submersible bladder that is towed behind the *Ram*. There is also the need to discover why each of the last 20 submarines sent on such a mission was lost. The classification of the story depends on the capabilities of the submarine, which were in advance of those existing at the time, and of certain equipment employed within the story.

The final story appearing in this category is *The Ayes of Texas* by Daniel da Cruz. The story, which takes place in the closing years of the 20th century, involves an independent Texas in an attempt to embarrass the efforts to have the United States sign a treaty with a Soviet Union that has managed to dominate most of the world. This process involves the use of the dreadnought-era battleship U.S.S. *Texas to* demonstrate the true plans and nature of the Soviets. But this is a *Texas* whose hull has been smoothed and coated to reduce friction, equipped with atomic reactors and water jet propulsion that allows it to exceed 60 knots, and is armed with electron beam weapons which are able to convert portions of Soviet ships to molten slag. The surviving ships of a visiting Soviet fleet that has sailed up the Houston Ship Channel, their numbers already reduced by other means, are totally destroyed by the *Texas*, although it also meets its end in the battle.

We now come to the region of overlap between the two ellipses. This region represents stories in which the naval technology being used is somehow in advance of that of the present (as in *The Ayes of Texas*) and the story, exclusive of the naval features, can clearly be seen to be science fiction (as in *Final Countdown*). The best example of this is G. Harry Stine's Starsea Invaders trilogy (*First Action, Second Contact,* and *Third Encounter*). The action occurs in the mid-21st century and involves the crew of the U.S.S. *Shenandoah*. The *Shenandoah* is an SSCV, an aircraft carrier submarine capable of launching and recovering VTOL naval aircraft. The submarine is equipped with a new super-secret device, the MASDET (or mass detector), which passively senses the presence of objects. Communication between members of the crew is enhanced by use of the N-phone (or neurophone) which creates a form of artificial telepathy.

While investigating the disappearance of Americans in the vicinity of Sulawesi in the Southwest Pacific, the crew discovers the presence of aliens on Earth. As the story unwinds, they also discover that Earth has actually been in contact with aliens since the time of the sighting of UFOs in the years after World War 2. There are over 70 different alien races known, and some of them are not particularly friendly to humans. The technologies behind the MASDET and N-phone are revealed as being the result of earlier contact with aliens.

Alternative timeline stories are closely related to alternative history as they permit any number of such potential histories to coexist. Although I had place alternative history in the first category that was discussed, there is one novel which I feel belongs in the intersection of the two major categories. This is *Patton's Spaceship*, which is one of a trio of novels by John Barnes that consider an organization combating threats to timelines such as ours. The villains of the story are known as Closers as they attempt to close off the possibilities for the various timelines. The protagonist is trapped on a timeline in which the Axis forces, with the help of the

Closers, were able to gain control of most of the planet in their version of World War 2. The story does briefly relate conventional naval battles that occurred during the attempts to defend the United States. If these battle descriptions were the only mention of the Navy, the story would belong in the first category that was discussed. What places it in the intersection of the two main categories is the appearance of a U.S.S. *Arizona* that never had to endure a sinking at Pearl Harbor and which has been converted to a super-submarine through the installation of atomic reactors (as well as other unspecified engineering changes).

Other stories which are placed in the area representing the intersection involve submarines. The first is *Voyage to the Bottom of the Sea*, which appeared as a movie in 1961 and then as a television series from 1964 through 1968. The second is *SeaQuestDSV*, which appeared as a television series with some variations in title and cast from 1993 through 1996. If one is to count the individual episodes of both series, the number dominates all of the other works of science fiction that I have mentioned.

Why do all of the stories so far placed in the area of intersection involve submarines? This is possibly the case because the submarine is the form of naval craft that lends itself so easily to science fiction. Mankind has been familiar with surface craft of all types for thousands of years. Even today most people have some acquaintance with travel on the surface of a body of water, even if it is limited to a rowboat on a pond. Practical submarines are fairly recent in human history and are still limited to the upper layers of the world's oceans. The number of people that have traveled beneath the sea is a very small segment of humanity. We have all read books and seen movies and television shows, but that is not the same as being there. The operation of a submarine involves a trip into a great unknown. The situation is similar to that of mankind's efforts in space. We have seen the landings on the moon, the shuttle flights and the space station. But how many of us have actually been in space? Even with the possibility of space tourism, the numbers making such trips will remain small. The hull of a submarine totally encloses the crew, protecting them from the sea and its perils, just as the hull of a spacecraft protects its crew from vacuum and radiation. The perils lurking in the depths of the world's oceans can find their counterpart in imagined threats of deep space.

In spite of my efforts, the number of stories presented in any form of media that I have been able to classify as naval science fiction is quite small. One might ask why the number *is* so small. Although it is possible that my search has failed to discover some number of stories that might be so classified, the real reason is that very little true naval science fiction has actually been written. It seems strange that the number is small when we consider the interwar years, which includes the beginning of the Golden

Age of science fiction. This was the time when the airplane as a serious weapon of war was still in its formative stage, and it was the Navy that represented modern technology in defense of the nation. With the connection between technology and science fiction, why did that dominance of naval technology fail to manifest itself in the form of more naval science fiction?

I suggest that the absence of a large quantity of naval science fiction is due the lack of those who were qualified to write it. Practically any science fiction author would appear to consider himself or herself qualified to write a story of travel to another planetary system or time travel or contacting life on another planet. Since no one has traveled through interstellar space or through time or set foot on a planet inhabited by alien life, who is qualified to question your assumptions or correct your errors? Unless your science fiction author has failed to do adequate research into the physics, chemistry and biology required for the tale and as a consequence commits some obvious technical faux pas, the result will pass muster with most of the readers. But now consider how many people have served in the Navy at one time or another. This means that there are a lot of potential critics waiting to pounce on your slightest technical or procedural errors in a work of naval science fiction.

How then does one write naval science fiction? As with any type of writing, one does research. One example of this is Frank Herbert's "Under Pressure." His knowledge of submarines came from research performed at the Library of Congress. Even though Herbert had served in the Navy for a number of years, he did not set foot on a submarine until after the publication of his story. The other way to write successful naval science fiction is to make use of one's actual naval experience. This might strike many of you as a sneaky way to lead up to the works of Robert Heinlein and any influence his naval career might have had upon certain of those works.

Let us first consider any of Heinlein's writings, fiction or not, that make direct reference to either his time at the Naval Academy or to his time on active duty prior to his medical discharge in 1934. If we begin with his years at the Naval Academy, we must look at "Tale of the Man Who Was too Lazy to Fail" which appeared as a chapter in *Time Enough for Love*. This chapter takes the form of Lazarus Long's memories of his acquaintance David Lamb, consisting of his Academy years and subsequent naval career. It had been stated by Ginny Heinlein that the basis for the David Lamb character was Heinlein's classmate Delos Wait. Like the character Lamb (and of course Heinlein), Wait had been a member of the fencing team at the Academy. Wait flew the large patrol craft such as Catalina flying boats described in the chapter. The identification of Wait with Lamb is confirmed by the fact that Wait was the first of the Class of 1929 to reach flag rank with a tombstone promotion to Rear Admiral when he retired in June 1948. Note that the story of David Lamb does not, however, contain anything to correspond to Wait's postgraduate training in electronics as described in the previous chapter. I have always felt that David Lamb also contained a little bit of Caleb Laning and possibly Heinlein himself. It should be noted that like David Lamb, and unlike Heinlein, both Laning and Wait had been enlisted men before receiving an appointment to the Naval Academy. This is a key component of "Tale."

The work *Expanded Universe* contains several naval references. Sticking with the theme of the Naval Academy, we have the paragraph from "The Happy Days Ahead" concerning his classmates that was quoted in the previous chapter. If we then move to the Afterword of the short story "Searchlight," we find Heinlein's recollection of being radio compass officer on the *Lexington* and trying to help guide back a group of lost planes, including one piloted by his close friend Buddy Scoles. Then we return to "The Happy Days Ahead," where Heinlein relates that when he was in the Canal Zone a very short time after the incident related in the Afterword to "Searchlight," he would relax on some evening by floating in a swimming pool. The comfort provided to him in such a situation, contrasted with the discomfort endured during his later hospitalization for tuberculosis, led him to develop the concept of the water bed.

We may then turn to *For Us, The Living*. Perry is relating the details of his former life in the Navy and tells Diana that:

> A classmate of mine at the Naval Academy joined the navy because he got tired of walking behind a mule and plowing. So he walked fifteen miles to town barefooted and slept on the doorstep of the post office. When the postmaster arrived in the morning he enlisted. He was selected for the Naval Academy and became one of the most brilliant young officers in the fleet and expert in the use and design of equipment that makes your automatic door seem simple.

It sounds like a very condensed version of "Tale of the Man Who Was too Lazy to Fail." But it does include an implied reference to working with electronics that was missing from the tale of David Lamb.

Once we look over Heinlein's stories, we discover that almost all of his naval references are actually in space. We begin with "Misfit." Although Libby and the other young men are in the Cosmic Construction Corps, there are many distinct naval features to the story. The ranks of "gunner's mate" and "marine gunner" are mentioned. The rank of Captain would of course apply to the master of a civilian as well as military craft, but the navigator is identified as Commander Blackie Rhodes. Finally, at the end of the story, we have the messages from the Admiral observing the final orbital change process.

We then come to the story that I have previously identified in my introduction to the works of Robert Heinlein and science fiction in general, *Space Cadet*. As with "Misfit," it is possible to infer some naval connection by the ranks mentioned. We have "Lieutenant" and "Captain." Some officers are referred to as "Commander," and the Commandant of the Patrol Academy has the rank of Commodore. I remember reading somewhere, but have been unable to recall where, that Heinlein wrote of the experience of Matt Dodson and his classmates as he would have liked the Naval Academy to have been, without the hazing by the upperclassmen.

The references to naval craft in "Methuselah's Children" are few and brief. Slayton Ford, as one of his last acts as Administrator, sends out a false alarm of an attack on an orbiting power plant to divert police and naval craft. Then, as the *New Frontiers* is trying to make its escape with all of the members of the Howard Families aboard, they must continually monitor the presence of naval craft in the inner solar system.

If I refer to the naval portions of *Starship Troopers*, most of you will probably remember the space battle scenes from movie that bore only a passing resemblance to Heinlein's novel. Within the novel, most of the action focuses on Juan Rico and his fellow Mobile Infantrymen. But they must be transported between planets. Rico mentions the ships on which the Mobile Infantry travels such as the *Rodger Young*, *Ypres*, and *Valley Forge*. There are a few direct mentions of the Navy, if there should be any doubts.

Now let us return to Earth. In "Goldfish Bowl," the opening and closing action takes place on board a ship investigating two mysterious pillars of water that have appeared near Hawaii. There is no doubt what type of ship it is, as Heinlein states at the very opening of the story that:

> In addition to the naval personnel of the watch, the bridge of the hydrographic survey ship U.S.S. *Mahan* held two civilians. . . .

Brief mention is also made of the disappearance of a naval aircraft.

We now come to the story with the greatest naval content of any of Heinlein's stories, "If This Goes On—." Those of you who are familiar with the story will object that there is no waterborne naval action in the entire story. And you would be correct, as all of this "naval" action takes place on land. Since I began the chapter by disallowing the type of story that has transposed naval warfare into space, how can I justify transposing naval warfare to land?

To begin with, it is easy to demonstrate Heinlein's intent in the matter. The narrator of the story, John Lyle, states that the craft available to the forces of the revolution consist of:

> thirty-four land cruisers, thirteen of them modern battle wagons, the rest light cruisers and obsolescent craft—all that was left of the Prophet's mighty East Mississippi fleet. . . .

But the idea of such a connection between land and sea warfare is not original to Heinlein. There were several earlier presentations of the idea, any one of which could have influenced Heinlein in his development of this story.

The steam-powered, armor-plated ships developed during the Civil War, such as the U.S.S. *Monitor* and the C.S.S. *Virginia* (known to many people as the *Merrimac*), were called ironclads. They were seen as representing something new in naval warfare. So when H. G. Wells wrote in 1904 proposing something new in ground warfare, he called his short story "The Land Ironclads." As we know that Heinlein was a great fan of Wells, it can be safely assumed that he had read this story.

If we had stayed in England for about a decade after Wells' story appeared, we would have seen the emergence of the tank. It would be tempting to consider that his story was the inspiration for the tanks, but there were many different variations proposed. The idea of some form of mobile, protected and armed structure can be traced back to the belfry or siege towers first developed by the Assyrians. The most modern developments simply substituted mechanical power for human or animal power, armor plate for wood construction, and cannons and machine guns for catapults and battering rams.

As modern designs were proposed, the biggest variation appears to have been in the means of propulsion. The ironclads proposed by Wells "sailed forward on huge pedrail wheels hung 'with elephant-like feet'." One of the designs which appeared at the time of World War I involved a three-wheeled monster weighing three hundred tons, and extending a hundred feet long in length. The next design was for a smaller wheeled craft, with a design finally emerging which employed the familiar caterpillar treads. All of this development work would be interesting enough if it were the work of the British Army, but in the absence of interest by the Army, it was done by the Admiralty Landships committee that was set up in February 1915.

This same year an article appeared in an American publication which took the land ironclad to its extreme by speculating on the possibility of land warships apparently larger than what Heinlein had in mind. I say "apparently" as a careful reading of "If This Goes On—" reveals that Heinlein was vague about the size of the craft appearing in his story. The article, which appeared in *Popular Science Monthly* in October 1915, was written by Admiral Bradley Fiske. Fiske's naval career began during a period of stagnation following the end of the Civil War. As America began its movement towards a modern navy, Fiske was involved with many of the technical advances. For his entire life he was an inventor, the details of which will be presented in Chapter 10. The article "If Battleships Ran on Land" was an extension of some ideas on naval power that Fiske had presented some five years earlier. The following paragraph from the article, quoted in Fiske's autobiography, definitely gets the idea across:

> *Inherent Power of a Battleship.* Possibly the declaration may be accepted now that a battleship of 30,000 tons, such as the navies are building now, with, say, twelve 14-inch guns, is a greater example of power, under absolute direction and control, than anything else existing; and that the main reason is the concentration of a tremendous amount of mechanical energy in a very small space, all made available by certain properties of water. Nothing like a ship can be made to run on shore; but if an automobile could be constructed, carrying twelve 14-inch guns, twenty-two 5-inch guns, and four torpedo-tubes, of the size of the *Pennsylvania*, and with her armor, able to run over the land in any direction at 20 knots, propelled by engines of 31,000 horse-power, it could whip an army of a million men just as quickly as it could get hold of its component parts. Such a machine could start at one end of an army and go through to the other, like a mowing-machine through a field of wheat; and knock down all the buildings in New York afterward, smash all the cars, break down all the bridges, and sink all the shipping.

The article was accompanied by an illustration of such a land battleship, as shown in Figure 4. As you can see, the craft is completely enclosed in armor with one large single turret with two massive guns visible and a collection of broadside guns. The size is hard to judge, but the turret appears to be over 100 feet above the ground. How many of the details of this sketch may be attributed to the artist and how many to Fiske, we may never know.

Figure 4. Land Battleship (*From Midshipman to Rear-Admiral* by Bradley Fiske, published in 1919.)

Fiske then attempts to take some credit for the idea of tanks. He stated that:

> This article attracted considerable attention in England from the military papers and others. The British "tanks" or "land battleships" appeared in somewhat less than a year afterward.

A simple comparison of dates shows, however, that the idea was being explored by the Landships Committee months before Fiske's article even appeared.

Although the British employed small numbers of tanks in various operations, the first large tank battle took place at Cambrai starting on November 20, 1917. The details of the battle are not important here except to note that 476 tanks were employed on the first day. But the battle served as one of the bases for a lecture given in February 1920 by Colonel (later General) J. F. C. Fuller. A bit of a strange character, Fuller was at various times interested in the occult, yoga, the Kaballah and fascism. I think that relevance of the lecture may be inferred by its title "The Development of Sea Warfare on Land and Its Influence on Future Naval Operations."

In his lecture, Fuller recounted details of the Battle of Cambrai and other World War I actions and then made a series of comparisons between land and sea warfare beginning with:

> What is a Tank? A mechanically propelled battery on land!
> What is a Battleship? A mechanically propelled battery on water!

After enumerating the features of the Tank, he then commented:

> you will understand why the Tank rightly has been called the Land Ship. It has superimposed naval tactics on land tactics, that is; it has enabled men to discharge their weapons from a moving platforms protected by a fixed shield.

At the end of his lecture, Fuller referred to the professional fortune teller and then made his own attempt to look into the future:

> I see a fleet operating against a fleet not at sea but on land: cruisers and battleships and destroyers.

We may speculate whether Heinlein ever encountered Fuller's article in *The Journal of the Royal United Service Institution* in the stacks of the Naval Academy library. Would he also have encountered Fiske's autobiography *From Midshipman to Rear-Admiral*, which was published in 1919?

This demonstrated connection between true naval warfare and land warfare by Fiske and Fuller, as opposed to the arbitrary transposition into outer space justifies, in my opinion, the choice to include "If This Goes On—" in the ranks of naval science fiction. But where to place it in Figure 3? The general background of the story, exclusive of the assault upon New Jerusalem, identifies it as a SF environment. It takes place in a not-too-distant future with a political and social structure drastically different than ours. The story contains devices such as passenger rockets, blasters and disintegrators in advance of the existing technology.

So the key question is whether the Navy should be considered Conventional or SF. Consider the devices described in the battle, which will be analyzed in a later chapter as part of the process to identify the mystery device. Connections are shown with the naval technology with which Heinlein was familiar. But the devices described by Heinlein are not exactly as employed by the Navy of his time, so they justify the classification of SF Navy. This means that "If This Goes On—" should be placed in the area of intersection between the two ellipses.

One area of technology that will not be analyzed elsewhere, but which I feel deserves discussion, is the propulsion of the craft employed in the battle. When describing the actual attack on New Jerusalem, Heinlein makes no reference to how the various craft were propelled. Earlier in the story, however, the character John Lyle hitched a ride during his escape westward to the General Headquarters of the Cabal. The vehicle on which he rides employs Waterburies. Although the Waterburies are explained in a non-military situation, John Lyle comments that:

> I filed away in my mind the idea that freighter jacks could be trained as military ground-cruiser pilots in short order, if the Cabal should need them.

The logical conclusion is that the military craft employ the same type of propulsion system as the freighter. In the analysis of the Virtues essay, it was pointed out that Heinlein said that he was familiar with such devices:

> For example, in one story I described a rather remarkable oleo-gear arrangement for handling exceedingly heavy loads. I was not cheating, the device would work; it had been patented about 1900 and has been in industrial use ever since. But it is a gadget not well known to the public and it happened to fit into a story I was writing.

A sentence crossed out in the original draft of the Virtues essay stated "I was required to learn to sketch and describe it at the US Naval Academy back in the twenties."

The use of such devices may be explained by a quote from *Between Human and Machine* by David Mindell:

> Waterbury's hydraulic gear moved turrets for large naval guns and shell hoists, cranes and numerous other shipboard machines; one ad called them the "nerves" and "muscles" for superhuman tasks.

The driver of the freighter explains in detail:

> See these here speed bars . . . . they tilt the disks in the Waterburies, and that controls the speed of each tread . . . . It's a Diesel-electric hookup. The Diesel runs the generator at constant speed, and the generator charges the main battery. The port and starboard motors run off the battery and deliver their power to the treads through the waterburies. The Waterburies ain't nothing more nor less than a device to deliver the power from the motors to the treads at whatever rate you need it; they're variable speed gears that work hydraulically. This way the Diesel runs all the time at its most economical speed and the treads use power just as they need it.

The Waterbury, developed and patented by the Waterbury Tool Company, was a device which converted rotary motion, most likely from an electric motor, to hydraulic pressure and then back to rotary motion. The primary unit, called a Waterbury A, is what the driver is describing when he speaks of the "speed bars" changing the angle of the disk. This disk is mounted on the shaft rotated by the motor, with the attachment made using a universal joint. Also mounted on the shaft is a metal cylinder into which a number of smaller cylinders have been cut parallel to the shaft, each containing a piston. Each individual piston is part of the mechanism used to pump the hydraulic fluid, and is connected to the disk. By varying the angle of the plate with the "speed bar," it is possible to control the amount by which each piston moves as both the disk and cylinder are rotated by the motor. This design allows for a very precise control of the motion of the pistons and therefore of the hydraulic pressure.

A second unit, called a Waterbury B, was then mounted in a location where the rotary motion was required. The Waterbury A and B units were connected by hydraulic lines. In the case of the freighter in the story, the Waterbury B is driving the treads. Inside the Waterbury B, there are also pistons and a disk, although in this case the disk is maintained at a fixed angle. As the hydraulic fluid acts upon the pistons, the forces exerted against the tilted disk cause the shaft to rotate. By controlling the hydraulic pressure, the rotation obtained from the Waterbury B is controlled.

Why go through all of this trouble? Why not just mount the electric motor where you actually needed the rotary motion? One place where you would not want to employ an electric motor is a naval gun turret, where an electric spark could possibly cause an explosion. The electric motor could be safely located in an adjacent compartment with only the hydraulic lines coming through a bulkhead. This is one application with which Heinlein would have been very familiar as a gunnery specialist.

The Waterbury is just a means of converting rotary motion to hydraulic pressure and back again. Something has to generate the rotary motion in the first place. Heinlein does not state the size and weight of his naval craft. The above description of the civilian freighter puts me in mind of the familiar 18-wheeler, which also employs a Diesel engine. The general impression is that the naval craft are considerably larger. At the end of the battle, John Lyle is exiting the ship to try to join the battle:

> I hurried down the ladders from the turret, ran down the passageway between the engine rooms, and located the escape hatch in the floor plates . . . .

If we have a craft large enough to contain engine rooms, what is the source of power? Although Diesel propulsion would be suitable for the freighter, it must be remembered that we are in a future with "blasters," "vortex guns" and refuse disposal systems where an object is "reduced to its primordial atoms in the fierce disintegration blast." Concurrent with such futuristic technology, one might at least expect a propulsion system such as the atomic reactor used in submarines. But Heinlein never says exactly what serves as the ultimate power source for his land-based naval craft.

Although the analysis to be presented in subsequent chapters will focus on all of the stories published no later than "The Roads Must Roll," the naval connection which occurs in the second installment of "If This Goes On—" has always made it the most likely story in which the mystery device may be found.

The next chapter will consider how inventions are related to science fiction and science fiction authors.

8

SCIENCE FICTION AND INVENTIONS

As presented in Chapter 3, many people including Heinlein have attempted to develop a definition of the term "science fiction." One other attempt was made by J. O. Bailey in his 1947 work *Pilgrims Through Space and Time*. Although he was aware of other terms for the genre, such as Hugo Gernsback's "scientifiction" and "science-fiction" (note the hyphen), he preferred the slightly expansive term "scientific fiction," reversing Gernsback's contraction. His definition was:

> A piece of scientific fiction is a narrative of an imaginary invention or discovery in the natural sciences and consequent adventures and experiences.

If strictly applied, it would seem that such a definition would exclude many stories normally considered science fiction. The argument could be made, however, that if you make the definition of invention or discovery wide enough or concentrate on the consequences of the invention or discovery, it would be possible to include almost any type of science fiction story. For example, any encounters with aliens could be classed as discovery - of course the question would then be exactly who had discovered whom. In contrast with Wells' *The Time Machine* in which we have the story of the machine's inventor, any meeting with a time traveler could be classed as an invention story, even if you didn't know anything about the supposed principle involved in time travel or when or by whom it was developed. I am not saying that I prefer Bailey's definition to any of the others that exist. I have quoted it since it provides me with an introduction to the discussion of how inventions and inventors are presented in science fiction.

One problem with the use of Bailey's work in looking at how inventions are portrayed is the range of authors he covered. As was noted in Chapter 3, Bailey's attempt to extend the original scope of his work to cover through the 1940s omitted well-known authors from that period. The works from Campbell's early career as an author include such invention tales as *The Mightiest Machine* and *The Black Star Passes*. Similarly, some of Heinlein's early works such as "Life-Line" and "Let There Be Light" can be classed as invention stories. One may speculate that Bailey did not have access to the issues of the magazines in which those stories first appeared.

As the ultimate intent of this work is to attempt to discover a device that was built - an invention rather than scientific discovery - the focus of this chapter will be on the invention portion of Bailey's definition rather than the scientific discovery.

What are the similarities or differences between creating a science fiction story and making an invention? One way to view it is expressed in a quote from article, "Growing Up in the Future" by Michael Swanwick:

> The late Will Jenkins, who wrote under the name of Murray Leinster, was also an inventor. He told me once that he'd get an idea for something new and then think about it for a long time, puzzling it over, until he could make it work or he understood why it never would. If it worked, he'd patent it. If he didn't, he'd write a science fiction story in which it did.

This quote, while it attempts to show a connection between inventing and writing a story, has a problem discussed later in this chapter.

The one thing that both processes - creating a plausible science fiction story and making a real invention - have in common is the need for technical knowledge. As pointed out by Heinlein in the Virtues essay, it is necessary for a science fiction writer to have such knowledge to be able to write a plausible story. One could create some trivial invention for household or amusement purposes without the need for any great degree of technical knowledge. But for a non-trivial invention with a serious academic, scientific or industrial application, technical knowledge is essential. There is, of course, one very important difference between creating a story and successfully developing an invention. In working only with words, one has no constraints at all in how the story is laid out, how you have the characters act and speak, and so on. But in developing a physical device, you may have a clear picture in your mind what you want it to do but your implementation is limited by the properties of materials or how fast electronic devices operate or by the laws of chemistry and physics.

The invention process in stories from the early days of science fiction was not portrayed in a realistic manner. How many of you have read an old story where the inventor conceives, develops and constructs the fully realized device within days of his original discovery or idea? Fortunately, we see very few stories of that type today. John W. Campbell, Jr. pointed this out in his editorial "Invention and Imagination" that appeared in the August 1939 issue of *Astounding*. Campbell's observation was that:

> Today's authors tend to recognize that long and arduous - and undramatic! - period of delay and development. They take up their story after the great principles have been worked out, and most of the infinite multitude of accessory inventions made. The hero makes one small, but vital invention - and therein lies a story.

If we were to look at some of Campbell's early works such as previously mentioned *The Black Star Passes* and *The Mightiest Machine*, however, we would find that he was also guilty of creating inventors who were capable of instant or very rapid invention.

Two other authors must be mentioned whose stories were invention oriented. These authors were George O. Smith (1911-1981) and G. Harry Stine (1928-1997).

The works of George O. Smith with which I am most familiar are the Venus Equilateral stories, of which all except one were written during the 1940s and most of which originally appeared in *Astounding*. The stories assume that both Mars and Venus are habitable and have been colonized. As Venus, Earth and Mars proceed in their orbits, there occur situations where direct line-of-sight interplanetary communications between planets is not possible. To enable communications to be maintained at all times required the construction of a relay station in the orbit of Venus located sixty degrees ahead of Venus. This station was placed in one of the Lagrangian points with regard to Venus and the Sun, in this case L_4. A Lagrangian point is one the small number of stable solutions which have been determined for the generally intractable three-body problem. From its location, L_4 occupies one vertex of an equilateral triangle with respect to Venus and the Sun.

If such a communications relay was found to be necessary today for some reason, it would be constructed as an unmanned automated satellite employing solid-state electronics wherever possible. As written in the 1940s, Venus Equilateral was a manned station employing vacuum tubes or similar devices. The protagonists were concerned with maintaining interplanetary communications, but always found time to cope with emergencies which required that they invent some new device to save the day.

The workings of this group of inventors may best be illustrated by the story "Calling the Empress." The ship *Empress of Kolain*, en route from Mars to Venus must be contacted and ordered to divert directly to Earth. The problem consisted of two parts: locating the ship along its path between planets, and then contacting it. The first part of the problem was one of calculation of position and then constructing a means of directing the communication to the proper location in space. The second part of the problem was more difficult as the assumed impossibility of any type of communication with a ship in interplanetary flight meant that its radio would not normally even be turned on during flight. The exact details of the solution are not important to the discussion here, but part of the method of solution bears mentioning. The design session occurred in the restaurant/bar located on the station, making use of the tablecloth for sketches and calculation. The owner complained about their use of the tablecloths:

> It's tough, running a restaurant on Venus Equilateral. I tried using paper ones once, but that didn't work. I had 'em printed, but when the Solar System was on 'em, you drew schematic diagrams for a new coupler circuit. I put all kinds of radio circuits on them, and the gang drew plans for antenna arrays. I gave up and put pads of paper on each table and the boys used them to make folded paper airplanes and they shot them all over the place. Why don't you guys grow up?

Other stories considered other problems, such as dealing with interplanetary criminals, tapping the Sun for power, communicating faster than light or matter duplication. But the inventors of Venus Equilateral always delivered the goods. It is worth noting that "Identity," the only Venus Equilateral story mentioned by Bailey, had no inventions occur within that story. Why Bailey chose only "Identity" as opposed to all of Smith's invention-oriented stories will remain a mystery.

One invention story by G. Harry Stine (who also wrote stories as Harry Stine and Lee Correy) was "Galactic Gadgeteers," which appeared in the May 1951 issue of *Astounding*. This story concerned the crew of the future space navy battle cruiser *Sinbad* who were always tinkering and trying to develop devices such a perfect square-wave oscillator or a faster-than-light communication system to permit direct communication over long distances without the need for relay stations. During an interstellar rebellion, the need to land on a previously unknown planet to make battle damage repairs led to the discovery of strange metallic crystals. These crystals enabled the crew to develop a weapon which disabled the enemy fleet and quickly brought the rebellion to an end. At the close of the story it is revealed that the members of *Sinbad's* crew are participants, without their knowledge, in a top secret project. They are all highly intelligent and very creative types who have been placed on this ship to see what weapons and devices they are able to develop.

Even if we do not accept Bailey's definition of science fiction, the small sample of stories presented indicates that science fiction authors are fond of using the theme of invention in at least some of their stories. How successful they are in presenting the process of invention might depend on their personal familiarity with inventing. So the question then presents itself, how many science fiction authors have been or are inventors?

In a certain sense, ***anyone*** can be considered an inventor. Assume that you are doing something around the house or at work and are faced with a situation where you must accomplish some task. It may be trivial, but to save time or aggravation you manage to come up with an arrangement of electrical or mechanical assemblies that simplifies your job. You have just made an invention. Should you patent it?

Before going any further, let us consider what a patent is. Many people are still under the impression that a patent represents some form of official government approval of your invention. That is not the case. A patent is simply the statement that you are, as far as the Patent Office has been able to determine, the first to arrive at this idea, and that it satisfies certain conditions. A patent confers upon the recipient the right to sue anyone who attempts to employ the idea without permission for a specified period of time. That is all there is to it.

What are the conditions attached to an invention that makes it possible to obtain a patent?:

a. Be of patentable subject matter - The best was to define patentable subject matter is to quote the relevant segment of the law, Section 101 of Title 35 U.S.C.: "Whoever invents or discovers any new and useful <u>process, machine, manufacture, or composition of matter</u>, or any new and useful improvement thereof, may obtain a patent therefor, subject to the conditions and requirements of this title."

b. Be Novel - Something is not patentable if it is previously known. In the United States, if a description of your invention has been published more than a year ago, you may not obtain a patent, even if you were the one who had caused it to be published. The description must be such that someone having ordinary skill in the art required for its construction could do so on the basis of the description provided. If, on the other hand, the description only serves as a starting point for someone who performs additional research and development, then that person might be able to obtain a patent.

c. Be Non-obvious - The invention has to be different from what already exists in some fundamental way. Simply changing the color, size or physical arrangement in a way that has no effect on the functionality of some object will not allow you to obtain a patent. The usual test that is applied is that to be patentable it must not be obvious to someone who understands the technical field.

d. Be Useful - This means that the invention must actually perform the operation or function claimed. This prevents someone from obtaining a patent on something like a time machine or anti-gravity, unless it could be demonstrated that it actually accomplished the function.

So the home or office invention mentioned above would meet criteria **d**, that it is useful, in that it does perform the desired function or operation. Otherwise, why would you go through the trouble of making the invention? It is probably novel, at least to you. But did you see something like it or read about it sometime before? Even if you had not, was something like it described in a journal article or a newspaper? Whether it meets all of the criteria determines whether or not you should contact a patent attorney.

The ability of an author to invent is naturally not restricted to the genre of science fiction. One example of this is Mark Twain, who had three patents to his name: (1) Improved adjustable and detachable garment straps (121,992), (2) A self-pasting scrapbook (140,245) and (3) A game to help players remember important historical dates (324,535). But these were hardly inventions requiring some degree of technical knowledge.

I have made this minor excursion into the topic of patents because of the problem of identifying science fiction authors who were inventors. It would not have been practical to obtain and analyze the biography of each writer to determine if he or she had a basement workshop where inventions were made between stories, in the manner of Will Jenkins. If he or she is not otherwise known for having made a specific invention, the next best criterion is whether he or she had any patents.

In a perfect world, one could simply search the files of the U.S. Patent Office for those patents with an inventor whose name matches that of a science fiction author. The difficulty is that the search engine available on the U.S. Patent Office website will not permit you to search by inventor's name for any patents before 1976. If you happen to know the patent number, there is no such limitation. Alternatively, one could make physical searches of the patent records. Fortunately, there now exists another means of automated search which does not suffer from the date limits imposed by the government search engine. I am referring to the Google Patent Search™ service available at www.google.com. Search may be by inventors name, patent number, patent title or a number of other parameters without any date restrictions. Unfortunately, the site has a minor problem of its own. I am assuming that some sort of optical character recognition approach was used to scan the patent documents and convert them into the digital data that may be searched. This process has its limitations. Basically, the act of conversion occasionally results in minor garbling of information such as the inventor's name. This is described in more detail below. But even with that limitation, the service is very useful.

The first inventor to be discussed is one who should be familiar to anyone with an interest in science fiction - Hugo Gernsback (1884-1967). He was an inventor, author, and publisher. His publication of science fiction stories in his early technical magazines led to the publication of magazines devoted solely to science fiction. He is the person for whom the Hugo Awards presented at each year's WorldCon are named. My primary interest was in determining how many patents Gernsback had obtained. If you were to use your browser to search the Internet for "Gernsback" and "patents," some of the results will claim that he had "almost 80 patents" or "80 patents" or "more than 80 patents." As these would all have occurred prior to 1976, the Patent Office search engine was of no use to me in verifying the quantity. The numbers of a few of his patents were found in articles on the Internet. The search would have ended there if not for the discovery of an article in a publication of The Antique Wireless Association. This article contained lists of the U.S. patents of people involved in the early days of radio including, fortunately, Hugo Gernsback. This information was compiled by the article's author through the manual inspection of the U.S. Patent Gazette.

The problem is that the list for Gernsback only included 37 patents. Armed with the correct patent numbers, it was possible for me to use the U.S. Patent Office web site to locate and verify all of these patents. This occurred before I was aware of the existence of the Google patent site. But what about the problem with the number of patents? Even the author of the article, David W. Kraeuter, commented on this discrepancy between his count of 37 and the value quoted elsewhere, which he attributes to one of Gernsback's biographers. Unless the higher count was just someone pulling a value out of thin air, Kraeuter's suggestion that the value might also include duplication of certain American patents by English, French and German patents is the most likely. Readers with access to such information and a bit of time on their hands might wish to see if they can discover any foreign patents by Gernsback and resolve this mystery.

When I learned of the patent search available at www.google.com, I attempted to search on his name to see if I could find any in excess of the 37 known. To my surprise, the site returned less than that number. When I then searched for each invention by number and examined the inventor's name, I encountered variations such as Geensback, Gebnsback, Gernsboak, Gernsbacx, and Qebnsback. This is attributed to the document scanning process as mentioned above.

What were some of Gernsback's inventions? Many of them (only a few of which are given here) were electrical in nature: "Battery" (842,950), "Potentiometer" (988,456), "Variable Condenser" (1,562,629) or "Switch" (1,695,957). The remainder ranged from the mundane to the very strange: "Combined Electric Hair Brush and Comb" (1,016,138), "Postal Card" (1,209,425), "Submersible Amusement Device" (1,384,750), "Electrically Operated Fountain" (1,954,704) or "Hydraulic Fishery" (2,718,083). One very interesting device was his "Acoustic Apparatus" (1,521,287). This device, also sometimes called an ossophone, was a hearing aid which enabled a person to hear by the process of bone conduction. The sound was provided to a device that the person clamped between his teeth. Not a very practical approach. Contrary to the statement of Mike Ashley in *The Gernsback Days*, one of his patented inventions was not the "hypnobioscope." This remains a purely fictional device from *Ralph 124C 41+* which permitted information to be transmitted directly to the brain while the user was asleep.

The next most prolific author/inventor was Dr. Robert L. Forward (1932-2002). His fictional works, all examples of hard science fiction, include *Rocheworld, Dragon's Egg, Timemaster* and *Saturn Rukh*. Forward received his Ph.D. in Gravitational Physics in 1958 from the University of Maryland for work in constructing an antenna used in attempts to detect gravitational waves. The bulk of his scientific career was spent in the research labs of Hughes Aircraft. At the time of his death, he was Chief Scientist and Chairman of Tethers Unlimited, which he co-founded in 1994.

The number of patents given by Forward in the autobiography written shortly before his death was 28. Two of these are worth mentioning. The first is the Forward Mass Detector, patented as "Measurement of Static

Force Field Gradients" (3,273,397). The detector consists of two arms with weights at each end connected in the shape of an X. The weights closer to some external mass are naturally attracted with a slight greater force than those further away. The entire apparatus is rotated several times a second. Measurements of vibrations in the rotating arms can then be interpreted in terms of small angle changes between the arms. This can then be used to give the differential torque caused by the gravitational attraction.

The other patent is titled "Statite: Spacecraft that utilizes sight pressure and method of use" (5,183,225). A reading of the patent indicates that the title should actually read "light pressure." The idea is to use the pressure exerted by light upon a reflective light sail to balance the gravitational attraction of the Earth. Any object connected to the light sail would hover without having to be in orbit around the Earth. The potential for placing a "statite" (as opposed to satellite) in position is described in a short story "Race for the Pole" in Forward's book *Indistinguishable From Magic*.

The next author/inventor to consider is Will F. Jenkins. The statement by Michael Swanwick quoted earlier in the chapter would imply that Jenkins had obtained a large number of patents. A search for patents using the Google site yielded only two. The fact that Jenkins had actually obtained only two patents was confirmed by one of his daughters. It does seem that Jenkins was involved in developing various ideas, as described in his 1963 WorldCon Guest of Honor speech. It may simply be that the rights to many of his successful inventions were sold without resorting to the process of obtaining a patent.

The two patents obtained by Jenkins were "Apparatus for Production of Light Effects in Composite Photography" (2,727,427) and "Apparatus for the Production of Composite Photographic Effects" (2,727,429). The story behind the original idea, the development process, obtaining a patent, and licensing the idea is given in Jenkins' article "Applied Science Fiction," which appeared in the November 1967 issue of *Analog*.

As related in the article, Jenkins became aware of the problems connected with the construction and manipulation of physical scenery during the televising of some of his science fiction stories. He was also aware of the limitations of producing the required scenery by the process of rear projection. The front projection system that he developed made use of a flat screen composed of material which provides reflex reflection, such that a light beam is returned in the direction from which it came in the manner of a corner reflector. The camera was directed toward the screen, with a half-silvered mirror in the light path mounted at a 45 degree angle to the screen. To one side was a projector which supplied the background image, aimed at the angled mirror. The background image would strike the angled mirror and be directed to the screen. It would then be reflected by the screen and pass through the mirror to the camera. There would be some loss as the light passed through the mirror, but since the arrangement has the projector effectively aimed directly into the camera, such losses were acceptable. If any physical object or an actor were placed in the scene, any light that struck it would have been diffusely reflected, such that no detectable image of the background will be seen on its surface by the camera. The shadow from the projected background was always directly behind the actor or object as seen by the camera, regardless of its position, and therefore invisible to the camera. According to Jenkins, it was found to be useful at the time, but it is doubtful that any such systems are still in use. Advances in computer graphics have made it possible to provide any type of background image.

The theme of the title of the *Analog* article was carried over into a comment Jenkins makes at the end of the first paragraph:

> I think it's interesting because if anything ever came out of science fiction for a practical purpose—contrived as science fiction, looking like science fiction, and working like a mad scientist's dream—this is it!"

In spite of this comment, it does not appear that the device was directly related to or employed in any of his stories. If he had not be able to figure out how to accomplish the front projection system, it is likely that we *would* have seen a version of it in one of his stories, based on his earlier comment.

The converse of this situation exists in "Politics," Jenkins' naval science fiction story mentioned in Chapter 7. Was this story the use of an idea for a rangefinder that he was not able to develop into a successful device? As one reads the story, it would appear that the key detail of the rangefinders was that the photocells employed were sensitive to infrared light and were therefore capable of seeing through the enemy smoke screens. But if we ignore the infrared aspects of the rangefinder, we may still consider the basics of its operation which is described by Jenkins in some detail:

> All electrical . . . . No observer at all. Two telescopes, one at each end of a base-line, and mounted exactly parallel. Fitted with photoelectric cells instead of eyepieces. You swing the base-line around and they sweep the horizon. And a ship on the horizon changes the amount of light that goes through a narrow slit to the photoelectric cell. It registers the instant the first telescope hits the stern of the ship. A fraction of a second later—because the

telescopes are exactly parallel—the ship-image registers on the other cell. Both cells register exactly the same changes in current-output, but one is a fraction of a second behind the other. Knowing the rate of sweep in seconds or mils of arc, if one photoelectric cell lags behind the other one mil, and you know the base-line, you work out the distance in a hurry. . . .Those range-finders sweep their field ten time per second, ranging each way. We range the enemy ship twenty times per second and get electric impulses to read off.

Which at first sounds plausible, but then as you think about it, the difficulties begin to mount.

As stated in the quote, the telescopes would have to be perfectly parallel. He says that it swept its field ten times a second, ranging each way to give twenty ranges a second. I have interpreted that to mean that it is swinging back and forth very quickly. To hold the telescopes exactly parallel with the forces generated by such rapid reversals of the rotation, the mounting would have to be incredibly rigid and heavy. Rather than deal with these forces resulting from bringing it to a stop, reversing and then accelerating up to speed again, it would make more sense to continually rotate in one direction like a radar antenna. Finally, the field of view of each telescope would have to be extremely narrow; otherwise the object would appear in both telescopes with no rotation. With such a narrow field of view established by the slit as described by Jenkins, would sufficient light strike the photocells? Nothing remotely like this device was ever actually used. All navies made use of stereoscopic or coincidence rangefinders which operated on purely optical and geometric principles.

Another author/inventor was John W. Campbell, Jr. He had only one patent, "Electron Discharge Apparatus" (2,954,466). As described in the patent, it is a simple circuit involving two vacuum tubes for the stated purpose of generating different types of waveforms such as a square wave, a sawtooth or a stepped waveform. Interesting. Possibly useful in certain applications. But was it worth going through the trouble of obtaining a patent? Campbell thought it was. Perhaps he was just interested in saying that he had a patent.

The last science fiction author for whom I have been able to locate patents is, in contrast to those already mentioned, a living writer and inventor. This is Wil McCarthy (1966-), the author of such works of science fiction as *Murder in the Solid State*, *Lost in Transmission* and *To Crush the Moon*. He is also the author of *Hacking Matter*, which considers the possibilities presented by what is called Programmable Matter. This is the name given to matter whose physical properties may be altered by the application of electrical or magnetic fields.

Programmable Matter is also the focus of McCarthy's two patents which have the same name "Fiber Incorporating Quantum Dots and Programmable Dopants" (6,978,070 and 7,276,432). He also has a number of patent applications in the same area. A quantum dot is an extension of a quantum well into three dimensions, permitting electrons to be confined. The electrons, so confined, will arrange themselves as if they were in orbit around an atom. As it is the number of electrons and how they are arranged that determines the properties of the element which they represent, the ability to create desired arrangements of electrons presents the possibility to create "artificial atoms."

Although I have no more authors with known patents to present, there are several who have been recognized as being responsible for the introduction of interesting ideas, even if they did not obtain a patent or attempt to develop or promote the device themselves. The first of these was Sir Arthur Clarke (1917-2008). He is universally recognized as the developer of the idea of using satellites placed in a geostationary orbit around the Earth as communications relays, although he admitted his debt to others for the concept of the geostationary orbit itself. He described this concept in an article published in *Wireless World* magazine in 1945, but did not attempt to obtain a patent. The geostationary orbit used for communication satellites is sometimes called the Clarke Orbit.

Let us next consider L. Sprague de Camp (1907-2000). His familiarity with inventions began with the only job he was able to find following his obtaining his MS in Mechanical Engineering from Stevens Institute of Technology in 1932. The job was with the Inventors Foundation, a non-profit corporation intended to advise inventors. It accomplished this by creating a book, *Inventing and Patenting*, teaching courses and acting as consultant to inventors. De Camp was hired simply to perform editorial duties on the book, but became involved in the other aspects of the Foundation. Over more than twenty years following his involvement with Foundation, he was called upon to work with the surviving author on revisions and updates of the book.

After his entry into the field of science fiction in the late 1930's, de Camp's appearances in print were a mixture of science fiction stories and science fact articles. One of the articles was "Justinian Jugg's Patent," which appeared in the December 1940 issue of *Astounding*. It presented all of the pertinent steps connected with obtaining a patent and spelled out in some detail what the inventor might expect after he had been successful in obtaining his patent. One of the references listed for the article was

Inventions and Their Management by Berle and de Camp, which was the first re-write of the original work with which he was involved.

Inventions and patents figured in some of his other writings, both fiction and non-fiction. In the area of science fiction, consider "Finished," a *Viagens Interplanetarias* story which appeared in the November 1949 issue of *Astounding*. The inhabitants of the planet Krishna are under a technological blockade by the Interplanetary Council. A native prince of Sotaspé, one of the Krishnan nations, has journeyed to Earth in an attempt to acquire technical literature. Although this scheme fails, on his return he presents an alternative scheme:

> Why, thought I, should we strain every nerve to steal the secrets of Ertsu science? Why not develop our own? While reading that book on the history of Earthly law, I learned of a system whereby the Ertsuma have long promoted knowledge and invention on their own planet. 'Tis called a patent system, and as soon as the Privy Council can work out the details, Sotaspé will have one too.

The story ends with a citizen of Sotaspé being awarded a patent and a knighthood for a less than perfectly successful attempt to combine a glider with firework rockets.

Inventions also figure into some of de Camp's non-fiction works. His *The Ancient Engineers* is a well-researched work that considers technology beginning with the ancient Egyptians and then other civilizations leading up to modern times. The technology presented ranges from pyramids to windmills, canals to crossbows, temples to water pumps, and much more in between. De Camp considered that the terms engineer and inventor were interchangeable in the early civilizations as any technically capable person was usually making something that had never been seen before, an invention.

Although de Camp had no patents, he was clearly involved in the invention process. He related in his autobiography that while he was associated with the Inventors Foundation, he had an invention of his own. He described it as device for determining the radius of curvature of lines on a drawing. Although he determined, on the basis the basis of his newly acquired experience with patents, that the device was probably patentable, it was not practical to attempt to obtain one.

He also related the story of an idea that he had developed while still in the Naval Reserve following the war. One of his projects was to design a joint for high altitude pressure suits (space suits). The joint must maintain a constant volume as the joint is bent. Otherwise the internal pressure would cause all joints to have a tendency to resist a change from their fully extended position. It would require effort from the person wearing the suit to fight against this tendency to remain extended when making the simplest bending motion of any joint.

De Camp stated that he developed the design for such a constant volume joint, but was not involved in any work with it past that point. He later heard that such a joint was being used but was unable to determine if it was actually based on his design. As noted in Chapter 3, the "de Camp joints" are briefly mentioned in *Rocket Ship Galileo*. The operation of such joints is explained in *Have Space Suit, Will Travel*.

It may be safely said that even with his lack of any patents, L. Sprague de Camp was the most knowledgeable science fiction author concerning inventions and patents.

We cannot close the chapter without considering Robert Heinlein. As in the case of Clarke and de Camp, he had no patents. But he is known for having presented plausible sounding ideas in his stories. One of these ideas was the remote manipulators introduced in "Waldo." When remote manipulators were developed for the handling of radioactive materials in the Manhattan Project, the engineers and scientists, many of whom probably read science fiction, referred to them as "waldoes." In this case, we are apparently dealing with a name applied because of a general functional similarity.

The other idea for which Heinlein is known is the water bed. Most people have connected the water bed with its appearance in *Stranger in A Strange Land*, which was published in 1961. But descriptions of the water bed, perhaps not in as great a detail, appeared in a number of his earlier works: *Beyond This Horizon* (1942), the short story "Waldo" (1942), the short story "Sky Lift" (1953) and *Double Star* (1956).

Heinlein related the story behind the development of the water bed concept in his essay "Happy Days Ahead" which was published in *Expanded Universe*. The basic idea was to develop a more comfortable hospital bed, something that can only be appreciated by one who has been confined to such a bed for long periods of time, as he was after having contracted tuberculosis while in the Navy. Heinlein claimed that the idea was based on his experience in the Canal Zone. When temporarily stationed ashore, he would occasionally go in the evening to the swimming pool on the base and simply float there for a while to relax. In developing his design, Heinlein was attempting to duplicate the pleasant floating situation of his memories as much as technology would permit. The details of the design were described by Heinlein as:

> I designed the water bed during years as a bed patient in the middle thirties: a pump to control water level, side supports to permit one

to float rather than simply lying on a not-very-soft water-filled mattress, thermostatic control of temperature, safety interfaces to avoid all possibility of electrical shock, waterproof box to make a leak no more important than a leaky hot water bottle rather than a domestic disaster, calculation of floor loads (important!), internal rubber mattress, and lighting, reading, and eating arrangements — an attempt to design the perfect hospital bed by one who had spent too *damned* much time in hospital beds.

Let us now examine how the water bed was mentioned in his various stories:

Beyond This Horizon:

The water rose gently under the skin of the mattress until he floated, dry and warm and snug. . . . Hamilton became aware that the water had drained out of his bed, and that he lay with nothing between him and the spongy bottom but the sheet and the waterproof skin.

"Waldo":

The deceleration tanks which are now standard equipment for the lunar mail ships traced their parentage to a flotation tank in which Waldo habitually had eaten and slept up to the point when he left the home of his parents for his present, somewhat unique, home.

The tank was not a standard deceleration type, but a modification built for this one trip. The tank was roughly the shape of an oversized coffin and was swung in gymbals to keep it always normal to the axis of absolute acceleration. Waldo floated in water — the specific gravity of his fat hulk was low — from which he was separated by the usual flexible, gasketed tarpaulin. Supporting his head and shoulders was a pad shaped to his contour. A mechanical artificial resuscitator was built into the tank, the back pads being under water, the breast pads out of the water but retracted out of the way.

"Sky Lift":

Each tank was like an oversized bathtub filled with a liquid denser than water. The top was covered by a rubbery sheet, gasketed at the edges; during boost each man would float with the sheet conforming to his body.

Double Star:

Against one bulkhead and flat to it were two bunks, or "cider presses," the bathtub-shaped, hydraulic, pressure-distribution tanks used for high acceleration in torchships."

Stranger in a Strange Land:

.... transferred into a hydraulic bed ....

The patient floated in the flexible skin of the hydraulic bed.

"Sure, you're weak as a kitten but you'll never put on muscle floating in that bed." Nelson opened a valve, water drained out. ... "Here, help me lift him into bed. No — fill it first." Frame cut off the flow when the skin floated six inches from the top.

He went to a hydraulic bed in the center of the room. . . . Floating, half concealed by the way his body sank into the plastic skin and covered to his armpits by a sheet, was a young man.

A patient that old can smother in a water bed.

The last quote is included only because the term "water bed" is specifically used, as opposed to the earlier reference to a "hydraulic bed."
The water bed was presented in three different incarnations: a hospital bed in *Stranger* (the purpose for which Heinlein apparently intended it), as a personal bed in *Beyond This Horizon*, and as a cushion in high-gravity situations in "Waldo," "Sky Lift" and *Double Star*. There was never any attempt by Heinlein to either construct or patent such a device. At this point Heinlein ran counter to Will Jenkins' reasoning for developing and employing an idea. Heinlein successfully developed the idea and then, unlike Jenkins, *only* employed it in his stories.
In investigating the history of the water bed, it was discovered that the actual situation was very different from the story related by Heinlein that:

Some joker tried to patent the water bed to shut out competition, and discovered that he could not because it was in the public domain, having been described in detail in STRANGER IN A STRANGE LAND.

The particular portion of patent law which applies here is Novelty. As stated earlier in this chapter, if a published description of the invention would allow someone to construct it, then it is not possible to obtain a patent. But there are situations which might make it possible to obtain a patent. In the first case, a person uses the few published details as the starting point for additional research and development work, resulting in a final product which has new features not originally presented. In the second case, a person working in ignorance of the published work develops an invention, also with additional features not described in the published work. What must be considered is the amount of technical detail contained in a published work.

The actual story is that a gentleman named Charles Prior Hall had been experimenting with novel types of furniture, including chairs filled with material such as cornstarch or Jell-O. After developing the water bed, he attempted to obtain a patent. Contrary to the story as related by Heinlein, there was no problem at all in obtaining the patent. The patent was granted on June 15, 1971 for "Liquid Support for Human Bodies" (3,585,356). The abstract for the patent reads:

> An article of furniture comprising a flexible bladder which is substantially filled with a liquid. A supporting framework is provided for holding the liquid filled bladder in such manner that a body resting upon the bladder is floatably supported by the liquid. Heating means is provided for maintaining a temperature of the liquid at a temperature on the order of the temperature of the human body. In some embodiments, solid particles such as Styrofoam are disposed in the bladder to dampen shock waves in the liquid and to provide additional support for a body resting upon the bladder.

This particular patent, sometimes simply referred to as the "'356" patent, was later used by Mr. Hall as the basis of lawsuits filed against a number of other water bed manufacturers in an attempt to obtain damages on the basis of patent infringement.

As Mr. Hall has related to me, during the patent process and subsequent litigation, no mention was ever made of Robert Heinlein and his works. It would seem that neither the patent examiners nor those involved in subsequent attempts to invalidate the patent were aware of Heinlein's fiction as possible prior art. Someone is then bound to ask if the patent would have been granted if the examiners had known about Heinlein's stories. The Claims portion of a patent is what defines the patent and is used to distinguish it from similar previous patents. I have examined the claims contained in Hall's patent and compared it with the story quotes presented above. Although I am not presenting myself as an expert on patent matters, it seems clear to me that sufficient claims exist in the patent which cannot be related to details in the stories. My conclusion is that even if the examiners had been aware of Heinlein's stories, the patent would still have been issued to Mr. Hall. You should download a copy of the water bed patent and see if you agree with my conclusion.

We should also consider the details of the water bed presented by Heinlein in "The Happy Days Ahead," which was written well after the patent was granted. These details appear to be more extensive than was collectively presented in the five stories. If Heinlein had included this amount of detail regarding the water bed in any of his stories, it is possible that they might have constituted sufficient prior art to prevent the patent from being issued.

This chapter has presented what I hope have been some interesting connections between inventions and science fiction. The next chapter will explore a more direct connection.

9

PREDICTION AND INSPIRATION

The preceding chapter discussed, in part, the ways in which inventions and inventors are portrayed in science fiction. It may be that the invention portrayed, while serving as the basis of or at least a feature of the story, has no relationship with the world around us. In this chapter, the focus will be on the converse question. What relationship do the ideas presented in science fiction stories have with the real world?

One does not have to look very far for examples of attempts to answer that question. Before examining some of these, let us consider that there are three possible categories:

1. Science fiction did not anticipate a particular feature of the world as we know it today.

2. An idea or concept presented in science fiction has not yet been realized.

3. An idea which was first presented in science fiction exists in the world today.

The first category would appear to be a very difficult one to populate. We would have to be sure that we were not including devices or concepts which existed before the development of what we call science fiction. The submarine, for example, existed in primitive form even before the works of Jules Verne. One might have to be restrictive in the details of something which exists to be able to state the science fiction did not anticipate it.

To illustrate, some might argue that science fiction did not predict the Internet. But it is possible to point to a short story "A Logic Named Joe" by Will F. Jenkins that appeared in the March 1946 *Astounding*. It features a service available to the public which is very much like the Internet - you can communicate with others using it, call up the weather, view a television program, get sports results, or ask historical questions. The problem to be faced in the story is that a malfunctioning unit or "logic" is providing illegal and dangerous information to people and must be removed from the system. As described by Jenkins, which is to say obviously not in very much detail, it does not work the way the Internet does. Do the similarities with the Internet disqualify it from inclusion in the first category, or is what is portrayed sufficiently different? Perhaps there is very little in our world today that has not appeared first in science fiction, if we take the time and effort to look.

In the title of this chapter I used the term inspiration. I simply mean that the inventor has encountered an idea or a concept in a work of science fiction which inspires or drives him or her to develop a real world system/device that has a demonstrable connection, possibly in appearance but most likely in the function it performs, to the idea or concept that appeared in the story.

One must be careful how one employs the word "inspiration." In his essay "Science Fiction and the Future," James Gunn states that:

> . . . .scientists and explorers such as Igor Sikorsky, speleologist Norman Casteret, Admiral Richard Byrd, Lucius Beebe, Guglielmo Marconi, and Alberto Santos-Dumont credited Verne with inspiring their achievements.

Gunn also makes reference to submarine developer Simon Lake. If you look at Lake's autobiography, he claimed that "Jules Verne was in a sense the director-general of my life." You will find that he also said "But with the impudence which is a part of the equipment of the totally inexperienced I found fault with some features of Jules Verne's *Nautilus* and set about improving on them." One thing that Lake mentioned developing was a chamber and air-lock combination for a diver entering or leaving the submarine. This was described as an improvement on the diving chamber on Verne's *Nautilus*. But he did do much more in developing a successful submarine. Do we attribute all of his advances to the influence of Verne's story?

You might ask why I am interested in presenting cases concerned with the direct inspiration of science fiction. I hope, in the course of following my wanderings through the preceding chapters, you have not lost sight that the objective of this work has been to identify the real world naval system in such a case of direct inspiration by one of Heinlein's stories. During the course of my years of research I began to wonder (a) if what I was trying discover was actually possible and (b) if it existed in the case of Heinlein, how rare it was in all of science fiction? My objective is to not only prove that such cases existed, but also to discover the relationships between the idea and the final device. Understanding such relationships was considered to be an aid in identifying Heinlein's device.

I am not the first person to consider this particular question. We should recall that Bailey in *Pilgrims Through Space and Time* attempted to characterize all science fiction in terms of invention and scientific discovery. He wondered whether any invention had been inspired by an imaginary invention. Bailey did point out that imaginary inventions occur in the same period as the scientific and engineering work leading to the actual inventions. The example he mentioned is Verne using heavier-than-air flight in works such as *Robur the Conqueror* coincident with such real world experiments in the latter part of the 19th century.

The statement by Bailey which was presented in Chapter 3, that a direct influence of imaginary inventions cannot be demonstrated, is opposed to what I have been trying to accomplish. In this chapter, I will present a number of cases which might indicate such a direct influence. Some of these have been presented by others. In some of the cases it is possible to make a very strong case for direct inspiration.

Drawing a line between prediction and inspiration is difficult. Assume that a story contains an idea which is sufficiently in advance of the technology of the time, so that it cannot be immediately developed. Such an idea can then be considered to "float around" for years until it reaches a person who has no idea of its true origin. Someone could claim that the idea was in the public domain. In the meantime, technology has proceeded to the point where a person could develop the invention. This person then uses the idea as a basis for developing such an invention. If we were to look at the timing between the story and the invention, it might be concluded that it was only prediction. There may be many cases of inspiration which we would consider to be prediction, for which the lack of any direct evidence makes it impossible to prove the existence of inspiration.

H. G. Wells and the Tank.

This first case would appear to be representative of the difficulty in deciding between prediction and inspiration. The interval between the story and the real-world device was just over a decade. H. G. Wells' short story "The Land Ironclads" appeared in *Strand Magazine* in December 1903. To many readers, it was just another work from the pen of the author of *The*

Time Machine and *The War of the Worlds*. But unlike most of his other story concepts, this one saw practical realization in World War 1.

Any history of the tank will point out that the idea for an armored, or at least covered, war vehicle can easily be traced as far back as Leonardo da Vinci. One could go back further if the description could include medieval and classical siege equipment. Even if it was possible to decide that Wells had been a very strong influence on one of the developers, we would also have to look at the historical record and ask how these prior ideas and implementations had influenced the developers, in addition to "The Land Ironclads."

The device described by Wells was a steel frame with eight pair of ten-foot diameter pedrail wheels. Each set of wheels was driven by the engines and the axle pivoted to permit it to cope with the terrain. The ironclad was, as its name implied, heavily armored. The craft contained a number of gunners, each of whom made use of optical sights to aim his automatic rifle. This description of the device, past that of being an armored, armed vehicle capable of traversing a battlefield, bears no great similarity to tanks as they were developed. One particular feature of the tank which made it successful was the use of the caterpillar tread. This had been developed some years previously in America, but had not been proposed by Wells in the story.

The first step is to ask who invented the tank. This question was considered after the war by the Royal Commission on Awards for Inventors. It considered the claims of 12 individuals and divided awards totaling to £18,000 ($90,000 at the time) between six of them. The two largest recipients were Sir William Tritton and Major Walter Wilson. Together these gentlemen received £15,000 ($75,000). Early designs of the tank having proved unsuccessful, they were instrumental in incorporating the caterpillar tread and making other necessary design changes.

One other name mentioned in connection with tanks is Major Ernest Swinton (later Major General Sir Ernest). His wartime job was to write uplifting articles about the war for publication. He had an idea for a "machine gun destroyer" and tried to promote his ideas at the War Office. It is difficult to sort out how much influence Swinton's ideas had upon subsequent development.

Wells was a popular writer at the time and his stories were widely read. Even if we cannot say that each of those credited with the development of the tank had read "The Land Ironclads," it should be considered likely. Swinton said at one point that the work was done without knowledge of Wells' story, but later said that he had read it in 1903 "but looked upon it as pure fantasy and had entirely forgotten it." Since the Royal Commission had difficulty with the claims of individuals, it is not possible to say how much, if any, influence the story had upon the development of the tank. Perhaps the question to ask should be whether the tank would have been invented anyway, even if Wells had never written this particular story.

Hugo Gernsback and Sleep Learning

Whatever you might think of Hugo Gernsback's *Ralph 124C 41+* as science fiction, or even as literature, it does contain a large number of ideas for futuristic devices. One of these was the Hypnobioscope, a fictional device that would permit a person to learn while sleeping as a result of transmitting words, by some unspecified electrical process, directly into the brain.

Ralph 124C 41+ first appeared in monthly installments in Gernsback's magazine *Modern Electrics*, running from April 1911 to March 1912. This magazine was sold in 1913 and quickly replaced with a new magazine, *The Electrical Experimenter*. In 1920, the name of this magazine was changed to *Science and Invention*. It was in the December 1921 issue of *Science and Invention*, not quite 10 years after the last installment of *Ralph*, that an article appeared titled "Learn and Work While You Sleep." The author of this article was also Hugo Gernsback.

This article made no reference to *Ralph*, but presented in expanded form the idea first stated in the novel - that the senses may be affected while a person is asleep. With pseudo-psychological arguments on the part of Gernsback as the basis, the possibility of learning while listening to recordings while sleeping was suggested. One interesting feature is that Gernsback postulated that a phonograph would not be the ideal means of reproducing the sound. He suggested that better sound quality with less distracting noises could be obtained using a wire recorder (telgraphone). This article gave no indication that any sleep learning experiments had actually been tried.

Then, in October 1923, an article on this topic appeared in yet another of Gernsback's magazines, *Radio News*. This was the article "Learn While You Sleep," by Chief Radioman J. N. Phinney, stationed at the Navy Training School in Pensacola, Florida. The article related his experiments in using sleep learning to improve the performance of his students in reading Morse Code signals. The results were presented for a group of students who had failed to make the required progress in the course. According to the results stated by Phinney, almost all of the students showed some degree of improvement after receiving code through their earphones while sleeping.

Whether or not we believe that sleep learning (Hypnopaedia) actually works, we must ask if Gernsback's story or his 1921 article inspired Chief

Phinney. If you were to read a 1962 Gernsback article "Sleep Learning," which presented most of the details given above, you might get that impression. But if you actually read Phinney's article, the details he gave of his life appear to indicate that his work with what he called "subconscious learning" predated the 1921 Gernsback article. No mention is made of *Ralph*. The introduction to Phinney's article, no doubt written by Gernsback himself as Editor of the magazine, only says that his two earlier works "proved prophetic."

H. G. Wells and the Chain Reaction

Histories of the development of the atomic bomb credit the physicist Leo Szilard with the development of the concept of the chain reaction. These same works imply an influence on Szilard by H. G. Wells' work *The World Set Free*, published in 1914.

Szilard's own recollections list three influences in the years 1932 and 1933. The first is that he had read *The World Set Free*. The second was a conversation with Otto Mandl, an Austrian who had years before acquired the rights to publish Wells' works in German. Mandl explained to Szilard his theory for the salvation of mankind. Instead of continuing to fight war after war, man should concentrate his energies on finding a way to leave the earth. Szilard's reply was that if he wished to be a part of the enterprise, he would be become involved in nuclear physics since atomic energy was the only way that man could leave the earth and the solar system as well.

The final influence was the speech by Lord Rutherford at the meeting of the British Association for the Advancement of Science in September 1933. Rutherford was commenting on the transformation of elements by bombarding the nuclei with sub-atomic particles such as the proton. In 1932, Cockcroft and Walton had bombarded Lithium with protons. The capture of the proton by the Lithium nucleus caused it to fragment into two alpha particles - Helium nuclei. Rutherford's comment was that:

> We might in these processes obtain very much more energy than the proton supplied, but on the average we could not expect to obtain energy in this way. It was a very poor and inefficient way of producing energy, and anyone who looked for power in the transformation of atoms was talking moonshine.

Szilard reacted to the fact that Rutherford was claiming that something could not be done. He wondered how Rutherford could be so sure about something that someone else might one day discover or invent. It must be noted that this was six years before the discovery of the fission of the nuclei of elements such as uranium.

Szilard later claimed that as he was taking a walk in London and waiting for the traffic light to change:

> it suddenly occurred to me that if we could find an element which is split by neutrons and which would emit *two* neutrons when it absorbed *one* neutron, such an element, if assembled in sufficiently large mass, could sustain a nuclear chain reaction. I didn't see at the moment just how one would go about finding such an element or what experiments would be needed, but the idea never left me.

Having read *The World Set Free* enabled Szilard to realize the possible applications in both peace and war. The question to be considered is if it is possible to determine if any concepts presented in Wells' work were instrumental in developing the concept of a chain reaction.

Wells' story contains an episode of a lecture in Edinburgh where the gradual decay of radioactive elements is described and it is postulated that much could be done if a way could be found to release the energy at a higher rate. We then have one of the characters, Holsten, finding a way of causing atomic disintegration in bismuth which:

> exploded with great violence into a heavy gas of extreme radio-activity, which disintegrated in its turn in the course of seven days

Many years are then stated to have passed before a way was found to employ Holsten's discovery and a number of different devices are developed, all operating on different principles: Holsten-Roberts, Dass-Tata, Kemp and Krupp-Erlanger. Of course, the means of operation of any of these devices was never explained. It was only stated that they provided energy so cheaply as to begin to immediately replace all existing means of transportation and power generation. The eventual effect of such devices was to upset the world economy. The result was war.

The bombs employed were small and dropped by hand from aircraft. The description of their supposed operation is pure doubletalk with imaginary materials and a ludicrous triggering mechanism:

> Those used by the Allies were lumps of pure Carolinum, painted on the outside with unoxidised cydonator inducive enclosed hermetically in a case of membranium. A little celluloid stud between the handles by which the bomb was lifted was arranged so as to be easily torn off and admit air to the inducive, which at once

became active and set up radio-activity in the outer layer of the Carolinum sphere. This liberated fresh inducive, and so in a few minutes the whole bomb was a blazing continual explosion.

The one major difficulty with Wells' pseudo-scientific explanation is that he does not permit the explosion of the device, however powerful, to disrupt the material of the bomb, thereby stopping the reaction. The mass of the material, Carolinum, simply continues to release energy at a gradually decreasing rate.

We must conclude that there is nothing in the story that would have suggested the principle of chain reaction to Szilard. It is interesting to note that Wells' story has the industrial peacetime applications occurring first, and then the use of the bombs in the war that follows. Although it was recognized prior to World War 2 that there were peaceful applications of atomic power, all of the fission reactors constructed during and immediately after the war were either for experimental purposes or for the transmutation of uranium 238 into plutonium. The first practical use of atomic fission, if one can call warfare practical, was of course the use of the atomic bombs in 1945. Atomic fission first generated electricity in an experimental reactor in Idaho in 1951. It was then employed for the propulsion of the U.S.S. *Nautilus* in 1954.

David H. Keller and Royal Jelly

When I first started this search for cases of inspiration by science fiction, I posted an email to fellow members of the Science Fiction Research Association asking if any knew of such cases. I only received two replies. One was from James Gunn at the University of Kansas (the other will be discussed in a later case). Included with the response was a copy of his remarks delivered at the Campbell Conference in 2004. The talk contained the statement that:

> The discoverer of royal jelly, the food that turns female bees into queen bees, credited his inspiration to a story by David H. Keller.

My first step, as I saw it, was to get back in touch with James Gunn and find out more details. But he replied that he could not tell me anything more or even who had provided him with the information, although he thought that it might have been Fred Pohl. When I was able to get a message to him, Fred's reply was "It wasn't me!"

So I was stuck with an unknown story by David H. Keller and some unknown researcher who had worked with royal jelly. The wording of the sentence quoted above was considered suspicious in that it referred to the person as the "discoverer" of royal jelly. Most of the attempts to learn about the history of royal jelly resulted in ads for bee-related products and all sorts of claims for their healing powers and the supposed antiquity of the knowledge of these powers.

I was then fortunate to encounter a short *New York Times* article from 1928 concerned with royal jelly. The article quoted a Toronto beekeeper attending a convention of Ontario beekeepers in November of that year. The apiarist spoke of research being proposed into the properties of royal jelly and that "he believed the food provided by the worker bees for the queen and her larvae prolongs the life of the queen bee by several years, and might have similar properties in the treatment of humans."

Although the *Times* article did give me a little information about royal jelly, I did not have much hope in learning any more about the problem, so I was therefore quite pleased when I found an answer to the first part - the story. I had been performing some more general research into Hugo Gernsback and had acquired a copy of *The Gernsback Days* by Ashley and Lowndes. In the discussion of the state of science fiction in the 1929-1930 interval, I encountered the name of the story and a very brief description:

> Dr. Keller's short story, "The Boneless Horror," is as much fantasy as science fiction. The "science part" deals with the indefinite prolongation of life through the use of royal jelly, something that was considered possible at the time.

This was the key to the whole problem. I was then able to locate a copy of a collection of Keller's stories, originally published in 1947 and then reprinted in 1974. The collection, *Life Everlasting and Other Tales of Science, Fantasy and Horror*, contains an introduction by Sam Moskowitz. In it, Moskowitz stated that:

> When Dr. Thomas S. Gardner, one of the country's leading gerontologists, informed Doctor Keller that due to the inspiration from the story, "The Boneless Horror," he had experimented with "royal jelly," a food eaten exclusively by queen bees and which seemed responsible for their long life-span in contrast to the short life of the worker bee and that in experiments he had been able to greatly prolong the life of fruit flies by feeding them this food, Doctor Keller simply asked, "What will the fruit flies do with these extra days of life?"

Just as Gunn was in error in referring to the un-named Gardner as the "discoverer of royal jelly," Moskowitz was apparently wrong in referring to him as "one of the country's leading gerontologists." Gardner was undoubtedly a very bright guy, with a Ph.D. in Organic Chemistry from Ohio State. He was a member of the Gerontological Society, Inc., in whose Journal he published a few papers containing the results of his research, but as far as I was able to determine did not occupy any position of prominence or notoriety in the field.

Only a few days after having obtained the second half of the answer from the introduction by Moskowitz, I was quite surprised to receive a letter from Fred Pohl. Since he had told me that he was not the one who had given the information to James Gunn, I did not expect to hear any more from him on the topic. In the letter, he stated that the people who would have had the most knowledge of the works of the 1920s and early 1930s were *Hugo Gernsback* and *Sam Moskowitz* and that I should check their works for the answer. I immediately wrote back thanking Fred for his suggestion and explained that those two names were the key to the solution. I told him that his score was 2 for 2, but just a few days late.

In this particular case, we do have a demonstrated direct connection between the story and the subsequent research. But the concept of the use of royal jelly for life extension was shown to date from at least the *New York Times* article of November 1928, whereas Keller's story did not appear in *Science Wonder Stories* until the July issue of the following year. We may even consider the possibility that this newspaper article could have provided Keller with the idea for his story.

E. E. "Doc" Smith and the Combat Information Center

A recently published book, *Different Engines: How Science Drives Fiction and Fiction Drives Science*, states that one idea from the works of Edward Elmer "Doc" Smith had influence on American naval technology. The quote used as the basis for this conclusion is attributed to a letter to Smith from Admiral Chester Nimitz:

> Your entire set-up was taken specifically, directly, and consciously from the Directrix. Here you reached the situation the Navy was in — more communication channels than integration techniques to handle it. In your writing you proposed such an integrating technique and proved how advantageous it could be.

There are problems with this quote and the statement made in *Different Engines* regarding its origin. If the letter had been written by a naval officer, the phrase "Your entire setup" does not make sense. It should have said that "Our (the Navy's) set-up" was derived from Smith's work. As it turns out, the ultimate source of the quote was a letter dated June 11, 1947 which was actually written by John W. Campbell, Jr. Any problems in the wording of the quote are due to Smith's daughter Verna, who included a portion of the letter in a speech made at a science fiction convention in 1979. This speech was source of the quote which appeared in *Different Engines*.

When a copy of the original letter was located and examined, it was found that Campbell was claiming that Smith's work had directly influenced the development of the Combat Information Center (CIC) and that the person responsible for the CIC concept was Heinlein's classmate Caleb Laning.

The Directrix was the name given to the gigantic spaceship Z9M9Z which was meant to be the way of controlling the ships of the Grand Fleet in Smith's stories *Gray Lensman* and *Second Stage Lensman*. The key to the control was the "tank" - a means of representing planets and ships in a gigantic three-dimensional display. Smith does not describe the exact shape of the "tank", but says that it is 700 feet in diameter and eighty feet thick in the middle, with a volume of over 17 million cubic feet. These figures suggest a squat cylindrical segment capped by a dome. The objective in building the tank was to provide information on a million combat ships.

The "set-up" to which Campbell referred was the Combat Information Center (CIC) that was developed for use in combat vessels during World War 2. I would suggest that most of you have encountered a scene in a war movie of a darkened shipboard compartment with several men bent over radar screens and another standing at a clear vertical plotting board, plotting the tracks of enemy planes and ships. So whether you knew it or not, you were looking at a CIC. The objective of the CIC is to collect, manage and evaluate the information being received visually from shipboard observers, by radar and sonar, and from pilots of planes in contact with the enemy. The information would be used to control the movements of ships, and to direct the actions of both anti-aircraft guns and the aircraft whose job it is to protect the ships from attack. It is an idea which is obvious in retrospect, as many ideas are, but which required much in the way of experimentation and development.

It is clear that Smith was describing the same type of problem facing his Grand Fleet which was faced by naval officers in the years leading up to World War 2. The days were gone when the information available to the Commanding Officer in planning his actions was limited to what he could see with his own eyes. The information from multiple sources had to be collected and presented in such a way that it was understandable and useful in combat situations. Fortunately, the U.S. Navy did not have to deal with the massive number of ships that Smith's stories seemed to involve.

It is impossible to give a comprehensive history of CIC in the space available here. One important factor in the creation and evolution of CIC was the delivery of the first operational naval radars in May 1940. These six CXAM radars were sent to the aircraft carrier U.S.S. *Yorktown*, the battleship U.S.S. *California* and the cruisers U.S.S. *Chester*, U.S.S *Chicago*, U.S.S. *Northampton* and U.S.S. *Pensacola*. The Navy was fortunate in that the officers of these ships were interested in making use of radar and wanted to find the best way that it could be done. The arrangement of the equipment and the distribution of information were under the control of each Commanding Officer and not explicitly directed by headquarters. The efforts on these ships led to the development of what was first called radar plot, which then evolved into the Combat Information Center. Any study of the development of CIC shows that it grew from learning how to use the information properly and efficiently, rather than working to a preconceived plan in imitation of Smith.

Laning was heavily involved in the development of the Combat Information Center. From October, 1942 until November 1943, he was on the staff of Commander Destroyers, U.S. Pacific Fleet, and later during that same interval also on the staff of Commander Cruisers, U.S. Pacific Fleet. His many concerns in connection with CIC were the equipment to be placed on ships, how it should be organized, how the information should be distributed, and most importantly, how the men should be trained to use it. Because of his many accomplishments in making CIC a success, Laning received the Legion of Merit. But it is clear that he was not the originator of the CIC concept. During the time of the earliest experimentation with radars and the gradual development of CIC, Laning was the staff Radio Officer of a cruiser division, and then served on destroyers.

There does exist one statement by Laning concerning CIC and science fiction. It appears in a letter to Robert and Leslyn Heinlein, dated January 17, 1944. Laning had completed the assignment during which he was concerned with the development of CIC, and had received a combat assignment where he hoped to put what he had been working on into practice. The letter stated:

> For info, I have been the top man in "CIC" development for past year. You will be fascinated with the story, when it can be told. Basic ideas were frequently very similar to some of Amazing S.F. "brain-machine" ideas. And it works and sinks and shoots down Japs.

Three things should be noted with regard to the quote. First, Laning stated that he had been in CIC development, not that he originated the idea. Second, it stated that the ideas were similar to science fiction ideas, but not that they were derived from or based on science fiction. And finally, there is no mention made of any works of "Doc" Smith.

So we are left with a quote in a book which has been traced to a letter containing a number of erroneous statements regarding the influence of science fiction upon the Navy, all of which we must attribute to Campbell.

John Campbell, Robert Heinlein and Radioactive Dust

In July of 2008, I presented a paper at the conference held by the Science Fiction Research Association. The paper considered the details behind the creation of the story "Solution Unsatisfactory" and a minor connection with the U.S. atomic program in the period before the entry of the United States into the war. It appears as the essay "The Creation of Heinlein's 'Solution Unsatisfactory'" in *Practicing Science Fiction: Critical Essays on Writing, Reading and Teaching the Genre*.

The discoveries that were being made in the field of nuclear physics during the 1930s and early 1940s were often published in the daily press. This was before the security measures and censorship that were imposed due to the war and the Manhattan Project. One such story appeared in the *New York Times* on May 5, 1940, with similar articles appearing in other papers. These articles put forth the promise of almost unlimited energy possible through nuclear fission so strongly that it was necessary for subsequent articles to tell the readers that we weren't quite there yet.

In the August 1940 issue of *Astounding*, there was an article "Shhhhh --- Don't Mention It!" The article was by Arthur McCann, which was actually a pseudonym for John W. Campbell, Jr. The article began by commenting on the enthusiasm generated by the newspaper articles. Much of the article was concerned with engineering problems associated with power generation, such as the shielding from gamma rays.

But at one point, Campbell did turn to the question of weapons. He downplayed the possibility of bombs based on fission. As another possible military application, he turned to the Roman conquests of Carthage. The solution that was supposedly employed by the Romans to make sure that Carthage could not rise again was to destroy the city and then plow salt into the fields to prevent any crops from being grown. Campbell then suggested that:

The modern equivalent would probably be to bomb the undesired city with a few pounds of a long-lived radioactive isotope. There would undoubtedly be plant life left - rather weird stuff, probably - but humans would find it expedient to get out and stay out for one hundred years or so. A few uranium power plants could rather easily manufacture the necessary isotope bombs.

We then consider a letter from Robert Heinlein to John Campbell and his wife Doña, dated December 1, 1940:

I've just reread John's letter of November 12th . . . . Such nice ideas he has, radioactive dust to wipe out all of modern civilization.

Campbell's letter spelled out his idea for long story based on his idea of using radioactive dust as a weapon. The plot outline began with the dusting of Berlin and then other German and also Italian cities. The dustings were done in an attempt to end the war, and it appeared at first that it had worked. But then there were retaliatory dusting, followed by more and more nations becoming involved. The final result was a collapse of centralized governments and a decrease in the world's population.

Heinlein made use of at least the initial dusting in his creation of "Solution Unsatisfactory." He chose to write a shorter story employing a different view of the problems resulting from such a weapon. He felt that it would have taken a novel or even a series of novels to properly present Campbell's idea. But many of the technical details employed by Heinlein can be traced back to Campbell's August article.

The story appeared in the May 1941 issue of *Astounding*, which meant that it went on sale on April 18th. At almost the same time (the various sources only say mid-April), a committee was formed to consider the possible military applications of nuclear fission. The report that they delivered a month later suggested bombs, a power source for submarines and ships and the "production of violently radioactive materials . . . . carried by airplanes to be scattered as bombs over enemy territory."

Was this coincidence, or did someone connected with committee read either "Shhhhh - Don't Mention It!" or "Solution Unsatisfactory"? Although the short time interval between the story and the report has been noted by other such as H. Bruce Franklin and James Gifford, no one appears to have investigated it any further. It turns out that there is one other possibility.

Heinlein identified his two sources for the atomic physics used in the story as John Campbell and Dr. Robert Cornog. Cornog had just received his Ph.D. in Physics from the University of California at Berkeley. During the late 1930s, he worked as a graduate student at the Radiation Laboratory, now known as the Lawrence Berkeley Laboratory in honor of its first director, Ernest O. Lawrence. Lawrence had received the Nobel Prize in Physics in 1939 for the invention of the cyclotron.

We don't know how much technical help Cornog gave to Heinlein when he was writing the story. But any conversations would have made Cornog familiar with the basic concept of radioactive dusting. Why is this important? One of the members of the committee that developed the government report was Ernest O. Lawrence. It is likely that at some point between his work with Heinlein and the creation of the report Cornog would have mentioned the idea to Lawrence or others at the Laboratory so that it was considered for inclusion into the report.

The Allies decided not to make use of radioactive dust during the war. There was some concern, based on limited information, that the Germans were developing such a weapon. As it turned out, such fears were unfounded.

My opinion is that the last stated possibility is the most likely. We may then credit Campbell with an idea which had an admittedly minor effect on the U.S. atomic program and that we may also credit Robert Heinlein with an assist.

Ivan Yefremov and Volume Holography

The second response from my query about inspiration by science fiction posted to members of the SFRA elicited a response from Larisa Mikhaylova, a Senior Researcher from Lomonsov Moscow State University who was at the time a Fulbright Scholar at The University of Wisconsin at Eau Claire. She told me of a story by the Russian writer Ivan Yefremov (1907-1972) which had inspired a Russian physicist to make years later some fundamental developments in the field of holography. The physicist was Yuri Denisyuk (1927-2006), and he is credited with the development of Volume Holography, or as it is sometimes known in his honor Denisyuk Holography.

Both Yefremov and Denisyuk acknowledged the connection between a story and the science. But this is where the situation becomes interesting. In his writings, Yefremov identified the story as "Shadow of the Past," which was written in 1944 and published in 1945. A group of paleontologists exploring a region of the steppes are doing some blasting. They encounter a nearby gully in which their blasting has caused the collapse of the cliff face, exposing a mass of resinous material. When the sun was at the proper angle:

> Against the bluish-black slab of fossilized rosin, as from a yawning abyss there appeared a gigantic gray-green ghost. A huge dinosaur was hanging motionless in the air, above the upper edge of a craggy precipice, rearing 30 feet over the heads of the stupefied little group below.

The chief character of the story attempts to discover the natural process that would have permitted such an image to be formed, and then must convince the scientific world of the validity of what he has discovered.

The problem in trying to connect this story to the later developments in holography is that Denisyuk identified a different story by Yefremov as his source of inspiration. The story is "Star Ships" (sometimes translated as "Stellar Ships") also listed as being written in 1944, but not published until 1948. The story hinges on the recovery by a professor of a notebook belonging to a former student killed in a great tank battle during the war. The student, who had switched to the field of astronomy, had developed theories about the motion of the solar system within the Milky Way Galaxy. At approximately 70 million years ago, according to this theory, the solar system was in an area of the Galaxy where there was a greater density of stars, making travel between stars more likely. This is first viewed as an interesting theory, but it then serves to explain how dinosaur bones that were recently recovered showed the marks of weapons similar to that of modern man. It is then concluded that the Earth was visited during this time and that the visitors had engaged in a bit of dinosaur hunting. Additional excavation reveals the remains of one of the visitors, apparently killed by a dinosaur, and some artifacts. When the surface of an artifact is cleaned, they see the image of an alien:

> From a deep, absolutely transparent layer, a strange face was looking at them. The face was enlarged by some unknown optical method to its natural size and was three dimensional in its shape. The most striking feature of this face was its unbelievable animation, especially in its eyes.

Although Dennis Gabor received the Nobel Prize in Physics in 1971 for his "invention and development of the holographic method," a complete history of the field must also include the work of Emmett Leith and Juris Upatnieks in the United States and Yuri Denisyuk in Russia. Gabor's basic work in the late 1940s came from the area of electron microscopy. The discoveries by Leith and Upatnieks came from the fields of Synthetic Aperture Radar and Optical Processing. Leith and Upatnieks were aware of the work of Gabor and built upon it. When he began his work in 1958 on the reconstruction of images, however, Denisyuk was unaware of the earlier work by Gabor. In Gabor's work, the hologram was recorded upon a photographic plate positioned behind the object. In Denisyuk's approach, the plate was positioned between the source of illumination and the object to be recorded. The interference between the source of illumination and the wavefront reflected from the object are recorded within the volume of the photographic plate.

Because the works of Yefremov are not well known in the United States, the story of his inspiration by a work of science fiction is similarly unknown. But in many references which give the historical background of holography, you will find that several will refer to the stories of Yefremov.

Frank Herbert and the Dracone

Most people are no doubt familiar with Frank Herbert through his monumental work *Dune* and its sequels. Many of these same people have probably never read, or possibly never even heard of, his first novel *Under Pressure*, which also appeared as *21st Century Sub* and *Dragon in the Sea*. In the story, the United States has been trying to solve its energy problems by secretly stealing oil from the eastern powers. This was accomplished by underwater drilling by nuclear submarines. The oil was transported in a very long flexible plastic barge called a "slug" which was towed behind the submarine. At the beginning of the story, it was revealed that the last twenty such missions have failed. The main character, John Ramsey, is a psychologist who is sent under cover aboard one of the submarines to attempt to determine why the preceding missions have failed. The remaining details of the story will not be presented here, as it is the barge which is the important factor.

First consider the statements of Brian Herbert, Frank Herbert's son, in his book *Dreamer of Dune: The Biography of Frank Herbert*:

> Early in the 1960s, Dad learned that a British company had developed flexible underwater barges based on his concept in *The Dragon in the Sea*. The company was marketing them under the trade name "Dracone," and, as this name suggested, they freely admitted the source of the idea. Science fiction authors Arthur C. Clarke and Fritz Leiber, friends of Dad, recommended that he take legal action to invalidate Dracone's patents. Dad consulted a number of people on this, including John W. Campbell, and learned from them, to his dismay, that he should have filed formal patent papers within two years of publication of his idea. The

publication gave him "discovery rights" for that period, but his failure to file proper documents sent the idea to the public domain.

Before presenting the details of the use of Frank Herbert's idea, it is necessary to correct a misstatement by his son. The publication did not provide Frank Herbert with any type of "discovery rights." As explained in Chapter 8, once the idea was presented in a publication, he would have had exactly one year (not two) from the date of publication to file a patent application.

Now, let us consider the story of the British firm. The details of the development of the "dracone" barge are contained in a paper which appeared in the *Proceedings of the Institute of Mechanical Engineers* in 1961. The author of the paper was William R. Hawthorne, Sc.D., F.R.S. (later Sir William). In the paper, he stated that "The Dracone project was born in two casual conversations on 23 November 1956." He did not state what, if anything, inspired the two conversations. Was it Herbert's story?

"Under Pressure" appeared in serial form in *Astounding* from November 1955 through January 1956. It was published just a month later by Doubleday as *Dragon in the Sea*. "Under Pressure" then appeared again, in the British edition of *Astounding* between April and June of 1956. If we accept the fact that Hawthorne had been inspired by Herbert's work, any of the above mentioned publications could have served as the influence. If it had been the book version, he would have also been supplied with the inspiration for the name "dracone." In his paper, however, Hawthorne stated that the name was suggested to him by a Cambridge fellow in early 1957. The exact date was not specified, but the implication is that it occurred between tests at the beginning of March and other tests at the beginning of April. But Hawthorne translates Greek word $\Delta\rho\alpha\kappa\omega\nu$ as serpent rather than dragon, which might be an obvious reference to its snakelike appearance.

Hawthorne and his colleagues subsequently filed for and obtained patents in both Britain and the United States. If it was not possible for Herbert to have obtained a patent more than one year after the publication of the idea, which would have been November 1956, how was it possible for Hawthorne? The British Patent GB884,566 states that "This invention relates to flexible barges intended primarily for the transport and/or storage of liquids or solids such as wheat or other grain . . . . The present invention aims at improving the stability of the barge and to this end provides means . . . ." Similarly the U.S. Patent 3,056,373 begins by stating "This invention relates to totally enclosed barges of flexible material for the transport of fluid or granular or like portable cargo by towing. More particularly, it is concerned with measures to counter snaking and other flexural oscillations of such barges." (***My emphasis***)

The stability problems to which each patent refers were observed during Hawthorne's development work on the dracone. A picture in his paper shows the "snaking" action that was observed on the very first experimental model. The paper contains much discussion and analysis regarding this problem. So what was being patented was not just the basic barge idea (which would not have been possible) but the barge idea along with the means of reducing or eliminating potentially damaging oscillations.

But what if Frank Herbert *had* acted quickly enough? Could he have obtained a patent on the basic barge idea? Probably not. Both Hawthorne's U.S. Patent and paper reference an earlier U.S. Patent for a Nonrigid Barge. The patent (2,391,926) was granted on January 1, 1946 to William Edmiston Scott, a U.S. Naval officer. The patent figures show much shorter barges, and the text does not discuss oscillations or the means to combat them. If Herbert had attempted to patent the basic barge idea, the existence of Scott's patent would have represented prior art.

Finally, consider the possibility that Herbert would have filed in time and had been granted a patent for his flexible barge idea. Would he have had a successful product? Remember that Herbert's background was as a journalist. If he had built simple barges of the same dimensions as Hawthorne's, he would have encountered the same oscillations shown in Hawthorne's paper. Without the background in fluid dynamics of a person such as Hawthorne, it is not likely that he would have been able to develop the same type of solution. He would have been led to conclude, incorrectly as it turns out, that the flexible barge idea was impractical.

Conclusions

Of the eight cases presented, we can say that an adequate connection between science fiction and a subsequent invention or scientific research has been shown for four: Keller, Campbell/Heinlein, Yefremov, and Herbert. In the case of royal jelly and radioactive dust, the concept did not originate in a science fiction story. But the story was apparently the means by which the concept was passed to others. For the remaining four: Gernsback, the two for Wells and then Doc Smith, it does not appear that a judgment of inspiration is justified by what is currently known.

There may be additional evidence that would permit the judgment to be modified in some of the above cases. It may also be that other cases of demonstrable inspiration exist that have not come to my attention. I feel, however, that the evidence is strong enough in the cases cited to show that the very idea of Heinlein inspiring one of his Academy classmates to develop a naval system by means of a science fiction story is not one to be dismissed.

The next chapter will consider the processes by which ideas have been reduced to practice in the Navy.

10

NAVAL INNOVATION

The previous two chapters have considered the relationships between science fiction and invention. In the last chapter, I addressed the possibility of a concept contained within a science fiction story inspiring a real invention. Information was presented to show that in some small number of cases such direct inspiration had occurred. This allows us to consider the first step in Heinlein's claim, as best expressed in quote from the Virtues essay, that his fictional electronic device served as the inspiration for a real naval system, and to state that such a claim is at least plausible.

Let us look at the next step in the same quote - the part played by the classmate. One problem that I have with this portion of the Virtues quote is that Heinlein has the classmate "directing such research." This problem was discussed in Chapter 4. While it is not impossible that a classmate could have occupied such a research position at the time, let us just consider if *any* naval officer could have created or proposed a technical idea with the chance that it might be adopted by the Navy as an operational system.

First consider how such a situation is presented in the works of Heinlein. In the very first quote presented in Chapter 2 from the Heinlein letter of December 21, 1941, we have Heinlein stating:

> Nevertheless the brasshats are not quite as opposed to new ideas as the news commentators would have us think. The present method of anti-aircraft fire was invented by an ensign. Admiral King encouraged a warrant officer and myself to try to invent a new type of bomb (Note: We weren't successful). You may remember that one of my story gags was picked up by a junior officer and made standard practice in the fleet before the next issue hit the stands.

Previous analysis focused on the sentence regarding the "story gag." But consider the balance of the quote in which Heinlein states the receptivity of higher ranking naval officers to new ideas. Does Heinlein present any other references to such development work by naval officers in the correspondence file? The only such mention found was regarding the invention of the method of anti-aircraft fire in the above quote, for which the investigation led nowhere. But in his works of fiction, we do have the point in "Tale of the Man Who Was too Lazy to Fail" where Heinlein refers to the work done by the character David Lamb:

> I haven't mentioned the automatic pilot he thought up, then had developed years later when he was in a position to get such things done.

In Chapter 7, the possible connection between David Lamb and Perry's classmate from *For Us, The Living* was noted with him being:

> one of the most brilliant young officers in the fleet and expert in the use and design of equipment that makes your automatic door seem simple.

I believe that the important phrase in this quote is "in the fleet" as it implies that this officer was not tucked away at some research facility such as NRL. This is just the type of officer in which we are interested.

As also noted in Chapter 7, there is not that much real naval content in Heinlein's work. For one final mention of such development work in connection with Heinlein, we must step into the real world. We know from the service record of his classmate Caleb Laning that he was commended for developing a torpedo targeting system.

So we have a statement by Heinlein, the accomplishments of a fictional character, and the accomplishment of one classmate. Is this sufficient to permit us to evaluate the possibility of the classmate having developed the device as stated by Heinlein? I maintain that it is not. It is necessary to look at the broader picture of such development work within the Navy. Would a naval officer, not specifically engaged in a line of research, have the opportunity to propose and develop a device? In using the word "opportunity" I am considering more than him having the time to do such work and the access to the materials to make it possible to perform the work. Another word that perhaps better describes the overall situation is "culture." So what I am asking is, did the Navy of the interwar years present such a culture in which innovation would be possible and even desired?

Before proceeding any further, it is necessary to make a distinction between the types of innovation or invention within the Navy. Although these definitions would apply to any time in the existence of the Navy, this chapter will consider the period from 1919 to 1945. This extends the period of interest from the interwar years (which is still the primary interval of interest) through the end of World War 2. The first type we can call *institutional innovation*. The second would have to be called *improvisational ingenuity*. The third, and the one of greatest interest, I will call *individual innovation*.

The first type, *institutional innovation*, is the one addressed in nearly all discussions of naval innovation. This involves the changes in the design and construction of ship, planes, navigational equipment, guns and types of electronics such as radio and radar. These would be developed at places such as the Bureau of Ships, The Naval Research Laboratory, The Naval Aircraft Factory (which existed during our period of interest), or at the firms which supplied the Navy. This type of innovation is discussed later in the chapter.

The second type, *improvisational ingenuity*, is that most encountered in time of war, or at least in light of a dangerous situation. It does show true inventive spirit, but may be seen as the response to an urgent or threatening situation. The survival of the improviser and possibly all of his shipmates may have depended upon the invention made. All of the cases in this category are taken from the war years, and are the reason for extending the period of interest.

Considering improvisational ingenuity, the primary example we might be most familiar with through either TV shows or movies is Damage Control. Although procedures exist for such efforts to keep the vessel afloat and functional in the case of damage, whether as a result of combat or not, such procedures cannot possibly consider every eventuality. Those involved in damage control must look at the situation that exists, draw on their training and experience, consider the material and equipment available, and then improvise.

Let us consider some specific instances of improvisational ingenuity which occurred during World War 2. The first two cases may be drawn from the defense of Wake Island in December 1941. When the 12 Wildcats (Grumman F4Fs) of Marine Fighter Squadron VMF-211 arrived on Wake Island on December 4, they found very primitive operating conditions. Although intended as a fighter, dependent on its six .50-caliber machine guns, the F4F was also capable of carrying two 100 lb. bombs. On Wake, it was discovered that some of the bombs stockpiled were Army bombs. This presented a problem, as the two-point Army bomb attachment was incompatible with the single-point Navy bomb racks. The improvisation in this case involved taking the suspension bands from Navy practice bombs and fitting them to the Army bombs. You might consider such an improvisation minor or perhaps even trivial, but it was then possible to use these bombs in attacks on Japanese naval vessels in the days that followed.

One of the early Japanese attacks on Wake Island destroyed quantities of the oxygen supply employed by the F4F pilots. Also available on the island, however, were cylinders of oxygen used for welding by the civilian workman who had been engaged in constructing facilitates when the war began. A senior VMF-211 pilot, Captain H. C. Freuler, devised a means of transferring oxygen from the cylinders to the aircraft oxygen bottles. This was a small improvisation, but one that kept the Marine planes flying.

For another example of improvisation, we must move below the surface of the sea. On July 6, 1943, the submarine U.S.S. *Gurnard* was on a patrol to the Palaus. As a result of a bombing attack by a Japanese aircraft, the bow planes of the submarine were jammed by an electrical problem. With the jammed planes, the only means of controlling the attitude was to move groups of men either forward or aft. The depth of the *Gurnard* during this time was estimated to be in excess of 500 feet, which was below test depth. Power to the dive plane circuits was restored by one the boat's electricians, Chief W. F. Fritsch, who squeezed into a very tight spot and laid a toothbrush between two electrical connections. Again this was a simple improvisation, but one that saved the crew of the *Gurnard* and resulted in a Silver Star being awarded to Chief Fritsch.

Finally, let us consider a number of improvisations made aboard aircraft carriers in the early days of the Pacific war. Much was done to improve the operation of the aircraft and the protection to the pilots. More desirable reflector gunsights were somehow acquired and installed in the cockpits, and 3/8" boiler plate was installed as armor behind the seats. But improvisation in the area of engines was not neglected. Many aircraft engines of the time employed the Coffman starter, which used a blank cartridge loaded with gunpowder to provide the starting impulse to the engine. (Remember the movie *The Flight of the Phoenix*?) Because of similarity of the cartridge to a shotgun shell, these were also known as "shotgun" starters. On one early carrier mission in 1942, it was discovered that there was a shortage of such cartridges. The existing supply of cartridges was kept for use only for combat missions. But for the routine yet necessary patrol flights, the aircraft engines were started with a block and tackle arrangement involving elastic line, similar to pull-starting an outboard motor or lawn mower.

Now let us turn to *individual innovation,* the primary area of interest. As the name implies, it is an idea that is proposed and developed by an individual officer or seaman outside of the context of any of the areas considered under institutional innovation. This could be ashore at a naval base, but here is considered to have likely occurred aboard a ship of any type, from a submarine all the way up to a battleship or carrier.

In 1925, when Joseph M. Reeves assumed the position of Commander Aircraft Squadrons Battle Fleet, the full extent of his command was the U.S.S. *Langley*, the U.S. Navy's first aircraft carrier. He discovered that the *Langley*, still performing in an experimental role, was operating at most only 12 aircraft. He realized that to be of use a carrier must be able to operate a larger numbers of planes and be able to employ them as efficiently as possible. During his time of connection with the *Langley*, many of the procedures and devices employed during World War 2 were proposed and developed. After each plane landed, it was moved towards the bow to an area called the deck park (a *Langley* innovation) and protected by a crash barrier (another *Langley* innovation). Once all planes had landed, the aircraft could be returned to the aft portion of the flight deck, refueled and reloaded, and be ready to launch again. This was a great improvement over previous operational procedures. Use of these procedures and an increase in the number of aircraft made it possible for the *Langley* to become an operational carrier. It is not clear whether any of these advances were the direct suggestion of Reeves or were originally proposed by various officers under his command, but they represent the type of innovation of interest to us.

An important tactical innovation was the circular formation for ships, which arose from analysis of the problems with the type of sailing formation that had been employed in the Battle of Jutland. Although this idea has been attributed to Commander (later Admiral) Chester Nimitz during his time the Naval War College from 1922 to 1923, it was in fact due to his Academy and War College classmate Roscoe MacFall. It was Nimitz, however, who upon his return to the Fleet actively pushed for tests of this idea at sea. These tests revealed both the advantages and disadvantages of such a formation, and the idea languished for a number of years. It was the emergence of the aircraft carrier in World War 2 as the principal ship, as opposed to the battleship, that led to the use of the concept. A circular formation with the carrier at the center, surrounded by a screen of other types of ships, eventually became the standard formation in most navies.

If we are to look at electronics, radar more specifically, we encounter a number of innovations more concerned with how such devices were to be employed rather than their original development. As was noted in Chapter 5, the tests performed during the Fleet Problem of early 1939 indicated the superiority of the Naval Research Lab's XAF radar over the CXZ radar developed by RCA. The decision was made to procure a number of copies of the successful NRL unit. The preliminary model was delivered in November 1939, and the first production model in May 1940. The initial six units, designated CXAM, were followed in 1941 by 14 additional improved units, designated CXAM-1.

The form of display employed by these early radars, such as the CXAM, was the Type A or A-scope (or some variant) in which the distance to the target was indicated as the distance across the display screen from the beginning of the radar trace. Now consider the case where a return was obtained at a range greater than that represented by the time between two successive transmit pulses. This could result from atmospheric conditions which permitted radar signals to be returned from objects that would normally be beyond the horizon. If an object such as an island or coastal mountain existed at that range, the operator would obtain a strong echo in the next (or succeeding) interval, known as a second-time-around echo. Note that the echo from a normal target such as a ship or plane at this increased range would be too weak to detect. This second-time-around echo could have misled the operator, based on what he was able to see on his display, into thinking that he was seeing a real target at short range. But there was no such short range target.

The technical solution was to introduce the range-changing push button. By momentarily changing the repetition rate (based on the time between transmit pulses) the existence of a second-time-around echo could be seen. A proper short range echo would not change position when the button was pressed. But the change in the rate would mean that the second-time-around echo would now occur at a different distance from its nearest transmit pulse. This would cause the pulse on the radar display screen representing the false echo to abruptly change its position.

While this was an interesting and necessary modification to the CXAM, the real innovation involved its use in communication. The radar operators discovered that if they attached a pair of headphones to their receiver, they could hear a tone which was the repetition rate of another ship's radar. If one operator pressed his range-changing button, the other operator would then hear the change from one tone to another. By pointing their radar dishes at each other, the operators could then use their buttons as telegraph keys and communicate in Morse Code. This was a very secure means of communication due to the high frequency and the directionality of the radar beams. The same method was employed at a later point in the war by submarines with their SJ periscope radars.

Another example of innovation involved the further development of radar plots. In *Angel on the Yardarm*, the author John Monsarrat relates details of his naval career, including the fitting out of the U.S.S. *Langley* (CVL-27) in 1943. (The original Langley (CV-1) had been converted to a seaplane tender (AV-3) in 1936-37 and was critically damaged by Japanese bombers on February 27, 1942. She was abandoned and sunk by friendly fire.) When Monsarrat and the other officers assigned to the *Langley* as fighter director officers arrived at the shipyard where she was being built, they were faced with a number of problems. It was not clear that they would be assigned the qualified enlisted radar operators that they would need, and so took steps of their own to obtain what they considered qualified men and to send them for training. They also found that the radar plot of the *Langley* was an empty room. Although the concept of a radar plot had been around for several years, there was still no plan for the optimum arrangement of equipment within such a space. The officers had the opportunity to innovate in developing the layout for the *Langley* radar plot, based on their own judgment and the inspection of the layouts developed for other ships.

There are two similar stories of innovation and the effect that it had upon the naval careers of the persons involved. Irwin McNally was a young man who had the misfortune to graduate from college during the Great Depression. Although in possession of a bachelor's degree in Electrical Engineering, he was unable to find a job. It was suggested to him that he attempt to enlist in the Navy, and he was fortunate to be accepted. During his first few years in the Navy, he was able to obtain training and practical experience in many areas of electronics. He had the unique experience of occasionally being assigned as an instructor at the training schools he attended, on the basis of his engineering degree. By 1937 he had attained the rank of Warrant Officer. After considerable pre-war training in radar and shipboard experience including the *Lexington*, he was assigned, still a warrant officer, to the task of establishing the radar school in Hawaii. By July 1943, the efforts of senior officers had resulted in an officer's commission for McNally, with the rank of lieutenant junior grade. Just two weeks later, a spot promotion advanced him to the rank of lieutenant.

Aside from his school duties, McNally was interested in how radar was actually being employed by various vessels, including submarines. He developed the design for a small radar antenna for the SJ radar to be mounted on the periscope. This was an improvement over the existing larger rotating antenna first developed for the submarine radar. He had completed the tests of his prototype when Vice Admiral Lockwood, Commander Submarines Pacific Fleet, paid a visit to the radar school. Lockwood asked if it was possible to develop a small radar antenna to be mounted on the periscope. McNally showed the admiral his prototype, and the next day he was on his way to Washington, D.C. with an assignment to the Bureau of Ships. Shortly after his arrival in Washington, he received another spot promotion, this time to Lieutenant Commander. After many years of working on a variety of naval command and control systems, McNally retired with rank of Commander.

Then there was the case of George Hoover, who enlisted in the Navy at approximately the same time as Irwin McNally, first becoming an aviation machinist's mate. By 1938, he had earned his wings as an enlisted pilot (AP). He became very interested in the problem of navigation. As he had also become an instrument instructor, his solution was to develop a new piece of instrumentation - the automatic dead-reckoning tracker. This would perform the task usually performed by the pilot using a manual plotting board in the cockpit. As Hoover put it, "You could crank in information and it would show you how to get from here to there." Although he had developed such a unit on his own, it was too large to fit in the cockpit.

In the summer of 1942, he was ordered one day to fly Admiral Bellinger from Pearl Harbor to the Naval Air Station at Kaneohe. The admiral was impressed with Hoover's ability to successfully navigate in spite of bad weather. Hoover then explained to the admiral what he was trying to accomplish with his automatic dead-reckoning tracker. Although Hoover's departure was not as abrupt as McNally's, the conversation with Admiral Bellinger eventually resulted in his being transferred to Washington as well. In the course of events, he discovered that he had received a series of promotions, from chief to warrant officer and then to ensign. His next wartime assignment was in the Special Devices Branch of the Bureau of Aeronautics. His post-war assignments eventually led him into the beginnings of the U.S. space program. Like McNally, Hoover retired with rank of Commander.

A broader look at the role of innovation in the Navy requires that we start with the period following the U.S. Civil War. One might assume that a conflict which saw the development of the ironclads C.S.S. *Virginia* (sometimes mistakenly referred to as the *Merrimack*, the Union ship on which it was based) and U.S.S. *Monitor* would be followed by a period of exploitation of the ideas which those vessels represented. But for more than a decade following the war the ships of the Navy were allowed to deteriorate and little, if any, technical progress was made. This situation had many causes, the chief of which were uncertainties about the post-war role of the Navy, political disputes, the appointment of inadequate Secretaries of the Navy, economic problems such as the Panic of 1873, and just plain corruption.

It was not until the early 1880s that any real effort was made to improve the condition of the Navy. In 1883, construction was authorized of what were called the ABCD ships - 3,000-ton protected cruisers U.S.S.

Atlanta and U.S.S. *Boston*, 4500-ton protected cruiser U.S.S. *Chicago*, and 1500-ton dispatch boat U.S.S. *Dolphin*. It was the beginning of the modern steel Navy. These ships are worth mentioning only because of their connection with the person who may be called the greatest American naval inventor and innovator, Bradley Fiske (1854-1942).

Fiske graduated from the Naval Academy in 1874, but under the then current system, was required to serve as a midshipman for two years before taking the examination for ensign. His naval career started in the midst of the post-war problems of the Navy. But his career also coincided with the era of invention, as characterized by the incandescent light bulb and the telephone. With the rank of Lieutenant junior grade, Fiske began his duties at the Bureau of Ordnance in the fall of 1883. He had completed a one year leave for the purpose of studies in the area of electrical engineering.

Fiske's tasks were connected with design of the ordnance for the three cruisers, specifically how electricity could be applied to gunnery systems. The work that Fiske did regarding design and installation of ordnance equipment for these ships should be classed as institutional innovation. What are of greater interest are those inventions which Fiske made on his own. Fiske stated in his autobiography *From Midshipman to Rear Admiral* that he had obtained sixty U.S. patents. Some were for devices with no direct application to the operation of a ship or naval warfare, such as a mechanical pencil (226,607), an electrical insulator (286,801) and a printing telegraph (389,142). His last 10 patents, obtained after the end of his naval career, were all for the "Reading Machine" in which books and other text would be stored in a reduced format and then enlarged for viewing. The majority of his inventions had naval applications and may be divided into the areas of signaling, fire control and weapons delivery. These inventions were not the result of any direction to do so by his superiors. They came from Fiske recognizing that a problem existed, and the development of such devices occurred at the expense of his own time and money.

One of Fiske's early ideas, apparently never patented, was for signaling at night by means of a box containing a light with a mechanical shutter which may be opened and closed to transmit the messages by flashes of light. The idea was accepted and should be familiar to anyone who has seen a Navy signalman in action. Other devices that were patented were for transmitting helm or engine information within a ship and improvements on the use of semaphores to signal between ships.

Fiske's inventions with regard to fire control were concerned with finding the bearing and range of a target, usually optically, and then properly aiming the gun. The entire group of distinct inventions and improvements will not be presented here. Only one will be considered, the stadimeter (523,721), which is primarily used to determine distance to an object if the distance between two points on the object is known. Conversely, if the distance is known, it may be used to determine the distance between the two points. The stadimeter works by measuring the angular separation. The primary application was to determine the distance between ships sailing in a formation. Since you know the identity of the ship you are sighting through the instrument, you can look up its masthead height, which is then set on the stadimeter. By then turning a knob as you look at the ship until the image of the masthead is brought down to the waterline, you have determined the angular separation. The distance to the ship is then simply read off the indicator. As with any device that determines distance by means of angles, the accuracy of the result decreases as the distance to the object increases.

In the area of weapons delivery, Fiske obtained patents for the control of torpedoes by radio (660,155 and 660,156) and for the concept of employing aircraft in torpedo attacks upon ships (1,032,394). He realized that the airplanes of 1912 were not capable of lifting a torpedo, but was also convinced that planes were becoming larger and that it was only a matter of time before his idea could be implemented. He was reluctant to apply for a patent as he felt that such an obvious idea must have already been suggested by someone else and patented. But, as he discovered, he was the first to propose such an idea. After obtaining his patent, he was unable to convince the U.S. Navy to develop the torpedoes and planes which would be necessary. It was the British who were the first to employ air dropped torpedoes during World War 1. In 1919, Fiske at least had the satisfaction of receiving the Gold Medal of the Aero Club of America for the invention of the Torpedo Plane, although he stated in the closing paragraphs of his autobiography that he was "chagrined" that the British Navy had used his idea to establish superiority over the American Navy.

One may point to the inventions of two other officers who began their naval careers in the latter part of the nineteenth century. The first is Admiral Frank Friday Fletcher (1855-1928), the uncle of World War 2 Admiral Frank Jack Fletcher. The elder Fletcher had five patents, all of which concerned guns - mounting, sighting and breech mechanisms. In the second case, a patent for a Ship's Telegraph (1,163,191) was granted to Admiral Harris Laning (1873-1941), the uncle of Heinlein's classmate Caleb Laning. Is this an indication that inventing ran in the Laning family?

All of the above discussion has focused on the U.S. Navy. As might be expected, innovation was occurring in other major navies. If we concentrate on the British Navy, a comparison with American naval innovation may be found in the article "Anglo-American Naval Inventors, 1890-1919: Last of a Breed." Fiske and Sims are mentioned on the

American side and Percy Scott for the British. The article gives a good picture of the various technical innovations of the time and the difficulties faced in getting some of these innovations accepted. My one quibble with the article is that the author appears to be of two minds with regard to the technical qualifications of Bradley Fiske. In the first paragraph, he makes a comparison of Fiske (and Scott) with Thomas Edison in their lack of a significant scientific or engineering background. But he later states that Fiske had better training in science and technology than the average naval officer of the time, even if had to acquire this training himself during the course of his naval career. The article noted that many of the innovators in both countries had retired or died either during the years of World War 1 or shortly thereafter. It closed by referring to the technical innovation which occurred in the American and Japanese (not British) navies during the interwar years.

We may attribute several causes to the innovation which occurred in the Navy during the interwar years. One cause was the obvious advance of technology, in fields such as aviation and electronics following World War 1. Many of the details of the developments in the field of electronics, both in general and with respect to the Navy, were presented in Chapter 5. The results of the yearly Fleet Problems were used to judge the effects of new technology and to discover problems that additional technological or tactical innovations would be required to solve. But the interwar years are primarily characterized by attempts to control by international agreement the ships and weapons that nations could employ.

There were a number of conferences on naval arms limitation during the 1920s and 1930s - The Washington Conference of 1921-22, the Geneva Naval Conference of 1927, the London Naval Conference of 1930, and the London Naval Conference of 1935. As a result of the conferences, several treaties were developed and agreed to by the attendees, but the one that dominated the interwar years was the Washington Treaty of 1922. The signatories were the United States, Britain, Japan, France and Italy. Such were the effects of this and the other treaties on the size and composition of the United States Navy during the interwar years that it gave rise to the term "treaty navy." The primary effect was to control the number, size and armament of capital ships (battleships and battle cruisers), but there were additional provisions to the treaty. The major provisions may be summarized as follows: (1) Retain certain named capital ships, (2) Britain and U.S. could complete specified capital ships but must dispose of others, (3) No new capital ships (except to replace accidental losses) for 10 years, (4) Tonnage ratios between nations for capital ships, (5) Replacement capital ships limited to 35,000 tons and 16-in guns, (6) Limits on individual and total tonnage of aircraft carriers, (7) Other warships limited to 10,000 tons and 8-in guns, and (8) Status quo on fortifications. The last of these meant that fortifications could not be made or improved on any island bases west of Hawaii.

The interwar years have been analyzed by many naval historians, either as part of a larger history of the Navy or as an individual work. Three very good works in the latter category are *The Treaty Navy* by James Hammond, *Battle Line: The United States Navy 1919-1939* by Thomas Hone and Trent Hone, and *Agents of Innovation* by John T. Kuehn. The first two works give a more general view of the interwar years, and in Hammond's work any discussion of innovation is restricted to one chapter. Kuehn's work, as the title indicates, is more directly concerned with the problem of innovation. He presents a review of the works by the other major researchers of the history of this era, and carefully analyzes their various claims and conclusions. Kuehn claims that the most influential provision of the treaty with regard to innovation was the last clause, the prohibition on the construction or improvement of island bases. It is his contention that this forced the development of type of navy that was able to range far and wide and to be able to provision at sea, without being dependent on island bases. This was in fact the type of navy that enabled the United States to win the war in the Pacific.

The constraints on the type of ships, their tonnage and their armament would have been bad enough, even if the U.S. Navy had been actually built up to the limits stated by the Treaty. But few new ships of any type were constructed by the United States during the 1920s and the early 1930s. Two important exceptions were the aircraft carriers U.S.S. *Lexington* and U.S.S. *Saratoga,* which were constructed using the hulls of battlecruisers that were prohibited by the Washington Treaty. Part of the problem was the failure of Congress to pass certain bills authorizing the construction of ships. Then there was the uncertainty of how to build within the limits. In the case of aircraft carriers, for example, the question was whether to build additional large carriers or a greater number of smaller carriers (such as was done with U.S.S. *Ranger*). Then there was the limitation on naval appropriations due the Great Depression. It was only when Franklin D. Roosevelt became president that things began to change. The world situation had begun to deteriorate and it was becoming clear to many people that the size of the Navy had to be increased, even if it only meant building up to the treaty limits as Britain and Japan had always been doing. One means which Roosevelt used to obtain funding to build ships was to employ National Industrial Recovery Act funds, so that men out of work because of the Great Depression would obtain jobs. The collapse of the treaty system finally occurred in 1935, with Japan stating that it would no longer adhere to the treaty limitations.

As one reads all of these works on the interwar years, it is discovered that any discussion of innovation focuses on what was earlier called the institutional variety. Ships are the main focus of these discussions. Much attention during the 1920s was focused on the conversion of earlier battleships from coal to oil. There was interest in modifying the gun turrets to increase the maximum range of the guns. One innovative ship design that was proposed but never developed was the flight deck or flying deck cruiser. The idea was to begin with a design for a 10,000 ton cruiser with either 6-in or 8-in guns, and then modifying the design to permit a small number of planes to be carried. This was seen as a means of making more planes available for support of operations without the need to construct island bases and without placing the very few large aircraft carriers then in existence at risk. One problem was whether the resulting design could be counted as a cruiser (on which there were no limits) or an aircraft carrier (which would count against the tonnage limit of the Washington Treaty). The entire project fell victim to the tight naval budgets, but some of the designs proposed at the time led to the light aircraft carriers built during the war using cruiser hulls.

The general attitude towards innovation in the Navy is summed up very well by Kuehn in his concluding chapter where he states that:

> The U.S. Navy of the interwar period was predisposed toward technological solutions to the problems posed at tactical, operational, and strategic levels of war—more so than the bulk of the U.S. Army (with the significant exception of its Air Corps). This is because navies generally are technologically oriented institutions. Even more than armies, navies rely on their equipment, not only in battle but in peace, to protect them from the enemy and the sea.

None of these discussions of interwar innovation that I have been able to locate make any mention of the individual variety suggested by the development of the mystery device. Such innovation did occur, as indicated by the examples presented. But what triggered the innovation in these cases, and other cases yet to be discovered? Was the system or device developed as the logical application of the improvements in technology occurring at the time? Or was it driven by a realization that to win battles with a Navy limited by treaties it was necessary to make improvements wherever possible, such as in communications and fire control? Or was the innovation inspired by something as unlikely as a science fiction story?

If anyone reading this were to decide to study the interwar years on their own in a bit more detail, it should be remembered that the naval education of Heinlein and his classmates occurred during this period, as well as the first dozen years of their naval careers. As the various events and conditions of the period are studied and analyzed, the reader should ask what effects there were upon the thinking of the members of the Class of 1929. We know the type of technical training that they received, but we do not know if the "treaty navy" environment in which they developed as naval officers in any way led them to become innovators of the type that have been presented in this chapter.

I close this chapter by emphasizing that unlike the naval innovators of the period when officers such as Bradley Fiske had to acquire on their own the technical training to supplement their naval training, the officers of Heinlein's era received improved technical training. Their training included the latest technologies such as radio, and they were also in a position to obtain postgraduate training in a number of fields. As stated in the chapter on the classmates, such advanced training would not be absolutely necessary for any innovation to have occurred, but would have placed the classmate in question in a better position to succeed as an innovator.

In the next chapter, Heinlein's stories are analyzed in an effort to identify the mystery device.

11

ANALYSIS OF STORIES

It has not been possible to say on the basis of the limited knowledge available concerning the classmates of Robert Heinlein which one may have been responsible for the development of the naval system - although Caleb Laning remains the front runner. The approach that remained for the identification of the gadget was to make a detailed analysis of the stories and attempt to select probable technology candidates for further analysis. Based on the information extracted in Chapter 2 from the letters between Heinlein and Campbell and a knowledge of the publishing schedule of *Astounding*, we are able to restrict ourselves to the first six of Heinlein's published works instead of having the consider the full range of his pre-war stories. The one serialized story in the group, "If This Goes On—," is presented as two distinct segments.

A very basic process was employed in analyzing the stories. Each story was read very carefully, multiple times, and every mention of *any* type of technology was noted. Lists were compiled of the sentences or sentence fragments containing these mentions. These lists are shown below. The lists were then reviewed and most of the items were discarded for the following reasons:

- Description too vague ("eye")

- Too general or obvious (radio, television)

- Pre-existing at time of story (bone conduction receiver)

- Unrealizable technology

- Derived from earlier work of SF (efficient power from sunlight)

- Technically feasible but no apparent naval connection

Only the ones that remained were considered for further analysis. These are the ones marked with **N** for Navy. I felt, however, that a few of the discarded items were of sufficient interest to consider in the next chapter. Such items are marked with **I** for Interesting.

The weaknesses of this approach have been recognized. First, it is possible that an item may have been missed on reading the story. For this reason, each of the stories was reviewed multiple times at intervals sufficient to provide some freshness to the process of examination. There were cases of items being missed on the first or second reading that were extracted on subsequent readings. It is hoped that no other instances of any mention of technology will have eluded my eye.

Second, although an attempt has been made to be as objective as possible, it might be that a particular mention of a technology has been rated such that it was discarded when it should have been retained for further examination. It should be obvious that the mental image or idea that was suggested to the classmate may not be identical to that produced in the mind of another reader such as myself. It is for this reason that the entire list for each story is being presented rather than just those items ultimately selected. I suspect that the greatest amount of feedback and discussion generated by this work will be connected with the story material, with someone questioning why a particular item was not considered for further analysis.

Another factor which must be considered is that the evaluation of the technology is being done from a distance of more than 70 years. This makes each of the technology evaluations very difficult. It requires a very broad knowledge of the level of technology in 1939 and 1940. I am in the position of evaluating references to technology that may or may not have existed 10 years before I was born.

Life-Line *Astounding Science-Fiction* August, 1939

Heinlein's first published story was concerned with the effects of the invention of the "chronovitameter," a device capable of predicting with great accuracy when a person will die. The inventor, Hugo Pinero, refuses to reveal the secrets of his invention to either a scientific association or to the press, only presenting in the latter case vague analogies to indicate its means of operation. It is demonstrated that having such precise knowledge concerning a person's death is not a good thing. Pinero's invention is the object of attempts by the insurance industry to prevent it from being used, first by legal means to suppress it and then finally to destroy it. The destruction of the machine also results in Pinero's death, and it is made clear to the reader that he knew that his own death was imminent. The very few mentions of technology are connected with descriptions of the device's operation.

1 The mass of equipment . . . . resembled a medico's office X-ray gear   (87)

2 the fact that electrical engineers can, by certain measurements, predict the exact location of a break in a transatlantic cable without ever leaving the shore   (87)

3 manner in which one measures the length of an electrical conductor   (88)

4 like measuring the length of a long corridor by bouncing an echo off the far end   (88)

Misfit *Astounding Science-Fiction* November, 1939

The story contains the first appearance of Andrew Jackson Libby, known in subsequent stories as "Slipstick" Libby. In this tale, he is one of a number of young men being sent to perform work in space converting an asteroid for use as a safe haven for travelers between the Earth and Mars. They are members of the Cosmic Construction Corps, an obvious analogy to the Depression-era Civilian Construction Corps. The story is primarily that of the education and maturation of Libby, and the discovery of his unique mathematical talents. The mentions of technology are, as might be expected, mostly connected with the spaceship used to transfer the workers, details of the operation of space suits, with a few concerned with the operations to convert the asteroid.

5 **I**   a line of old-fashioned glow-tubes   (54)

6   loud-speaker   (54)

7 **I**	the glow-tubes turned red	(54)
8 **I**	the glow-tubes flashed white	(54)
9	announcer	(54)
10	communicator on the bulkhead	(55)
11	television	(55)
12	composite conoid curve	(57)
13	potential energy of your fuel	(57)
14	plot the basic paraboloid	(57)
15	the ponderous integral calculator	(58)
16	blue glow of the instrument dials	(58)
17 **I**	stereoscopes	(58)
18 **I**	stereoscope	(59)
19	he brought two illuminated crosshairs in until they were exactly tangent to the upper and lower limbs of the disk	(59)
20	The suit is equipped with two-way telephony of a half mile radius	(60)
21	use of the external controls	(60)
22	continuous conveyor belt	(61)
23	portable atomic heater	(61)
24	clean it out with the blowers of the air conditioning plant	(62)
25	circular slide rule	(63)
26	his phones picked up the gunner's instructions	(63)

27	pressed his transmitter button	(63)
28	tore the electrodes from the detonator	(63)
29	durite . . . . which — usually — would confine even atomic disintegration	(65)
30	ballistic calculator, three Earth-tons of thinking metal that dominated the plotting room . . . . its integrators, three-dimensional cams, its differential gear trains, and silent gyroscopes	(65)
31	helio	(66)
32	gyros tumbled	(66)
33	audio circuit from Communications	(67)

Requiem *Astounding Science-Fiction* January, 1940

"Requiem" concerns the efforts of Delos D. Harriman, an elderly businessman, to get to the Moon. His interests since his younger days were in astronomy and the possibilities of space travel, but he was forced by the death of his father to forgo an academic or technical career and enter the world of business. By the time that he was able to consider taking such a trip, his advanced age and frail state of health would not permit him to make the trip legally. The story may be divided into his attempts to plan and finance an illegal trip, and then the trip itself. Harriman makes it to the Moon, but dies shortly after his arrival. As in "Misfit," most of the technical mentions are concerned with the details of spaceflight.

34	a single-jet type with fractional controls around her midriff	(80)
35	keys of the console and the semicircle of dials above	(80)
36	We don't even use standard juice in her—just gasoline and liquid air	(83)
37 **I**	interoffice 'visor	(85)

38	stratosphere yacht	(85)
39	install the extra fuel tanks, change the injectors and timers	(86)
40	pressure tests on the new tanks and the fuel lines	(87)
41	vacuum suits	(87)
42 **I**	a sextant and a good stadimeter and I'll set you down any place on the moon	(87)
43	radio hams, they were, and telescope builders, and airplane amateurs. We had science clubs, and basement laboratories, and science fiction leagues . . . . we wanted to build spaceships	(87-88)
44	desert runabout	(88)
45	strato yacht	(88)
46	auxiliary motor	(89)
47	involute approach curve	(89)
48	gave a short blast on two tangential jets opposed in couple to cause the ship to spin slowly about her longitudinal axis, and thereby create a slight artificial gravity	(89)
49 **I**	punch the stadimeter	(91)

If This Goes On— (Part 1) *Astounding Science-Fiction* **February, 1940**

Heinlein's first serialized story concerns the exploits of John Lyle in a future America ruled by a religious dictatorship. Originally a loyal member of the Army, stationed at New Jerusalem, Lyle is led by his love for Sister Judith into joining the Cabal, an underground force devoted to the overthrow of the Prophet Incarnate and the re-establishment of democratic government. Both installments of this story contain a large number of technical mentions, most in a military context, with others setting the general technical background. The first installment concludes with Lyle's efforts to escape the government authorities during his attempt to reach the Headquarters of the Cabal in the southwestern United States.

50	vortex guns and blaster, drilled with tanks	(10)
51	vortex pistol	(10)
52	paralysis bombs	(10)
53 **N**	telechronometer strapped to my wrist	(11)
54 **N**	My telechronometer, animated by the master clock at the Naval Observatory, tinkled its tiny chimes	(11)
55	characterless uniform script of the common lectrowriter	(14)
56	eye read it . . . . electrostated it	(14)
57	contents of my pockets must have been photographed	(15)
58	a small instrument which glowed with a dim violet radiance	(15)
59	neither eye nor ear	(15)
60	thin pencil of light flashed out	(17)
61	vibroblade	(18)
62	incinerator . . . . reduced to its primordial atoms in the fierce disintegration blast	(18)
63	air conditioner	(19)
64	hypodermic	(20)
65	vibroblade	(20)
66	a blade of cold energy	(20)
67	read it with my flash	(24)

68	covered with fine script which glowed with a faint radiance (24)	
69	paralysis bomb	(24)
70	incinerator chute	(25)
71	disintegrator	(25)
72	(paralysis) bomb	(25)
73	general alarm gongs	(26)
74	chronometer	(26)
75	cinema records	(27)
76	psychoanalysts were plotting curves	(27)
77	the bite of a hypodermic, the bruise of the injection	(28)
78	a rubber bandage tight about my upper arm, electrodes to my wrists, a tiny mirror to the pulse on my throat	(29)
79	a shadow show of my inner working sprang into view	(29)
80	heterodyne your normal senses	(29)
81 I	visiphone	(31)
82	supplies, modern machinery and modern weapons	(31)
83	applied miracles	(32)
84	psychodynamics	(32)
85	watched the card-sorter go through several thousand cards	(32)
86	old phonographic tutor stunt and wear earphones to bed	(34)

87 **I**	telechronometer	(36)
88	(passenger) rocket	(36)
89	transtube station	(36)
90	empty cartridge	(36)
91	station chronometer	(36)
92 **I**	the news broadcast flashing on the television screen at the forward end of the car .... My seat mate flicked a thumb towards the televue screen .... I snatched up the headphones hanging behind the seat in front of me (37)	
93	thin bulkhead of molded plastic	(39)
94	A small ship appeared on the horizon, swelled at once to a gaudy streamer of fire, circled the field, and landed about a quarter of a mile away. ... a speedy little pursuit job with fractional controls as well as gyros, seven tail jets set in a three-degree cone (40)	
95	vibrobolts	(40)
96	necessary power leads, and trigger connections	(40)
97	contact alarms	(40)
98	selenium circuit	(40)
99 **I**	retinal	(40)
100	telestat	(40)
101	lifted her bow ten degrees with the gyros	(40)

If This Goes On— (Part 2) *Astounding Science-Fiction* **March, 1940**

The second installment begins with John Lyle's continuing efforts to escape from the authorities. Following his arrival at Headquarters, the story line switches to the means by which the Cabal is preparing for its efforts to overthrow the Prophet Incarnate. The final portion of the installment is the attack on New Jerusalem and the destruction of the Prophet Incarnate. The attack is made on land, but the enormous tank-like vehicles presented are obvious land-based analogs of naval vessels. This casting of the battle in a pseudo-naval context, as well as the large number of technical mentions, has always made this the most likely story or story segment in which the device might appear.

102   the front of their closed composite search curve   (119)

103   cordons around every field, and retiring search curves from each (119)

104   old-fashioned, internal-combustion type plane   (119)

105 **I**   set the robot and jump   (119)

106   parachute jump from a rocket   (119)

107   rocket blast   (119)

108   (rocket) power plants   (119)

109 **N**   I examined the dead-reckoner and saw that the bug was on a point seventy-five miles west of Denver   (119)

110 **I**   set the altitude for twenty-five thousand feet and clamped the robot (119)

111   fire-proof crash suit   (119)

112   high-altitude pressure suit   (119)

113   police planes   (120)

114 **I**   I tripped the robot, and flung her about her gyros, tilting her nose up at a sharp angle. I set the robot to level off at fifty thousand feet (120)

115 **I**   set the robot to pick up to six hundred in five minutes   (120)

116	some sort of a flier	(122)
117	Ford family skycar	(122)
118	internal-combustion engines	(122)
119	cut the locked switch out of the circuit with a jury rig that would permit the engine to run	(122)
120	started the electric auxiliary	(122)
121	main engine started readily enough, and the rotor unfolded its airfoils	(123)
122	a bad valve knock in the engine, and a vibration in the rotor	(123)
123 I	any navigating equipment other than an old-style, uncompensated Sperry robot	(123)
124	radio receiver	(123)
125	pilot's alarm	(123)
126	helicopter	(123)
127	rocket plane	(123)
128	There were the same port and starboard Waterbury hydraulic universal speed gears controlling the traction surfaces, much the same instrument board—engine speed, port and starboard motor speeds, torque ratios . . . . See these here speed bars . . . . they tilt the disks in the Waterburies, and that controls the speed of each tread . . . . It's a Diesel-electric hookup. The Diesel runs the generator at constant speed, and the generator charges the main battery. The port and starboard motors run off the battery and deliver their power to the treads through the Waterburies. The Waterburies ain't nothing more nor less than a device to deliver the power from the motors to the treads at whatever rate you need it; they're variable speed gears that work hydraulically. This way the Diesel runs all the time at its most economical speed and the treads use power just as they need it.	(124)

129	ground-cruiser (124)	
130	I pressed the announcer, and heard the clicking whir of an out-of-date type of scanner (126)	
131	the televox inquired (126)	
132	helicopter (126)	
133 **N**	squeal of a radio beam (126)	
134	vortex of a tripod-mount blaster (127)	
135	elevator (127)	
136	recorder (128)	
137	blasters, pistols, squad guns, and siege guns (128)	
138	calipers and feather gauges and micrometers (128)	
139	in those branches of physical science commonly called "miracles" because of their application in producing effects calculated to awe the ignorant masses (131)	
140	sensitive eye and ear devices and by automatic mines (132)	
141	a passenger transtube of the progressive magnetic field type, and a little electric railroad (132)	
142	electrical equipment, laboratory supplies, and a constant stream of vortex pistols, paralysis bombs, portable blasters, and small arms of every sort (132)	
143	rocket and disintegrator (133)	
144 **I**	dictaphone and dictawriter (133)	
145	the television and radio stations (133)	
146	the power supply of forty-six of the largest cities (133)	

147	major surface transportation and freight routes	(133)
148	phoning the data to the calculating room	(133)
149	ticker	(133)
150	main communications room	(136)
151	television screen . . . . stereoscopic and in full color	(137)
152	film . . . . made a print	(137)
153	giant television screen	(137)
154	trick cinematography	(138)
155	network of telecasters	(138)
156	telecasts	(138)
157	telecasting stations	(138)
158	televisors	(138)
159	telecast projections	(138)
160	short blast from a tripod mounted on the hillside	(138)
161	the miracle telecast	(140)
162	Rockets are not well adapted to attack on fortified positions in any case. They can't carry enough pay load for heavy bombing, and must travel at too high a speed for accurate bombing, too. They are principally useful for high-speed, long-range reconnaissance; protection of bombing helicopters against enemy rockets, and fighting among themselves for control of the air.	(142)
163	heavy bombing helicopters	(142)
164	antiaircraft battery	(142)

165	thirty-four land cruisers, thirteen of them modern battle wagons, the rest light cruisers and obsolescent craft	(142)
166	armored transports	(142)
167 N	We had improvised a flag-plotting room in the communications room just abaft of the conning tower, tearing out the long-range televisor to make room for the battle tracker and concentration plot.	(142)
168 N	my jury-rigged tracker	(142)
169	telescreens	(143)
170 N	At 12:32 the televisors went out. The enemy had analyzed our frequency variation pattern, matched us and blown every tube in the circuit	(143)
171 N	Radio went out at 12:37, jammed and then blown.	(143)
172 N	Shift to light-phone circuits	(143)
173 N	Keep contact in formation with sonics.	(143)
174 N	He hooked us up via telephone, using infrared beams for the ship-to-ship circuits.	(143)
175 N	Bi-aural sonic range-finders kept the formation intact, each craft sending out its own sonic frequency.	(143)
176 N	I passed on the order, and cut my tracker out of the circuit for fifteen minutes. It wasn't built to handle so many variables at such high speeds, and there was no sense in overloading the relays. Nineteen minutes later the last transport had checked in by phone; I made a preliminary setup on the tracker, threw the starting switch and let the correction data come in. For a couple of minutes I was very busy balancing the data, hands moving swiftly among the keys and knobs; then the integrators took hold with a satisfying hum, and I reported: "Tracking, sir!"	(144)
177	booster guns . . . . In an ordinary single-explosion gun the propelling gas pressure is highest when the shell is near the breech,	

and falls off rapidly as the shell approaches the muzzle. The booster gun has a series of firing chambers located along the side of the barrel in addition to the main firing chamber at the breech. The charge in each of these is fired through an electrical timing gear by the passage of the shell itself so that they fire in order as the shell passes them. Thus the booster charges maintain maximum pressure on the base of the shell right up to the time it leaves the muzzle, giving it an enormous muzzle velocity and terrific striking power   (144-45)

178   periscope   (145)

179 **N**   Telephone circuits using infrared-beam transmission   (145)

180 **N**   we checked our dead reckoning by means of the data given by the sonic range-finders   (145)

181 **N**   Even after the sonics failed   (146)

182   The dead reckoners of a tread-driven cruiser are surprisingly accurate. It's like this—every time the tread lays down it measures the ground it passes over. A little differential gadget to compare the speeds of the port and starboard treads, another gadget to do vector sums, and a gyro compass hook-in, to check and correct your vector addition, and you have a dead reckoner that will trace your course over fifteen miles of rough terrain and tell within a yard where you have ended up.   (146)

183   gas helmets   (147)

184   the setup shown by my battle tracker   (147)

185 **N**   torn off the current plot from my tracker   (147)

186   full communication mesh   (147)

187   fire-control station   (147)

188   chronograph   (147)

189   chronometer   (148)

190   forward hydraulic jacks   (149)

191   fire control tower in the turret (149)

192   blasters   (149)

193   engine rooms   (149)

194   radio, television, and other means of influencing masses of people simultaneously   (151)

Let There Be Light *Super Science Stories* May, 1940

    This short story, the only one of the group not to appear in *Astounding*, is a basic invention story. The original objective of the main characters was to develop "cold" light, a more efficient means of converting electricity into light than the incandescent bulb. The discovery, once made, led to a similarly efficient means of converting sunlight into electricity. The villain of the story is presented as the power industry, which fears the effects of such a device upon their revenues and possible survival. The technical mentions are mainly concerned with the supposed principles of such an invention and how it is developed and tested.

195   cold light   (34)

196   centrifuge   (36)

197   Even if you could manage to work out an inductance-capacitance circuit with a natural resonant frequency within the visual band (38)

198   quartz crystal that has a natural frequency of its own   (38)

199   crystal that would have a natural frequency in the octave of visible light   (38)

200   a gray screen, about the size and shape of the top of a card table . . . . The screen glowed brilliantly, but not dazzlingly, and exhibited a mother-of-pearl iridescence   (38)

201 **I** Look, Dad—do you know what that screen up there is made out of? Common, ordinary clay. It's an allotropic aluminum silicate; cheap and easy to make from any clay, or ore, that contains aluminum. I can use Bauxite, or cryolite, or most anything. (38-39)

202 rigging two cold light screens face to face (40)

203 **I** The sun pours out about a horse power and a half, or one and one eighth kilowatts on every square yard of surface on the earth that is faced directly towards the sun. Atmospheric absorption cuts that down about a third, even at high noon over the Sahara desert. That would give one horsepower per square yard. With the sun just rising we might not get more than one-third horsepower per square yard here. At fifteen percent efficiency that would be about five hundredths of a horsepower. The screen is a yard square; it gives five hundredths of a horsepower. (40-41)

204 another that will be atonic—one that will vibrate to any wavelength (41)

205 screens to radiate in the infra-red . . . . heating units of any convenient size or shape (41)

206 take power from the sun at nearly one hundred percent efficiency . . . . deliver it as cold light . . . . as heat . . . . as electric power (42)

207 electric runabout that gets its power from the sun while its (sic) parked at the curb (43)

The Roads Must Roll *Astounding Science-Fiction* June, 1940

The final story is concerned with the operation of the Roads, the conveyor-strip means of transport which are a feature of a future United States. Seen as an answer to the growing problems of automotive travel, the Roads are powered by the Douglas-Martin Solar Reception screens introduced in "Let There Be Light." Although the technical details of the Roads form a large part of the story, the primary focus is political. The main character is the Chief Engineer of the Roads in a section of California, who must deal with a seizure of control of the Roads. The seizure was made by a group of the workers who maintain and operate the Roads, led by a dissatisfied member of the Chief Engineer's staff. The workers have been led to feel that they deserve more respect and power because of the great dependence of society and the economy upon the Roads.

208   tell a rotor bearing from a field coil   (10)

209   antinoise helmet   (10)

210 I   office intercommunicator   (11)

211   replaced the handset . . . . faded from the visor screen   (11)

212   Antipodes ship   (12)

213   large visor screen mounted on the opposite wall   (12)

214   semicircular control desk, which was backed by a complex instrument board   (12)

215   electric staircase   (13)

216   conveyor strip   (13)

217   glassite partition . . . . wind break   (13)

218   the driving mechanism concealed beneath the moving strips   (13)

219   portable telephone   (13)

220   Sun-power screen   (14)

221   moving stairways, powered with the Douglas-Martin Solar Reception Screens   (15)

222   first mechanized road   (15)

223   wide, low buildings whose roofs were covered with solar power screens   (15)

224	Tensiometer readings .... synchrotachometer readings	(15)
225	moving model of the road, spread out before him in the main control room	(15)
226	control board chronometer	(17)
227	rotors	(17)
228	strip can't part .... built up of overlapping sections	(17)
229	strip was hardly more than a conveyor belt	(17)
230	signal light of the portable telephone glowed red	(19)
231	television theaters	(20)
232	the Sun-power screens glowed with a faint opalescent radiance, their slight percentage of inefficiency as transformers of radiant Sun power to available electrical power being evidenced as a mild induced radioactivity	(21)
233	electromechanical integrator	(22)
234	glowed a green line of arrows	(23)
235 I	glow tube	(23)
236 I	public telebooth .... visor screen	(23)
237	tumblebugs, pistols and sleep-gas bombs	(24)
238	reconnaissance car	(24)
239	red monochrome of a neon arc	(24)
240	its great, drum-shaped armature revolving slowly around the stationary field coils in its core	(24)
241	Bridging the gaps between the rotors were the slender rollers, crowded together like cigars in box, in order that the strip might have a continuous rolling support. The rollers were supported by	

steel girder arches through the gaps of which he saw row after row of rotors in staggered succession, the rotors in each succeeding row turning over more rapidly than the last.   (24)

242   flashlight . . . . the beam focused down to a slender, intense needle of light   (25)

243   ovoid in shape, and poised on two centerline wheels   (25)

244   built-in communicator   (25)

245   tumblebugs—small, open monocycles   (26)

246   Each rotor . . . . is to be cut out, then hooked into the Stockton control board. It will be a haywire rig, with no safety interlocks   (28)

247   helmet . . . . leaving the antinoise ear flaps up   (28)

248   A tumblebug does not give a man dignity, since it is about the size and shape of a kitchen stool, gyro-stabilized on a single wheel. But it is perfectly adapted to patrolling the maze of machinery down inside, since it can go through an opening the width of a man's shoulders, is easily controlled, and will stand patiently upright, waiting, should its rider dismount   (30-31)

249   television and audio communicator   (31)

250 I   a hush-a-phone which he had plugged into the telephone jack . . . . He snatched at the soft rubber mask of the phone, jerking it away from the man's mouth so violently that he could feel the bone-conduction receiver grate between the man's teeth.   (31)

251   electric push button, attached to a long cord   (33)

252   the strips must be cross-connected with safety interlocks   (34)

253   emergency-stop button   (35)

254   relay station   (35)

255   televisor at the control desk   (37)

256   they had to cross-connect around two wrecked subsector control boards   (37)

The next chapter will consider those items marked with an **I** in the preceding list.

12

INTERESTING, BUT NOT THE ANSWER

In his works, Heinlein made extensive mentions of different types of technology. A large part of my research was to become familiar with the types of technology of his time so that it could be determined if any concept was in advance of the level of the available technology and would therefore be a candidate for the mystery device. A number of the devices or concepts mentioned in the stories were eliminated as possible candidates on that basis. Others are worth mentioning only because I felt that their background was particularly interesting.

Glow-Tubes

In "Misfit" we have several mentions of what Heinlein calls glow-tubes:

> There were no ports, but a line of old-fashioned glow-tubes ran around the junction of bulkhead and ceiling and trisected the overhead....

> By the time each boy had found a place on the deck and the master-at-arms had checked the pad under his head, the glow-tubes turned red....

> An indefinite time later the glow-tubes flashed white....

And then we have a single mention in "The Roads Must Roll":

. . . . to a door let in the wall, which gave into a narrow stairway lighted by a single glow tube.

If we were to only consider the first quote from "Misfit" and the single quote from "Roads," I would be willing to say that Heinlein was simply speaking of the type of fluorescent lights that we still use today. They first appeared on the market in 1938. They were demonstrated in 1939 at the New York World's Fair and the San Francisco Exposition. The one problem is that simple fluorescent lights would not be able to change between red and white as described in "Misfit." Although fluorescent lighting had just appeared at the time that Heinlein was writing this story, he establishes the sense of the future by referring to them as "old-fashioned."

Stereoscope

In "Misfit" we have the following scene, with the Captain entering the control room as they are attempting to locate a particular asteroid:

> He walked over by the lookouts at the stereoscopes and peered out at the star-flecked blackness . . . . His mate read the exterior dials of the stereoscope. "Plus point two, abaft one point three; slight drift astern." . . . . The lookout hurriedly twisted the knobs of his instrument, but the captain nudged him aside.
>
> "I'll do that, son." He fitted his face to the double eye guards and surveyed a little silvery sphere, a tiny moon. Carefully he brought two illuminated crosshairs in until they were exactly tangent to the upper and lower limbs of the disk. "Mark!"

Here we have a case where we can be misled by the term used by Heinlein. A stereoscope is the name given to the means of viewing a 3-dimensional image by presenting a slightly different view to each eye. Some of my older readers might remember the Viewmaster with the disk of photographs.

What Heinlein seems to be describing is a type of rangefinder. Given his naval background, it makes sense to consider how range was found optically, in the days before radar.

The British were the first to employ a two-man rangefinder which used the length of the ship as the baseline. One viewer was at the bow and one at the stern. Each pointed the rangefinder at the target and noted the angle to the centerline of the ship. Knowing the distance between the two observers and the two angles, it was possible to determine the distance. There are several drawbacks. If there are multiple targets available, you must be sure that both are pointing at the same one. The information must be communicated rapidly to some location where the calculation can be made. Finally, the system is useless if the target is located almost or directly ahead or astern.

A <u>coincidence</u> rangefinder consists of a long horizontal tube, with lenses and prisms at each end. The image of the target is brought in from each end. A split image is developed with the upper part of the image from the optics at one end and the lower part from the optics at the other end. These two images are viewed in a single eyepiece. Adjustment is made to the angle of the line of sight of one input to bring the two split images together - into coincidence. When this is done, the distance separating the optics and the angle determine the range. The longer the tube the more accurate it is at a greater range, but there is a practical limit to how long you can make such a tube which is sufficiently rigid and still able to be able to be manipulated.

The <u>stereoscopic</u> rangefinder may be thought of as a pair of binoculars with the inputs widely separated as in the coincidence rangefinder. Each input feeds a separate eyepiece. Operation depends on the user having perfect binocular vision. In each optical path within the rangefinder were located reticles with markings. The images coming in along each optical path are adjusted until they appear to be at the same distance as the reticle markings. Then one reads the distance from the instrument.

During World War I, the British used coincidence rangefinders and the Germans used stereoscopic rangefinders. During the 1930s, the United States adopted the stereoscopic rangefinder. Can we assume that this is the type with which Heinlein would have been familiar?

We must be careful in interpreting what Heinlein says in "Misfit": "Carefully he brought two illuminated crosshairs in until they were exactly tangent to the upper and lower limbs of the disk." The reference to double eye guards would imply that a stereoscopic rangefinder is being used. Once the range has been found using the rangefinder function, the crosshairs would be used to determine the angular width. Knowing the range and angular width would give the true size. In the revised story, the determination of the range is performed using radar.

Dictawriter

In the original version of "If This Goes On—," we have a description of one of the duties of the principal character, John Lyle:

It was part of my duties to be present at these meetings and record them by dictaphone and dictawriter.

Here we have two devices being mentioned. The name Dictaphone was applied in 1907 to devices which used wax cylinders for the recording of dictation for business purposes. The wax cylinder system was used until 1947 when it was replaced by a new recording technique. The second device, the dictawriter, is given a different name in the revised version of "If This Goes On—":

My own girl was ill and I had borrowed Maggie from G-2 to operate the voicewriter, since she was cleared for top secret.

What is being described is a device that would convert speech to some form of readable text, either English or some phonetic language. Calling it a dictawriter in the first case is just a logical assumption that if some device existed in the future, it would be made by the same company that made the real Dictaphone. But then one must ask the question, if the dictawriter was sufficiently reliable, why would the Dictaphone still be needed? Heinlein seems to have realized this in the revision and only mentions the voicewriter.

At the beginning of the original version of "Coventry" we have a similar device:

MacKinnon glanced with distaste at the tiny microphone hanging near his face. The knowledge that any word spoken in its range would be broken down into typed phonetic symbols by a recording voder somewhere in the Hall of Archives inhibited his speech.

All of these means of converting speech to text or symbols appear to derive from one of the many futuristic devices featured in *Ralph 124C 41+*. Although Ralph never gives a specific name to his invention, in Chapter IX he describes the marks which the machine makes as the phonolphabet, i.e. phonetic alphabet.

Stadimeter

In "Requiem," during their preparation for the flight to the moon, Captain McIntyre informs Delos D. Harriman that they have not yet received the lunar ephemerides, tables which give the positions of heavenly bodies, in this case the moon. He then states:

This guff about how hard it is to navigate from here to the Moon is hokum to impress the public. After all, you can *see* your destination—it's not like ocean navigation. Gimme a sextant and a good stadimeter and I'll set you down any place on the Moon you like—without opening an almanac or a star table—just from a general knowledge of the speeds involved.

You should recognize the stadimeter from Chapter 10 as an instrument for determining the distance to an object on the basis of a measurement of its angular extent. Invented by Bradley Fiske for naval purposes, it was proposed by Heinlein for use in travel to the moon. A measurement of the angular width of the moon and its known diameter would allow one to determine its distance. The accuracy of the distance measurement depends on how well the instrument could be used to determine the angular width.

Visiphone

In quite a few of his stories, Heinlein made use of two-way visual communication, what he usually but not always called the "visiphone." The first appearance of such a device is in "Requiem," where Delos D. Harriman is contacted in his office by his secretary. This is not accomplished by a simple intercom, as the story states that "The interoffice 'visor flashed into life." It is just a brief mention, almost lost in the scene, but there is no doubt as to what he is describing.

The first explicit use of the term "visiphone" occurs in the first installment of "If This Goes On—" where John Lyle, recently rescued from the clutches of the Chief Inquisitor, is investigating the working of the Cabal. He states that the Cabal is able to make use of the visiphone circuits of the department store run by a member.

In "The Roads Must Roll," extensive use is made of visual telephone conversation, although the term "visiphone" is never used once in the story. Chief Engineer Gaines uses such devices to communicate with his wife, his subordinates and the leader of the faction who have taken over control of the roads. When talking to his wife, it first appears that he is only using a conventional telephone, but then mention is made of the conclusion of the conversation at which point the image of his wife "faded from the visor screen." Gaines' assistant takes the hourly reports from the various sectors over the "visor screen." During the confusion resulting from the stopping of one of the strips, Gaines loses contact with his headquarters and to place a call is forced to make use of a public "telebooth," after first ejecting the person who was using it. Successive uses of such visual devices occur using a large screen in a subsector watch office and the communication device built into cars used to travel in the service ways beneath the roads.

Two way visual communication also occurred extensively in *FUTL*. The use of visual communication of this type continued through many of Heinlein's works. Other stories featuring the idea include "Blowups Happen," "Sixth Column," "—We Also Walk Dogs," and "Methuselah's Children."

As we know that Heinlein was familiar with the works of Hugo Gernsback, we may assume that this is where he got the idea. In *Ralph*, we have many instances of two-way visual communication. It is how Ralph actually meets Alice the first time. The device is called the telephot.

Inflight Entertainment

In the first installment of "If This Goes On—" John Lyle is traveling on a passenger rocket from Cincinnati to Kansas City. The flight is nearly full and Lyle does not have the luxury of an unoccupied seat next to him. He comments on the actions of his seat mate:

He gave his attention to the news broadcast flashing on the television screen at the forward end of the car.

I felt a nudge some ten minutes later, and looked around. My seat mate flicked a thumb toward the televue screen. There displayed was a scene in some large city, presumably in the United States. . . . I snatched up the headphones hanging behind the seat in front of me and listened.

Anyone who has flown commercially should be familiar with the screens and earphones used for inflight entertainment. The first stated use of a movie in flight was a promotional film for the city of Chicago shown on an amphibious aircraft conducting tour flights in that city. This occurred in August 1921 and was obviously a silent film. A flight in May 1932 made use of a television receiver instead of a film projector. It is not clear when the use of headphones became standard. So the concept of providing some form of inflight entertainment would have been known to Heinlein from a newspaper or magazine article.

Retinal

At the very end of the first installment of "If This Goes On—," we have John Lyle, disguised as Adam Reeves by plastic surgery and fingerprint modification, being detained by the authorities. A blood sample was taken, and while Lyle is being held, he overhears the conversation from an adjacent room:

"Oh-o! Make a priority call to Main Laboratory; we're taking him into town for a retinal."

I needed no one to interpret these cryptic remarks. I was caught! Since my blood type didn't check, they knew positively that I was not Reeves. Once in Denver, and the blood-vessel pattern of the retina of either of my eyes photographed, it would be just a matter of time until they knew with certainty, my real identity—the time necessary to telestat it to the Bureau of Investigation, and receive a report.

There are existing security systems which make use of the uniqueness of the patterns of the blood vessels of the retina. Here we have the use of the concept in a story from 1940. But what was the source of this concept?

Two ophthalmologists from New York State, Drs. Carleton Simon and Isodore Goldstein, described the use of the retinal blood vessel patterns in their 1935 paper "A New Scientific Method of Identification." It may be assumed that Heinlein became familiar with the concept through either a 1936 *New York Times* article or a similar article which no doubt appeared in other newspapers that presented its possible use in identifying criminals who had made use of plastic surgery to change their appearance or attempted to modify or obliterate their fingerprint patterns.

Is it possible that a detective story published in the late 1930s made use of this concept, or was Heinlein the first to employ identification by retinal patterns in any work of fiction?

Robot

In the second installment of "If This Goes On—" we have multiple appearances of the word "robot" as John Lyle is attempting to escape in the rocket craft he has stolen. He first states that in an older type of plane, he could just "set the robot and jump." As Lyle begins to work out the details of his escape, he "set the altitude for twenty-five thousand feet and clamped the robot." When he had figured out how to safely bail out, he then "tripped the robot, and flung her about her gyros, tilting her nose up at a sharp angle" and "then set the robot to level off at fifty thousand feet." Just before he jumped at fifty thousand feet and three hundred miles an hour, he "set the robot to pick up to six hundred in five minutes."

After Lyle reaches the ground, he has a chance to steal a skycar, a vehicle cable of both ground travel and flight. After he takes to the air, he discovers that the craft is somewhat limited in its capabilities with a "lack of any navigating equipment other than an old-style uncompensated Sperry robot." But he still makes use of the robot to permit him to continue to travel while he sleeps.

Heinlein is clearly speaking in both instances of some sort of automatic pilot. But why the use of the term "robot"? It was finally possible to locate two *New York Times* articles from just before Wiley Post's solo around the world flight in 1933 which speak of his intended use of a "robot" pilot. Although the maker of this automatic pilot was not mentioned in either of the articles, it was developed and built by the Sperry Corporation, which matches with the robot for the family skycar.

In the revised version of the "If This Goes On—," all mentions of "robot" in reference to the stolen rocket plane are omitted. The method of escape was changed in a manner that required a more complex autopilot involving electronic circuitry employing transistors. The only mention of the term "robot" that is retained is with regard to the stolen skycar.

"Robot" also appears in *FUTL* on pages 98, 200 and 201. All cases refer to the very intelligent autopilot used in the personal skycar.

In *Rocket Ship Galileo*, the autopilot of the *Galileo* is referred to as a robot.

Light and Power

An examination of "Let There Be Light" did not reveal any concept which could be connected with the mystery gadget. It is suggested, however, that this is yet another case where Heinlein was influenced by Hugo Gernsback. In his novel *Ralph 124C 41+*, Gernsback described the means by which electric power is generated from sunlight:

In 1909 Cove of Massachusetts invented a thermo-electric sun-power-generator which could deliver ten volts and six amperes, or one-sixtieth kilowatt in a space of twelve square feet. [Error here – 60 watts is not one-sixtieth (0.0166...) of a kilowatt, but is six percent (0.060) of a kilowatt.] Since that time inventors by the score had busied themselves to perfect solar generators, but it was not until the year 2469 that the Italian 63A 1243 invented the photoelectric cell, which revolutionized entire electric industry. This Italian discovered that by derivatives of the Radium-M class, in conjunction with Tellurium and Arcturium, a photo-electric element could be produced which was strongly affected by the sun's ultraviolet rays and in this condition was able to transfer heat directly into electrical energy, without losses of any kind.

What we have is a double-talk explanation of the first order, even invoking the use of nonexistent elements such as the "derivatives of the Radium-M class" and "Arcturium." The approach developed by Heinlein's characters, while vague in the details of the manufacture of the screen, does not invoke any mystical elements. As explained by Archie Douglas:

Look, Dad—do you know what that screen up there is made out of? Common, ordinary clay. It's an allotropic aluminum silicate; cheap and easy to make from any clay, or ore, that contains aluminum. I can use Bauxite, or cryolite, or most anything.

Gernsback's explanation does not make direct use of the ultraviolet content of the sunlight to generate the electricity, but uses it to put his material into some condition that will convert the heat generated by the absorption of visible and ultraviolet into electric current. Heinlein's device responds, in the earlier version, to visible light only, but the discovery is then made which means that the screen will respond to a wider range of the spectrum of sunlight, giving a higher power output.

No figures are given for the ultimate system in use in Gernsback's work, only for the original system of 1909 explained by Ralph. It was stated that this device could generate 60 watts from twelve square feet. Heinlein also gives figures only for the visible light system. The panel under the conditions of sunrise as opposed to high noon, produced about 37.5 watts from a square yard or 50 watts from 12 square feet. It would be assumed that a larger output would be obtained at high noon. Although it is stated that the screen capable of converting over the wider range could produce a thousand horsepower for the area of the factory roof, we cannot calculate its efficiency without knowing that area.

Bone Conduction Receiver

In "The Roads Must Roll," there are many descriptions of the high noise level under which the engineers and technicians must operate among the machinery which drives the strips. Ordinary conversation would not be possible when one considers the hearing protection which would be worn under such circumstances. For face-to-face communication, a specialized sign language is described in one scene. In a later scene, during the attempt to retake control of the strips from the technicians who have seized control of a sector, another means of communication is briefly described. The advancing forces encounter a technician communicating with special type of phone suited to the environment:

> He snatched at the soft rubber mask of the phone, jerking it away from the man's mouth so violently that he could feel the bone-conduction receiver grate between the man's teeth.

The problem is not in the person speaking, as the rubber mask would contain what Heinlein refers to in a preceding paragraph as a hush-a-phone. This simply channels the voice of the speaker into the telephone transmitter. The problem is providing the response to the person in the high noise environment. One solution would be to amplify the sound from the telephone receiver and feed it into the ear protectors being worn. This approach would not have been practical in Heinlein's time, with the user required to carry around a vacuum tube amplifier and the bulky batteries necessary to power it. His solution was to make use of a device described in Chapter 8. This was the "Acoustic Apparatus" patented by Hugo Gernsback. Also known as the "ossophone," it enables a person to hear by the process of bone conduction, with the receiver clamped between the teeth.

The next chapter considers those items marked with **N** in Chapter 11, indicating that they should be analyzed in greater detail for a possible naval connection.

13

DEVICE ANALYSIS

The purpose of this chapter will be to provide a detailed analysis of all of the devices marked **N** in Chapter 11, meaning they appeared to be technically feasible and had a possible naval connection. The first device is from the first installment of "If This Goes On—," and the other six are from the second installment of "If This Goes On—." The last four occur during the final land assault on New Jerusalem.

All of these devices must be interpreted in a naval context. This is particularly true in the case of the assault, where it is important to recognize that it is a naval battle that has been transposed by Heinlein to land. Heinlein did not attempt to disguise this as the large ground attack vehicles are referred to as cruisers, light cruisers and battle wagons (battleships). Therefore, each description of a device that appears within the story must be interpreted not as presented, but in the context of its possible use in a naval environment.

The process for presenting each candidate device and then analyzing it to determine the likelihood of it being the mystery device will be according to the following steps:

1. Presentation of all references to that device within the first installment of "If This Goes On—" for the telechronometer or within the second installment for all other devices (with page numbers in *Astounding Science-Fiction* from February 1940 or March 1940).

2. Presentation of all references to that device, if any, in the later version of the story (with page numbers from the Baen paperback edition of *Revolt in 2100 and Methuselah's Children*).

3. Discussion of any relevant differences between the versions, and what these differences might imply.

4. Any other possible references to the device, either in other stories not within the time frame being considered or in other material from the Heinlein Archives.

5. Historical and Technical analyses.

6. Related naval systems from World War 2, if any.

One thing that makes any analysis difficult is that we do not know the degree to which Heinlein was familiar with work being performed in any of the technical areas to be discussed. He had received a good technical education at the Naval Academy from 1925 through 1929 and had served in the Fleet until his medical discharge in 1934. But his specialty was gunnery. It is impossible to know the degree to which he would have become familiar with equipment or development work outside of his area of specialization during his period of active duty. There is also the question as to the extent he was kept apprised of new developments after 1934 by classmates still serving on active duty or by such material that was released to the public. Any of his suggestions could have been made in ignorance of actual work being performed by the Navy.

Also to be considered are the different views of the device description. First, we have what was on Heinlein's mind when he wrote it. Then we must consider the classmate, who was a person with a nearly identical naval education to Heinlein and who had over ten years of active duty experience. What came to the classmate's mind when he read the portion of the story containing the device description? Finally, we have below my own interpretation of the device descriptions. To lead to the correct device, my interpretation must correlate closely with that of the classmate.

A. Telechronometer

1. I glanced at the telechronometer strapped to my wrist.   (11)

    My telechronometer, animated by the master clock at the Naval Observatory, tinkled its tiny chimes.   (11)

    I glanced at my telechronometer, and was surprised to see how late it was.   (36)

2.   I had glanced at my wrist chrono . . . .   (9)

. . . . when my chrono had chimed the quarter hour.   (11)

3. The first two quotes from the serialized version clearly establish that what Heinlein was describing was a timepiece that was small enough to fit on the wrist and was controlled by radio signals from the Naval Observatory. The third quote adds nothing to this description. The two quotes which appear in the later version remove any reference to the synchronization to the Naval Observatory. The shorter term "chrono" could be seen as slang for telechronometer, but could as easily just mean chronometer, with no implication of external synchronization.

4. The term "telechronometer" also appears in the original versions of "Coventry," "Blowups Happen" and "Methuselah's Children."

5. The telechronometer corresponds to the radio-controlled watches that were made possible by advances in electronic miniaturization. These watches first appeared for sale in 1990. Such watches (and radio-controlled clocks) receive time signals in the United States from WWVB, which is operated by NIST, not the U.S. Naval Observatory.

But this is not to say that Heinlein was wrong in specifying the Naval Observatory. Beginning in 1865, Western Union began transmitting time signals from the Naval Observatory by telegraph to various locations in Washington, DC. This service was expanded to railroads and then to other cities. In these early cases, a person would have to set the clock manually on the basis of the received signals. This still allowed for some degree of variability in accuracy. In 1879, however, Western Union made clocks available to railroads that would be directly set by telegraph time signals. Just before the time designated for synchronization, a message would be sent out for all telegraph operators to switch their local clocks to the main telegraph. A master synchronizing pulse would then be sent to all clocks.

Transmission of time signals by radio did begin with the Naval Observatory in 1904, with a regular service established in 1905. These signals were employed in the same manner as the original telegraph time signals, to assist in setting a clock or watch manually. The concept of using radio to set the clock directly, as in the Western Union clock, was presented in an article published by an Englishman in 1910. Various techniques were tried over the years by inventors in different countries. A clock incorporating any one of these experimental techniques might have been described in the literature or even demonstrated, but none ever went into production. The first production radio-controlled clock did not appear until 1986, followed in a few years by watches.

6. On a ship, knowledge of the accurate time is necessary for proper navigation. Navigational matters are the job of the Quartermaster. This included, in the past, the daily winding and checking of the ship's chronometers. The chronometer is a sturdy, accurate timepiece with a gimbal mounting to minimize disturbances by the ship's motion. Large ships had as many as three chronometers. One way to check the accuracy of a chronometer is by determining local noon by the position of the sun. But this is possible only if you know your exact position. The other method, as outlined in the 1946 training book for *Quartermaster 3rd Class and 2nd Class* (NAVPERS 10023) involves the use of the time signals from the Naval Observatory. The time signals commence five minutes before the end of the hour. Each minute is identified by the omission of certain ticks within the last 10 seconds. Quoting from the training book:

> The minutes are identified as follows:
>
> 55th minute . . . . 51st-second beat omitted
> 56th minute . . . . 52nd-second beat omitted
> 57th minute . . . . 53rd-second beat omitted
> 58th minute . . . . 54th-second beat omitted
>
> In all but the last minute, there is also a silence for the 56th through 59th second; in the LAST (59th) minute, there is a 9-second silence preceding the end-of-hour signal.

Clearly, the vacuum tube technology of the 1930s and 1940s did not permit the development of a radio-controlled watch such as worn by John Lyle. A naval system inspired by the telechronometer would have been a piece of electronic equipment on a ship that would provide accurate time on the basis of signals from the Naval Observatory or other source. But I can find no indication that any such work was done in the World War 2 time frame. An Internet search revealed a reminiscence from the U.S.S. *Hancock* in 1963 which still has the Quartermaster using radio signals to manually set the chronometers:

> It would all start in the Chart house, where the three ship's chronometers were kept. At least once a day the Quartermaster would crank up a radio receiver and tune it to a special frequency to listen in on a special transmitting station. The station in the

Western Pacific had the call letters of JJY and stateside WWV, plus one other. These stations broadcast the Greenwich mean time in one minute increments. A little voice would announce the upcoming minute after-the-hour and then a series of clicking tones would be transmitted sounding like a ticking clock. Hence the term getting a time-tic. One special highlighted tone would announce the exact time by the minute. The Quartermaster would have his pocket/stop watch set for the upcoming minute, and listen carefully for the upcoming ticks and final tone signal. When the tone was heard, the QM would start the watch.

The writer then speculated whether it is currently done on a purely electronic basis. Whether it is or not, and when such a change might have taken place, it was clearly after 1963. So we can definitely say that no such system existed in World War 2.

B. Airborne Dead-Reckoner

1. I examined the dead-reckoner and saw that the bug was on a point seventy five miles west of Denver.   (119)

2. The dead-reckoner showed me some seventy-five miles from Denver and headed north of west . . . .   (85)

3. The only observation is that the original story is a bit more precise in its reference to the "bug" which indicates the position of the craft. Neither of these quotes or any others to be presented contain the term "airborne," but this may be inferred from the context.

4. There are two quotes which must be considered, one major and one minor. The first quote occurs in *For Us, The Living* (*FUTL*):

> Below the ground flowed past in plastic miniature, each detail sharp. It looked remarkably like the illuminated strip map that unrolled on the instrument board. A glowing red dot floated on the surface of the map. Perry recognized this as a dead-reckoner of some sort and wondered how the trick was done. Air speed? Hardly. Earth induction? Possible but difficult, especially in latitude made good. Radio? More likely, but still a clever trick.

The content of the quote indicates that in this earlier work, Heinlein had a very clear picture of what he meant by an airborne dead-reckoner. In

FUTL, the main character Perry is transported from the 1930s to some point considerably in his future. At one point in the story, Perry is traveling on a passenger aircraft and has requested permission to observe in the cockpit. What Heinlein described was the airborne equivalent of a ship's Dead Reckoning Tracer (DRT), which plots the calculated position of the craft on a map or chart. Heinlein was frustratingly ambiguous about the actual technology to be employed in the portion of the system that determines the position, although he did present a number of possibilities.

In *FUTL*, the technology being presented is new to the character Perry, and Heinlein was therefore able to get away with a bit of detailed description and speculation by the character in the usual author's trick for explaining the technology to his readers. In "If This Goes On—," the character John Lyle has previously stated his great familiarity with the particular aircraft that he has stolen in his escape attempt. As he is familiar with its instruments and their means of operation, there is no need for him to speculate about the operation of the dead-reckoner in the presentation of that story. It is accepted by the character and very briefly presented as a part of the scene.

Why should this mention of an airborne dead-reckoner in *FUTL* be connected with the brief mention of such a device in "If This Goes On—"? The answer is that a careful reading of *FUTL* will show that Heinlein made use of many ideas and concepts from his unpublished manuscript for *FUTL* in his later stories that were sold and published.

The minor quote appears in the novel *The Puppet Masters*. It is included as the only other direct mention of an airborne dead-reckoner that has been located in Heinlein's works:

> He adjusted his dead-reckoner bug, checked his board, and set his controls. (171)

5. How would someone develop an airborne dead-reckoner to perform navigation automatically? Remember that this is the period before inertial guidance systems and the Global Positioning System. The problem may be broken into two segments. The first is to obtain the proper inputs required for the navigational calculations. The second is to present these calculations in a form that is useful to the pilot or the navigator of the aircraft. In Heinlein's quote from *FUTL*, we may recognize each of these segments.

Let us begin by considering the process of dead-reckoning as applied to a ship. You take as the starting point the known position of your ship. If you know both the compass heading at which you are proceeding and your speed, it would seem to be a simple matter to calculate your position at any later time. However, there are disturbing influences acting upon your ship, such as wind and currents. For a ship, the most likely disturbing influence would be ocean currents. Acting from ahead or astern, they could either retard or augment the speed of the ship through the water. Other currents would act at an angle to the longitudinal axis of the ship, causing a deviation from the intended course. The result of such external influences is that you are not where the dead-reckoning calculations have said that you are.

Heinlein would have been familiar with dead-reckoning from his instruction in navigation at the Naval Academy, where one his instructors was Philip Van Horn Weems, an expert in the field. Although the actual navigation of a ship would be the duty of the Navigator, the procedures and equipment would also have been known to Heinlein from duties required of him as a newly commissioned officer standing watch. The Dead Reckoning Tracer (DRT) would have been a familiar piece of equipment located on or near the bridge of the ship. Such navigation equipment employing electromechanical means of calculation are closely related to equipment employed for fire control, which was Heinlein's area of specialization. In addition, his service aboard the aircraft carrier U.S.S. *Lexington* would have acquainted him with some of the problems of aircraft navigation.

The navigational situation is the same in an aircraft, where the disturbing influence is the wind. Like a current acting on a ship, the wind can speed up or slow down the aircraft, and push it to one side or the other of the intended course. If you can see the ground and are able to plot your actual track and groundspeed, and know your airspeed and heading, you can solve for the wind. But what if you cannot see the ground, or are flying over the ocean? How does one estimate drift?

One must have accurate measurements of the magnitude and direction of the various quantities. A detailed analysis could be presented of the various types of instruments developed over the years such as the drift meter, airspeed indicator and a practical compass. The relatively slow motions of a ship allow the compass to follow its motion accurately. On an aircraft, however, the rapid motions would mean that time must be allowed after each maneuver for the compass to settle on the new heading. Other than the usual magnetic compass, by the mid-1920s versions of the earth inductor compass (mentioned in the *FUTL* quote) and the gyrocompass had been developed that were possible to employ in aircraft.

The literature indicates that there were various types of navigational systems under development in different countries by the time of World War 2. The British developed the Direct Reading Compass (DRC), which was able to provide its heading information to equipment performing the navigational calculations. Also developed was the Air Mileage Unit (AMU) to provide an airspeed signal. Heading and mileage information were combined in the Air Position Indicator (API) and used to determine true air miles flown east-west and north-south, which could then be converted into longitude and latitude. Advances by the British were shared with the United States, where the effort was to improve the British AMU and develop a version of the API suitable for carrier aircraft.

Various U.S. patents have been located from the World War 2 era regarding airborne dead-reckoning, some even from Bell Laboratories. Considering the implied connection with Bell Laboratories in the development of the system inspired by Heinlein's story gadget, the demonstration of any connection of any of these patents with Heinlein's classmates or any fielded Navy system could be very important. Unfortunately, no such connections have been found.

6. The story of the career of Commander George Hoover, as related in Chapter 10, referred to his efforts in developing such equipment. In the article "Let George Do It," it is stated that in 1944 he was able to demonstrate a system that could be used in an aircraft. In another article in *Naval Aviation News* from December 1948, a description is given of the system developed by Hoover. The device is called an automatic position plotter:

> a boxlike affair, over which a sectional map is superimposed. The pilot, by using the E-W and N-S knobs, places the spot of light, contained within the device, behind the departure point of his flight. The compass heading, true air speed, wind direction and wind velocity are then automatically fed into the device as the plane is flown, and the point of light follows the course of plane. By looking at this point the pilot can immediately determine his position at any given time enroute.

This sounds very much like what Heinlein described in *FUTL*. The article goes on to state that this was the first version of the device and that testing was to be performed to determine the feasibility for use by carrier aircraft. We may assume that any system placed in service would have appeared no earlier than 1949 or possibly even 1950.

A search was made for airborne navigation systems that were placed in naval service. It was possible to discover references to an automatic dead-reckoning system, the AN/ASA-14, which dates from the 1950s. While other systems may have been placed in service before the AN/ASA-14, no information on such systems has been located.

The general impression obtained from all of the material encountered is that no airborne dead-reckoning system, either based on British systems or independent American development efforts, saw service by the U.S. Navy until well after the end of World War 2.

C. Radio Beam

1. The squeal of a radio beam told me that we were arriving. We slid down it, hovered for a moment, and bumped gently to a landing. (126-127)

2. At last I heard the squeal of a landing beam. We slid along it, hovered, and bumped gently to a stop. (101)

3. There is no appreciable difference between quotes.

4. Use of a radio beam for navigation does appear in "Solution Unsatisfactory" and "Methuselah's Children." We may also consider the narrative in *Expanded Universe* related in Chapter 5 with regard to Buddy Scoles and the location of aircraft by radio compass. This episode in his duty aboard the *Lexington*, as with the Airborne Dead-Reckoner, would have made Heinlein familiar with the problem of guiding a plane to a successful return and landing.

5. Although Heinlein's description of a landing beam involved a helicopter, the obvious purpose of a landing beam would be to provide a radio signal that a pilot of any type of aircraft could use to find his way at night or in conditions of limited visibility to the point of making a safe landing. The beam would have to permit the pilot to approach at the proper heading *and* to descend at the proper rate.

The development of such systems may be traced back, at least in the United States, to 1918. Although an airmail service had been established, the planes were unable to fly in condition of bad weather and poor visibility. Various radio devices were developed through the 1920s and 1930s to help pilots navigate along their intended route and, more importantly, to land safely. The landing beam as described by Heinlein was one of the systems developed during this period. Such a system made use of a highly directional radio beam or collection of beams. This required the use of special antennas and high frequencies. The higher the frequency was, the tighter the beam. The plane would be led into its approach by other systems until it encountered the landing beam, which it would then use to descend to the runway. There is no mystery regarding Heinlein being aware of such systems, as the experiments would have been featured in the press. One newspaper article from 1939 described the use of the recently developed klystron to generate landing beams at 750 MHz.

6. If we consider the problem of landing naval aircraft at a land base, we would most likely employ the same type of systems that were developed for commercial aircraft. Considered in a naval context, we are talking about homing systems developed to guide planes back to the carrier. This is worth mentioning even though it differs appreciably from the simple landing beam mentioned by Heinlein.

Finding one's way back to the carrier over open water is a difficult problem, complicated by the fact that the carrier will probably have moved from the point of launch. The first attempts involved simple radio direction finders mounted on the planes to home in on signals transmitted by the carrier. Small planes employed fixed loops built into the body of the aircraft, but this required turning the entire plane to obtain the signal bearing. Large planes could mount rotatable loops, but these caused drag.

The system developed by the Naval Research Laboratory was the Model YE-YG/ZB. The experimental model was tested on the U.S.S. *Saratoga* in 1938 and, based on the recommendation of Admiral King, was placed into production and used on all aircraft carriers throughout the war.

The carrier employed a rotating antenna that transmitted coded signals, each one identifying a 30-degree sector. The standard transmitter was Model YE, with Model YG employed on smaller carriers. The signals were received by an aircraft using a frequency converter (Model ZB) to feed the signal to the standard aircraft communication receiver. The pilot would listen for the strongest signal and know by the code which of the 12 sectors he was in relative to the carrier.

D. Battle Tracker

1. We had improvised a flag-plotting room in the communications room just abaft of the conning tower, tearing out the long-range televisor to make room for the battle tracker and concentration plot. (142)

    I was sweating over my jury-rigged tracker, hoping to heaven that the makeshift shock absorbers would be sufficient to cushion the concussion when we opened up. (142)

    I passed the order, and cut my tracker out of the circuit for fifteen minutes. It wasn't built to handle so many variables at such high speeds, and there was no sense in overloading the relays. Nineteen minutes later the last transport had checked in by phone; I made a preliminary setup on the tracker, threw the start switch and let the correction data come in. For a couple of minutes I was very busy balancing the data, hands moving swiftly among the keys and knobs, then the integrators took hold with a satisfying hum, and I reported: "Tracking, sir!" (144)

I had torn off the current plot from my tracker and brought it along. It had on it the predicted positions for Formation E. (147)

2. .... so we had improvised a flag plot just abaft the conning tower, tearing out the long-range televisor to make room for the battle tracker and concentration plot. (165)

I was sweating over my jury-rigged tracker, hoping to Heaven that the makeshift shock absorbers would be good enough when we opened up. (165)

I passed the order and cut my tracker out of circuit for fifteen minutes; it wasn't built for so many variables at such high speeds and there was no sense in overloading it. Nineteen minutes later the last transport had checked in by phone, I made a preliminary setup, threw the starting switch and let the correction data feed in. For a couple of minutes I was very busy balancing data, my hands moving among knobs and keys; then the machine was satisfied with its own predictions and I reported, "Tracking, sir." (166-167)

I had torn the current plot from my tracker and brought it along. It had the time-predicted plots for Formation E. (170)

3. Most of the changes seem concerned with improving the structure of the sentences. The only technical difference in the later version is the omission of a reference to the integrators.

4. There is no mention of a similar device in any of Heinlein's other works.

5. During the attack upon New Jerusalem, it was necessary to provide the overall commander, General Huxley, with information on the position of the other attacking craft. This was accomplished by what Heinlein called a **battle tracker**. From the above quotes which describe John Lyle operating the device, it is understood that the battle tracker is capable of plotting the position of a number of craft in the attacking formation, although the exact

number is never given. This choice of name points directly to the earlier Sperry Battle Tracer described in Appendix 2 "Electromechanical Computing." By the implied connection of the Battle Tracker with an earlier device, the means of constructing navigation and fire control devices prior to and in the early stages of the war, and Heinlein's known familiarity with such devices, it is concluded that the battle tracker featured in the story was electromechanical in nature. This is reinforced by the reference to the hum of the integrators, as purely electronic integrators would be silent in their operation. Although the one direct reference to the nature of the device in the Virtues essay identifies it as being electronic, I have relaxed that particular constraint to include electromechanical.

There are several features of the battle tracker which must be considered. The first is that it is capable of plotting the position of more than one craft. The second concerns how the data is input to the tracker. We have John Lyle initially receiving the information by messages from the other craft and inputting their information. But it also stated that the dead reckoning is checked by means of the sonic range-finders. Heinlein does not specify how this information is provided to the tracker.

6. The Dead Reckoning Tracer (DRT) used before, during and after World War 2 was capable of plotting only "own ship" position on the basis of compass and speed inputs. The position of any other ships, either friendly or hostile, would have to be plotted manually on the basis of range and bearing information determined by other means.

The naval system which eventually replaced the DRT was the NC-2. This early version of this system was capable of projecting colored lights which represented "own ship" as well as two targets. A later model was capable of projecting four targets. Quoting from the *Training Manual for Quartermaster 1 & C* (NAVTRA 10151-D), we first have:

> The NC-2 Plotting System comprises four units: plotting table, target plot attachments (TPA), data converter, and dead reckoning indicator.

The plotting table has a glass plate above the projectors. One projector indicates the position of own ship. Each of the target plot attachments is a projector of a different color which shows the position of a target relative to own ship. The TPAs are mounted on the portion of the mechanism which moves to display own ship's position. The indicator, as in the older model DRT, displays longitude and latitude. Unfortunately the description of the data converter given in the manual is very brief:

The data converter receives range and speed information from the ship's radar indicators, sonar, and log and then converts this information into a form usable by the plotting table and target plot attachment systems.

At one point, the Battle Tracker was considered the solution to the mystery, with the naval system that it inspired being the NC-2. To confirm the solution, an attempt was made to locate information on how and when the NC-2 was developed and when it went into service with the Navy. Although it was possible to locate the Quartermaster Training Manual quoted above and one published paper which gave a more detailed description of its inner workings of the NC-2, it has been nearly impossible to find any historical data on the device. Queries directed to various former naval personnel only indicated that it came into service in the mid-to-late 1950s. A work on the history of Network-Centric Warfare had just one brief mention of the NC-2 and indicated that it was a Canadian system that was then adopted by the U.S. Navy. I had earlier discovered manuals for the NC-2 which at least indicated the companies which had manufactured them, one of them being named Marsland. A little more searching led to an online listing of Canadian archives which identified the manufacturer as Marsland Engineering Limited based in Canada. The description of the archived document referred to a component of the Plotting Tables MK NC-1 MOD.0, MK NC-2 MOD.0, which would be the earliest versions of the system. The date associated with this document was 1957.

E. Frequency Variation

1. At 12:32 the televisors went out. The enemy had analyzed our frequency variation pattern, matched us and blown every tube in the circuit. It's not supposed to be theoretically possible, but they did it. Radio went out at 12:37, jammed and then blown. (143)

2. At 12:32 the televisors went out. The enemy had analyzed our frequency variation pattern, matched us and blown every tube in the circuits. It is theoretically impossible; they did it. At 12:37 radio went out. (166)

3. The differences between the first three sentences in each version appear to be minor and would appear to reflect a desire by Heinlein to improve the style: "circuit" versus "circuits" "It's not supposed to be theoretically possible . . . ." versus "It is theoretically impossible . . . ."

The original version includes the phrase "jammed and then blown" in reference to the radio. The revised version omits that phrase. This also appears be a question of style, as we may assume that the actions with regard to the televisors apply to the radio.

4. No apparent references to frequency variation or jamming exist in any other of Heinlein's works or letters.

5. The other descriptions of story devices that are analyzed in this chapter each point to a single device or concept. In this case, there is difficulty in determining which portion of the description should be our point of focus. Should we consider the frequency variation mentioned by Heinlein? It is assumed that this variation was intended to provide some degree of security to the operation of the televisors. Or do we consider how such frequency variation might be analyzed and matched? Finally, do we consider how jamming signals might be applied to affect either the televisors or the radio?

No matter which portion of the story quote we consider, we would clearly be in the area of Radio Countermeasures (RCM). It is necessary to make the distinction between Nonradar and Radar applications. Nonradar applications include communications, radio navigation and radio-controlled devices. The various types of RCM facilities include:

- Receivers (search, monitoring, warning, and homing or direction-finding types.)

- Jamming transmitters.

- Confusion and deception types.

- Antijamming techniques.

Someone might suggest that even though Heinlein presented a countermeasures concept in the area of communications, it was applied by the classmate to radar. The problem with such a suggestion is the timing of events. By the analysis conducted in Chapter 2, the story idea would have appeared and been recognized as having a naval application in the first part of 1940. The delivery of the first of the CXAM radars to the Navy only began in mid-1940. It would have been necessary to gain some experience with radars before considering vulnerability to jamming and the need to develop countermeasures.

Jamming of a radio signal was not a new concept even then. It goes back to the early days of radio. Before the development of the means of tuning both transmitters and receivers to operate only at desired frequencies, it was almost impossible to avoid interfering with other radio transmissions. During World War I, air-to-ground transmissions were interfered with by both friendly transmitters as well as intentional jamming. A technical development that made it possible for the tone of the Morse Code signal from a particular aircraft to be differentiated from other friendly aircraft was also of some benefit with regard to intentional jamming.

Some work was done at the Naval Research Laboratory (NRL) with regard to jamming in the period between the wars. Jammers were created from existing naval transmitters, with the assumption that a similar approach could be used to construct jammers in time of war. An interest in combating the problem of remote-controlled weapons led to the development of a receiver to determine the control frequencies of such a device so that it might be jammed. An existing receiver was modified to repeatedly scan over the frequency range of interest. At the end of the constantly rotating tuning shaft was a disk with a radial slot. A neon bulb was connected to the receiver output and placed behind the disk. When a signal was received at a particular frequency, the bulb would glow and the light would be visible through the slot. The direction in which the slot was pointed when the bulb lit up would indicate the frequency.

After the attack on Pearl Harbor, as might be expected, the interest in Radio Countermeasures greatly increased. The major portion of this effort was focused upon the problems of radar jamming, most specifically how to detect, analyze and then jam the enemy's radar. Of course, there was also interest in the problems of communications. The greater interest in radar is indicated by the content of the available literature. Efforts for both radar and nonradar applications were directed by Division 15 of the National Defense Research Committee (NDRC), with the work performed by various electronics firms such as RCA, Federal Telegraph and Radio Corporation, and Bell Telephone Laboratories. The work included the determination of the best jamming signals and the means of overcoming the jamming. The considerable effort devoted to such problems, both for radio communications and radar, would indicate that the engineers at NRL were a bit naïve in their pre-war assumptions regarding the ease by which equipment could be converted for jamming in wartime.

You should recall that the Heinlein quotes imply a connection with Bell Labs with regard to the development of the naval system. It would be useful if one of the contracts with NDRC could somehow be connected with the story idea. Unfortunately, the contracts listed for Bell Labs appear to be general studies rather than being concerned with a particular system. A few which may be listed are OEMsr-626 "Study of Interference Generation," OEMsr-940 "Radio barrage jamming and anti-jamming studies," and OEMsr-993 "Scanning reception in radio countermeasures." While it is possible that one of these studies may have led to a system employed by the Navy, it must be noted that all of the efforts mentioned above were initiated after Pearl Harbor, perhaps as late as 1943, whereas Heinlein's letter quotes were in the immediate time frame of Pearl Harbor and imply an even earlier time frame for the development of the system inspired by his story device.

One might change the frequency over which a system operates to minimize the effects of jamming. As discussed in the literature on wartime activities, it is interpreted as having different transmitting and receiving equipment available so that changes could easily be made to frequencies not affected by the jamming. What Heinlein seems to be implying with his mention of frequency variation is something like the concept of frequency hopping (FH). In a FH system, both the transmitter and receiver make a series of rapid, synchronized changes between a number of frequency bands (channels).

A broadband noise jammer is one that transmits random noise covering the full frequency range over which a communication system is operating. Under many circumstances, random noise is the best type of jamming signal to apply. Use of this type of jammer does not depend upon the pattern with which the transmitted frequency changes. All the person attempting to jam has to know is the total frequency range over which the transmitter operates. Of course, using this approach means that you are transmitting jamming signals at frequencies that are not in use most of the time. For example, if there were 20 possible frequency bands, at any point in time 19 of the frequency bands would not be in use, so 95% of your jamming energy would be wasted. With the need to apply power in all bands all of the time, it might not be possible to apply sufficient power to any one band to properly jam the communications.

It would be possible to be more efficient in the application of the jamming signal if one were to somehow monitor the transmitted signal and then jam only in the frequency band that was detected. Such a jamming system would have to detect the frequency used in a particular time interval and then apply the jamming signal before the transmitter changed to a different frequency band in the next time interval. As opposed to simply following the pattern as it occurred, it would be better to be able to determine the means by which the pattern was generated. Regarding the complexity of the frequency variation pattern, if the pattern at which the transmitter changed was too simple, it would not take very long to be able to determine it and then be able to predict it for all future times.

6. It has not been possible to find a particular naval system that could be traced with any degree of confidence to the concepts presented in the story quote.

Heinlein's mention of frequency variation does enable us to look at a frequency hopping concept which was proposed at roughly the same time. If one searches the Internet for information on FH, it is impossible to avoid the story of the invention by actress Hedy Lamarr (Hedy Kiesler Markey) and composer George Anthiel. The patent application, filed June 10, 1941, was titled "Secret communications system," but actually concerned a radio control system for devices such as torpedoes which made use of a randomized frequency hopping code. The concept was patented in 1942 and we may assume that the Navy was aware of it, but nothing came of the idea at the time. It is stated in the technical literature that a FH communication system was not employed operationally by the Navy against jamming until 1963. This was a system called BLADES, which was developed by Sylvania and only delivered for shipboard testing in 1962.

F. Infrared

1. Shift to light-phone circuits.   (143)

    He hooked us up via telephone, using infrared beams for the ship-to-ship circuits.   (143)

    Telephone circuits using infrared-beam transmission are very fine things, simple, secret, and don't get out of order, but a thick cloud of smoke will stop the beam.   (145)

2. Shift to light-phone circuits.   (166)

    .... our audio circuits were now on infra-red beams, ship to ship.   (166)

3. Although the references to the infrared light-phones are considerably simplified in the later version of the story, the simplification does not imply anything has changed with regard to the nature of the device or how it was being used. The communication system involved voice rather than Morse Code blinker signals.

4. No apparent references to infrared communication exist in any other of Heinlein's works or letters.

5. First, let us consider such a communication system from an engineering standpoint. One end of the communication process involves applying a voice modulation from a microphone to a beam of light. This would be accomplished by amplifying the voice signal from a microphone and then either applying this directly to the light emitter or by using it to modulate a constant beam of light after it has been emitted. The light may or may not be visible to the naked eye. At the receiving end, a material which is sensitive in the proper wavelength range is used to create a voltage or current that varies with the same modulation according to the light that strikes it. One then amplifies the received signal and uses it to drive a speaker or headphones. The advantage of communication using infrared rather than visible light is that unless the enemy possesses a receiver sensitive to the wavelengths at which the message is being sent, the signal will not be detected.

The quote from the Virtues essay states that the bread-boarded unit was being tried out aboard ship within a month. This would be possible for an infrared communication system if you already have both a suitable emitter and detector on hand and are just constructing the electronics that are required to use those components. It would be impossible in that period of time if you were trying to develop the entire system, including the emitter and/or the detector, from scratch as a result of the inspiration of Heinlein's story device. Development of a detector material would be a process more appropriate to a university or industrial laboratory, as is indicated by the historical record, than to the experiments of a naval officer.

A system for communicating by visible light was developed by Alexander Graham Bell in 1880, only four years after the invention of the telephone. During World War I, work on various systems for communicating with light was done by Germany, Britain and the United States. The British and German systems that were developed included voice systems, but at visible wavelengths. A system developed by the United States included an infrared system for keeping convoys together, but this did not involve voice communications. An infrared code blinker system was demonstrated to the Army and Navy in 1917. This used a Thalofide cell developed by T. W. Case. The Thalofide cell is an oxidized thallous sulfide photoconductive cell. This system was capable of operating over a range of 18 miles.

In 1939, at both the World's Fair in New York City and at Treasure Island in San Francisco, one of the General Motors' exhibits was the transmission of voice and music on a beam of light. So we may safely conclude that Heinlein was familiar with the concept of communication by light.

One of the wartime contracts with the National Defense Research Committee (NDRC) was for the development of a voice and code communication system operating in the near infrared (0.8 μ to 1.5 μ). This was done at the request of the Bureau of Ships and was handled by Section 16.4 of the NDRC. The development of this system was initiated in May 1943 by means of the Contract OEMsr-990 "Infrared communication system with electrically modulated lamps" issued to Northwestern University.

As the Heinlein letters referred to work being done AT&T, the primary reference for wartime infrared work was examined for any contracts to that firm. Four contracts existed with Bell Laboratories, both in New York City and Murray Hill, New Jersey. None of these contracts involved communication systems. Two were concerned with devices known as thermistor bolometers, used for the sensing of small quantities of radiant heat energy. The third contract involved techniques for the manufacture of silicon photoconductive cells. The final contract, which did concern the Navy, was for the development of infrared range and detection (IRRAD) equipment, an optical equivalent of radar. The limited range possible with the system that was developed meant that it had no military value and the contract was terminated.

6. The system developed by Northwestern University was given the name of Type E Voice System. We may find it described in a manual from 1945, *This is NANCY* (NAVSHIPS 250-222-10). "NANCY" is defined as the name applied to equipment for night signaling, recognition and reconnaissance, developed under the code name "NAN." After some pages of description of the nature of light and infrared in particular, the manual presents the section "NANCY'S Family Album," which describes the various systems. There is a Signaling Searchlight, Beacon System, Beachmarker, Course Marker, Type D Code System, and Type E Voice System. There are also brief descriptions of the phosphor or electronic receivers. Although a number of technical details of the Type E system are given, let us simply note that the range under average weather conditions is given as approximately 8,000 yards or 4.5 miles.

Several infrared communication systems are briefly described in the *Catalogue of Electronic Equipment* (NAVSHIPS 900,116 - Supplement Number 5), which bears a date of October 1952. This catalogue is described as containing both World War 2 and post-war equipment. The voice systems listed are the AN/SAC-1 Type E Infrared Voice System (which is identical to the system described in *This is NANCY*), AN/SAC-4 (which is a lightweight version of the AN/SAC-1 with a lower wattage lamp), and the AN/PAC-1 (which is a portable self-contained version of the larger types of equipment).

For a listing of similar systems at an even later date, we may consider the manual *Shipboard Electronic Equipment*, (NAVPERS 10794-B). This manual is specifically identified as being for naval personnel who are not electronics specialists. In Chapter 9 - Miscellaneous Facilities, there is a section on Infrared equipment:

> Some of the infrared devices in use in the fleet today are the blinker equipments AN/SAR-( ), AN/SAT- ( ), and VS-18 ( )/SAT; the voice/tone equipments AN/SAC - ( ), AN/PAC - ( ), and AN/PAR - ( ), and the detection tracking equipment AN/ SAQ - ( ).

The manual states that with the exception of the blinker category, all such systems are classified.

Unfortunately, none of these sources of information indicated when the units such as the Type E came into use. It may be inferred that the AN/SAC-4 and AN/PAC-1 came into use sometime after 1945, otherwise they would also have been described in the *This is NANCY* manual. A number of newspaper articles appeared immediately after the war, however, which revealed the existence of an infrared communication system. The security of communications when using such a system was the primary focus of the articles. It is stated that the one system described was not developed in time for use during the war. As it appears that the Type E system was the only infrared voice system developed for the Navy during World War 2, then it must be identified with the system described in the newspaper articles. One point of confusion resulting from the newspaper articles is that the development work was attributed to the Westinghouse Electric Corporation.

G. Sonic Range-Finder

1. Keep contact in formation with sonics.   (143)

    Bi-aural sonic range-finders kept the formation intact, each craft sending out its own sonic frequency.   (143)

> Thereafter we checked our dead reckoning by means of the data given by the sonic range-finders. (145)

> Even after the sonics failed, we were well enough off. (146)

2. No mention of sonic range-finders in the later version.

3. Was the elimination of sonic range-finders from the later story significant, or was Heinlein simply recognizing that in the land environment implied in the story, the use of radar would be more logical than a system based on sound?

4. No references to sonic range-finders exist in any other of Heinlein's works or letters.

5. Let us begin by trying to understand exactly what Heinlein is saying in the quote:

> Bi-aural sonic range-finders kept the formation intact, each craft sending out its own sonic frequency.

A range-finder is a device which emits a signal - which may be either acoustic or electronic, but will be acoustic in this case. It is also equipped to receive the echo (reflection) of the signal from the surface of some distant object. This echo will most likely be greatly attenuated with respect to the original signal, so some amount of amplification is required. By knowing the total travel time to and from the object and the velocity of propagation of the signal, it is a simple matter to determine the distance.

If the range-finder in every craft in the formation was emitting the same frequency, it would not be possible to separate the echo from your signal from the signals emitted by others. Having each craft emit a different frequency signal would be required to prevent interference between the various range-finders.

The description of the device includes the term "bi-aural." The bi-aural (or more correctly binaural) effect describes the means by which a person uses both ears to determine from which direction a sound is coming. The process depends on the relative timing of the signals reaching each ear, and also upon the differences in sound intensity.

Up to this point it has not been necessary to consider the medium in which Heinlein's sonic range-finders would be operating. In the land battle, the range-finders would be operating in the air. This is the one case where we must consider the naval environment, in which case the range-finders would be operating in water. This of course leads us to SONAR. The term SONAR, like RADAR, is an acronym created to describe the function of the system. SONAR stands for **SO**und **N**avigation **A**nd **R**anging. Its purpose is to locate objects below the surface of the water, where systems such as radar are limited by the attenuation of electromagnetic waves in water.

There are two types of systems - passive listening and active sonar. Passive listening, as the name implies, does not depend on the emission of any signal by the craft doing the listening. The purpose is simply to detect any sound source in the vicinity. It is capable of determining direction. To be capable of determining the precise distance to the object, it would be necessary to know exactly when the sound which is being received was emitted from the object. Active sonar depends upon the emission of a sound pulse which, as previously described, will be reflected from an object. Active sonar is therefore capable of determining both the direction and range to an object.

Passive listening systems were developed in World War I for the purpose of locating submerged enemy submarines. In one early version, the sound receptors were simply short sections of pipe capped with rubber. These were located at the ends of an inverted T-shape of metal extending below the hull of the ship. The sound was simply conducted through tubes to the earphones of the operator - similar to the inexpensive earphones which you plug into your armrest when traveling by air. No electronics. No amplification. The operator simply rotated the T until he heard equal sounds in each ear. The sound emitter would then be on a bearing perpendicular to the crossbar of the T. Without any form of signal amplification, these early primitive systems had limited range.

Later versions of such systems, known as hydrophones, converted the received sounds to electrical signals which were then amplified. This increased the sensitivity of such systems, and of course their ranges. Although the structure of such systems was internally more complex than in the early acoustic systems, the principle of orienting the hydrophone until a balanced signal was received remained the same. The signals could be provided to headphones or to a visual display which would indicate the direction to which the array should be turned and then when the two signals were equal.

While the purpose of a hydrophone is to convert sound into an electrical signal, active sonar makes use of transducers which perform the conversion in both directions - electrical to acoustic and then acoustic back to electrical. There are two types of transducers - magnetostrictive and piezoelectric.

The sonars of the World War 2 era operated in a searchlight mode. This meant that they projected sound in a fairly narrow beam in a specific direction. Such a mode of operation was due to the limited acoustic power that could be generated. The implication of this is that active sonar did not require the use of the binaural effect. If an active sonar transducer was pointed at a particular azimuth and you received an echo, you then had all the information you needed. Employing the binaural effect would not provide you with any more information regarding the bearing to the object.

According to the preceding discussion, it appears that Heinlein, intentionally or not, combined the principles of the passive listening and active sonar into one system which he called the sonic range-finder.

6. The various systems installed on most World War 2 submarines are mentioned in the *Submarine Sonar Operator's Manual* (NAVPERS 16167). Detailed technical descriptions are contained in *Naval Sonar* (NAVPERS 10884), which also considers surface ship equipment:

J-Series Listening Equipment:

JP is sonic - works with audible sounds. JT works with sonic and ultrasonic sounds.

The JT hydrophone consists of 10 coils, each surrounding a nickel cylinder. The coils are connected in series so that the signals add, with the maximum signal when the hydrophone is oriented perpendicular to the bearing to the sound source, so that all coils are responding the same to the incident sound.

WCA Sonar Equipment:

NM is a magnetostriction transducer aimed downward for depth sounding.

QC and JK are two separate devices contained in one housing called, as might be expected, the QC-JK. QC is a magnetostriction transducer, and JK is a Rochelle-salt hydrophone. The QC is used for echo ranging, and the JK for listening. The QC and JK cannot be used at the same time.

QB, mounted in a separate housing, is a Rochelle-salt transducer. The QB is used for echo-ranging.

The QB sonar was installed on some U.S. destroyers as early as 1934. Although the destroyers on which it was initially installed did not include the U.S.S. *Roper* on which Heinlein served, it is possible that Heinlein could have acquired some knowledge of sonar principles prior to the end of his active duty service. Even if this was not the case, we might assume that during his time at the Academy the use of passive devices during the World War 1 would have been mentioned. Another possible source of information is Cal Laning, who had training and service in submarines.

The final point to consider is the reference to "each craft sending out its own sonic frequency." In the manual *Naval Sonar* (NAVPERS 10884), the frequency of operation is discussed. A low frequency, less than 10 kHz, has little attenuation in the sea, but the signals do not provide the directivity required in locating targets. As the frequency is increased, the directivity improves, but the signal is attenuated by a greater amount. For long ranges, the signal could not be higher than 25 to 30 kHz. The value of 24 kHz was given as the compromise selected by the Navy. It was then stated that newer equipment was being installed that would be capable of working at low frequencies at long range and higher frequencies at closer range, when improved directivity and accuracy are required.

Regarding the ability to change frequencies of a particular sonar installation, it should be noted that the determining factor is the resonant frequency of the transducer. In a discussion in *Naval Sonar* of a surface ship installation, Model QGB, it is noted that the electronics which interface with the transducer are capable of operating over a range of 17 kHz to 26 kHz. But to operate at different frequencies within that range, one has to physically replace the transducer. The resonant frequencies available for the Model QGB were 20, 22, 23 and 26 kHz. An alternative approach was represented by another surface ship installation, Model QGA, which was composed of two systems, one operating at 14 kHz and the other at 30 kHz.

The preceding discussion would appear to indicate that Heinlein's suggestion of operation at different frequencies is definitely possible, subject to the limits imposed by the propagation of sound through the water and the availability of a sufficient number of different transducers.

The final chapter will consider the results of the analysis presented in this chapter and propose a solution to the Mystery.

14

WHAT IS THE ANSWER?

From the very beginning of the search, it has been known that there were four parts to the solution: the story in which the mystery device appeared, the naval officer responsible for recognizing that a real naval system could be based on the device, the identity of the device and the naval system inspired by the device. Each of these is considered and my solution to each presented.

Of the four parts of the solution, the strongest case can be made for the story in which the mystery device appeared. My conclusion is that the device appeared in the second installment of "If This Goes On—." The most important step taken in arriving at this conclusion was the use of Heinlein's statements regarding his mention of the existence of the device to Campbell in the spring of 1940. This allowed me to restrict the search to stories no later than "The Roads Must Roll." Working from this subset of stories, it was then possible to construct a list of all items of technology, as presented in Chapter 11. The named story segment contains the largest number of such items, which makes it more likely that it contains the device. In addition, this segment features a land battle scene that is a disguised naval action. I have always felt that the device that would inspire a naval system would be found in that scene. Even though this conclusion is contrary to statements made by Heinlein in the Virtues essay regarding "1939" and the "next installment," I will stick firmly with it. Should I be proven wrong with regard to the actual identity of the device, I expect this part of the solution to stand.

Next, we will consider the naval officer who was responsible for taking the story idea and using it as the basis for a naval system. The focus on Cal Laning began with the suggestion made by Virginia Heinlein at the very start of my search. I have kept Laning as the prime candidate because of his known technical expertise, his position as Radio Officer during the interval of interest and his contact with Heinlein. The possibility of other classmates was considered in Chapter 6. Although others were suggested because of their postgraduate education, no additional evidence such as contact with Heinlein has been found for any of them.

Why is there no mention of the device in any letters between Heinlein and Laning? Although they kept in touch, large gaps exist in the communication between Laning and Heinlein as preserved in the Heinlein Archives. After a letter from Laning dated October 24, 1938, no other letter in either direction has been found until a short note from Laning in September 1940. The note has no date, but Laning used it to inform Heinlein that he had been transferred from the U.S.S. *Philadelphia* to the U.S.S. *Sicard*, which definitely places it in September 1940. For two friends who maintained contact during the war and later, a gap of almost two years stands out.

As stated above, the mystery device is considered to have appeared in the second installment of "If This Goes On—" in the March 1940 issue of *Astounding*. Based on the type of analysis done in Chapter 2, this issue would have appeared on the fourth Friday in February, which was the 23rd.

So why do we not have a communication from Laning dated March or April 1940 concerning the device? To suggest a reason, it is necessary to consider the movements of the U.S.S. *Philadelphia* during the first few months of 1940. Remember that Laning had been on the *Philadelphia* since June 1938. The *Philadelphia* was in the Atlantic and the Caribbean until June 1939. It then operated from the West Coast of the United States until April 1940, when it was shifted to Hawaiian waters.

The log of the *Philadelphia* was examined for the first half of 1940. The general pattern was that it would anchor at some location for a few days, and then spend a short period of days at sea. From January 1940 through March 1940, the log indicates it was moored at various times at Los Angeles Harbor, San Clemente Island, Santa Barbara Island, or Monterey Bay. An important detail is that during this interval, most weekends were spent in port. This is consistent with the practice of the time described by the slogan "Week out, weekend in," where an effort was made to balance operational readiness and low fuel budgets.

The *Philadelphia* was anchored in Los Angeles Harbor for the first two weekends in March as well as most of the last half of the month. With the Heinleins living in Hollywood, I feel that we may confidently assume that Cal Laning was able to have gone ashore and met with them in person. This would explain the absence of a letter concerning the device. The device would have been discussed face-to-face.

If we assume that a similar pattern of movements existed for the *Philadelphia* for the interval from June 1939 until 1940, the occasional presence of Laning in the Los Angeles area could explain at least part of the gap in their letters mentioned above.

There is indirect evidence for such contact in another letter. Following the short note from Laning in September 1940, Heinlein responded with a letter on October 25. In it he told Laning of their recent activities, beginning with their departure for the East Coast at the beginning of May and ending with their return home at the end of August. It is important to note that in this letter Heinlein did not list any activities prior to May. I conclude that Laning had already been made aware of their activities up to the end of March, prior to the departure of the *Philadelphia* for Hawaii. Since there are no letters for that period, such information could only have been obtained by direct contact.

The time interval between February 23 and the end of March (before the departure of the *Philadelphia* for Hawaiian waters) is consistent with the one month bread-board time frame mentioned in the Virtues essay. Therefore, Laning could have told Heinlein not only that he had picked up the idea from the story, but also that it was successfully bread-boarded.

In the letter to Campbell on January 4, 1942, Heinlein referred to the development work done on the device. The one remaining question is where and how Heinlein obtained information about the development of the naval system in the interval between April 1940 and January 1942. If Laning was the source, we must also consider how Laning would have obtained such information. During this interval, Laning was on the *Philadelphia*, then the U.S.S. *Sicard* and then the U.S.S. *Conyngham*, all operating out of Hawaii. I suppose that as the person who presented the idea to the Navy, he might have been told something like "By the way, your idea is being worked on by AT&T." No letter has been found in the Archives that provided Heinlein with such information on the naval system. I maintain, however, that the inability to answer this particular question does not eliminate Laning.

We can also speculate about one more possible connection between Laning and the mystery device. Did it have any effect upon his future assignments? Following the *Conyngham*, he became a Communications Officer on the staff of Commander Destroyers, U.S. Pacific Fleet and later also on the staff of Commander Cruisers, U.S. Pacific Fleet. By its title, this position would appear to be in line with his postgraduate training in Communications and his previous staff assignment as Radio Officer. However, it is known that this new assignment involved important work on the development and implementation of the Combat Information Center. What determined Laning's selection for the duty assignment involving the

Combat Information Center? Was it based on his prior service record and his postgraduate training? Or might we assume that his connection with the naval system developed from Heinlein's story device was the reason for his selection?

In the absence of any evidence to the contrary, I will repeat my conclusion that the naval officer in question was Heinlein's classmate, Caleb Barrett Laning.

The identities of the device and the naval system are too closely related to be considered separately in any discussion which follows. In the preceding chapter, detailed information was presented for each of the seven selected story devices. Let us consider what that information means as we evaluate each of those devices as the possible solution to the mystery and suggest the naval system to which it may be connected.

The first story device to examine is the telechronometer. As a candidate for the solution of the mystery, it has several problems. The primary difficulty is that the concept of using external signals to synchronize a timekeeping device without human intervention was shown not to be original with Heinlein. Such a device could not have been constructed at the time as described in "If This Goes On—" in the form of a watch because the technology required to miniaturize the electronics did not exist. This would not have been a problem for a naval system, as the story device could have served as the inspiration for a larger but functionally equivalent system constructed using the vacuum tube technology of the time. Such a system would have been used to maintain the accuracy of shipboard chronometers. The greatest difficulty is that I was not able to find any indication of the existence of such a naval system in the period of interest or considerably thereafter. Synchronization of chronometers was done using radio signals, but these signals were used by the Quartermaster to perform the operation manually. So out goes the telechronometer.

One interesting question remains concerning the telechronometer. As noted in Chapter 13, such a device was also mentioned in the original versions of "Coventry," "Blowups Happen" and "Methuselah's Children" as published in *Astounding*. Quotes from the revision of "If This Goes On—" show that the telechronometer was replaced by a timekeeping device with no implication of synchronization to an external signal. Such a replacement of the telechronometer also occurred in the other stories, with the exception of "Blowups Happen."

Why would Heinlein have modified his early stories in such a manner? One explanation is that in the years since the stories had been written he would have gained experience as an author and could see various ways of improving how each story was told. Characters would be added or removed or the relationship changed between characters. A prime example is Sister Magdalene, "Maggie." In the original version of "If This Goes On—," she is a major character in the first installment, but effectively disappears in the second installment, being mentioned only once. In the later version, she is prominently featured in the second half of the story and even winds up marrying John Lyle just before the assault upon New Jerusalem. Another reason for modifying the story is to update the technology, as in the introduction of transistors and radar into the revised "If This Goes On—."

Let us consider one more reason for modifying the story. Is it reasonable to assume that in updating a story for later publication Heinlein would remove any mentions of the "story gag" that had inspired the actual naval system? Care must be exercised in following this line of reasoning as applied to the telechronometer. "Blowups Happen" was written in early 1940, at approximately the time that Heinlein would have become aware of the naval system based on his story device. If the telechronometer had been related in some way to the naval system, Heinlein would have had a chance to remove it from "Blowups Happen" prior to its publication in the September 1940 *Astounding*. Why feature a device in a story if it was already known that it had inspired a secret naval system? On the other hand, such a change to an accepted manuscript could have indicated to Campbell that this was the device mentioned by Heinlein in May or June. However, consider "Methuselah's Children," which was written even later. According to the material from the Heinlein Archives, the first installment was not sent to Campbell until early March 1941. If the telechronometer was the mystery device, then why even include it at all in the original version of that story?

The next step is to look at naval systems which may be linked to story devices, but which predated the appearance of the stories. If such a system already existed, either with or without Heinlein's knowledge, then it is not possible for his story device to have influenced its creation or development. The two story devices that fall into this category are the landing aid and the sonic range-finder.

The concept of using radio beams for the landing of aircraft, at least in the civil sector, was known for many years before the story appeared. That is all that Heinlein seems to be implying in "If This Goes On—" to guide the helicopter. If we expand from the simple story device to consider it as the possible inspiration for a more complex naval system to guide aircraft back to the carrier, it was found that such a system also predates the story. So much for the landing aid.

The sonic range-finders in "If This Goes On—" are the equivalent of sonar, which was introduced into the U.S. Navy in the early 1930s. It is not known what knowledge Heinlein had acquired with regard to these early systems, either while on active duty or following his discharge. As pointed out in the technical discussion, his brief description mixed the features of passive and active underwater sound systems. This indicates to me that he had only vague knowledge of such systems, rather than any real experience. The transducers in such systems could be constructed to operate at different frequencies within the accepted frequency band. However, it was not possible to locate any indication of operational or tactical significance of employing multiple ships or submarines with different frequencies. Therefore, we may also dispose of the sonic range-finder.

The sonic range-finder, like the telechronometer, is a device for which there is a substantial difference between the two versions of the story. The sonic range-finder was totally eliminated from the later version and replaced by radar. This will be discussed in some detail below with regard to the battle tracker.

Let us now consider the system that was developed during the war, perhaps saw some wartime service, and which was confidential/secret. I am referring, of course, to the infrared light phones. At this point, many of you reading this will say "***STOP!!! This meets the conditions and must be the answer.***" If I had only encountered a very brief mention of the Type E Voice System, with no details of its development or use, I might agree with you. But as indicated in Chapter 13, it was discovered that the development work for the Type E did not begin until May 1943, was performed by Northwestern University rather than AT&T, and it did not enter service until very late in the war. I would say that the starting date of such work relative to Heinlein's statements in late 1941 and early 1942 is the greatest factor against this being the solution. There was also the work done by others on communication by light well before the story appeared. So again, the concept was not something new that was introduced by Heinlein. I consider it highly unlikely that his brief mention of infrared light phones served as the inspiration for the actual development work performed in the area of naval infrared communication.

Finally, we must consider those three remaining systems that, like the infrared light phones, did enter naval service. The distinction is that in each case this occurred much later than suggested by Heinlein's statements. For each story device, the analysis of the corresponding naval system has indicated some considerable gap between the end of World War 2 and when each such system appeared. I will admit, however, that in spite of my research efforts, the possibility exists that some earlier version of one of these systems might exist.

These remaining three story devices are the airborne dead-reckoner, frequency variation and battle tracker. The first to be disposed of is the airborne dead-reckoner. The best available evidence has shown that although such systems were being developed during the war in both the United States and England with the capabilities assumed by Heinlein (based on the description in *For Us, The Living*), no such system appears to have entered U.S. naval service before the end of the 1940s.

With regard to the airborne dead-reckoner, there remains an additional unanswered question. In Chapter 4, the letter from Heinlein's friend William Corson was discussed. The letter referred to the device being employed by Scoles and Heinlein at the NAF as "your gadget." Keeping in mind that these were Corson's words and not Heinlein's, does this indicate a connection with the mystery device? Based on the vague description in Corson's letter, the only of the seven candidate devices with which it seems to have *any* chance of connection is the airborne dead-reckoner. It is concerned with obtaining information on position and speed and it involves an airplane. However, it is clearly not an airborne dead-reckoner. So what is it? Or am I simply wrong in assuming that it is related in any way to the mystery device?

The next device to be considered is covered under the term of frequency variation, but also includes the possibility of jamming and anti-jamming. As with the infrared light phones, much work in this area was done under the auspices of the NDRC. Unlike the infrared case where it was possible to point to the Type E Voice System, it was not possible to identify specific jamming or anti-jamming naval systems for communications in use during World War 2. If such systems could be identified, they might fall into the same category as the infrared light phones regarding secrecy and wartime service. As with the infrared phones, the start of the research and development well after Heinlein's statements makes it unlikely that any such system would be the solution. No mention was found of any system that could have been based on the story idea being developed prior to the NDRC work. Having eliminated any connection with jamming or anti-jamming, we are left with the reference to a secure communication system involving frequency variation. As stated in Chapter 13, the first such system that saw naval service did not appear until the early 1960s.

Finally, we come to the battle tracker. As mentioned in Chapter 13, it had once been assumed that the solution was simply that the battle tracker had inspired the development of the NC-2 Plotting System. The point of similarity was the ability to plot multiple targets. However, the appearance of the NC-2 in the mid-1950s and its initial development by a Canadian firm means that it cannot be the naval system to which Heinlein is referring in his comments shortly after Pearl Harbor. Nevertheless, I would like to propose a solution that is a combination of the battle tracker with one of the other candidates.

Let us consider the problems of navigation and tracking of the formation during the attack on New Jerusalem. A search of the original story reveals that there are several sections of text concerned with these tasks. Some of these have already been quoted in the battle tracker section in Chapter 13. In each of these cases, comparison of the quotes indicates there is no significant difference between the two versions of the story. However, there is another block of text from the original story that should be considered. Three portions of this block appear in the listing in Chapter 11. Two items, Nos. 180 and 181, were selected because of their reference to the sonic range-finder. The other item, No. 182, was concerned with the operation of the dead-reckoner and was not selected for further analysis. The entire block occurs as smoke has reduced visibility during the battle:

> Shortly we were hooked up with the transports and second-line craft, as well as with the bombers and the rocket assigned to spot the fall of shot. The rocket reported that smoke had reduced visibility to zero. I told him to stand by, as a favorable sea breeze at sunup might make him useful again.
>
> We weren't very dependent on direct observation in any case. We knew to an inch the geographical location of every angle and surface of our objective. We had made our departure with reference to the nearest benchmark of the geodetic survey, and had performed accurate triangulation up to the time the televisors blew. Thereafter we checked our dead reckoning by means of the data given by the sonic range-finders. That is to say that we knew our positions relative to each other; therefore, whenever any craft in formation had an opportunity to fix its position with reference to the ground by recognizing a building, bridge, or other fixed point, every other craft would immediately know its own exact position relative to every point in New Jerusalem.
>
> Even after the sonics failed, we were well enough off. The dead reckoners of a tread-driven cruiser are surprisingly accurate. It's like this—every time the tread lays down it measures the ground it passes over. A little differential gadget to compare the speeds of the port and starboard treads, another gadget to do vector sums, and a gyro compass hook-in, to check and correct the vector addition, and you have a dead reckoner that will trace your course

over fifteen miles of rough terrain and tell within a yard where you have ended up.

Shot was falling all around us.

The above quote and those sections quoted in Chapter 13 have allowed me to come up with an impression of how the battle tracker would have operated. This block diagram is shown in Figure 5. Only data inputs and flows are shown, with no attempt to describe how any functions are performed.

Heinlein referred to the plotting of the positions of the craft in the formation without describing the operation of the plotting mechanism or specifying how many craft were being plotted. In the block diagram, the plotter is simply represented by showing four lines being plotted, with inputs being received on four channels. Channel 1 is used for the plotting of "own craft," which in the story corresponds to the flagship.

The starting position, course and speed of the flagship would be set by manual controls, the "keys and knobs" in the story, which would also be used to apply corrections at later times. Course and speed inputs are also provided by the dead-reckoner, which operates from the different speeds of the treads. Heinlein's claim of accuracy to within a yard after fifteen miles is clearly unrealistic. Any driving mechanism operating over uncertain ground is going to have some amount of slippage, which will introduce errors. The manual controls and dead-reckoner both feed one channel of the computation section, which provides its results to the plotter.

The problems arise when the plotting for the other craft is considered. Each of the other three channels is associated with a different craft in the formation. The manual controls permit the entry of the position, course and speed data, as was done for "own craft." Where would such information come from? First, it should be noted that both versions of the story mention a growing pile of dispatches as John Lyle works at the tracker. Second, we can see in one of the items of quoted text for the battle tracker in Chapter 13, Lyle restarts the tracker after "the last transport had checked in by phone." My interpretation of these two references to messages is that he was receiving navigational data from the other craft in the formation. Each craft would have derived the data from its own observations and the operation of its own dead-reckoner. This data would have been provided first by radio, then by infrared light phone and finally by the telepathic "sensitives."

Now consider the sonic range-finder. Heinlein referred to the use of the dead-reckoner "after the sonics failed." It is interesting to note that no mention is actually made in the story of the failure of the sonics. Perhaps

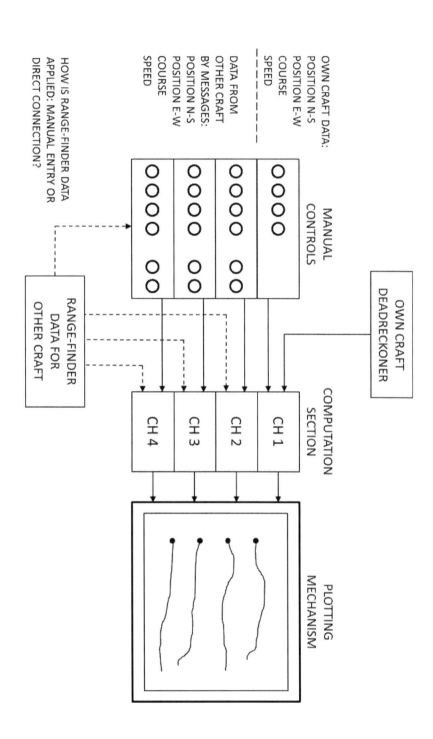

he should have said, "*if* the sonics failed." In the section of text quoted above, Heinlein stated that the range-finders permitted each craft to know the position of every other craft in the formation relative to itself. This is inherently more accurate than each craft reporting its position as derived by dead-reckoning.

To help understand this, consider the flagship and one other craft. Assume that each starts from a correctly known position and proceeds for a period of time, perhaps fifteen minutes. Based on what the dead-reckoner on each craft shows, they assume that they are at locations A and B, respectively. However, locations A and B are both incorrect due to errors caused by slippage of the treads when moving over rough ground. The two craft are actually at slightly different locations, which will be called A' and B'. The flagship then receives a message from the other craft saying that it is at location B. If the flagship attempts to determine the heading and distance of the other craft, any calculations will be based on the flagship's assumed location A and the other craft's reported location B, rather than the true values of A' and B'. Unless the differences in both distance and direction between A and A' are precisely the same as the differences between B and B', the calculations will give an incorrect result.

This problem vanishes if the sonic range-finder is used. The range-finder tells the flagship that the other craft is actually X yards distant at a bearing of Y degrees. It does not matter that each craft may be in error about its own absolute location. The range-finder enables the flagship to plot the other craft's correct position, relative to itself.

How is the sonic range-finder data provided to the battle tracker? The two possibilities are shown as dotted lines in Figure 5. If the data is supplied to the operator, it will be in distance and bearing format. This is incompatible with the controls used to input the position, course and speed data contained in the messages. It is possible, of course, for additional controls to exist for each channel to permit range and bearing data to be entered manually. You will note that in Figure 5 extra manual controls are provided for the other craft in the formation. However, providing some form of direct connection between the sonic range-finder and the computation section of the battle tracker would reduce the workload upon the operator and eliminate human error.

What is in the corresponding section of text in the later version of the story? The most significant change is the elimination of the sonic range-finders and the insertion of references to radar. One thing to note is that the radar was not simply used as direct replacement for the sonic range-finder.

Figure 5. Block Diagram of Battle Tracker based on description in "If This Goes On—"

The sonic range-finders were used primarily for navigation and keeping the formation intact, whereas the radar was used for observing the fall of shot and targeting:

> Shortly we were hooked up with the transports and second-line craft, as well as with the bombers and the rocket-jet spotting the fall of shot. *The jet reported visibility zero and complained that he wasn't getting anything intelligible by radar.* I told him to stand by; the morning breeze might clear the smoke away presently.
>
> We weren't dependent on him anyway; we knew our positions almost to the inch. We had taken departure from a benchmark and our deadreckoning was checked for the whole battle line every time any skipper identified a map-shown landmark. In addition, the deadreckoners of a tread-driven cruiser are surprisingly accurate; the treads literally measure every yard of ground as they pass over it and a little differential gadget compares the treads and keeps just as careful track of direction. *The smoke did not really bother us and we could keep on firing accurately even if radar failed. On the other hand, if the Palace commander kept us in smoke he himself was entirely dependent on radar.*
>
> *His radar was apparently working;* shot was falling all around us.

I have indicated in italics the only mentions of radar during the attack upon New Jerusalem. The only other mention of radar in the entire story occurs much earlier during John Lyle's escape in the stolen rocket as he speculates about its use by the authorities in tracking him.

When I looked at the later version of the story, I noticed that there was **absolutely no mention of the flagship or any other attacking craft having radar**. Only the jet observing the fall of shot and the Palace were explicitly stated as having radar. The attacking craft are known to be analogs of warships, and Heinlein clearly knew of the use of radar on ships during World War 2. In such cases, radar was used for navigation and keeping formations intact as well as targeting. It seems to me that Heinlein could have used the radar for the same purposes as the sonic range-finders. The absence of radar on any of the attacking craft is therefore very puzzling.

The key point I wish to make is that if the flagship and the other craft did not possess radar, then there would have been no need to consider interfacing radar with the battle tracker. If we accept that Heinlein was concerned about preserving the secrecy of the naval system, his revision of the story would have allowed him to eliminate the connection in the original story that served as the inspiration for the naval system.

Therefore, I am proposing that the solution is a naval system that provided an interface between the existing dead reckoning tracers and sonar. This would have been an interim approach to the plotting of targets before the appearance of the NC-2. That such a system existed is conceivable, but it gives rise to a question of implementation.

If you have the information from sonar for just one target provided to the DRT, which is capable of only plotting the track for own ship, how do you indicate the target? In other systems capable of plotting or displaying own ship and at least one target, these operations were performed simultaneously. To plot the location of the target, the Sperry Battle Tracer used an arm capable of pivoting around the head that was plotting the position of own ship. In the NC-2, as described in Chapter 13, the positions of own ship and targets are indicated at the same time by colored lights.

However, there is nothing to prevent plotting operations from being performed sequentially. A DRT could indicate the most recent position of own ship and then move to the location necessary to indicate the position of the target. The principle is the same as a multi-pen plotter, which draws the lines in one color and then switches to a pen of a different color before plotting additional lines. I am not claiming this sequential process as part of the proposed solution. I am only mentioning it to show that I am aware of the plotting problem.

How many targets could be handled? The original battle tracker was capable of plotting own ship plus target. Even the later model of the NC-2 was capable of only plotting four targets in addition to own ship. The number of craft plotted by the battle tracker in the story, although never stated, always seemed to me to be more than four.

Another detail to consider is that the battle tracker was electromechanical in nature. If we are to accept Heinlein's statement from the Virtues essay that both the story device and naval system were electronic, the battle tracker alone would appear to present a problem. However, if we accept the solution as involving the connection of the battle tracker with the sonic range-finders, this connection would have to be electronic or electrical in nature.

There was definitely wartime interest in interfacing sensor information directly with the dead reckoning information. This was described in "The Interconnection of Dead-Reckoning and Radar Data for Precision Navigation and Prediction," which appeared in the *Journal of the Franklin Institute* in 1946. Some examples in the paper referred to ship navigation, and employed the same speed and bearing information that would be employed by a DRT. As in the DRT, the course vector was resolved into

N-S and E-W components, although this resolution was done electronically instead of mechanically. These components were used by circuitry that controlled a Plan-Position Indicator (PPI) radar display. In the first example, a point on the coastline was kept in the center of the display as the image of the ship moved away, rather than the normal approach of keeping own ship in the center. Another example was concerned with displaying the relative motion of two ships. As these examples made use of a PPI display, which did not come into use until 1942, they cannot be part of the system directly inspired by Heinlein's story. They have been mentioned only to show the types of ideas being developed and to give an indication of the level of technology at the end of the war.

Since I cannot point to an actual naval system of the period of interest that was concerned with the combination of DRT and sonar, I cannot claim to have arrived at a definite solution. All I have is speculation. However, this speculation is based on the elimination of other story devices, how the operation of the battle tracker and its various inputs were described by Heinlein and the differences between the versions of the story.

==================

I fully expect that there will be disagreement with the various parts of my solution, particularly the identity of the mystery device. Therefore, I ask that you consider some of the following points.

Secrecy

Some of you might suggest that I have been unable to discover the correct answer because the naval system in question is still secret. Even if I had correctly picked the proper story device, the secrecy surrounding the naval system would have prevented me from making the connection. Considering the time elapsed since World War 2 and the large amount of material that has been declassified, I would say that this is extremely unlikely. Advances in technology in so many areas make it reasonable to conclude that the Navy would have developed newer systems of all types and functions. If the older systems were rendered obsolete, this means that they would no longer be covered by a cloak of secrecy. Finally, we cannot say that Heinlein's many claims of secrecy were actually valid.

Problems with material in letters or essay

As discussed in Chapter 4, there are several problems with the clues provided by Heinlein. The existence of inconsistencies between various clues required me to make certain assumptions to be able to proceed. Perhaps one or more of my assumptions regarding the nature of the naval system or its development was incorrect and has led me down the wrong path. If, as suggested in Chapter 4, various statements were made solely so that the device would be difficult to identify, is there any way to untangle the web of deception?

Candidate device missed in story

As previously stated, each of the stories was reviewed multiple times in the course of compiling the list of story devices. In spite of this, it is conceivable that I may have read right past a mention of some device within a story. However, I do not consider it very likely.

Misinterpretation of device description

Having compiled the list of all story devices in Chapter 11, it was then necessary to go through and select any of those that appeared to have a naval connection. To do so required knowledge of naval systems, a topic to be discussed in the next section. However, the process also depended on my interpretation of the description of the story devices. My interpretation of some device may not have been what Heinlein meant or, more important, how it was interpreted by the naval officer who was involved in the development of the system. This could have led me to eliminate that device from further analysis and research. It could also have led me to link it with the wrong naval system.

Lack of knowledge of existence of naval system in question

I would by no means present myself as an expert on World War 2 naval technology. The state of my knowledge in this area at the start of my attempt to solve the mystery was very limited. A large portion of my research has been in gathering information on naval technology of the period. I do feel that, based on the books, articles and other material that I have collected and examined, and the various people I have consulted, I have obtained a fair picture of the technology from the period of interest. This picture is only partly represented by what was discussed in Chapter 5. I realize, of course, that it would be impossible to have knowledge of every single system in use by the Navy during the war. An alternative solution might be suggested by someone else involving a naval system that is outside the range of my studies.

Link between story device and naval system is very tenuous

Where I have been able to connect a naval system to a story device, I feel that I am justified in saying that the connection is obvious. This corresponds to the case of the dracone as presented in Chapter 9, where that invention was directly linked to the flexible tank presented in Herbert's *Under Pressure*. It was shown in the same chapter, however, that not every case that was investigated has such a clear connection between story concept and the invention or discovery. The best example presented of this type of connection was Yefremov's "Star Ships" and Denisyuk's invention of volume holography. If the connection between the story device of Heinlein and the naval system is of the type represented by Yefremov and Denisyuk, I think that most of you will agree that discovering that connection in the absence of additional data might be impossible.

===================

As I have related at the beginning of this work, and as I hope should be obvious from the range of material presented, this research has involved much time and effort on my part. Even though a definite solution has not yet been found, I am not inclined to simply toss it all out and walk away.

I would hope that it is clear to all that I would like to be the person to present a definite solution to the Heinlein mystery. I still might be. Even though I have collected and organized this material for publication, I will keep working to find a solution. The desire to arrive at the solution has kept me working on this problem longer than I probably should have. Aside from certain details regarding the relationship between inventions and SF and additional data on selected naval systems, I could have written this book in essentially the same form a few years earlier. On the other hand, there is the feeling that if one checks just one more source or pursues just one more lead, it might provide the answer.

I have learned a great deal in the course of my research. There are many interesting details contained in the correspondence between Heinlein and Campbell. Then there are the accomplishments of the members of the Class of 1929. I have always had an interest in both military history and the history of technology, so most of the material that I have collected fed those interests. I have been able to write a number of short articles that I hope have added in some small way to the study of science fiction and of Robert Heinlein in particular. I have traveled to many interesting places in search of information. I have communicated with many people in the course of these studies, and met many in person. None of which would have happened if I had simply read the Virtues essay and *Grumbles* and then gone on to something else instead of thinking "What is the naval system that Heinlein was talking about?"

What are the different types of information that I have accumulated during the course of my research?

Archive material from the letters and the Virtues essay

When I first started this research, all I had to work with was *Grumbles from the Grave* and the book containing the Virtues essay. It took a trip out to the Heinlein Archives when they were located at UCSC to be able to look at even a small amount of the material during the few days I was there. Now all of this and much more is available online from the Heinlein Archives, to be examined at leisure. My research would have been accelerated if such access had existed earlier. You now have the opportunity to search the material from the Archives yourself to see if I have missed something or that you disagree with some of my assumptions or conclusions.

Classmate information

The greater part of such information concerns Caleb Laning and includes his service record. For those classmates who made it to flag rank, even if only upon retirement, it was possible to obtain their naval biographies. Of course, these fall short of the material contained in a service record. For the majority of Heinlein's classmates, the available information has been limited to what is contained in the *Register of Alumni* or what I was able to locate in the Nimitz Library at the Naval Academy. I still consider it possible that a descendant or relative of a member of the Class of 1929 may be in possession of information that points to the mystery device or at least suggests a new direction for research. I would have great difficulty finding such people, but the publication of this book to put the question out there to the public could conceivably cause something new to be revealed.

Material extracted from original published version of stories

You can accept my list of devices as presented in Chapter 11, or examine the early stories and compile your own list. I had collected copies all of required early issues of the pulp magazines before the Heinlein Archives were available online. You now have it much easier, and cheaper as well. A file exists in the Archives for each of the stories. Such a file contains a copy of Heinlein's manuscript and should also contain a copy of the published story. Perhaps someone will find a story device that I simply missed.

Naval Technology

This material was compiled from a large number of sources, which are contained in the Bibliography. However, you are obviously not restricted to those sources. Here is an area where someone may have knowledge of a particular naval system of which I am unaware or additional information on one of those systems that I selected as a possible solution but then rejected after additional research.

==================

I hope that some of you will also consider the material I have presented that is not directly related to the Heinlein mystery. There is the material on Naval Science Fiction as presented in Chapter 7, which could serve as the starting point for additional research. In pursuit of the solution to the mystery, I had begun to wonder if, as stated by J. O. Bailey, that it was not possible to establish connections between inventions and science fiction. This is what led me to consider inventions possibly related to works by other authors. The material that I presented in Chapters 8 and 9 definitely indicates that such connections do exist. Even if a definite solution is never found to the Heinlein mystery, this represents an area for research that has not been explored in sufficient detail.

==================

If you wish to be the one to find a definite solution to the Mystery, you will have to go back through the material I have presented, re-examine my assumptions and conclusions, and perhaps develop new ones of your own. You will consult some of the same reference material that I employed. And probably find new sources of data, if they exist. And even if you do not succeed in finding your own solution to The Great Heinlein Mystery, I think that you will discover that such searches for knowledge are never a wasted effort.

I wish you luck!!!!!

APPENDIX 1

GRADUATES OF THE CLASS OF 1929

The following pages identify the 240 graduates of the Class of 1929 of the United States Naval Academy. The rank shown is at the time of retirement or death. Number in boldface is the graduation number and indicates relative standing in the class at graduation. (**09356** to **09595**)

This information was obtained from the 1992 edition of the *Register of Alumni* and is presented with the permission of the U.S. Naval Academy Alumni Association, Inc.

1. Adamson, Frank Marshall RADM 09367	21. Britt, Jacob William LCDR 09534
2. Akin, Harvey Davidson LT 09449	22. Brown, Melvin George Col USMC 09471
3. Allen, William Carlton LCDR 09361	23. Brown, Winston Seaborn CAPT 09461
4. Anderson, Samuel Clay CAPT 09373	24. Brownlee, Robert Carson LT 09400
5. Andrews, John CAPT 09477	25. Brunton, Charles Edward RADM 09551
6. Armbrust, Carl Raymond CAPT 09571	26. Bryson, William Franklyn LT USMC 09568
7. Arthur, William Samuel LTJG 09509	27. Buckalew, William Dorsey 09484
8. Ashford, George Woodson RADM 09411	28. Burke, Edward Joseph RADM 09514
9. Bacher, Edward Johnson RADM 09393	29. Bush, Burt Heber CDR 09423
10. Baird, Abraham Lincoln CAPT 09357	30. Bush, Donald Porter LTC USAR 09370
11. Baldauf, Laurence Charles RADM 09413	31. Butler, Edward Francis CDR 09463
12. Ballinger, Richard Robert RADM 09469	32. Butts, Whitmore Spencer RADM 09548
13. Beardsley, George Francis VADM 09468	33. Canty, Joseph Patrick RADM 09396
14. Benson, Roy Stanley RADM 09458	34. Carlson, Daniel RADM 09511
15. Berkley, Joseph Berzowski CAPT 09398	35. Carmichael, George Kennedy RADM 09505
16. Bermingham, John Michael LCDR 09494	36. Carver, Lamar Peyton RADM 09426
17. Bernet, Howard Cavender CAPT 09460	37. Cashman, William Arthur CDR USNR 09521
18. Bond, Awtry Lawrence LTJG 09590	38. Christie, Carl Guilford CAPT 09581
19. Brandley, Frank Albin RADM 09576	39. Clark, Robert Nicholson RADM 09486
20. Briant, Granville Charles CAPT 09472	40. Coe, Benjamin RADM 09457

41. Coffin, Harry Nelson RADM **09495**	61. Dickinson, Milton Carey CAPT **09589**
42. Coleman, William Francis BGEN USMC **09381**	62. Dieter, George Hedwig **09404**
43. Collett, John Austin LCDR **09438**	63. Dodson, Edwin Neil **09493**
44. Collins, Ernest Clifford CDR **09552**	64. Dowling, Dean Barrow CDR **09545**
45. Cone, Gordon LT USMC **09480**	65. Duborg, Francis Rahr RADM **09401**
46. Cone, Henry Shipman RADM **09572**	66. Duffy, Leonard Vincent LT **09591**
47. Conley, Edwin Gus CAPT **09524**	67. Duval, Joseph Berwick CAPT **09459**
48. Connell, Robert Joseph CDR **09547**	68. Duvall, Gordon Franklin LCDR **09517**
49. Crichton, Charles Helmick RADM **09473**	69. Dye, Williston Lamar CAPT **09407**
50. Crist, Raymond Fowler BGEN USMC **09535**	70. Dyer, Edward Colston BGEN USMC **09464**
51. Curry, Manley Lamar BGEN USMC **09474**	71. Easton, William Thomas CAPT **09470**
52. Darnell, William Irvin CDR **09487**	72. Eller, Donald Temple RADM **09502**
53. D'Avi, Joseph Arthur CAPT **09541**	73. Epps, William Bunyon CAPT **09490**
54. Davidson, John Frederick RADM **09439**	74. Farrin, James Moore RADM **09358**
55. Davis, Royce Purinton CAPT **09492**	75. Fenton, Charles Rudolph RADM **09540**
56. Davison, John Walter CAPT **09386**	76. Ferrier, David Tweed CDR **09427**
57. Davison, Thurlow Weed RADM **09563**	77. Fitzgerald, Charles Tuckerman CAPT **09419**
58. Denbo, Robert Wayne RADM **09523**	78. Flatley, James Henry VADM **09556**
59. Denham, Walter Sam CAPT **09392**	79. Foley, James Louis CAPT **09557**
60. Dennett, Eric Van Emburgh RADM **09616**	80. Foley, Paul RADM **09397**

81. Folger, Edward Clinton CDR **09420**	101. Hiemenz, Herbert John CAPT **09366**
82. Fox, Leonard Oron CAPT **09384**	102. Hill, Arthur Sinclair CAPT **09436**
83. Frank, Nickolas John RADM **09512**	103. Hinman, Maurice Blackwell CDR **09379**
84. Frankel, Samuel Benjamin RADM **09475**	104. Hogle, Reynold Delos VADM **09446**
85. Galbraith, William Jackson RADM **09488**	105. Hood, Alexander Haldeman CAPT **09527**
86. Garland, Guy Puett CAPT **09432**	106. Huelskamp, Wilfred James CDR **09453**
87. Garner, Howard Robert LCDR **09415**	107. Huff, Gerald Lewis RADM **09376**
88. Garrett, Kenneth Howard **09467**	108. Humphrey, Pat List **09409**
89. Gates, William Shinn LTJG **09387**	109. Hutchins, Edward Francis CAPT **09424**
90. Giese, Carl Emil CAPT **09570**	110. Hutchison, Charles Kenneth CDR **09564**
91. Gray, Allan McLeod CAPT **09519**	111. Jackson, Roy CAPT **09429**
92. Greenamyer, Lloyd Keys LCDR **09501**	112. Johansen, Gustave Norman RADM **09503**
93. Griffith, Samuel Blair BGEN USMC **09531**	113. Johnson, Carl Arthur CAPT **09550**
94. Hall, Finley Elliott CDR **09485**	114. Johnson, Chandler Wilce LTC USMC **09489**
95. Hannon, Robert Edward CAPT **09444**	115. Johnson, Francis Joseph RADM **09554**
96. Hardin, James Thomas CAPT **09496**	116. Johnson, Roy Lee ADM **09434**
97. Hart, Russell Armour CDR **09579**	117. Jones, Lloyd Hoadley **09476**
98. Hastings, William T. **09431**	118. Jordan, Francis Dixon LCDR **09515**
99. Heinlein, Robert Anson LTJG **09375**	119. Junghans, Earl Austin CAPT **09372**
100. Hezlep, James McBurney LCDR **09578**	120. Kabler, William Leverette RADM **09389**

121. Karrer, Harold Edward **09416**	141. Mains, MacDonald Crawford CDR **09414**
122. Keatley, John Hancock RADM **09360**	142. Marchant, William Alexander **09594**
123. Keeler, Frederic Seward RADM **09482**	143. Marcy, Clayton Clifton CAPT **09455**
124. Kennedy, Marvin Granville RADM **09422**	144. Martin, Edwin Prather LCDR **09454**
125. Kent, Thomas Everett LT **09378**	145. Martin, Melvin Micajah LCDR **09546**
126. Keyes, Raymond Stedman **09567**	146. Mattie, Dominic Lewis RADM **09588**
127. Kirk, Oliver Grafton RADM **09428**	147. McAlpin, John Volney **09561**
128. Kohr, George Lester CAPT **09553**	148. McCauley, Clayton Chot CAPT **09483**
129. Kuhn, Frederick William CAPT **09466**	149. McClure, William Howard CAPT **09408**
130. Lake, James Bushrod CAPT USMC **09573**	150. McCoy, Robert Bruce **09380**
131. Lake, Richard Cross CAPT **09403**	151. McElroy, John Harper CAPT **09582**
132. Lang, Harry Cox MAJ USMC **09565**	152. McGinnis, Robert Devore RADM **09430**
133. Laning, Caleb Barrett RADM **09394**	153. McGregor, Rob Roy RADM **09508**
134. Ledbetter, Otho Christoper LTC USMC **09559**	154. McIntyre, Lee Emerson **09451**
135. Lincoln, Samuel Ankeny LCDR **09497**	155. McRoberts, Henry Johnston CDR **09536**
136. Lippert, Frederick George CAPT **09395**	156. Meeker, Charles Alton LCDR **09574**
137. Loomis, Almon Ellsworth RADM **09522**	157. Miller, Adolph Jerome CAPT **09520**
138. Lucas, Albert Davis CAPT **09539**	158. Miller, Clair Lemoine CDR **09382**
139. Lynch, Ralph Clinton RADM **09417**	159. Miller, Cleaveland F. LCDR **09575**
140. MacFarlane, Harold Archibald LTJG **09374**	160. Mills, James Herve CAPT **09478**

161. Mitchell, Frank Paull RADM **09507**	181. Peterson, Carl Arthur CAPT **09418**
162. Moore, Clarence Joseph **09405**	182. Phillips, Charles Frederick CDR **09583**
163. Moore, John Raymond RADM **09388**	183. Prause, Jack Hamilton CDR **09526**
164. Morgan, Charles Claude CDR **09542**	184. Pryor, Knight CAPT **09359**
165. Morse, Leonard Townsend CAPT **09377**	185. Raby, John RADM **09525**
166. Murray, Homer Carr COL USMC **09406**	186. Ramsbotham, Robert Joynson CAPT **09402**
167. Nash, Herbert LCDR **09504**	187. Ray, Herman Lamar RADM **09425**
168. Nelson, Hugo Adolphus **09555**	188. Rembert, John Patrick RADM **09518**
169. Nelson, Paul John CAPT **09498**	189. Richardson, Leslie Edward CAPT **09362**
170. Nielsen, Harold CDR **09544**	190. Richter, William Julius CAPT **09584**
171. Novak, Frank CAPT **09385**	191. Ricketts, Claude Vernon ADM **09399**
172. O'Donnell, Edward Joseph RADM **09437**	192. Roberts, Clyde Cameron **09538**
173. Oliver, William LTJG **09593**	193. Roberts, Deane Carroll COL USMC **09586**
174. Osborn, Phillip Ransom CAPT **09580**	194. Rodimon, Warner Scott RADM **09442**
175. Parish, Elliott Walter CAPT **09391**	195. Rooney, Roderick Shanahan CDR **09529**
176. Patrick, G. Serpell RADM **09456**	196. Roth, Egbert Adolph LCDR **09530**
177. Pennewill, William Ellison LCDR **09500**	197. Roughton, Emery CAPT **09549**
178. Perkins, Albert Carson CAPT **09412**	198. Schreiber, Earl Tobias RADM **09433**
179. Perreault, Seraphin Bach LCDR **09481**	199. Schwable, Frank Hawse BGEN USMC **09441**
180. Persons, Henry Stanford RADM **09371**	200. Sharp, George Arthur RADM **09558**

201. Shute, Corben Clark CAPT **09363**	221. Walker, Calvin Alexander LCDR **09543**
202. Simpler, Leroy Coard RADM **09562**	222. Walker, Hiram Street **09587**
203. StAngelo, Augustus Robert RADM **09569**	223. Walker, Phillip Andrew CAPT **09447**
204. Stephan, Edward Clark RADM **09533**	224. Waltermire, William Glen **09537**
205. Stephens, Frank Briscoe CDR **09452**	225. Warfield, Charles Dorsey COL USAFR **09506**
206. Stewart, Claude Weaver LCDR **09566**	226. Waterhouse, Jacob Wilson RADM **09421**
207. Stillman, Donald Frederick ENS **09592**	227. Watson, William Henry CAPT **09448**
208. Stone, Lowell Thornton RADM **09465**	228. Weakley, Charles Enright VADM **09368**
209. Stovall, William S. RADM **09560**	229. Webster, John Bartholomew **09356**
210. Strahorn, Albert Wesley LT **09435**	230. Weiss, Donald Frederick RADM **09532**
211. Strong, Stanley Carter CAPT **09491**	231. Welsh, David James RADM **09499**
212. Sullivan, Raymond Brooks 2ndLT USMC **09513**	232. White, Albert Francis RADM **09595**
213. Tolley, Kemp RADM **09479**	233. White, William Waldron CAPT **09445**
214. Trescott, Charles Edward CAPT **09364**	234. Wilkinson, Robert Holden RADM **09510**
215. Triebel, Charles Otto RADM **09443**	235. Wilson, Thomas Payne CAPT **09390**
216. Twohy, Henry Bell LT **09410**	236. Wilson, Thomas Rex ENS **09450**
217. Van Voorhis, Bruce Avery CDR **09440**	237. Woerner, Paul Leslie CDR **09528**
218. Visser, Richard Gerben RADM **09577**	238. Wotton, Albert Harry LT **09585**
219. Wait, Delos Edwin RADM **09369**	239. Wyatt, Mathias Beally LTJG **09383**
220. Wales, George Herrick RADM **09365**	240. Yoho, John Richard LCDR **09462**

APPENDIX 2

ELECTROMECHANICAL COMPUTING

The performance of mathematical calculations by purely mechanical means is outside the scope of our search for the mystery device, which has been described as electronic in nature. The mention of such devices in several of Heinlein's early works, however, has been the subject of quite a bit of interest and research and I feel it is worth presenting to provide some feel for the level of technology with which Heinlein was familiar. This clearly shows how Heinlein was applying his naval training and experience to his works of science fiction.

In the foreword to *Expanded Universe*, we find the oft-repeated story of his submitting "Life-Line" to *Astounding* instead of submitting it to a contest sponsored by another magazine. In relating this story, Heinlein stated:

> I was highly skilled in ordnance, gunnery, and fire control for Naval vessels, a skill for which there was no demand ashore . . . .

A similar statement occurs in the letter written by Heinlein to John Campbell on May 1, 1939 following the sale of "Life-Line":

> You may possibly wish to know who a new author is. I am a retired naval officer. When I was in the fleet my specialty was ballistics, with emphasis on the electro-mechanical integrators used in fire control.

At the same period in his life when he was beginning his career as a science fiction author, Heinlein was also interested in the subject of

General Semantics. He and Leslyn Heinlein attended a General Semantics seminar in Los Angeles in the summer of 1939, and another in Chicago in July 1940 as they were returning from their trip to the East Coast. In his application to the first seminar, he stated that one of his former positions had been "Ensign and Lieut (jg) US Navy, various line job[s], specializing in electro-mechanical integrators." In the second application, he similarly stated that he "specialized in electromechanical integrating machines."

In referring to these electromechanical devices in his applications, Heinlein was employing a euphemism for the systems that he would have employed in the process of Fire Control. Naval gunfire has long since progressed past the point where a cannon was visually aimed from one relatively slow moving vessel to another at very close range. As both the speed of naval vessels and the range of their guns increased, the problem of properly aiming these guns became more and more difficult. The basic fire control problem consists of taking the available information, which is the speed and course of your ship and the estimated speed and course of the enemy ship, and to attempt to predict the position of the enemy ship at some time in the very near future. This position determines where your guns should be aimed and when they should be fired.

A duck hunter performs the same type of calculation when he aims at a point ahead of a duck in flight. His problem is simplified as the duck is most likely flying at a reasonably constant speed and course. In the case of naval surface fire control, the problem is complicated by the fact that neither vessel is likely to be moving with an easily predictable path and speed. Your vessel is maneuvering to avoid enemy gunfire at the same time that the enemy is performing his own maneuvers to avoid your gunfire. If we then consider the application of fire control to anti-aircraft fire, we are faced with the much higher speed of the target, its ability to maneuver drastically, and the addition of a third dimension to the calculations.

The means of solving the problem of fire control today is based upon the use of radar and electronic computers. At the time that Heinlein's writing career was beginning, radar was being developed and installed on naval vessels. Radar developed specifically for use in controlling naval gunfire appeared at the end of 1940. But electronic computers of sufficient speed and reliability to be employed on naval vessels were many years in the future. Throughout World War 2 and for years afterward, there was still total dependence on electromechanical calculating devices.

The means of determining a ship's position in the era before GPS and other electronic aids was celestial navigation. This determination was based on careful observations of the sun or the stars. But there will always be times when such observations are not possible. This is when the process of dead-reckoning is used. It attempts to determine the current position of the ship on the basis of a known starting point and successive measurements of its speed and bearing. This process may be done manually or may make use of electromechanical computing to perform the required calculations and to plot the estimate of the ship's position.

The first such mention of electromechanical computing falls outside the range of stories that are being considered for the mystery device, as it occurs within Heinlein's long unpublished work *For Us, The Living*. The character Perry is attempting to explain what was actually possible with the fire control technology of his time:

> the most amazing technical devices—mechanical brains that could solve the most involved ballistic problems, problems in calculus using a round dozen variables, problems that would have taken an experienced mathematician days to solve. The machine solved them in a split second and applied the solutions . . . .

We next encounter a mechanical computing device in Heinlein's second published story, "Misfit." Here the problem is one of navigation, although in space rather than at sea. As the story reaches the point where the change in the asteroid's orbit is to be performed, we are told that:

> Libby was assigned to the ballistic calculator, three Earth-tons of thinking metal that dominated the plotting room. He loved the big machine with its integrators, three-dimensional cams, its differential gear trains, and silent gyroscopes.

It is the failure of a component of this machine in the midst of the orbital transfer operation which forces Libby to make use of his extraordinary mathematical talents, so recently discovered.

The next mentions of mechanical computing occur in the second part of "If This Goes On—," with regard to the attack on New Jerusalem. This story contains the most detailed mention of such devices in any of Heinlein's stories. Lyle's duty station is on the "flagship" of the attacking "fleet," keeping in mind that the attack is occurring upon land:

> We had improvised a flag-plotting room in the communications room just abaft the conning tower, tearing out the long-range televisor to make room for the battle tracker and concentration plot. I was sweating over my jury-rigged tracker, hoping to heaven that the makeshift shock absorbers would be sufficient to cushion the concussion when we opened up.

A bit later:

> I passed the order, and cut my tracker out of the circuit for fifteen minutes. It wasn't built to handle so many variables at such high speeds, and there was no sense in overloading the relays. Nineteen minutes later the last transport had checked in by phone; I made a preliminary setup on the tracker, threw the start switch and let the correction data come in. For a couple of minutes I was very busy balancing the data, hands moving swiftly among the keys and knobs, then the integrators took hold with a satisfying hum, and I reported: "Tracking, sir!"

Other quotes clearly indicate that the battle tracker is being used to plot the positions of the various craft in the formation employed in the attack upon New Jerusalem. If the objective was to plot the position of enemy craft, this would be part of a fire control problem. However, since the craft are all friendly, the focus is on navigation and maintaining the formation.

Even later in the same story we encounter a device known as the differential:

> The dead reckoners of a tread-driven cruiser are surprisingly accurate. It's like this—every time the tread lays down it measures the ground it passes over. A little differential gadget to compare the speeds of the port and starboard treads, another gadget to do vector sums, and a gyro-compass hook-in, to check and correct the vector addition, and you have a dead reckoner that will trace your course over fifteen mile of rough terrain and tell within a yard where you have ended up.

Any applications which occur in later works are either performing some unspecified calculation or involve problems of navigation. A brief mention of mechanical computing systems occurs in "The Roads Must Roll," where a comparison is made to the mental processes of Chief Engineer Gaines. No such computing devices are actually employed within the story. We then move beyond the range of stories considered in the basic search. In "Methuselah's Children," reference is made to a "ballistic calculator," the same type of device mentioned in "Misfit." In this case, the device operates with no moving parts. We again encounter mechanical components in "Beyond This Horizon," with references to the "settings of three-dimensional cams" and then later in comparing the computing of the

Great Research to "ordinary ball-and-plane integrators and ordinary three-dimensional cams."

I had first thought that descriptions of such mechanical computing did not exist in the works of Heinlein which appeared after World War 2. As it turns out, a few such descriptions do exist. In *Space Cadet*, Matt Dodson must solve an astrogation problem and has to convince an officer to let him use a "ballistic integrator." Reference is also made in the story to the giant "ballistic calculator" located at Terra Station. In *Rocket Ship Galileo*, the robot pilot which is guiding the *Galileo* to the moon makes use of a three-dimensional cam. Finally, three-dimensional cams also form part of the automated vacuum cleaner Hired Girl in *The Door Into Summer*.

If we wished to perform the required calculations for the purposes of navigation or fire control today, we would employ a digital computer running either specialized software written for the purpose or a mathematical package such as MATLAB.

The ingenuity in the pre-electronic days was the use of purely mechanical systems to perform the mathematical operations. Variables such as speed, direction and distance were represented by the rotation of shafts. The basic mathematical operations performed by mechanical means were (1) Multiplication by a Scalar using Gears, (2) Addition and Subtraction of two Variables using a Differential, (3) Arbitrary Functions using Cams, (4) Multiplication of two Variables, (5) Integration and (6) Resolution of a Vector using a Component Solver. Rather than attempt to explain each here, I will refer you to the 1944 Naval Ordnance pamphlet *OP1140 Basic Fire Control Mechanisms*, which may be found online at www.hnsa.org. If you have trouble with the explanations in this training pamphlet, there are World War 2 training videos available to view at www.eugeneleeslover.com/VIDEOS/fire_control_computer1.html and also www.eugeneleeslover.com/VIDEOS/fire_control_computer2.html.

I will briefly describe three types of electromechanical systems that have been employed by the U.S. Navy. These are the Battle Tracer, the Dead Reckoning Tracer and the Rangekeeper. For those who are interested in the background of Fire Control systems developed by the United States and other nations, I can recommend in *Naval Firepower: Battleship Guns and Gunnery in the Dreadnought Era* by Norman Friedman.

Battle Tracer

The Battle Tracer was developed by Sperry Gyroscope. The purpose of the Battle Tracer, as part of the Fire Control System they had developed, was to plot on paper the course of the ship on which it was installed ("own ship") and the position of the target ship. The Battle Tracer was tested on a few battleships in 1915. It was more successful in displaying the position of "own ship" than the target, and was therefore seen as more useful for navigational purposes. The inventor of the Battle Tracer (U.S. Patent 1,293,747) was Hannibal Choate Ford, who then left Sperry Gyroscope to form his own company. Only 20 Battle Tracers were purchased by the U.S. Navy from Sperry Gyroscope.

Dead Reckoning Tracer

The Dead Reckoning Tracer (DRT) was a means of automating the process of dead-reckoning. It is considered the descendant of the Battle Tracer. It based its determination of the ship's position on the continuous input of its heading and speed. This represented a vector, which was resolved into its N-S and E-W components, each of which was integrated to give the position as a function of time. This would drive an X-Y plotting arrangement. One of the manufacturers of DRTs was the ARMA Engineering Company.

The DRT consists of three main parts: Dead Reckoning Analyzer (DRA), Indicator and Plotter. The Analyzer determined and displayed the N-S and E-W components of travel as well as the total distance traveled. The Indicator displayed the longitude and latitude. The Plotter displayed a spot of light representing the ship's position upon a glass plate on which a sheet could be placed for manual marking of the position. A successor to the DRT, the NC-2, returned to the intended function of the Battle Tracer. The NC-2 did not appear until well after World War 2. It was capable of plotting "own ship" position, plus the position of two targets. A later model was capable of plotting four targets in addition to own ship. For anyone with an interest in a more detailed description of the NC-2, I would suggest the article "Mk NC-2 Navigational Plotting System" by Poppe and MacDonald.

Rangekeeper

The Rangekeeper was developed by Hannibal Ford as a means of performing targeting calculations. It was presented as a way to *assist* the gunnery officers, not to replace them, and so found a high degree of acceptance. The first to appear in 1916 was the Ford Mark 1 Rangekeeper. The Mark 2 Rangekeeper, developed in 1917, was a simplified version known as the Baby Ford. There were many later Marks intended for use on different classes of ships, and for different purposes such as the Mark 4 for anti-aircraft gunfire. The Mark 8 appeared by the early 1930s.

The Mark 8 began by performing the same functions as the Mark 1, but then included additional calculations with more variables in an attempt to account for more real-world factors. The tracking section determined the present target position, in a manner similar to that to be described below. The output of the tracking section fed the prediction section, which determined the future target position and converted this prediction into the settings to properly position the guns. The correction section then accounted for the fact that you were not firing from a stable and level platform, but from a deck whose inclination changed with time with the motion of the ship. As might be expected, such inclination changes would affect accuracy, and a final set of corrections would need to be determined and applied. A good, detailed explanation which illustrates the principles employed by the Mark 8 Rangekeeper may be found online at www.eugeneleeslover.com/FIRE-CONTROL-PAGE.html.

Instead of the Mark 8, let us take a look at the operation of the much simpler Mark 2 (Baby Ford). Figure 6 illustrates the operation of the Mark 2 and is based on the manual for the 1922 version which may be found online at www.eugeneleeslover/ENGINEERING/OD-460-1922.html. The input stage of the Mark 2 has the same basic arrangement as the input stage of other Marks.

Figure 6a shows the basic variables involved in the calculations for the Mark 2. Unfortunately, this early manual was not very clear in explaining or illustrating the operation of the Mark 2. Although it is anachronistic, the variable names shown in the figure are those employed in the description of the Mark 8. The most important feature of Figure 6a is the line of sight between own ship and the target. We have the speed of our ship, S_O, and its bearing *relative to the line of sight*, cBr. Then we have the speed of the enemy ship, S, and the bearing of enemy ship also *relative to the line of sight*, A. Also shown is how the X and Y variables are related to the line of sight, where the subscripts O and T indicate Own Ship and Target, respectively.

Figure 6b shows all of the mechanical operations performed in the Mark 2. S_O and cBr represent the magnitude and direction of a vector and are resolved by a component solver into the components along the line of sight, Y_O, and perpendicular to the line of sight, X_O. Each of the two L-shaped output portions of the component solver would cause shafts to move according to the value of each component. In a similar manner, S and A are resolved into Y_T and X_T. The sum of Y_O and Y_T gives us dR, the range rate, which is displayed to the operator on the Range Rate Dial. This type of addition, as with all others within any Rangekeeper or similar device, is performed by a differential. The range rate is also integrated to give what is called the increment of generated range ΔcR. In the Baby

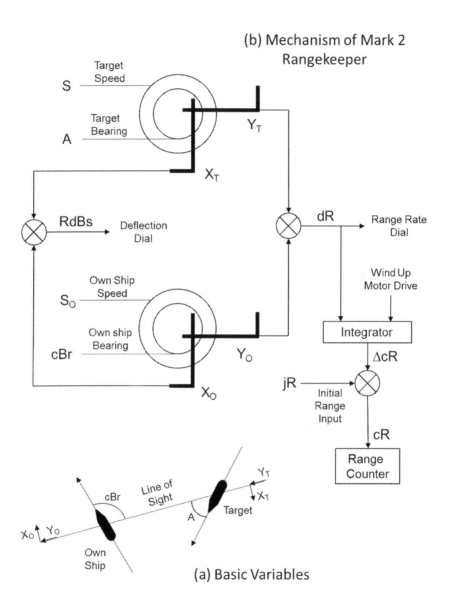

Figure 6. Mark 2 (Baby Ford) Rangekeeper

Ford, the Integrator was driven by a wind up motor. The initial range, jR, is set manually and added to ΔcR to give the present generated range cR, which is displayed on a Range Counter. At the same time, X_O and X_T are added to give the linear deflection rate, RdBS, which is displayed on the Deflection Dial.

The operation of the Mark 2 did not involve the feedback of any calculated values to the earlier stages of the calculation. Other Marks of the Rangekeeper employed some form of internal feedback. The Mark 1, for example, converted the deflection rate into a change of bearing, which was then integrated and both displayed and fed back to the input section to adjust the bearing data for both own ship and target ship being fed to the component solvers.

A key feature of the Ford Rangekeepers, however, was that the calculated values were displayed in such a way that easy comparison could be made with observed values. This would enable the operator to continually refine his estimates of enemy course and speed to improve the accuracy of the calculations. If both the calculated range and bearing matched the observed range and bearing, then the mathematical model of the target's motion would be considered correct and the values could be used to accurately project its future position. In addition, this type of display meant that any change of the enemy course and speed would be reflected in a divergence of the calculated and observed values, requiring new adjustments by the operator.

Electromechanical versus Electronic

It is important to consider how such devices differ from the electronic computers of today. The first is the most obvious. The fire control systems containing the devices of the type that I have just described would not be small systems. The weight of the Mark 8 was over three thousand pounds. Their operation would require a degree of physical rigidity to ensure the accuracy of computations, which implies a considerable amount of metal. Although they operated by different principles, the original digital computers were also massive devices. To reduce the size of those first digital computers required a transition from electromechanical switches (relays) to vacuum tubes, then to transistors, then to integrated circuits, and finally successive waves of further miniaturization of those integrated circuits. No such reductions were possible in the case of the mechanical systems. The next time you are tempted to complain that your laptop is too heavy, remember the mechanical fire control systems of Heinlein's Navy.

Next, consider the way that mathematical variables are handled. The electromechanical fire control system dealt with variables that changed in a continuous manner from value to value and also continuously in time from second to second. This is the definition of an *analog* system. Shafts and gears and integrators and cams were always turning with a smooth motion. In a *digital* system, on the other hand, all numerical values must be represented by a finite number of discrete binary digits. An increasing signal which could be represented by a smooth rotation or other continuous motion in an analog system would have to be represented by a staircase of a finite number of discrete steps in a digital computer. Changes in a digital computer also must occur in discrete steps in time. These steps in time have gotten shorter and shorter as the speed of electronic components has increased. It is the high speed at which digital computers now operate that masks the discrete nature of their operation.

The final, and I would say the most important, distinction between the fire control system and today's computers is that the naval systems were special purpose. Unlike a modern computer, where the function is changed simply by running a different piece of software, these electromechanical systems were each designed and built with a very specific set of calculations in mind. The inputs could be varied, but the calculations would always be performed in a manner totally determined by the physical arrangement of the components of the machine. The only way to perform a completely different calculation would be to disassemble the components of the system and then to reassemble them into a different arrangement.

NOTES

Chapter 1

4 "Early in the war": "Obituary: Caleb Barrett Laning '29."

Chapter 2

9 "The Navy is an involved profession": CORR218-3, 48; *Grumbles*, 28.

11 "And --- you did <u>not</u> tell me": CORR218-3, 57.

11 "Lots of civilians": CORR218-3, 76; *Grumbles*, 34.

14 "Your very request": CORR218-3, 81-82.

15 "We are leaving": CORR218-1, 68-69.

15 Trip east, Arwine: Chapdelaine, 551-52.

16 "On Monday, July 18": Asimov, 200.

16 "On my way out": Ibid., 242.

17 "Re the request": CORR218-3, 95.

17 Scoles letter: ANNA210a-09, 25-26.

18 Problem described by Campbell: Wysocki, "Astounding," 163.

18 "This much I can say": CORR218-3, 115.

Chapter 3

19 "I had a completely": Heinlein, "Virtues," 28-29.

22 "science fiction being": Ibid., 16.

23 "Are the speculations": Ibid., 24.

25 "For example, in one story": Ibid., 28.

25 "science fiction not infrequently": Ibid., 28.

25 "then was relieved": Ibid., 30.

26 "Even before the": Ibid., 31.

28 "Of what use": Ibid., 40.

30 "Even though a direct": Bailey, 262.

32 "For example, in one story": Opus129, 18, 74.

32 "A space suit": Ibid., 78.

33 "I had a completely": Ibid., 18, 76.

34 "I asked Heinlein": Knight, 301.

36 "at the Academy": Heinlein, *Expanded Universe*, 453.

36 "my classmate": CORR218-3, 85.

Chapter 4

40 "I have been a long time writing": ANNA201a-09, 25-26.

42 "Which reminds me, Robert": CORR328-09, 124-25.

Chapter 5

47 Compton effect: Kevles, 158-59.

47 Uncertainty principle: Ibid., 166.

47 Complementarity: Ibid., 166-67.

49 Number of radio sets: Dunlap, 69, 71, 126.

49	Hertz: Gebhard, 5.
49	Marconi: Douglas, 13-19, 54-57.
50	Poulsen arc: Hong, 164-65.
51	Edison effect: Ibid., 121-34.
51	De Forest: Lessing, 58.
54	Navy radio firms: Howeth, Ch. IV, Sec. 8 and 10.
54	CW 936: Gebhard, 14.
55	Bureau of Steam Engineering: Wolters, 76.
55	Western Electric tube contract: Howeth, Ch. XVII, Sec. 8.
56	Birth of NRL: Gebhard, 28-31.
56	Other facilities to NRL: Ibid., 31-32.
57	LF and MF: Ibid., 6.
57	AM band: Ibid., 43-44.
57	MF and HF boundary, battleships: Ibid., 49.
57	XA: Ibid., 54.
57	RG: Ibid., 60-61.
58	VHF, TBS: Ibid., 94-97.
58	UHF, Leary: Ibid., 100-101.
59	Remote Control: Ibid., 223-26.
60	Radio Direction Finder: Ibid., 263-68.
60	Radio altimeter: Ibid., 276.
60	LORAN: Ibid., 280-83.
60	Radar: Wolters, 215-216.

61	Fire control radar: Gebhard, 196.
62	IFF: Ibid., 251-55.

Chapter 6

64	Class Size of 243: Franklin, *Heinlein*, 12; Stover, 2; Gifford, 32; Patterson "Sketch," 9.
64	Class Size discussion: "Class News: 29."
65	"240 of my class graduated": Heinlein, *Expanded Universe*, 537.
66	Officers and men in 1922: Chisholm, 609.
66	Academy 1923: Ibid., 617.
68	Appropriations law 1924-25: Ibid., 619.
68	BuNav recommendation: Ibid, 657.
68	1938 limit: Ibid., 708.
68	Character Names: Wysocki, "Source."
69	"Cyrus Fielding . . . .": Heinlein, *For Us, the Living*, 88.
69	"Powerman 2/C Florence Berzowski.": Heinlein, *The Puppet Masters*, 136.
69	"But don't trip": Heinlein, *The Door Into Summer*, 105.
72	Ship information primarily from Dictionary of American Naval Fighting Ships at http://www.history.navy.mil/danfs/index.html.
73	NA Curriculum structure: *United States Naval Academy*, 28-31.
74	Junior officer: Hone, 52-56.
77	Tombstone promotion: Blair, 122n, 884.
81	Postgraduate instruction: Rilling, 166-72.

Chapter 7

90	"To the President": Leinster, "Politics," 279.

99   "A classmate of mine": Heinlein, *For Us, The Living*, 30-31.

100 "In addition to the": MacDonald, "Goldfish Bowl," 77.

101 "thirty-four land cruisers": Heinlein, "If This Goes On—," 142.

102 "Inherent Power of a Battleship": Fiske, 488-489.

104 "This article attracted": Ibid., 489.

104 "What is a Tank?": Fuller, 283.

104 "you will understand": Ibid., 290.

104 "I see a fleet": Ibid., 291.

105 "I filed away": Heinlein, "If This Goes On—," 124.

105 "For example, in one story": Heinlein, "Virtues," 28.

106 "I was required to learn": Opus129, 18.

106 "Waterbury's hydraulic gear": Mindell, 81.
     Besides gunnery and other applications on surface ships, Waterburies also found use on submarines. A good description of the operation of the Waterbury is in the manual *Submarine Hydraulic Systems* (NAVPERS 16169), 21-35.

106 "See these here speed bars": Heinlein, "If This Goes On—," 124.

107 "I hurried down the ladders": Heinlein, "If This Goes On—," 149.

Chapter 8

108 "A piece of scientific fiction": Bailey, 10.

109 "The late Will Jenkins": Swanwick.

110 "Today's authors tend": Campbell, "Invention and Imagination," 6.

111 "It's tough, running a restaurant": Smith, 50-51.

114 Gernsback patents: Kraueter, 174-75.

114 Discrepancy in patent counts: Ibid., 155.

115 Hypnobioscope: Ashley, 29.

117 "I think it's interesting": Jenkins, "Applied," 109.

117 "All electrical": Leinster, "Politics," 273.

119 De Camp background: De Camp, *Time*, 122-27.

120 "Why, thought I, should we": De Camp, "Finished," 162.

120 Constant volume joints: De Camp, *Time*, 193.

121 Water bed background: Heinlein, *Expanded Universe*, 516-18.

122 "I designed the water bed": Ibid., 517.

122 "The water rose": Heinlein, *Beyond This Horizon*, 19-20.

122 "The deceleration tanks": MacDonald, "Waldo," 16.

122 "The tank was not": Ibid., 33.

123 "Each tank was like": Heinlein, "Sky Lift", 119.

123 "Against one bulkhead": Heinlein, *Double Star*, 29.

123 "transferred into a hydraulic bed": Heinlein, *Stranger*, 11.

123 "The patient floated": Ibid., 14.

123 "Sure, you're weak": Ibid., 17.

123 "He went to a hydraulic": Ibid., 50.

123 "A patient that old": Ibid., 58.

124 "Some joker tried": Heinlein, *Expanded Universe*, 516.

Chapter 9

127 "scientists and explorers": Gunn, "Future," 210.

127 "Jules Verne": Lake, 10.

127 "But with the impudence": Ibid., 10.

129   Awards: Wright, *Tank*, 24.

129   Tritton and Wilson: "British award"; Wright, *Tank*, 28.

129   Swinton: Gannon, *Rumors*, 63-67.

131   Szilard and Mandel: Lanouette, 106.

131   Rutherford: Ibid, 133.

131   "We might in these": Ibid, 133.

132   "it suddenly occurred": Ibid., 133-34.

132   "exploded with great violence": Wells, *World*, 30.

132   "Those used by the Allies": Wells, *World*, 100-01.

133   "The discoverer of royal jelly": Gunn speech.

134   "he believed the food": "Longevity Secrets."

134   "Dr. Keller's short story": Ashley, 284.

134   "When Dr. Thomas": Moskowitz, 21-22.

135   "Your entire set-up": Brake, 96-97.

137   "For info, I have been": CORR305-1945, 77-78.

139   "The modern equivalent": McCann, 113.

139   "I've just reread": CORR218-1, 158. The letter to which Heinlein referred appears in the same Archives file on pages 162 and 163. It has a handwritten date notation of "Circa Dec 15, 1940," but by its content it is clear to me that it is the correct letter.

139   Story timing with report: Gifford, 173-74; Franklin, *War Stars*, 142.

141   "Against the bluish-black": Yefremov, 28.

141   "From a deep": Denisyuk, 425. This is the version of this segment as provided by Denisyuk in his *Leonardo* article. In the collection of Yefremov's stories, on page 259, it appears as:

From the deep bottom of the absolutely transparent layer, magnified by some mysterious optical device to its natural proportions, there looked out at them a strange but an undoubtedly human face. Its dominating features were its huge prominent eyes, which looked straight ahead.

Note that in Yefremov's version there is no mention of the image possessing any three-dimensional property.

141 Gabor, Leith and Upatnieks: Benton.

142 "Early in the 1960s": Herbert, *Dreamer*, 200.

143 "The Dracone project": Hawthorne, 53.

Chapter 10

146 "Nevertheless, the brasshats": CORR218-3, 48; *Grumbles*, 28.

147 "I haven't mentioned": Heinlein, "Tale," 96.

147 "one of the most": Heinlein, *For Us, The Living*, 31.

148 Wake Island: Elliott, Bombs, 28; Oxygen, 30.

149 Toothbrush fix: Blair, 441-42.

149 Aircraft improvisation: Lundstrom, *Pearl Harbor to Midway*, Gunsights, 55-56; Armor, 63.

149 Coffman starter: Ibid., 86

150 Reeves: Hone, 93-94.

150 Circular formation: Potter, 138-40

151 Signaling by radar: Page, 144-50

151 Radar plot: Monsarrat, Men, 47-52; Layout, 53-55.

152 McNally: Boslaugh, 24-34, 39, 42-44.

153 Hoover story: Wilbur.

153 "You could crank in": Wilbur, 11.

153 Post Civil War navy: Love, 322-34, 336-38, 341-44.

153 ABCD ships: Ibid., 352.

154 Number of patents: Fiske, 515.

154 Signal shutter box: Ibid., 56.

154 Helm and engine information: Ibid, 209-12.

154 Semaphore: Ibid., 129.

155 "chagrined": Ibid., 688.

156 Naval Treaty: Hammond, 37-38.

158 Flying Deck Cruiser: Kuehn, 101-23.

158 "The U.S. Navy of": Ibid., 175.

Chapter 11

All quotes are identified within the body of the chapter.

Chapter 12

181 "There were no ports": Heinlein, "Misfit," 54.

181 "By the time each boy": Ibid.

181 "An indefinite time": Ibid.

182 "to a door let": Heinlein, "Roads," 23.

182 "He walked over by": Heinlein, "Misfit," 58-59.

182 Stereoscope: Freidman *Naval Firepower*, 22-27.

184 "It was part of my": Heinlein, "If This Goes On—," 133.

184 "My own girl": Heinlein, *Revolt in 2100*, 135.

184 "MacKinnon glanced": Heinlein, "Coventry," 56.

185 "This guff about": Heinlein, "Requiem," 87.

186 "He gave his attention": "If This Goes On—," 37.

186 Inflight entertainment: White.

187 "Oho! Make a priority": "If This Goes On—," 40.

187 Retinal: Hill, 124.

187 Retinal ID: Kampffert.

188 Robot: Post ; "Robot to Aid."

188 "In 1909 Cove": Gernsback, *Ralph*, 101.

189 "Look, Dad - do you": Monroe, 38-39.

190 "He snatched at the": Heinlein, "Roads," 31.

Chapter 13

193 The telechronometer appears in "Coventry" in the July 1940 issue of *Astounding* on page 93, in "Blowups Happen" in the September 1940 issue of *Astounding* on page 75, and in "Methuselah's Children" in the July 1941 issue of *Astounding* on page 11. The fact that it disappears from all except "Blowups Happen" was noted by Gifford, 62.

193 Telegraphic time signals: Bartky, 105, 113-14.

193 Radio controlled clocks: Boullin, 12, 17, 18.

194 "The minutes are defined": NAVPERS 10023, 272.

194 "It would all start": Milliken.

195 "Below the ground flowed": Heinlein, *For Us, The Living*, 211.

196 "He adjusted his": Heinlein, *Puppet Masters*, 171.

197 Weems: Wright, *Most Probable*, 147-48, 147n.

197 Drift meter: Ibid., 50-51, 78-80, 139-41.

197 Airspeed indicator: Ibid., 47-50, 134.

197 Compass problems: Ibid., 42-47.

197 Earth inductor compass: Ibid., 134-37.

197 Gyrocompass: Ibid., 137-38.

197 British navigational systems: Ayliffe, II, 465-68.

198 "a boxlike affair": "Vision Unlimited," 15.

199 Radio beam is mentioned in "Solution Unsatisfactory" (May 1941) on page 69 and in "Methuselah's Children" (August 1941) on pages 79-80. In *Expanded Universe*, the radio compass is mentioned on pages 452-54.

199 Radio landing: Launius, 81-87.

200 Klystron radio beam: Crider.

200 YE-YG/ZB: Gebhard, 271-74.

202 "The NC-2 Plotting": NAVTRA 10151-D, 42.

203 "The data converter": Ibid., 43.

203 NC-2 Reference: Friedman, *Network-Centric*, 69.

204 RCM table: *Radio Countermeasures,* 9.

205 Air-to-ground: Price, 6.

205 Scanning receiver: Gebhard, 300.

205 NDRC RCM contract list: *Radio Countermeasures,* 498-500.

207 Hedy Lamarr: Simon, 60-62.

207 BLADES: Ibid., 62, 71-76.

208 IR background: Huxford, 256-60.

209 Voice / code system contract: *Non-Image Forming Infrared,* 118.

209 IR contract list: Ibid., 384.

210 "Some of the infrared": NAVPERS 10794-B, 157-158.

210 IR articles: "Navy Built Phone on Infra-Red Rays", "New Lamp Sends Secret Messages."

212 Early passive listening: Kevles, 122-123.

213 Underwater sound systems: NAVPERS 10884, J-Series, 241-45; WCA Equipment, 260-61.

214 Sonar Frequencies: Ibid, 76.

214 Transducers: Ibid., QGB, 123; QGA, 128.

Chapter 14

216 Unfortunately, letters between Heinlein and Laning are not contained in one Archives file but appear in many different files, such as CORR220-1, CORR305PREWAR, CORR305J, and CORR305-1945.

216 October 1938 letter: CORR305J, 107-12.

216 September 1940 letter: CORR305-1945, 83-84.

216 The log of the USS *Philadelphia* shows that during the month of March 1940, its movements were as follows:

> March 1. (16 - 20). Anchored Berth D-8, Los Angeles Harbor.

> *Weekend 2, 3*

> March 4. (8 - 12). Underway.
>   (16 - 18). Anchored Berth B-1, Pyramid Cove, San Clemente Island.

> March 5. (4 - 8). Underway.
>   (16 - 18). Anchored Pyramid Cove.

> March 6. (4 - 8). Underway.
>   (16 - 18). Anchored Pyramid Cove.

> March 7. (8 - 12). Underway.
>   (20 - 24). Anchored Berth C-7, Los Angeles Harbor.

> *Weekend 9, 10*

> March 11. (8 - 12). Underway.
>   (20 - 24). Anchored Berth C-5, Pyramid Cove, San Clemente Island

> March 12. (8 - 12). Underway.

(20 - 24). Anchored Berth C-5, Pyramid Cove.

March 13. (4 - 8). Underway.
(8 - 12). Anchored Berth C-5, Pyramid Cove.

March 14. (12 - 16). Underway.

March 15. (0 - 4). Anchored Berth F-5, Los Angeles Harbor.
(12 -16). Moved to Berth A-3, San Pedro Harbor.

Weekend 16, 17

March 17. Log says A-2, not A-3.

Weekend 23, 24

March 29. (8 - 12). Underway.
(12 - 16). Anchored Berth F-5, Los Angeles Harbor.

Weekend 30, 31

217 October 1940 letter: CORR305J, 89.

222 "Shortly we were hooked . . . .": Heinlein, "If This Goes On—," 145-46.

226 "Shortly we were hooked . . . .": Heinlein, *Revolt in 2100*, 168-69.

227 Electronic resolution of course vector: Chance, 355-56.

228 First PPI example: Ibid., 361-64.

228 Second PPI example: Ibid., 366.

Appendix 1

233 *Register of Alumni,* 1992 Edition, 216-17.

Appendix 2

240 "I was highly skilled": Heinlein, *Expanded Universe*, 4.

240 "You may possibly wish": CORR218-1, 4.

240 "Ensign and Lieut (jg)": Gladstone, 7.

241 "specialized in electromechanical": Ibid., 8.

242 "the most amazing": Heinlein, *For Us, the Living*, 30.

242 "Libby was assigned": Heinlein, "Misfit," 65.

242 "We had improvised": Heinlein, "If This Goes On—," 142.

243 "I passed on the order": Ibid., 144.

243 "The dead reckoners": Ibid., 146.

BIBLIOGRAPHY

Archives

AT&T Archives

    Biographical Data for John W. Campbell, Sr.

National Archives

    Log of U.S.S. *Philadelphia*

    Service Record of Caleb Barrett Laning

Robert A. and Virginia Heinlein Archives (http://www.heinleinarchives.net/).

    CORR201a-09
    CORR218-1
    CORR218-2
    CORR218-3
    CORR218-4
    CORR305-1945
    CORR305J
    CORR328-09
    Opus129

Unpublished Dissertations

Rilling, Alexander W. "The First Fifty Years of Graduate Education in the United States Navy, 1909-1959." Diss., USC, 1972.

Wolters, Timothy S. "Managing a Sea of Information: Shipboard Command and Control in the United States Navy, 1899-1945." Diss., MIT, 2003.

Navy Manuals

Basic Fire Control Mechanisms, OP1140, 1944.

Fire Control Equipment Ford Range Keeper, Mark II, OP460, 1922.

Naval Sonar, NAVPERS 10884, 1953.

Quartermaster 1 & C Rate Training Manual, NAVTRA 10151-D, 1972.

Quartermaster 3rd Class and 2nd Class, NAVPERS 10023, 1946.

Shipboard Electronic Equipment, NAVPERS 10794-B, 1965.

Submarine Hydraulic Systems, NAVPERS 16169, 1946.

Submarine Sonar Operator's Manual, NAVPERS 16167, 1944.

This is NANCY, NAVSHIPS 250-222-10, 1945.

Articles and Stories

Ayliffe, Alec. "The Development of Airborne Dead Reckoning. Part I: Before 1940 - Finding the Wind." *The Journal of Navigation* 54.2 (2001): 223-33.

—. "The Development of Airborne Dead Reckoning. Part II: After 1940 - Staying on Track." *The Journal of Navigation* 54.3 (2001): 463-76.

Benton, Stephen A. "Holography Reinvented." *Proceedings of SPIE* 4737 (2002): 23-26.

Bester, Alfred. "Science Fiction and the Renaissance Man." In *The Science Fiction Novel: Imagination and Social Criticism*, 77-96. Chicago: Advent, 1971.

Bloch, Robert. "Imagination and Modern Social Criticism." In *The Science Fiction Novel: Imagination and Social Criticism*, 97-121. Chicago: Advent, 1971.

Boullin, David J. "An Introduction to Radio-Controlled Timekeeping and Timekeepers." *NAWCC Bulletin* 41.1 (1999): 5-22.

"British Award $75,000 To Designers of Tank." *New York Times*, November 28, 1919.

Campbell, John W. and Linus E. Kittridge. "War Emergency Stocks in the Bell System." *Bell Telephone Magazine,* September 1943, 178-87.

Campbell, John W. Jr. "Invention and Imagination." *Astounding Science-Fiction,* August 1939, 6.

Chance, Britton. "The Interconnection of Dead-Reckoning and Radar Data for Precision Navigation and Prediction." *Journal of the Franklin Institute* 242.5 (1946): 355-72.

"Class News: 29." *Shipmate,* October 1973, 63.

Crider, John H. "Land Blind with Radio." *New York Times,* March 19, 1939.

De Camp, L. Sprague. "Finished." *Astounding Science Fiction,* November 1949, 146-62.

—. "Justinian Jugg's Patent." *Astounding Science-Fiction,* December 1940, 68-79.

Denisyuk, Yu. N. "My Way in Holography." *Leonardo* 25.5 (1992): 425-30.

Elliott, John M. "Wake Island: A Gallant Defense." *Naval Aviation News,* January-February, 1992, 26-31.

Fuller, J. F. C. "The Development of Sea Warfare on Land and Its Influence on Future Naval Operations." *The Journal of Royal United Services Institution* 65 (1920): 281-98.

Gernsback, Hugo. "Learn and Work While You Sleep." *Science and Invention,* December 1921, 714+.

—. "Sleep Learning." http://www.hugogernsback.com/aug2000learn.html. (accessed February 9 2010).

Gladstone, Kate. "Words, Words, Words: Robert Heinlein and General Semantics." *The Heinlein Journal* 11 (July 2002): 4-8.

Gunn, James. "Science Fiction and the Future" In *Inside Science Fiction,* 209-23. Lanham, MD: Scarecrow Press, 2006.

—. 2004 Campbell Conference Speech.

Harrison, Charles W. Jr. and James E. Blower. "Electronics - Your Future." *Journal of the American Society of Naval Engineers, Inc.* 62.1 (1950): 99-137.

Hawthorne, W. R. "The Early Development of the Dracone Flexible Barge." *Proceedings of the Institution of Mechanical Engineers* 175 (1961): 52-83.

Heinlein, Robert A. "Blowups Happen." *Astounding Science-Fiction,* September 1940, 51-85.

—. "Coventry." *Astounding Science-Fiction,* July 1940, 56-93.

—. "If This Goes On—." *Astounding Science-Fiction,* February 1940, 9-40.

—. "If This Goes On—." *Astounding Science-Fiction,* March 1940, 117-51.

—. "Life-Line." *Astounding Science-Fiction,* August 1939, 83-95.

—. "Methuselah's Children." *Astounding Science-Fiction,* July 1941, 9-43.

—. "Methuselah's Children." *Astounding Science-Fiction,* August 1941, 63-109.

—. "Methuselah's Children." *Astounding Science-Fiction,* September 1941, 133-162.

—. "Misfit." *Astounding Science-Fiction,* November 1939, 53-67.

—. "Requiem." *Astounding Science-Fiction,* January 1940, 80-91.

—. "The Roads Must Roll." *Astounding Science-Fiction,* June 1940, 9-37.

—. "Science Fiction: Its Nature, Faults and Virtues." In *The Science Fiction Novel: Imagination and Social Criticism*, 14-48. Chicago: Advent, 1971.

—. "Sky Lift." In *The Menace From Earth*, 115-128. New York: Signet, 1964.

—. "Tale of the Man Who Was too Lazy to Fail." In *Time Enough for Love*, 74-97. New York, Putnam, 1973.

Herbert, Frank. "Under Pressure." *Astounding Science Fiction,* November 1955, 6-66.

—. "Under Pressure." *Astounding Science Fiction,* December 1955, 79-126.

—. "Under Pressure." *Astounding Science Fiction,* January 1956, 80-135.

Hill, Robert. "Retina Identification." In A. Jain, R. Bolle and S. Pankanti (eds.). *Biometrics: Personal Identification in Networked Society*, 123-142. Boston: Kluwer Academic Press, 1999.

Huxford, W. S. and John. R. Platt. "Survey of Near Infra-Red Communication Systems." *Journal of the Optical Society of America* 38.3 (1948): 253-68.

Jenkins, Will F. "Applied Science Fiction." *Analog Science Fiction / Science Fact*, November 1967, 108-24.

—. "A Logic Named Joe." *Astounding Science-Fiction*, March 1946, 139-54.

Johnson, Hubert. "Anglo-American Naval Inventors, 1890-1919: Last of a Breed." *International Journal of Naval History* 1.1 Apr. 2002. http://www.ijnhonline.org/wp-content/uploads/2012/01/pdf_johnson1.pdf

Kaempffert, Waldemar. "Science: Eye Pictures in Place of Fingerprints." *New York Times*, August 2, 1936.

Kornbluth, C. M. "The Failure of the Science Fiction Novel as Social Criticism." In *The Science Fiction Novel: Imagination and Social Criticism*, 49-76. Chicago: Advent, 1971.

Kraeuter, David W. "The U.S. Patents of Alexanderson, Carson, Colpitts, Davis, Gernsback, Hogan, Loomis, Pupin, Rider, Stone, and Stubblefield." *The AWA Review* 6 (1991): 155-84.

Laning, Captain Caleb B., U.S. Navy and Lieutenant Robert A. Heinlein, U.S. Navy, Retired. "Flight Into the Future." *Collier's*, August 30, 1947, 18+.

Leinster, Murray [Will F. Jenkins]. "Politics." *Amazing Stories*, June 1932, 268-79.

"Longevity Secrets Sought in Queen Bee 'Royal Jelly'." *New York Times*, November 29, 1928.

Lyman, Lauren D. "Land Blind in New Beam." *New York Times*, March 12, 1933.

MacDonald, Anson [Robert A. Heinlein]. "Goldfish Bowl." *Astounding Science-Fiction*, March 1942, 77-93.

—. "Sixth Column." *Astounding Science-Fiction*, January 1941, 9-41.

—. "Sixth Column." *Astounding Science-Fiction*, February 1941, 117-55.

—. "Sixth Column." *Astounding Science-Fiction,* March 1941, 127-55.

—. "Solution Unsatisfactory." *Astounding Science-Fiction,* May 1941, 56-86.

—. "Waldo." *Astounding Science-Fiction,* August 1942, 9-53.

—. "We Also Walk Dogs." *Astounding Science-Fiction,* July 1941, 126-43.

Milliken, Dennis F. "A true Shipboard story how Hancock kept time." http://www.usshancockcv19.com/histories/timekeeper.htm (accessed September 20, 2011).

McCann, Arthur [John W. Campbell Jr.]. "Shhhhh—Don't Mention It!" *Astounding Science-Fiction,* August 1940, 104-14.

Monroe, Lyle [Robert A. Heinlein]. "Let There Be Light." *Super Science Stories,* May 1940, 34-45.

Moskowitz, Sam. Introduction to *Life Everlasting and Other Tales of Science, Fantasy and Horror*, by David Keller. Westport, CT: Hyperion Press, 1974. 9-33.

"Navy Built Phone on Infra-Red Rays." *New York Times,* November 25, 1946.

"New Lamp Sends Secret Messages." *New York Times,* August 18, 1946.

"Obituary: John S. Arwine, III '29." *Shipmate*, February 1966, 23.

"Obituary: Caleb Barrett Laning '29." *Shipmate,* July-August 1991, 120.

Patterson, Bill. "Robert A. Heinlein: A Biographical Sketch." *The Heinlein Journal* 5 (July 1999): 7-36.

Phinney, J. N. "Learn While You Sleep." *Radio News,* October 1923, 375+.

Poppe, C. W. and C. H. MacDonald. "Mk NC-2 Navigational Plotting System." *Navigation: Journal of the Institute of Navigation* 15.2 (1968): 136-49.

Post, Wiley. "Wiley Post Tells of Faith in Robot." *New York Times*, July 16, 1933.

"Robot to Aid Post on World Flight." *New York Times,* July 5, 1933.

Stine, Harry. "Galactic Gadgeteers." *Astounding Science Fiction,* May 1951, 6-46.

Swanwick, Michael. "Growing up in the Future." http://www.michaelswanwick.com/nonfic/future/html. (accessed July 15, 2006).

"'Talking Lamp' Used From Shore to Ship." *New York Times,* November 20, 1946.

"Vision Unlimited." *Naval Aviation News,* December 1948, 13-17.

Wells, H. G. "The Land Ironclads" In Richard Curtis (ed.) *Future Tense,* 11-33. New York: Dell, 1968.

Westover, T. A. "New Airborne Dead Reckoning Tracer Plots on A Mercator Chart." *Navigation: Journal of the Institute of Navigation* 5.3 (1956): 140-47.

White, John N. "A History of Inflight Entertainment." http://apex.aero/LinkClick.aspx?fileticket=y9eVk3lI1ac%3d&tabid=397. (accessed March 8, 2012).

Wilbur, Ted. "Let George Do It." *Naval Aviation News,* December 1971, 8-19.

Wysocki, Edward. "*Astounding* and World War II." *Science Fiction Studies* 39.1 (March 2012): 162-65.

—. "The Creation of Heinlein's 'Solution Unsatisfactory.'" In Karen Hellekson, et al. (eds.). *Practicing Science Fiction: Critical Essays on Writing, Reading and Teaching the Genre,* 74-86. Jefferson, NC: McFarland, 2010.

—. "The Great Heinlein Mystery." *Shipmate,* January-February 1995, 32-34.

—. "John W. Campbell, Jr., E. E. 'Doc' Smith, and the Combat Information Center." *Science Fiction Studies* 38.3 (November 2011): 558-62.

—. "A Source for Heinlein's Character Names." *The Heinlein Journal* 4 (January 1999): 4-5.

Books

Ashley, Mike and Robert A. W. Lowndes. *The Gernsback Days.* Holicong PA: Wildside Press, 2004.

Asimov, Isaac. *In Memory Yet Green: The Autobiography of Isaac Asimov, 1920-1954.* Garden City, NY: Doubleday, 1979.

Bailey, J. O. *Pilgrims Through Space and Time: Trends and Patterns in Scientific and Utopian Fiction.* New York: Argus Books, 1947.

Bartky, Ian R. *Selling The True Time: Nineteenth-Century Timekeeping in America*. Stanford: Stanford University Press, 2000.

Blair, Clay, Jr. *Silent Victory*. New York: Bantam, 1976.

Boslaugh, David L. *When Computers Went to Sea: The Digitization of the United States Navy*. Los Alamitos, CA: IEEE Computer Society, 1999.

Brake, Mark L. and Neil Hook. *Different Engines: How science drives fiction and fiction drives science.* London: Macmillan, 2008.

Bretnor, Reginald, ed. *Modern Science Fiction: Its Meaning and Its Future*. New York: Coward-McCann, 1953.

Bywater, Hector. *The Great Pacific War: A History of the American-Japanese Campaign of 1931-1933*. Bedford, MA: Applewood Books, n.d.

Chapdelaine, Perry A. Sr., ed. *The John W. Campbell Letters with Isaac Asimov and A. E. van Vogt, Volume II.* Franklin, TN: AC Projects, 1993.

Chisholm, Donald. *Waiting for Dead Men's Shoes: Origins and Development of the U.S. Navy's Officer Personnel System, 1793-1941*. Stanford: Stanford University Press, 2001.

Clark J. J., and Clark G. Reynolds. *Carrier Admiral*. New York: David McCay, 1967.

Da Cruz, Daniel. *The Ayes of Texas*. New York: Del Rey, 1982.

De Camp, L. Sprague. *Ancient Engineers*. New York, Ballantine, 1984.

—. *Time and Chance (An Autobiography)*. Hampton Falls, NH: Donald M. Grant, 1996.

Douglas, Susan J. *Inventing American Broadcasting, 1899-1922*. Baltimore: Johns Hopkins University Press, 1989.

Dunlap, Orrin E., Jr. *Dunlap's Radio and Television Almanac*. New York: Harper & Brothers, 1951.

Ewing, Steve. *Reaper Leader: The Life of Jimmy Flatley*. Annapolis: Naval Institute Press, 2002.

—. *Thach Weave: The Life of Jimmie Thach*. Annapolis: Naval Institute Press, 2004.

Fagen, M. D. *A History of Engineering and Science in the Bell System: National Service in War and Peace (1925-1975)*. Bell Telephone Laboratories, 1978.

Fiske, Bradley A. *From Midshipman to Rear-Admiral*. New York: Century, 1919.

Forward, Robert L. *Indistinguishable From Magic*. New York: Baen, 1995.

Franklin, H. Bruce. *Robert A. Heinlein: America as Science Fiction*. New York: Oxford University Press, 1980.

—. *War Stars: The Superweapon and the American Imagination*. New York: Oxford University Press, 1988.

Friedman, Norman. *Naval Firepower: Battleship Guns and Gunnery in the Dreadnought Era*. Annapolis: Naval Institute Press, 2008.

—. *Network-Centric Warfare: How Navies Learned to Fight Smarter through Three World Wars*. Annapolis: Naval Institute Press, 2009.

Gannon, Charles E. *Rumors of War and Infernal Machines: Technomilitary Agenda-setting in American and British Speculative Fiction*. Lanham, MD: Rowman and Littlefield: 2005.

Gannon, Robert. *Hellions of the Deep: The Development of American Torpedoes in World War II*. University Park: Pennsylvania State University Press, 1996.

Gebhard, Louis A. *Evolution of Naval Radio-Electronics and Contributions of the Naval Research Laboratory*. Washington: Naval Research Laboratory, 1979.

Gernsback, Hugo. *Ralph 124C 41+: A Romance of the Year 2660*. Lincoln: University of Nebraska Press, 2000.

Gifford, James. *Robert A. Heinlein: A Reader's Companion*. Sacramento: Nitrosyncretic Press, 2000.

Hammond, James W., Jr. *The Treaty Navy: The Story of the U.S. Naval Service Between the World Wars*. Victoria, B.C.: Trafford, n.d.

Hayward, John T. and C. W. Borklund. *Bluejacket Admiral: The Naval Career of Chick Hayward*. Annapolis: Naval Institute Press, 2000.

Heinlein, Robert A. *Beyond This Horizon*. New York: Signet, n.d.

—. *The Door Into Summer*. New York: Signet, n.d.

—. *Double Star*. New York: Signet, n.d.

—. *Expanded Universe: The New Worlds of Robert A. Heinlein*. New York: Grosset & Dunlap, 1980.

—. *For Us, The Living*. New York: Scribner, 2004.

—. *Have Space Suit, Will Travel*. New York: Ace, n.d.

—. *The Puppet Masters*. New York: Signet, 1963.

—. *Revolt in 2100 and Methuselah's Children*. Riverdale, NY: Baen, 1999.

—. *Rocket Ship Galileo*. New York: Ace, n.d.

—. *Space Cadet*. New York: Ace, n.d.

—. *Stranger in a Strange Land*. New York: Avon, 1966.

Heinlein, Virginia, ed. *Grumbles From the Grave / Robert A. Heinlein*. New York: Ballantine, 1990.

Herbert, Brian. *Dreamer of Dune: The Biography of Frank Herbert*. New York: Tor, 2004.

Hone, Thomas C. and Trent Hone. *Battle Line: The United States Navy, 1919-1939*. Annapolis: Naval Institute, 2006.

Hong, Sungook. *Wireless: From Marconi's Black Box to the Audion*. Cambridge: MIT Press, 2010.

Howeth, Linwood S. *History of Communications in the United States Navy*. Washington: GPO, 1963.

Kevles, Daniel J. *The Physicists*. New York: Vintage, 1979.

Knight, Damon, ed. *Turning Points: Essays on the Art of Science Fiction*. New York: Harper & Row, 1977.

Kondo, Yoji, ed. *Requiem: New Collected Works by Robert Heinlein and Tributes to the Grand Master*. New York: Tor, 1992.

Kuehn, John T. *Agents of Innovation: The General Board and the Design of the Fleet that Defeated the Japanese Navy*. Annapolis: NavalInstitute Press, 2008.

Lake, Simon and Herbert Corey. *Submarine: The Autobiography of Simon Lake*. New York: D. Appleton-Century, 1938.

Lanouette, William and Bela Szilard. *Genius in the Shadows: A Biography of Leo Szilard: The Man Behind the Bomb*. Chicago: University of Chicago Press, 1994.

Lessing, Lawrence. *Man of High Fidelity: Edwin Howard Armstrong*. New York: Bantam, 1969.

Launius, Roger D., ed. *Innovation and The Development of Flight*. College Station: Texas A&M University Press, 1999.

Love, Robert. W., Jr. *History of the U.S. Navy 1775-1941*. Harrisburg: Stackpole Books, 1992.

Lundstrom, John B. *The First Team: Pacific Naval Air Combat from Pearl Harbor to Midway*. Annapolis: Naval Institute Press, 1990.

—. *The First Team and the Guadalcanal Campaign: Naval Fighter Combat from August to November 1942*. Annapolis: Naval Institute Press, 1994.

Mindell, David A. *Between Human and Machine: Feedback, Control and Computing Before Cybernetics*. Baltimore: Johns Hopkins University Press, 2002.

Monsarrat, John. *Angel on the Yardarm: The Beginning of Fleet Radar Defense and the Kamikaze Threat*. Newport, RI: Naval War College Press, 1985.

Non-Image Forming Infrared. Summary Technical Report of Division 16, NDRC, Volume 3. Washington: 1946.

Page, Robert Morris. *The Origin of Radar*. Garden City, NY: Doubleday, 1962.

Panshin, Alexei. *Heinlein in Dimension*. Chicago: Advent, 1972.

Patterson, William H., Jr. *Robert A. Heinlein: In Dialogue With His Century: Volume I, 1907-1948: Learning Curve*. New York: Tor, 2010.

Potter, E. B. *Nimitz*. Annapolis: Naval Institute Press, 1976.

Price, Alfred. *The History of US Electronic Warfare, Volume 1*. The Association of Old Crows, 1984.

Radio Countermeasures. Summary Technical Report of Division 15, NDRC, Volume 1. Washington, 1946.

Register of Alumni, 1992 Edition. The United States Naval Academy Alumni Association, Inc.

Simon, Marvin K., et al. *Spread Spectrum Communications Handbook, Revised Edition*. New York: McGraw-Hill, 1994.

Smith, George O. *The Complete Venus Equilateral*. New York: Ballantine, 1976.

Stover, Leon. *Robert Heinlein*. Boston: Twayne, 1987.

The United States Naval Academy. Annapolis: Capital Gazette Press, 1926.

Tolley, Kemp. *Commissars and Caviar*. Annapolis: Naval Institute Press, 2003.

—. *Cruise of the Lanikai: Incitement to War*. Annapolis: Naval Institute Press, 2002.

Trimble, William F. *Wings for the Navy: A History of the Naval Aircraft Factory, 1917-1956*. Annapolis: Naval Institute Press, 1990.

Turtledove, Harry (ed). *Alternate Generals*. New York: Baen, 1998.

United States Naval Academy Postgraduate School Catalog 1938-1939.

Wells, H. G. *The World Set Free*. London: Macmillan, 1914.

Wright, Monte Duane. *Most Probable Position: A History of Aerial Navigation to 1941*. Lawrence: University Press of Kansas, 1972.

Wright, Patrick. *Tank: The Progress of a Monstrous War Machine*. New York: Viking Penguin, 2002.

Yefremov, I. *Stories*. Moscow: Foreign Language Publishing House, 1954.

ACKNOWLEDGEMENTS

I became aware of *The Heinlein Journal* shortly after it first appeared in 1997. Until that time, my research had been conducted in isolation. My contact with Bill Patterson began with my subscribing to the *Journal* and submitting a short Note that described my research. I probably would not have continued my research without the contact with Bill and through the *Journal* with information and concepts presented by others. I thank Bill for the assistance that he provided to me when I traveled to UCSC in 2003 to examine portions of the Heinlein Archives. This assistance continued after the Archives became available online, as Bill pointed out items that he had discovered in the course of the research for his biography of Heinlein. Then there were the countless email discussions over the years. Thank you, Bill, for all of the above and for the feedback, positive and otherwise, to my various ideas and theories.

I have had contact with many people and organizations kind enough to provide me with information and assistance. I wish to spare the reader the need to examine a very long list, but I feel that there are some who deserve special mention and thanks:

The Naval Academy Alumni Association, Inc., which provided me with the contact information for the surviving members of the Class of 1929 at the start of my research. And those members of the Class of 1929, all since deceased, who responded to my questions.

Dr. Yoji Kondo, who presented my original questions about the Mystery Device to Virginia Heinlein. And of course, the late Virginia Heinlein, both for the information that she provided to me on many occasions and for being such a gracious hostess when I visited her in 2001.

The descendants and relatives of RADM Caleb Barrett Laning.

The staff of the Special Collections & Archives Department, Nimitz Library, United States Naval Academy for their assistance during my many visits.

The people who provided comments on portions of my evolving manuscript, but particularly Marlo Sablad.

And my friends and co-workers and relatives who had to put up with my rambling on and on about my research over these many years.

To all of the others who I have not mentioned above or elsewhere in my work, please accept my apologies.

Every item of Heinlein material contained in this book, either from his published works or taken from the Heinlein Archives, is reproduced with the permission of the Robert A. & Virginia Heinlein Prize Trust.

I would like to specifically thank both of Cal Laning's daughters: Judith Laning Polatty, for permission to obtain his service record, and Jillian Giornelli, for permission to quote from his records and papers.

I wish to thank all of those who granted me permission to employ various quoted material. Again, I would like to spare you the need to examine another long list, and will just mention the following:

Perry Chapdelaine at AC Projects Inc., for permission to quote material by John W. Campbell, Jr.

Brian Herbert, for permission to quote from *Dreamer of Dune*.

John Keuhn, for permission to quote from *Agents of Innovation*.

Will F. Jenkins' daughter, Billee Stallings, for permission to quote from "Politics" and "Applied Science Fiction."

Finally, I would like to thank my editor, Sarah Bewley, for rounding off the rough edges of my manuscript.

INDEX

A

Airborne dead-reckoner, 195-99, 221
Alternate Generals, 94
Alternative history, 94
Arwine, John, 15, 65-66
Angel on the Yardarm, 151
Asimov, Isaac, 3, 5, 16, 18, 25, 26, 28, 29, 30, 44
Astounding Science-Fiction, 3, 5, 16, 17, 18, 24, 39, 40, 42, 93, 95, 110, 111, 119, 120, 127, 138, 139, 143, 160, 191, 216, 218, 219, 240
AT&T, 10, 11, 13, 14, 41, 209, 217, 220
The Ayes of Texas, 95-96

B

Bailey, J. O., 28-30, 108-09, 111, 112, 128, 232
Barnes, John, 96
Battle Tracer, 202, 227, 244-45
Battle Tracker, 173, 174, 200-03, 220, 221-28, 242, 243
Bell Laboratories, 14, 198, 205, 209
Bester, Alfred, 21
Beyond This Horizon, 4, 22, 121, 122, 123, 243
Bloch, Robert, 21-22
"Blowups Happen", 16, 186, 193, 218, 219
Bone conduction receiver, 115, 160, 189-90
Bowen, J. Hartley, 5
Bread-board, 19, 33, 36, 41, 74, 208, 217
Bretnor, Reginald, 22, 29
Bywater, Hector, 89, 91

C

California, U.S.S. (BB-44), 137
Campbell, Doña, 17, 18
Campbell, John Wood, Jr., 3, 21, 29, 30, 87, 142
    Article on nuclear fission, 138-40
    Letter from Heinlein May 1, 1939, 240
    Letter from Heinlein May 4, 1940, 15
    Letter from Heinlein December 1, 1940, 139
    Letter from Heinlein December 9, 1941, 9
    Letter from Heinlein December 21, 1941, 9-10, 146
    Letter from Leslyn Heinlein January 4, 1942, 14-15
    Letter from Heinlein January 4, 1942, 11-13
    Letter from Heinlein January 17, 1942, 17-18
    Letter to Heinlein December 29, 1941, 11
    Letter to Heinlein January 8, 1942, 17
    Patent, 118
Campbell, John Wood, Sr., 9-14
Chester, U.S.S. (CA-27), 137
Chicago, U.S.S. (CA-29), 137
CIC (Combat Information Center), 4, 83, 135-38, 217-18
Classmates (Class of 1929) in text:
    Anderson, Samuel, 69
    Ballinger, Richard Robert, 76, 77
    Beardsley, George Francis, 71
    Benson, Roy Stanley, 71
    Berkley, Joseph Berzowski   see Berzowski, Joseph
    Bermingham, John Michael, 70, 72
    Berzowski, Joseph, 69, 70, 76, 77, 85
    Britt, Jacob William, 70
    Carmichael, George Kennedy, 85
    Collett, John Austin, 71, 72
    D'Avi, Joseph Arthur, 70
    Davidson, John Frederick, 71
    Davison, John Walter, 76, 77
    Dodson, Edwin Neil, 69-70
    Dye, Williston Lamar, 85
    Dyer, Edward Colston, 85
    Fenton, Charles Rudolph, 71
    Ferrier, David Tweed, 76, 77, 85
    Flatley, James Henry, 70, 71
    Foley, Paul, 71
    Folger, Edward Clinton, 85
    Frankel, Samuel Benjamin, 70, 72
    Galbraith, William Jackson, 70
    Hall, Finley Elliott, 71
    Hardin, James Thomas, 71

Hogle, Reynold Delos, 69
Hutchins, Edward Francis, 85
Johansen, Gustave Norman, 76, 77, 85
Johnson, Carl Arthur, 71
Johnson, Roy Lee, 70
Jordan, Francis Dixon, 70
Kabler, William Leverette, 36
Kennedy, Marvin Granville, 71
Kirk, Oliver Grafton, 71
Lake, Richard Cross, 71
Laning, Caleb Barrett   see separate listing
Mains, MacDonald Crawford, 85
McCoy, Robert Bruce, 85
McGregor, Rob Roy, 71
Miller, Adolph Jerome, 70
Moore, John Raymond, 71
Nelson, Paul John, 85
Parish, Elliott Walter, 70
Pennewill, William Ellison, 73
Raby, John, 71
Ricketts, Claude V., 72
Rooney, Roderick Shanahan, 71
Roth, Egbert Adolph, 70
Ramsbotham, Robert Joynson, 77, 80
Sharp, George Arthur, 71
Simpler, Leroy Coard, 71
Stephan, Edward Clark, 71
Stone, Lowell Thornton, 69, 71
Stovall, William S., 71
Tolley, Kemp, 70
Triebel, Charles Otto, 71
Van Voorhis, Bruce Avery, 73
Wait, Delos Edwin, 69, 85, 98-99
Wales, George Herrick, 71
Weiss, Donald Frederick, 71

Claude V. Ricketts, U.S.S. (DDG-5), 72
Cold light, 175, 176
Collett, U.S.S. (DD-730), 72
Conyngham, U.S.S. (DD-371), 79, 80, 217
Cornog, Dr. Robert, 139-140
Corson, William
    Connection with Heinlein, 42
    Reference to gadget, 42-44, 221
"Coventry", 16, 17, 184, 193, 218
"The Creation of Heinlein's 'Solution Unsatisfactory'", 138

D

Da Cruz, Daniel, 95
Davenport, Basil, 20, 22
Dead-reckoning, 196-97
Dead Reckoning Tracer   see DRT
de Camp, L. Sprague, 5, 11, 15, 18, 25, 26, 28, 29, 30, 44, 119-121
Denisyuk, Yuri, 140-42, 230
Denisyuk holography   see Volume Holography
"The Development of Sea Warfare on Land and Its Influence on Future Naval Operations.", 104
Dictawriter, 171, 183-84
Directrix, 135-36
Dodson, Matt, 69, 100, 244
The Door Into Summer, 69, 244
Dracone, 142-144, 230
DRT (Dead Reckoning Tracer), 196, 197, 202, 227-28, 245

E

Eldridge, U.S.S. (DE 173), 93
Electromechanical computing   see Appendix 2
Expanded Universe, 36, 60, 64, 74, 99, 121, 199, 240

F

Final Countdown, 91-93, 96
Fire Control   see Appendix 2
Fiske, Bradley, 102-05, 154-56, 159, 185
For Us, The Living (FUTL), 8, 69, 99, 147, 186, 188, 195-97, 198. 221, 242
Forward, Robert L., 70, 115-16
Franklin, H. Bruce, 64-65, 139
Frequency Variation, 173, 203-07, 221
Friedman, Norman, 244
Fuller, J. F. C., 104-05

G

"Galactic Gadgeteers", 111-12
Gardner, Thomas S., 134-35
General Semantics, 15, 241
Gernsback, Hugo, 108, 114, 134, 135, 144, 186, 188-89, 190
    Number of patents, 114-15
    Sleep Learning, 130-31
Gifford, James, 64, 139
Glow-tubes, 162-63, 181-82

"Goldfish Bowl", 100
"The Great Heinlein Mystery", 5, 64
The Great Pacific War, 89
Grumbles From the Grave, 2-3, 5, 7, 9, 11, 15, 39, 231
Gunn, James, 127, 133-135
Gurnard, U.S.S. (SS-254), 149

H

Hall, Charles Prior, 124-25
"The Happy Days Ahead", 64, 65, 99, 121, 125
Harriman, Delos D., 69, 164, 184, 185
Hartwell, David, 70
Hawthorne, William R., 143-44
Heinlein in Dimension, 2, 4
The Heinlein Journal, 6, 25, 68
Heinlein, Leslyn, 14, 15, 17, 38, 137, 241
    Letter to Campbell January 4, 1942, 14-15
Heinlein, Robert Anson
    Letter from Campbell December 29, 1941, 11
    Letter from Campbell January 8, 1942, 17
    Letter from Laning October 24, 1938, 216
    Letter from Laning September 1940, 216, 217
    Letter from Laning January 17, 1944, 137
    Letter from Scoles January 14, 1942, 17-18, 40
    Letter to Campbell May 1, 1939, 240
    Letter to Campbell May 4,1940, 15
    Letter to Campbell December 1, 1940, 139
    Letter to Campbell December 9, 1941, 9
    Letter to Campbell December 21, 1941, 9-10, 146
    Letter to Campbell January 4, 1942, 11-13
    Letter to Campbell January 17, 1942, 17-18
    Letter to Laning October 25, 1940, 217
    University of Chicago Lecture, 19, 20, 22
    Wings for the Navy, 71
Heinlein, Virginia (Ginny), 3, 4, 5, 6, 20, 65, 75-77, 78, 98, 215
Herbert, Brian, 142-43
Herbert, Frank, 95, 98, 142-44
Hoover, George, 153, 198
Hull, E. Mayne, 93

I

IFF (Identification Friend or Foe), 62
"If This Goes On—" Part 1, 34, 160, 165-68, 191, 196, 218, 219
"If This Goes On—" Part 2, 25, 34, 100-07, 160, 168-75, 183, 187, 188, 191,215,

216, 219, 242
Inflight entertainment, 186
Infrared communications, 173, 174, 207-10, 220, 221, 223
Infrared range finder, 89-90, 117-118
Innovation
    Improvisational ingenuity, 148-49
    Individual innovation, 148, 149-56
    Institutional innovation, 148, 158
Integrated Circuit, 36, 53, 54, 56, 248
Interwar years
    Naval academy class sizes, 66-68
    Science and Technology, 46-49

J

Jamming, 203-07, 221
Jenkins, Will F., 30, 89-90, 91, 95, 109, 113, 116-18, 123, 127
John M. Bermingham, U.S.S. (DE-530), 72

K

Keller, David H., 133-35, 144
Kemp, Earl, 20
Knight, Damon, 2, 22, 29, 34, 38
Kondo, Yoji, 3-4, 5
Kornbluth, C. M., 20-21, 28

L

Lake, Simon, 127
Lamarr, Hedy, 207
"The Land Ironclads", 101, 128-30
Langley, U.S.S. (CV-1), 150, 151-52
Langley, U.S.S. (CV-27), 151-52
Lawrence, Ernest O., 48, 140
Laning, Caleb Barrett
    Contact with Heinlein, 216-17
    Early information, 4
    Letter from Heinlein October 25, 1940, 217
    Letter to Heinlein October 24, 1938, 216
    Letter to Heinlein September 1940, 216, 217
    Letter to Heinlein January 17, 1944, 137
    My contact with family members, 4
    Naval biography, 4, 79
    Obtaining his service record, 78-79
    Suggestion by Virginia Heinlein, 4

Torpedo director, 79-80
Leinster, Murray   see Will F. Jenkins
"Let There Be Light", 18, 39, 109, 175-76, 188
Lexington, U.S.S. (CV-2), 99, 152, 157, 197, 199
"Life-Line", 3, 34, 80, 109, 161-62, 240
"A Logic Named Joe", 126-27
Lucky Bag, 64-65

M

McCann, Arthur   see John W. Campbell, Jr.
McCarthy, Wil, 118-19
McNally, Irwin, 152-53
"Methuselah's Children", 100, 186, 191, 193, 199, 218, 219, 243
"Misfit", 34, 99, 100, 162-64, 181-82, 183, 242, 243
Modern Science Fiction: Its Meaning and Its Future, 29, 30
Moskowitz, Sam, 134-5

N

NANCY, 209-10
Nantucket trilogy, 94
Naval Aircraft Factory (NAF), 5, 6, 18, 25, 26, 37, 39, 40, 42-44, 71, 148, 221
Naval Research Laboratory (NRL), 56-58, 60, 61, 62, 147, 148, 150-51, 200, 205
NC-2, 202-03, 221, 227, 245
Nimitz, Admiral Chester, 135, 150
Nimitz, U.S.S. (CVN-68), 91
Northampton, U.S.S. (CA-26), 137

O

Ossophone, 115, 190
Oklahoma, U.S.S. (BB-37), 79

P

Panshin, Alexei, 2, 4
Patent Law, 112-13
Patterson, Bill, 6, 42, 43, 64
Patton's Spaceship, 96-97
Peary, U.S.S. (DD-226), 72
Pennewill. U.S.S. (DE-175), 73
Pensacola, U.S.S. (CA-24), 137
The Philadelphia Experiment, 93
Philadelphia, U.S.S. (CL-41), 8, 79, 216-17
Phinney, J. N., 130-31

Pilgrims Through Space and Time, 28, 29, 30, 108, 128
Pohl, Frederik, 20, 133, 135
"Politics", 89-90, 95, 117-18
Pressure suit, 18, 25-26, 120-21, 169
The Puppet Masters, 69, 196

R

Radio, 48-62, 73, 74, 79, 80, 114, 148, 155, 159, 160, 170, 171, 173, 175, 193-95
Radio beam, 171, 199-200, 219
Radio countermeasures (RCM), 204-207
Radio direction finder, 60, 200
Radio navigation, 60, 204
Radar
    CXAM, 61, 137, 151, 204
    CXAM-1, 151
    CXZ, 61, 150
    XAF, 61, 150
    Second-time-around echo, 151
Ralph 124C 41+, 115, 130-31, 184, 186, 188-89
Rangekeeper
    Mark 1, 245, 246, 248
    Mark 2 (Baby Ford), 245, 246-48
    Mark 4, 245
    Mark 8, 245, 246, 248
Reeves, Joseph M., 150
Reinsberg, Mark, 19-20
Remote control, 59-60
"Requiem", 69, 164-65, 184, 185
Requiem: New Collected Works by Robert A. Heinlein and Tributes to the Grand Master, 3, 4
Retinal, 168, 186-87
"The Roads Must Roll", 17, 80, 107, 176-80, 181, 185, 189, 215, 243
Robot, 169, 170, 187-88, 244
Rocket Ship Galileo, 26, 121, 188, 244
Royal jelly, 133-35, 144

S

The Science Fiction Novel: Imagination and Social Criticism, 2, 20
"Science Fiction: Its Nature, Faults and Virtues", 2
    Essay analysis, 22-29
    Key quote as printed, 19
    Key quote as in lecture script, 33
    Material from Archives, 30-32, 34-35
Scoles, Albert "Buddy", 17-18, 36, 39-40, 42-44, 74, 99, 199, 221

Letter to Heinlein January 14, 1942, 17-18, 40
"Searchlight", 60, 99
SeaQuest DSV, 97
Secrecy, 11-13, 34, 38, 41, 44, 221, 226, 228
"Shadow of the Past", 140
Shipmate
    Arwine obituary, 65
    "The Great Heinlein Mystery", 5, 64
    Laning obituary, 4
"Sixth Column", 186
USS *Sicard* (DD-346), 79, 80, 216, 217
"Sky Lift", 121-23
Smith, Edward Elmer "Doc", 21, 87, 135-38, 144
Smith, George O., 25, 30 , 110
Solar power, 175-76, 188-89
"Solution Unsatisfactory", 24, 29, 138-40, 199
Sonar, 203, 212-14, 219, 227, 228
Sonic range-finder, 173, 174, 210-14, 219-20, 222-27
Space Cadet, 2, 69, 100, 244
Stadimeter, 155, 165, 184-85
Starsea Invaders trilogy, 96
"Star Ships", 141, 230
Starship Troopers, 100
Stereoscope, 163, 182-83
Stine, G. Harry, 96, 110, 111
Stirling, S. M., 93-94
Stover, Leon, 64, 69
Stranger in a Strange Land, 121, 123-24
Swanwick, Michael, 109, 116
Szilard, Leo, 131-33

T

"Tale of the Man Who Was too Lazy to Fail", 98-99, 147
Telechronometer, 166, 168, 191, 192-95, 218-20
"The Thirty Fathom Grave", 93
Tombstone promotion, 77, 99
Transistor, 36, 53, 54, 188, 219, 248
Transmitters
    Alternator, 50-51
    Arc, 50
    Spark Gap, 50, 55
    Vacuum Tube, 52
Turning Points, 29, 34

U

"Under Pressure", 95, 98, 142, 143
United States Naval Academy
    Class sizes, 64-68
    Department of Electrical Engineering, 73-74
    Nimitz Library, 8, 65, 78, 83, 231
    Register of Alumni, 8, 64, 65, 83-85, 231
United States Naval Academy Postgraduate School
    Communications, 82-85
    General Line, 79, 81, 83-85
    Radio Engineering, 82-85

V

Vacuum tube, 48, 51-55, 57, 62, 73, 83, 110, 118, 190, 194, 218, 248
Van Voorhis, U.S.S. (DE-1028), 73
Venus Equilateral, 110-11
Virtues essay   see "Science Fiction: Its Nature, Faults and Virtues"
Visiphone, 167, 185-86
Volume holography, 140-42
Voyage to the Bottom of the Sea, 97

W

Wake Island, 148-49
"Waldo", 24, 37, 121-23
Water Bed, 99, 121-25
Waterburies, 105-107, 170
    Mentioned in Virtues essay, 25, 32
"—We Also Walk Dogs", 186
Wells, H. G.
    Influence of "The Land Ironclads", 128-30
    Influence of *The World Set Free,* 131-33
Western Electric, 14, 55, 61, 62
"The Winged Man", 93

Y

Yefremov, Ivan, 140-42, 144, 230
Yorktown, U.S.S (CV-5), 137

ABOUT THE AUTHOR

Edward M. Wysocki, Jr. received his Ph.D. in Electrical Engineering from Johns Hopkins University. This was followed by over three decades with a major defense contractor. He has had a lifelong interest in science fiction, with a particular focus on the works of Robert A. Heinlein. Dr. Wysocki is a member of The Heinlein Society and the Science Fiction Research Association. This is his first book-length effort in the field of science fiction.

Made in the USA
Columbia, SC
17 February 2018